DEFENDER OF CROWNS

TANYA BIRD

Copyright © 2021 by Tanya Bird

All rights reserved.

No part of this book may be reproduced in any form or by any electronic or mechanical means, including information storage and retrieval systems, without written permission from the author, except for the use of brief quotations in a book review.

CHAPTER 1

a flash of silver in the creek made Eda still. She watched the water down her arrow, the string of her bow pressing into her fingers.

'Come on,' she whispered as she waited for the trout to reappear.

Birds took flight behind her. She whipped her head around to look. Nothing moved, but the small hairs on the back of her neck stood on end. She waited, gaze darting from tree to tree. Someone was watching her.

Lowering her bow, Eda stepped back from the water's edge and moved up the muddy bank, taking cover behind the thick trunk of an oak tree. She stood with her back pressed to it, holding her weapon in front of her.

Snap.

The sound of debris breaking underfoot had Eda holding her breath. Emerging from her hiding place, she swung her bow left and right, searching.

A defender swooped into her vision. She barely had time to register the face before her bow was torn from her hands and the tip of a sword was pointed at her neck.

Oh, he's good.

1

She ducked, reaching for the knife at her hip in the same motion. The sword came for her, and she fell backwards out of its way. She kicked out, forcing him back. That was her opportunity to get back on her feet. She shot up, knife pointed at Roul Thornton. His copper eyes locked on hers as they circled one another.

'Are you aware that you're fishing on private property?'

The corners of her mouth lifted. 'Oh, that's what this is about?'

'I've received complaints.'

'Complaints from whom, may I ask?'

'The commander who owns this land.'

Eda pressed her lips together to stop from smiling. 'I've no idea why Commander Wright would be complaining since the fish I'm catching is for his dinner.' Spinning her knife, she added, 'And what is the punishment for illegal fishing nowadays?'

'A finger.'

'But I didn't catch anything.'

'Then two fingers.'

Her eyebrows rose. 'Why two?'

'One for the crime and one for your terrible aim.'

Eda whistled, noting the amusement in his eyes. 'I guess I'm just going to have to make a run for it, then.' She sheathed her knife and took off, arms pumping.

Roul's feet pounded the earth behind her, less than six feet between them. She was fast, but his strides were long.

Through the trees she fled, until Wright House finally came into view. 'If I make it to the door, you have to catch the fish for dinner,' she called to him without turning her head.

'You won't make it to the door.'

He was just a few feet behind her now. She could hear his breath.

Leaping over a fallen log, she prayed he might trip. But

defenders were not allowed to fall. She heard his feet land right behind her, within reach of her, so she pivoted.

When she reached the soggy lawn, she realised she was not going to make it to the door. She reached for her knife and turned, swinging it at him as she ran backwards. But he was ready for her dirty moves. His sword was already drawn, and he stopped her knife in its tracks, then pushed her back. Eda's heel caught on the uneven ground. A moment later, her back slammed into the grass, but even in her slightly winded state, she managed to keep a hold of the knife. She fought him as she lay on the ground until he finally lost patience and disarmed her. She reached for the other dagger hidden beneath her skirt at the same time the tip of Roul's sword went to her neck.

'Yes,' he said, panting, 'I know all about the dangerous things you keep hidden beneath your skirts.'

She slowly raised her hands, breathing hard as she waited to see what he would do next.

The back door of the house swung open, and her mother stepped outside carrying a tub of wet laundry. She stilled when she caught sight of Roul standing over Eda with a weapon pointed at her neck. Then, shaking her head, she kept walking.

'Afternoon, Thornton,' Candace called as she went to hang the laundry.

Roul cleared his throat and sheathed his weapon. 'Afternoon.' He extended a hand to Eda, but she slapped it away.

'Don't try to be all chivalric now just because my mother's here.' Eda pushed herself up and went to retrieve her knife. Turning to him, she held up both hands and said, 'Which fingers will you be taking?'

Candace glanced in their direction. 'Do not dare cut off any of her fingers, defender. Her contributions here are already minimal.'

3

'That's not true,' Eda replied. 'I was just down at the creek catching our dinner.'

Candace laughed. 'And where are the fish you caught?'

Eda swallowed. 'In the creek, awaiting certain death.'

'My fault,' Roul said. 'I distracted her.'

Candace hung the final sheet and picked up the empty tub before turning to them. 'Well, if you intend to eat with us this evening, might I suggest you help catch the key ingredient.'

'Of course' was his reply.

'Better get the big pot out, Mother,' Eda said, taking hold of Roul's arm and dragging him off in the direction of the trees. 'There's about to be a massacre in the water.'

'Three fish is plenty,' Candace called to them as she headed to the door. 'Not every hunt and forage needs to end in warfare.'

Eda let go of him and broke into a run. He jogged after her. When they reached the trees, they slowed, walking in silence all the way to the creek, where they retrieved Eda's bow from the shrubbery before returning to the quiver of arrows she had left at the edge of the water. They removed their boots, Roul rolling up his trousers and Eda hitching up her skirts, then waded into the water, taking turns with the bow.

When Eda caught the first fish, Roul said, 'Took you long enough, soldier.'

She kicked water at him before fetching the dead fish, pulling the arrow from it, and tossing it onto the river-bank. It was always 'soldier' when he was in a good mood, 'Eda' in front of her family, and 'Suttone' when she was in trouble. 'Don't see you with any fish.' She handed him the bow. 'I'd improve much faster if you let me train at the barracks. I've been asking both you and Harlan for months.'

'And we've both been telling you no for months.'

Her feet were beginning to ache in the cold water. 'How am I to improve if the only people I ever spar with are you two?'

'Improve?' Roul stilled, took aim, and caught the second fish of the day. He rushed forwards to retrieve it, throwing it onto the bank beside the other one. He held the bow out for her. 'Your skills are more than adequate. I've watched you train with Harlan. He teaches you the same things he teaches the recruits—but in the safety of your home.'

'Can you hear yourself? "Adequate. In the safety of your home".' She loaded the bow and watched the water for a minute. 'Queen Artemisia did not settle for adequate in the safety of her home.'

'Was she the queen of Halicarnassus? The one who broke her own neck in the name of love?'

Eda glared in his direction. 'She fought and won the battle of Salamis.'

'Perfect. Will you be asking for a boat next?'

Glimpsing spotty scales beneath the water's surface, Eda released her arrow, catching the final fish of the day. She retrieved it, but instead of throwing it on the grassy bank, she threw it *at* Roul. He caught it a few inches from his face. His smug expression made her temper flare.

She splashed through the water towards him. 'You once told me I was better than some of your recruits.'

He threw the fish onto the riverbank. 'You are. But you're also half their size.'

'That just makes me nimble.'

'It makes you fragile.'

She flicked water up at him, hitting him square in the face.

He wiped a hand down it. 'You're also twice as tiresome. There would be no tolerance for your bad behaviour in that environment. You'd spend the whole time running off your bad attitude.'

5

'I happen to like running.'

'I've noticed.' He exited the water. 'Sure, you could probably knock some of the recruits off their feet in the first few weeks, but they'll get stronger and better—you won't.'

She followed him out and bent to collect both their shoes since he was carrying the fish. 'I might.'

He turned to face her. 'Then what? Will you be miraculously content then? Once you've proved yourself?'

It was a valid question. 'I don't know. Maybe.'

Roul exhaled and brushed the back of his hand over his clean-shaven jaw. 'There are no female defenders. And even if there were, you couldn't do the job. You going to put on a uniform and hang merchants from the wall?'

'No.'

He began walking, and she followed him.

'I thought your uncle was busy finding you a husband,' he said when she fell into step with him.

'He is. He wants me to marry some widowed boot-maker in the merchant borough.'

Roul squinted in her direction. 'At least you would be in the merchant borough. You always say you don't belong among the noble.'

She let out a breath. 'I'd quite like to live somewhere quieter, more reclusive.' She gestured behind them to the clearing by the creek where they had stood moments earlier. 'I've daydreamed about living right there.'

He stopped walking and looked back, eyebrows drawn together. 'You want to live in a creek?'

'Not *in* the creek.' She pointed. 'I'd build a house in that spot right there. When the sun returns, it'll be drenched in sunlight each morning. At night, I would have owls and insects for company.'

His eyes returned to her, his expression softer now, something resembling pity in his eyes.

Colour filled her cheeks. 'Perhaps I'll suggest it to the bootmaker.'

He searched her face for the longest time, then resumed walking without saying another word.

She jogged to catch up to him. 'But before I settle for my reclusive existence, I'd quite like to see what's outside Chadora's walls first.'

He sighed. 'Of course you would.'

'Don't you ever get restless inside these walls?'

'I've certainly noticed that you do.'

He was an expert at deflecting personal questions.

Eda looked up at the heavy clouds. 'Sometimes I imagine going over the wall or boarding a ship to Ireland.'

He stopped walking and turned to her, visibly agitated. 'What for? To witness more suffering?'

'They're just thoughts. I'm allowed to be curious about the world. Or is that a hangable offence now too?'

He ran a hand over his crop of black hair. 'Are they just thoughts though? You're always testing boundaries and trying to prove yourself in some way. You seem to think you have to fight men twice your size, scale a wall, or board a ship—'

'I don't *have* to do any of those things.' She searched his eyes. 'Did you hear the part where I said I *want* to?'

'You only want to because you're not allowed to. That's how your brain works. You hear the word "no" and off you go on one of your little tangents.' He took a step back from her. 'You've not even met the bootmaker, but already you don't want to marry him because someone is telling you to. You are your own worst enemy.'

That stung. 'My own worst enemy? For not wanting to marry a stranger whom my uncle has selected?'

He wet his lips and looked away.

When he did not speak, she went on. 'I'm not allowed to seek new experiences of any kind or step outside of what's comfortable for everyone else, is that right? To seek some purpose in this miserable life is selfish. Noted.'

Roul lowered his brows. 'You have the shop and the almshouse. Is that work not purposeful enough for you?' He shifted his feet. 'And you know what? You can always choose your own husband if you're unhappy with his choice. I imagine your uncle will agree to any match at this point.'

'Well, that's rude.'

'Or if being someone's wife is so below you, why not tell your uncle you're committed to keeping your mother company through her later years in place of marriage?'

Eda pressed her teeth together. 'So many inviting options.'

He rubbed his face tiredly. 'Forgive me for trying to prevent you from scaling the wall or stowing away on a ship thinking there's something out there that you're missing.'

Of course Roul knew what was out there. He had been born and raised in Carmarthenshire, a region that had been abandoned by King Edward when it was taken over by rebel groups. While the English king maintained control of the north, everything between River Wnion, the Welsh Marches, and Chadora was now referred to as the Carmarthenshire wastelands.

Roul had fled. He had boarded a ship along the coast and arrived at Chadora's port, where he had caught the interest of the warden. That was all she knew of his past, small snippets, mostly from other people. Whenever she asked Roul questions directly, he immediately grew uncomfortable. She would be met with vague responses or a change in subject. When she had asked Harlan about him during training once, he had said that sometimes people prefered to keep their pasts buried.

Roul was waiting for her to respond. She dropped his

boots on the ground and took the fish from him. 'I should get these cleaned up for dinner.' Then she walked off before he could reply.

'Wait.' He picked up his boots and followed her. 'I'll help you.'

'It's all right,' she said without looking back. 'You've helped enough for one day.'

CHAPTER 2

'*A*gain,' Roul called to the recruit who had turned to empty his stomach.

The young defender wiped his mouth with the back of his hand, nodded. 'Yes, sir.' Turning to face his opponent, the pair resumed the drill.

Harlan appeared next to Roul in the training yard, crossing his arms and watching the recruits for a minute before speaking. 'They've improved in the last week.'

'Until you give them a shield. Then you need to be ready to duck.'

Harlan chuckled. 'Better finish up soon or they won't be able to hold a sword tomorrow.'

Roul nodded. 'Watch your feet, Alveye! You're retreating!'

Harlan turned to him. 'I came to warn you that the warden's on his way. He wants to speak with you.'

Roul looked in the direction of the barracks, and sure enough, Shapur Wright was striding towards them. 'Great. Do you know what he wants?'

'Yes.'

Roul waited for him to elaborate, but Harlan said nothing further. Shaking his head, Roul shouted at the recruits. 'All right. You're done. Walk it off, then pack it up.' He turned and stood to attention as the warden approached. 'Sir.'

Shapur came to a stop in front of him, his sharp eyes going to the recruits who were now cooling off. 'How are they coming along?'

'Better in their second week.'

'Good.' The warden turned his scowling face to Roul. 'I came to tell you that you are now in command of the recruits.'

Roul blinked. 'You're making me a commander?'

'I have been watching you closely over the previous year,' Shapur said. 'You are ready for the responsibility.'

Roul looked to Harlan, whose face held pride. He knew Shapur would have discussed it with him before making the decision. 'What of Commander Wright?'

'I'll be around,' Harlan said, clapping him on the back. 'No need to fret.'

'Commander Wright will still be involved,' Shapur said, 'but his main focus will be on the outer-wall. We need more eyes looking outwards now.'

That was a big step up for Harlan. To command a borough was one thing, but to protect the outer-wall was quite another. He would be responsible for the safety of the entire kingdom.

'Are we expecting unwanted visitors?' Roul asked.

The creases on Shapur's face deepened. 'We certainly need to be prepared for it.' He paused. 'We have received reports that Prince Becket is staying at Harlech Castle.'

Roul's eyebrows rose. Harlech Castle was one of King Edward's homes in the north. 'I don't understand. Was he taken there at swordpoint?'

The youngest prince was the only living heir to the

throne. He had spent the previous two years since his brother's death dodging the crown aimed at his head.

'He willingly boarded a ship from Ireland. We have no reason to suspect foul play.' Shapur took a step back, signalling that question time was over. 'Make sure I do not regret this decision, Commander.' And with that, he strode off.

Roul stood processing the conversation. The correct reaction to being promoted was pride. He had accomplished something every defender wanted but most never got. But he felt only guilt. He was a fraud. In two years, when his minimum term was up, he planned on returning to his home in Carno. Of course, the warden did not know that. Harlan was the only person who knew anything of his plans, and he had advised Roul to say nothing of them to anyone until his five years were up.

'My plans haven't changed,' Roul said, meeting Harlan's gaze. 'My family's waiting for me to return.'

Harlan nodded slowly. 'You know, you get to leave regardless of your title.' He took hold of Roul's shoulder. 'You're allowed to feel good about this. It's an enormous achievement, especially at your age.' Letting go, he added, 'In fact, I think you should come to the house for dinner tonight. We'll celebrate.'

'There's really no need for fuss.'

'Before you feel too special, Lord Thomas will also be in attendance. I invite you for my own sanity.'

Roul frowned. 'I thought he avoided Wright House at all costs.'

'Except when trying to marry off a relative. The bootmaker will also be joining us.'

Roul shifted his weight. He had heard about the bootmaker firsthand from Eda, but witnessing their courtship would be something else. The nature of their friendship led him to protect her as a brother would. 'Does Eda know he's coming?'

'Even the high lord knows better than to try and spring a suitor on Eda Suttone.' Harlan crossed his arms. 'With her nineteenth birthday now behind her, the pressure to be married is at an all-time high. I suspect Thomas is trying to secure free boots for the rest of his life.'

Roul watched the recruits bend to collect the weapons, stiff with pain. 'I'm surprised she agreed.'

Harlan observed him a moment. 'Don't worry. I'll intervene if there's cause to. No one wants to see her unhappy.'

Roul had not considered the possibility of Eda finding happiness with the man. He had assumed he would fall short of her impossibly high standards. Maybe he would not. Maybe he would make her laugh, indulge her adventurous nature. Maybe he would even make her happy.

'So you'll come?' Harlan asked.

Roul swallowed, nodded. 'I'll come.'

It was a large family affair. Roul was seated at the table between Candace and Eda, except Eda's chair was empty, and she was nowhere to be seen.

'You did not happen to see her on your way in?' Candace whispered as she passed Roul the roasted carrots.

'Afraid not.' He glanced at the bootmaker. Leigh Appleton. A man of few words who was a few years older than him. Leigh was a gentle kind of man, perhaps too gentle for Eda. She would break him in the first year of marriage.

A glowering Lord Thomas rose from his chair and smoothed down his tunic. 'I shall go outside and find her.' There was no hiding the agitation in his voice.

'I can go if you like,' Blake said, moving to stand.

'No. I'll go,' Thomas replied, walking around the table.

He almost stepped on the baby, then collided with the duck. 'It is like a barnyard in here. Someone get rid of that animal and put that child somewhere sensible.'

Blake plucked Luella from the floor and placed her on her lap. Her daughter arched her back and cried, wanting to be on the ground with Garlic. A heavily pregnant Lyndal rose from her chair and went to lock the duck outside.

'Mother and I were so excited to discover a few flower buds on the apple trees in the orchard this morning,' Kendra said as she inspected the tray of pork. 'It is autumn, yet the trees seem to think it is spring.'

The seasons still did not mean much, despite the gradual easing of rain over the past few months, which apparently counted as summer.

Astin pushed the tray closer to Lyndal. 'Don't get too excited. Same thing happened last year, but no fruit came of it.'

'What a pillar of positivity you are,' Lyndal said as she returned to her seat.

Astin dragged her chair closer, a hand going to her belly. 'Next time let me deal with the animals. You're supposed to be resting.'

'How long until the birth now?' Lady Victoria said, smiling at the couple. 'You must be getting close to lying in.'

'Only noblewomen lie-in,' Lyndal said.

Astin glanced in Lady Victoria's direction. 'Lyndal will get plenty of rest on my watch, I assure you.'

'I have another month to go,' Lyndal said, her voice cheerful. 'And I feel great.'

Harlan walked into the room, collecting his crying daughter from Blake's lap before taking his seat.

'Uncle wanted Garlic locked outside,' Blake explained.

Harlan handed his daughter a piece of carrot to chew on. 'I've been wanting that for the previous three years.'

'Luella reminds me so much of Eda as a baby,' Candace said. 'Always too busy to sit still for even a moment.'

Lyndal took the tray of pork from her cousin. 'Eda as a *baby*? Sounds very much like Eda now.'

'I heard that,' Eda said, walking into the room ahead of her glaring uncle.

Leigh rose, fingertips resting on the edge of the table as he waited for her to reach her chair. Everyone stopped eating. Apparently no one wanted to miss Eda and Leigh's first exchange of words.

Candace's face fell when she caught sight of her daughter. 'Really, Eda. Perhaps you should go and change before joining us.'

Roul looked down at Eda's mud-soaked hem, and then his eyes travelled up her body to her freshly scrubbed face. She did not need any of the coloured pastes and tea leaf concoctions that many used. She had natural colour in her cheeks from time spent outdoors, and those eyes of hers were as bright as emeralds, eradicating the need for fancy jewels. Her dark hair was half pulled back and damp from the rain.

'No need,' Eda told her mother. 'I just had a wash out back.'

Lyndal narrowed her eyes at her. 'Ah, which part did you wash?'

'Hands and face. The important parts,' Blake answered for her. 'Leave her alone.'

Eda signed something at Lyndal that made Blake laugh and Candace shake her head. She spoke verbally nowadays, but Roul noticed that she slipped back into signing on three occasions: when she did not want others knowing what she was saying, whenever her uncle was visiting, and when she was afraid. One would think she had no fears judging by the way she charged through life, but everyone was afraid of something.

'You remember Leigh Appleton?' Candace said, gesturing to the standing man. 'He took over his father's business in the merchant borough.'

Eda stopped behind her chair and bowed her head. 'Of course. I was very sorry to hear about your wife. It must've been devastating to lose her at such a young age.'

'Thank you,' he said. 'It was certainly tough.'

Everyone looked at their plates then.

'You must forgive my niece,' Thomas said. 'She speaks without thinking.'

'Not at all,' Leigh said, waiting for Eda to take her seat ahead of him. 'I appreciate the kind words.'

Roul had nothing against the man—so far. He reached up and pulled a piece of grass from Eda's hair as she took her seat.

'Thank you,' she mouthed as he threw the grass under the table.

He winked at her.

'I have some old dresses put aside if you are in need of some,' Kendra said once Eda was settled in her chair. 'I had planned to drop them at the almshouse, but you are more than welcome to them, cousin.'

'Oh, she has plenty of dresses,' Candace said, picking up her knife and fork. 'She simply chooses not to wear them.'

'She has been wearing Kingsley's old clothes of late,' Lyndal whispered to Kendra. 'Mother is beside herself.'

Kendra stopped eating. 'Men's clothing?' She had not whispered.

Eda only shrugged and said, 'Trousers are more practical for hunting and chores.'

Thomas flicked his napkin—hard—and settled it on his lap. 'Let us not turn your guest off before we have even begun eating.'

'I'm not turned off, my lord,' Leigh said.

That made everyone else at the table smile—except

Roul. Eda's face also remained neutral as she reached for a tray of food.

Blake cleared her throat. 'I spent the afternoon with Birtle today. I worry about him being in that shop all alone. He's struggling to lift the reams of fabric nowadays.'

Thomas finished chewing his food, then replied, 'If he is no longer able to do the work, then he is no longer able to live there for free.'

'We wouldn't be able to keep the shop open without his help, Uncle,' Blake replied. 'If anything, we're in his debt.'

Thomas ignored her.

'We heard rumours that Prince Becket was spotted disembarking a ship in Gwynedd,' Lyndal said, looking to Harlan. 'Is it true?'

Harlan nodded, finishing his food before speaking. 'Harlech Castle, to be precise.'

'Seems the English got to him first,' Astin said. 'Good luck bringing him home now.'

Candace brought a napkin to her mouth. 'This is the closest he has been to home in some time.'

Eda had stopped eating. 'I don't understand why he's at Harlech Castle. Was he taken there at arrow point?'

It always amused Roul how similarly their minds worked at times.

'My sources tell me the prince is a *guest* there,' Thomas said. He liked to point out that he had sources outside the walls.

'So how are we supposed to get to him now?' Blake asked.

Roul cut into his pork. 'We don't. Queen Fayre can't leave the safety of Chadora's walls. If anything were to happen to her, we would have no one to rule. And we can hardly send an army in her place.'

Kendra sighed. 'I remember Prince Becket. Such a

sweet boy. He will likely hand the kingdom to King Edward with his best wishes.'

'Can Queen Fayre not send one of her advisors in her place?' Lady Victoria asked, looking to her husband.

Thomas swallowed his food. 'The prince must be prepared to accept the visitors sent his way.'

'I can't imagine King Edward will be receiving any other Chadorian guests at court any time soon,' Lyndal replied. She was trying to entice Luella to come to her with a piece of parsnip.

Eda was spinning her fork along her fingers, listening. The sound of her uncle clearing his throat made her stop.

'What's to stop King Edward from simply executing him and taking control of our kingdom?' Leigh asked, joining the conversation.

'King Edward's not the concern,' Harlan replied. 'It's his mother and her... companion who control England right now.'

'Lord Roger Mortimer,' Astin said on a long exhale.

Kendra touched her napkin to her lips. 'Why King Edward would relinquish control to those two I have no idea. I keep hearing how he is a better king than his father, but he is yet to prove it.'

Blake nodded in agreement. 'If he's old enough to marry, he's old enough to rule, surely.'

'He's not the first king to be controlled by his mother,' Eda said pointedly. 'But it's definitely time he hauled her arse off his throne and got on with the job.'

Leigh coughed. More of a choke, really.

Thomas's fork clanged on his plate. 'That is no way for a lady to speak.' He glared accusingly at Candace. 'Where did she learn such things?'

Eda stiffened in her chair, having clearly forgotten herself. 'Certainly not from Mother.'

Thomas's eyes went to Blake, who raised her hands.

'I taught her to sign it, not say it.'

Candace brought a hand to her forehead and closed her eyes.

'It is my understanding that Prince Becket has turned away every man Queen Fayre has sent to collect him,' Lady Victoria said, bringing the conversation back on course.

'Then she's clearly not sending the right people,' Blake replied. 'Perhaps she should send a woman.'

Thomas placed his knife and fork down. 'This is not an appropriate discussion for ladies.'

Eda was staring hard at Blake, one foot bouncing under the table. Roul knew what she was thinking without her saying one word. She was thinking she could do it—better than any man.

Her eyes met his, and her foot stilled.

Busted.

Eda resumed eating. She had barely managed a few mouthfuls before Leigh leaned in close and said, 'Shall we take a walk after dinner?'

She sat back in her chair, hesitating for some reason.

'Perhaps now is a good time to share your news, Roul,' Harlan said, picking up his cup.

Eda looked over at Harlan, head tilted and eyebrows pinched. 'What news?'

'He was made commander today. A much-deserved step up.'

Eda shot out of her chair. 'Commander? Why didn't you tell me?'

'It's not that big a deal,' Roul replied.

A smile spread across her face. 'Of course it's a big deal.' She threw her arms around his neck. 'I'm so proud of you.'

He sat frozen, aware of the entire room watching them. Leigh looked down at his lap. Thomas's face was etched with disapproval. Finally, Eda released him, still grinning.

She was either oblivious to her audience or simply did not care. Likely the latter.

'We're all very proud of you,' Blake said.

Lyndal nodded in agreement. 'Hear, hear.'

Astin raised his cup. 'To Commander Thornton.'

Everyone raised their cups in a toast, and then conversation resumed. Roul finished his drink, accepting everyone's congratulations before announcing his departure.

'I'll walk you out,' Eda said, rising.

Thomas exhaled loudly. 'I am certain the commander is capable of fetching his own horse.'

'We'll both walk him out,' Leigh said, stepping up beside Eda. 'It'll give us a chance to talk.'

'Very well,' Thomas said with a curt nod.

Roul eyed Leigh, suddenly irritated by the well-mannered man. His eyes met Blake's as he stepped back from the table. She appeared amused, like she could read his thoughts.

'Goodnight,' he said before leaving the room.

The three of them exited the house via the back door through the kitchen. Roul held the door open for Eda, tempted to let it close in Leigh's face. The bootmaker stepped past him and jogged to catch up to Eda. Roul followed them.

'Your uncle tells me you made the tapestry hanging on the wall,' Leigh said to Eda as they headed towards the stables.

Eda watched her feet, not one for small talk. 'Well, sort of. My mother ended up finishing the piece because I lost patience with it.'

Leigh glanced sideways at her. 'Oh.' He cleared his throat. 'Your uncle mentioned that you kept yourself busy with various leisure pursuits.'

'Archery, sparring, knife throwing...' Eda said, listing some of them.

She was so unashamedly herself, something Roul admired about her.

'It seems you enjoy weapons' was Leigh's reply.

'Mm.' She slowed to walk beside Roul when they reached the stables. 'Can I ask you something?'

'So long as it's not about Prince Becket.' Yes, he knew her that well.

'What will happen if he simply never returns?' She was undeterred by his warning.

Roul continued to the stall where his horse was housed. 'The people of Chadora are content with Queen Fayre as regent, as long as the meat continues to show up in the borough.'

Eda held the stall door open while Leigh stood awkwardly back from them. 'I'm asking about everyone outside of Chadora. Will King Edward come for our meat?'

That mind of hers just never stopped. 'You know, you don't have to carry the weight of this kingdom on your shoulders.' He led his horse out into the mounting yard. Leigh trailed behind them. As Roul gathered the reins, Eda's hand landed on his arm.

'I could do it,' she said. 'No one would feel threatened if I showed up at Harlech Castle.'

Roul turned to her. 'Stop.'

'Stop what?' Leigh asked, looking between them with a confused expression.

Eda's eyes never left Roul. 'I'm capable. Entirely self-sufficient. I could make it there safely and convince the prince to return with me.'

Roul shook his head. 'I said stop.'

'I'll make him listen.'

Roul mounted. 'Go inside.'

She took hold of the reins, preventing the horse from moving. 'Can you at least hear me out?'

'No.' He reached down and took her hand off the reins,

eyes meeting hers. 'The prince doesn't know you, nor does he have any reason to trust you. The entire idea is ludicrous, and I'm not indulging you any longer.'

She raised her chin and stepped back. 'Well, maybe Queen Fayre will indulge me.'

Roul levelled her with a stare that made it clear he was not messing around. 'You saw firsthand what happened to your sister when she played these games.'

Leigh took hold of Eda's arm. 'Come. I'll take you inside.'

Roul's eyes went to the hand wrapping her arm. 'She can walk herself inside.' The words had come out harsher than he had intended, but the second Leigh had put his hands on her, he could not stop it.

Leigh let go of her arm.

Eda stepped away from the horse, looking taken aback. 'We'll talk tomorrow.'

He nudged his horse forwards. 'Not about this we won't.'

The last thing he saw was her determined face before she turned and headed for the house.

CHAPTER 3

Queen Fayre did not indulge Eda. In fact, she would not even agree to see her to discuss it.

'Yes, I delivered your letter to her personally,' Lyndal assured her. 'And as I've said three times now, she did not send a response.'

So Eda moved to plan B. Or rather she came up with a plan B, then moved to it. The next day, she implemented it. She was suspended forty feet from the ground on the royal borough wall when she started to doubt the plan. Her fingernails were bending backwards as she pressed herself flat against the stone, waiting for the footsteps to fade overhead. If the queen regent was not going to invite her in, then she was going to break in. Breaching the wall would give them some talking points.

Glancing once at the ground below, Eda drew a breath and continued her climb. Blake had made it over the wall once without falling, and she had been malnourished with half of Eda's strength at the time.

Eda paused at the top, peering over the embrasure, arms and legs trembling. All was silent. She checked below her once more, ensuring no merchants or defenders on the ground had spotted her. Satisfied, she pulled herself up and over, looking both ways along the wall walk before dropping onto it. There was no time to waste. She ran straight to the other side, leaping up onto the embrasure so she was out of view. Peering down into the borough, she saw the ground was clear below. She had picked a spot away from the barracks to give herself the best chance of success.

How many times had she walked the grounds of the royal borough with her sister during their stay at Eldon Castle, imagining all the ways she could break in and out if she needed to? Now all that imaginative scheming was finally paying off.

Taking a few slow breaths, she lowered herself over the edge, feeling for uneven stone and crevices to anchor herself. She moved quickly, knowing every second she was on the wall increased her risk of being caught. When she was ten feet from the bottom, she let go and dropped to the ground. She landed with a soft thud, knees bent to ease the impact. She looked around, above, then tugged her hood up and stepped out from the shadows, heading to the main path that led to the castle. No one would question her so long as she looked confident, like she belonged there—until she reached the castle gate. Then the guard on duty would ask to see her papers. But that did not matter, because she was not going through the gate. She was going to enter via the secret entrance Roul had shown her the day she busted Lyndal out of her bedchamber.

The day King Borin had died.

Slightly less exciting than scaling a wall, but definitely the most sensible option.

She kept her head high as she walked, making eye contact with any defenders she passed along the way. Smiling. Saying good morning. They nodded back, assuming she was a maid or a cook on her way to work.

Eda turned off the path when the main gate came into

sight, walking to the base of the wall and following the muddy path all the way to the small door located on the east wall. Roul had told her it was only used by defenders and those who knew of its existence. It was hidden beneath thick ivy that covered the lower half of the wall. The tread in the path is what gave away its location. Anyone with basic tracking skills could have found it.

She had just found the door's latch when the sound of male voices on the other side made her freeze. There was nowhere for her to hide. She moved back, her mind racing. The door opened, and the men stepped through. They stopped talking when they spotted her.

'What are you doing out here?' asked the taller defender.

She glanced in the direction of the barracks. 'Waiting like a fool for him to show up. It was all confessions of love in his bed last night but another matter in the sober light of day.'

The other defender grinned at the ground, but the man questioning her looked her up and down.

'You work in the castle?' he asked.

Eda nodded, praying he did not ask to see her papers. 'In the kitchen.' She reminded herself to breathe as she waited for his response.

'What's the defender's name?' he asked.

She hoped her face did not convey her panic. 'You don't really expect me to rat the man out, do you?'

He crossed his arms and waited.

Oh. She was never going to hear the end of this. 'Roul Thornton. Now *Commander* Roul Thornton.'

The defender's face relaxed, his arms returning to his sides. 'We're heading to the barracks now. We'll let him know you're here. Name?'

There was no chance in hell she was giving them her real name. 'Beatrice.' She prayed to Belenus and any other listening god that Roul was nowhere to be found. He would lock her in the tower himself, and there would be a lot of angry family waiting for her when she got out.

The men continued on their way. The second they were out of sight, she ran to the door and pushed it open. Thankfully, no one was standing on the other side of it. She closed it behind her and moved quickly to the large tree in the middle of the lawn to collect herself and ensure the area was clear of defenders before proceeding.

She would enter the castle via the fountain court without drawing too much attention. From there she would climb the grand staircase to the terrace, where Queen Fayre would likely be playing chess with one of her ladies. Then she would share her daring plan to bring Prince Becket home.

Eda removed her cloak so as to better blend in, rolling it into a ball and tucking it at the base of the tree. She peered around the trunk, checking the area was clear before stepping out into the open once more. Walking quickly, she headed straight for the door ahead of her. She was ten feet from it when she heard a throat clear behind her. Sucking in a breath, she spun around. And there stood a slightly breathless Roul. His hands were tight fists, and she was sure she would melt beneath his coppery glare.

'Hello, Beatrice,' he said.

She swallowed.

'Are you going to tell me what in God's name you're doing here?' He looked ready to drag her off to the tower before she had even given her response.

'Just… paying Queen Fayre a visit.'

He looked up at the terrace above them. 'And is the queen expecting you?'

He already knew the answer to that. 'Actually, I was hoping to keep it a surprise. So if you could not spoil—'

He was upon her before she had even gotten the words

out, taking a hold of her arm and dragging her back towards the wall. 'Of all the foolish things you've done, this really beats all of them.'

'You say that, yet you don't even know half the things I've done.'

He gave her arm a tug, forcing her to walk faster. 'You're lucky those men you lied to came to find me or you'd be bleeding out in the fountain court by now.'

'I'm unarmed. No defender is going to kill an unarmed woman.'

His thunderous eyes returned to her. 'Clearly you're not as smart as you think you are. They've killed people for less.'

She looked over her shoulder, wondering how long it would take her to reach the door. She had proven many times that she could outrun him over short distances.

It was worth a shot.

Swinging her arm, she circled free of his grip and took off at a sprint for the front entrance of the castle. He had taught her that move. The irony was not lost on her.

'Suttone!' Roul shouted, proving just how much trouble she was in.

Perhaps she should have stopped. Perhaps she should have made a new plan, a safer one. But would it have the same impact?

She kept running.

Roul's feet pounded the earth behind her, but she did not let the noise trip her up. She glanced once over her shoulder. There was at least twelve feet between them. Unarmed, she had the advantage of less weight and better motion. His superior fitness and long legs could only carry him so far.

'I swear to God, if you don't stop this second, I'm going to start throwing knives at your back,' he said through his teeth.

She knew he would do no such thing. 'I just want to speak with her,' she puffed out as she burst into the fountain court and headed for the staircase. She took the steps two at a time. When she reached the top, she spotted a defender patrolling the corridor. He stopped when he saw her.

'Grab her!' Roul called to him.

Years of playing barley break had led Eda to this moment. If there was ever a time she needed to make it to the other side, it was now.

'She'll roll,' Roul warned the man, knowing her tactics well. He had gained on her. His long legs meant he could take the steps three at a time.

With Roul giving away her trade secrets, she was forced to pivot instead, turning just out of reach of the defender and gliding past his fingertips. Roul slowed to stop from colliding with the guard, but then she heard his boots find their rhythm once more.

'I'm going to make sure you never leave the house again,' Roul called to her. 'I'm going to tie you to a chair.'

Eda rounded the corner, leaping sideways to avoid colliding with a maid carrying a tray of food. Roul was not so lucky. The maid yelped, and a loud clang rang out as the silver tray landed on the ground.

'If you step one foot on that terrace—' Roul said, scrambling after her.

He did not have a chance to finish his sentence, because she was already through the terrace door and dashing past the guards standing either side of it. Queen Fayre looked up from her game. Eda's eyes were on the two guards behind her. That was twice as many as usual. The woman was queen regent now, and the kingdom could not afford to lose her.

The men drew their weapons and came for Eda.

'Halt!' they shouted, forming a wall of steel and muscle between her and the queen.

That was her time to stop, put her hands up, tell them she was unarmed. She already had Fayre's full attention, but she had one more point to make. Eda continued towards the guards, dropping to the ground at the last minute and rolling through the narrow gap between them. She was through before they realised what had happened, then back on her feet, hands raised as she skidded to a stop in front of Queen Fayre.

'I'm unarmed,' she breathed. Then she felt the points of two swords in her back.

The queen regent sat stiff in her chair, staring. 'Eda Suttone.'

'Oh good,' she puffed. 'You remember me.'

Fayre looked past her to where Roul was now standing, telling the guards to take it easy. 'Good morning, Commander.'

'Your Majesty,' Roul replied awkwardly.

Fayre's eyes returned to Eda. 'Can I trust you to behave if I tell my guards to sheathe their weapons?'

Eda kept her hands up. 'Absolutely. I only came to talk.'

Queen Fayre nodded to her guards, and the pressure on Eda's back eased.

'I gather you were not aware of Ms Suttone's plans to visit either, Commander?' Fayre asked Roul.

'No, Your Majesty. I'm happy to escort her out.'

Eda dared a glance back at him. His face was red and jaw clenched.

'Leave us.' Fayre looked to her stunned opponent, who was frozen in her chair. 'I am afraid we shall need to finish our game later.'

Eda had forgotten there was someone else there. The woman rose from her chair, curtsied, then rushed off. The queen's guards wandered to the far end of the terrace. Eda could feel Roul's eyes on her as he turned and left. Only then did she lower her hands.

'Forgive my interruption,' Eda began.

'I forgive nothing, Ms Suttone. Now, tell me how you got into the royal borough without an invitation from me. I gather from Commander Thornton's face that he was not your ally.'

'Quite the opposite.' Eda was not invited to sit, so she remained standing. 'I climbed over the wall.'

'You climbed a forty-foot wall? With what?'

Eda held up her hands again. 'With these.'

Fayre's eyes moved over her bloodied fingernails. 'Why?'

'To follow up on the letter I sent you.' She wet her lips. 'I would very much like to go to Harlech Castle and bring your son home.'

Fayre leaned back in her chair, watching Eda. 'So you said in your letter. There is a reason you received no response from me.' She straightened one of the chess pieces on the board. 'You see, I cannot in good conscience send you to your death.'

Disappointment sat heavy in Eda's chest. 'But I can do this. Who else will you send if not me? If you send soldiers, they'll be slaughtered before they reach the castle. Or an advisor? If by some miracle they survive the journey, Prince Becket won't receive them.'

'And he will receive you?'

Eda nodded. 'Just tell me who you want me to be. A merchant, a noble lady, a relative, a maid at the castle. I'll be whatever you need me to be.' She took a small step forwards. 'I'll find a way in.'

'So that is what this little display is all about.' She drew a tired breath. 'Even if my son did not turn you away at the gate, there is the matter of the royal family. They have their own agenda and will not appreciate any interference.'

Eda only shrugged. 'Welcomed or not, I promise you I'll get inside. Give me a few minutes alone with the prince, and I'll tell him exactly who I am and explain all the reasons he needs to return to Chadora.'

The queen regent looked her up and down. 'Does your family know you are here?'

'No. Though they won't be too surprised to learn of it.'

Fayre was silent as she stared at Eda, then said, 'The safest route would be via ship. However, if a Chadorian ship were to anchor in Gwynedd, it would likely be attacked before its occupants had a chance to disembark. That leaves horseback.'

'Then you're in luck, because I ride very well.'

Fayre frowned. 'Have you any idea how dangerous that journey is? There are barely any villages left, only ghosts. I had an entire cavalry disappear in the forests of Carmarthenshire last year. A rebel group killed every defender, then ate every horse.'

'Which is exactly why the only woman you can send is *me*. I can protect myself and anyone else travelling at my side.'

Fayre folded her hands in her lap. 'And what do you get out of all this? I know you have no interest in securing wealth or a place at court.'

It was a good question. 'Chadora gets a king, and I get to be useful for something other than laundry.'

Fayre nodded in understanding. 'You seek purpose.'

Air filled Eda's lungs. She felt seen. 'Yes.'

A knowing smile played on Queen Fayre's lips. 'Have you no plans to settle down like your sisters? A beautiful young woman such as yourself must be getting offers of marriage.'

'My uncle has a suitor in mind.' Eda clasped her hands in front of her. 'I'm not sure if you've noticed, but I'm a bit of a handful.'

'Yes, I have noticed.'

One corner of Eda's mouth lifted. 'I'd prefer to settle down *after* I bring Chadora their king.'

Fayre looked to the defenders at the far end of the terrace. 'You have said your piece. Now it is time for you to leave.' She signalled to her guards. 'I should warn you that if I find you in my home, uninvited, again, you will be locked up next time.' Her eyes met Eda's. 'Am I clear?'

Eda chewed her lip. 'Does that mean you'll consider it?'

Fayre waved her away. 'You are positively exhausting. Go.'

Eda lowered into a curtsy. One of the guards took her arm as she rose, and she was escorted from the terrace.

CHAPTER 4

*I*f you don't stop pacing, you'll wear away the stone,' Harlan told Roul.

They were waiting at the front entrance of the castle to find out what was to become of Eda. Harlan had come as soon as he had heard.

Roul stopped and turned in a circle, hands on hips, trying to calm himself, then resumed pacing. 'She never listens. I specifically told her to leave this thing alone.'

Harlan crossed his arms. 'There's your first mistake. You tried to tell her what to do.'

'She seems to think Lyndal's friendship with the queen makes her untouchable.'

He stopped walking when he spotted Eda and one of the queen's guards descending the steps towards them. The defender let go of her when he neared them. 'Make sure she leaves.' Then, turning on his heel, he climbed the steps.

'You all right?' Harlan asked her.

'I'm fine.'

Every muscle in Roul's body was tense as he tried to contain his temper. It took a lot to get him worked up, but Eda seemed to manage it easily enough. 'What the hell was that? Do you have any idea how lucky you are to still have a head after that little stunt of yours? Those guards were armed. What if Queen Fayre hadn't recognised you? What if she hadn't spoken up? Those men would've cut your throat without a moment's hesitation. Queen Fayre's all this kingdom has right now. In case you haven't noticed, no one's taking chances around here.'

'She listened. That's all I wanted.'

'Glad one of you has that ability.' He took a step towards her. 'I'm tempted to lock you in the tower for the afternoon to teach you a lesson.'

She tilted her head. 'The lesson didn't stick the first time I was locked in the tower. I wouldn't waste your time.'

Roul looked to Harlan. 'I think it best you escort her to the gate.'

'Are you serious right now?' Eda asked.

He met her eyes. 'Deadly.'

Harlan drew a breath and gestured for Eda to start walking. 'Come on. Let's go.'

Eda did not move. 'It's done now. There's no point staying angry at me. I *am* sorry you got caught up in it. That was never the plan.'

Before Roul could reply, a servant appeared at the top of the steps. 'Commander Thornton. Queen Fayre would like to speak with you on the terrace.'

Eda's face fell. 'She knows it was my terrible idea and you have nothing to do with it.'

A glare was Roul's only response before stepping past her and heading back into the castle.

'Come to the house tonight,' she called to his back. 'We'll talk.'

Roul did not reply. He did not even look back when he reached the top of the steps. He marched along the gloomy corridors of Eldon castle, mind racing with possibilities, until he reached the terrace where Queen Fayre sat alone.

Her two guards stood out of hearing range. He stopped in front of her and bowed his head. 'You wanted to see me, Your Majesty?'

She looked up at him, a thoughtful expression on her face. 'Firstly, congratulations, Commander. The title is much deserved. I knew when I met you, half starved, all those years ago, that you would make something of yourself.'

In reality, he would likely still be stealing livestock from the houses along the Toryn border if their paths had not crossed that day. 'Thank you.'

She offered him a small smile. 'I do hope you wrote your family to tell them of the news.'

He could not gauge if her sentiments were genuine or if she was simply reminding him that she was the reason he still had a family to write to. Her compassion had saved their lives a few years back, but her ever-changing agenda had ruined his. They never spoke about that part. They had agreed to never say those things aloud to anyone. It was safer for everyone to keep them buried. Roul considered Harlan his closest friend, but even he only knew the bare minimum. Eda knew even less—despite her constant probing.

'Not yet, but I will.'

'Good.' She regarded him a moment. 'Eda Suttone. You are well acquainted with her, are you not?'

He already did not like the direction of the conversation. 'Yes.'

'Did she share with you her plans to travel to Harlech Castle?'

'She did.'

Queen Fayre was silent a moment. 'Did she really climb the wall without aid of a rope to get inside the borough?'

Roul had not known that part. 'If she said she did, then yes.'

'What about weaponry? Can she handle a sword?'

It felt a lot like the queen was actually considering her insane suggestion. 'Yes, she can handle most weapons.'

'Really?' She tapped her finger on the arm of her chair. 'Did *you* teach her?'

'I spar with her on occasion. Her father taught her before his death, then Commander Wright.'

She watched him closely. 'Are you and Ms Suttone friends?'

'Yes, Your Majesty.'

'Nothing more?'

He hesitated. Were they lovers? No. Were they kindred spirits? It certainly felt like it. But the queen was not asking that. 'Nothing more.'

'Good.' A slow nod as she thought. 'Good.' She looked around before continuing. 'She seems quite sure that she can find a way to reach my son. I had not considered sending a woman. Now I am forced to admit that it is an interesting idea given where we find ourselves. Of course, we would need to think smart about how we proceed. We only get one chance.'

Roul grew increasingly uneasy at her words. 'Just because she can handle a sword, climb a wall, and wears dresses, that doesn't make her the right person to pull this off.'

Fayre's eyes returned to him. 'Oh I know. The girl is fractious. Unruly. She lacks the discipline needed.'

Roul released the breath he had been holding.

'Anyone can learn to use a sword. However, the discipline component is what makes a soldier unique,' she added. 'Do you agree?'

'Yes.'

She sat a little straighter in her chair. 'That is what you teach your recruits, is it not?'

Any relief he felt moments earlier dissipated. 'That's part of it.'

'And have you taught unruly men in the past? Made soldiers out of them?'

He grew uneasy. 'Yes. Though some men can't be taught. Some never make it past the training phase.'

Fayre thought on that for a moment, then said, 'I would like Eda Suttone to train under you. I would like to know if she is up to it, physically and mentally. I want to see if she is capable of following orders—*any* orders.' She paused. 'You know her, know her limits. I would like you to push her to those limits. By the end of the month, we should know if she is up to it.'

Roul felt winded. 'Those things you speak of can't be taught in a month.'

'We do not have the luxury of time, Commander. Who knows what plans Queen Isabella and her son are making as we stand here debating what is possible? Chadora needs a king. I cannot keep my son's throne warm forever. Will you help me with this?'

Everything inside him screamed no. 'The training we provide is designed to break grown men.'

'Better she break here inside these walls than out there.' She lifted her chin. 'Do you not agree?'

He could see he was not going to talk Queen Fayre off the ledge now. She had made up her mind. 'I'll train her if that's your wish.'

But could he break her?

She tilted her head, studying him. 'I can assign her to someone else if you are not comfortable.'

That would be worse—much worse. That someone would not know her limits as he did and would not care if he pushed past them. 'I'll do it. I'll train her.'

Queen Fayre's shoulders relaxed. 'Good. I shall inform the warden and write to Lord Thomas. I am certain he will agree to the arrangement under the right conditions.' Her tone suggested she knew him well. The man would do anything to keep the queen's favour, even sacrifice his niece. 'Good day, Commander.'

Roul's feet were heavy as he turned away. 'Your Majesty.'

CHAPTER 5

*H*er mother read the letter over and over while Eda's uncle paced the length of the room, looking slightly bewildered.

'The queen offers no specifics as to what the family will gain from this arrangement,' Thomas said. 'Perhaps it depends on Eda's success.'

Candace held the letter out to Blake, who snatched it from her hands and began to read.

'You will send me to an early grave,' Candace said, pressing a hand to her chest. 'This is my fault. I should have stepped in a long time ago. The day I saw Harlan teaching you how to fight with multiple swords, I knew it had gone too far.'

Eda was seated on the floor beside Blake, chewing her lip. 'Wouldn't that make it Harlan's fault?'

Blake dropped the letter on her lap and leaned back in her chair. 'You nagged him incessantly, day after day.'

'And he indulged me,' Eda said with a shrug.

Blake closed her eyes. 'This is like Lyndal's time at court all over again. Why must it fall on you to bring him home?

Let Queen Fayre go to England and retrieve her son herself.'

Thomas stopped pacing, linking his hands behind his back. 'Queen Fayre cannot go. If anything should happen to her, we may as well open the gates and invite King Edward's army in, hand them our food as a welcome gift.' He looked down at Eda. 'Though why she thinks sending a merchant girl without an ounce of propriety will be beneficial I still cannot fathom.'

'Propriety won't help me navigate the rebel-infested wastelands of Carmarthenshire, Uncle.'

Candace closed her eyes at the words.

'It's only a few weeks of training,' Eda said. She crawled over to her mother and took her hand. 'Nothing's been decided yet.'

Thomas tapped one foot. 'I assume we are to be duly compensated regardless of the outcome. If Eda is to train for the next month, we shall be forced to delay the wedding.'

Everyone looked at him.

'I shall seek some clarity when I send my response,' he finished.

'Wedding?' Eda said. 'I've only met the man once.'

'And surprisingly, Leigh agreed to return—despite your dismal efforts,' Thomas said as he headed to the door. He stopped and turned when he reached it. 'You will do the queen's bidding, and then we shall reassess. If you did play a part in bringing Chadora a king, I think we could aim higher than the bootmaker.' He opened the door, stepped through it, and closed it behind him without another word.

'Poor Leigh,' Candace said after a long silence, sitting back in her chair with a heavy breath.

Blake had picked up the letter again and was rereading it. Eda's heart pounded with nervous excitement. She would finally get to train with the defenders. It was already more than she dared hope for.

'Of course Uncle is in agreement,' Blake muttered. 'Anything to gain favour with the queen.'

'Why did you do this?' Candace said, looking at Eda. 'I am trying to understand. Why? To avoid marriage?'

'No.' Though that was a nice perk. 'I just want to help, feel useful.'

'What are you talking about?' Blake said. 'You're already useful.'

'Because there are easier ways to get out of marriage,' Candace added.

Eda rose to her feet. 'Again, this isn't about marriage, though surely you see that Leigh Appleton is the most boring man Uncle could've selected for me.'

Candace's eyebrows came together in disapproval. 'I think that was intentional on his part.'

Eda waved a hand and went to leave the room.

'Stay where you are,' Blake said, voice firm. 'You can't run away from this conversation. You're not a child anymore.'

Eda turned back to them, crossing her arms. Garlic chose that moment to fly into the room, crash-landing in the middle of the table and looking around. They all stared at the duck, not speaking for the longest time.

'My soul itches,' Eda said quietly. 'I used to think it was grief, then anger. Then I learned to live with the grief, and the anger subsided. Yet still I'm restless.'

Candace sighed and looked down at the floor.

Blake leaned back in her chair. 'Do you really think getting beaten up by soldiers for a few weeks is going to fix that?'

Eda stepped forwards and picked up Garlic, stroking the duck's silky feathers. 'I don't need your permission. Uncle has already given it. But I do need you to love me through this.' She looked between them. 'This might be the biggest mistake I've ever made. I might regret it. But I'd really like a chance to learn the hard way.'

Candace raised her eyes. 'Must all my children learn the hard way?'

Eda understood her mother's frustration. Her brother's mistakes had cost him his life. Her sisters' brazen acts had almost cost them theirs. And now Eda was reaching for trouble with both hands.

'The letter says you'll only be sent if you're deemed to be both physically and mentally capable,' Blake said. 'You do realise a quarter of the recruits never make it past the initial training period?'

That was admittedly higher than Eda had expected. 'They're good odds.'

'Roul and Harlan can't give you any special treatment,' Blake added.

Eda shrugged. 'I don't want special treatment. I want to find out what I'm capable of as much as they do.'

Candace smoothed her hair back. 'You will be stuck with a group of foul-mouthed men, day after day. There will be no ladies for company.'

'I don't need company, Mother. It's not a picnic.'

Candace rose abruptly. 'You live as if we have not lost enough members of this family.' She left the room.

Eda's hand stilled as she looked at her sister. 'I can't live half a life for her peace of mind. I'm sorry.'

Luella's cries reached them from upstairs, prompting Blake to stand. 'I guess we'll see if you survive the training before worrying about the rest.' She went to Eda, pulling her into her arms and kissing the side of her head. 'For what it's worth, I'm rooting for you.'

Eda watched her sister walk away, then released a long breath.

CHAPTER 6

*T*he frosty grass crunched underfoot as Roul strode across the training field to where the recruits were gathered. He blew warm air into his hands, then rubbed them together. At least the rain had slowed to a drizzle. He looked for Eda among the group, but she was not there.

'Morning,' he called to Harlan, who was fiddling with one of the shields.

The commander looked in his direction. 'Morning.'

'She's late.'

Harlan placed the shield down with a chuckle. 'It's barely light.'

That was true, but Roul was agitated anyway. He had not seen Eda since their tense encounter at the castle the day before. That had been intentional on his part. He had been too angry to go to Wright House that night. He was still angry, and everyone else seemed a little too calm about the whole thing.

Harlan walked over to him. 'These men are only a few weeks into their training. She'll hold up.'

Roul looked around at the recruits. It was true, they

were inexperienced—but they could still do plenty of harm.

They had all come from noble households, with the exception of Blackmane, who had arrived on a ship. It was Roul who had convinced the warden to give the ill-tempered nineteen-year-old a chance. Tatum was all but disowned by his family, and the army was a logical place for noble fathers to send unruly boys. Tollere, Alveye, and Hadewaye were all the youngest sons in their households, another common trend among nobility.

'I'm sure Commander Wright has told you we have a new recruit joining us,' Roul said, addressing the men. 'She'll be training with you for the rest of the month.'

Tatum and Alveye exchanged a smirk.

'Something funny you want to share?' Roul asked the pair.

The smile fell from Alveye's face, and Tatum looked at the ground. 'No, Commander.'

Blackmane looked far from impressed but knew better than to air his grievances aloud.

'Why's she training with the likes of us?' Hadewaye asked, frowning.

'Because that's Queen Fayre's wish.' Roul looked over at Blackmane, who was shaking his head. 'That's not going to be a problem for you, is it?'

Blackmane leaned his weight on one foot. 'No, Commander.'

Before Roul could continue, Eda emerged from the fog at a run. She was dressed in men's trousers that were a mile too big for her. Everyone turned to watch her approach.

'I'll leave you to it,' Harlan said. 'Don't break her on the first day.'

'You're the one who said she gets no special treatment.' Roul looked in Eda's direction. 'You're late!'

Eda's eyes met Harlan's as they passed one another.

'Good luck,' Harlan said over his shoulder.

Eda came to a stop in front of Roul, removing her cloak. 'Sorry. I had a little trouble getting through the gate, even with a letter from the warden.'

'Perhaps they thought you were trying to break in again.'

Eda tilted her head. 'And good morning to you too.'

He stepped back from her. 'Recruits. What's the consequence for tardiness?'

Blackmane crossed his arms in front of him. 'Ten laps of the training yard, Commander.'

Eda looked between them. 'But it wasn't my fault.'

'It wasn't my fault, *Commander*,' Roul corrected. 'Rules are rules. Off you go. You can join us when you're done.' He turned away to make it clear the conversation was over.

He expected an argument, but for once, he did not get one. She simply jogged off.

Roul got the recruits warmed up with some strength training, conscious of Eda flashing in and out of his peripheral vision. Every now and then she would slow to tug her trousers up.

When she had completed her laps, she returned to the group, trying very hard not to appear out of breath.

'Listen up,' Roul called to the men. He waited until he had their full attention. 'This is Eda Suttone. Don't let her gender fool you. She's as capable with a sword as any one of you.' He pointed around the group, doing introductions. 'This is Ryder Blackmane, Nixon Hadewaye, Kelton Alveye, Brock Tatum, and Graeme Tollere.' His eyes returned to Eda. 'We use last names around here. You'll be addressed as Suttone moving forwards. Any questions before we begin?'

She shook her head. 'No, Commander.'

'Good.' He gestured to the weapons laid out on the icy grass. 'Grab a sword and a shield, then pair off.'

Everyone moved to collect weapons. Blackmane took the shield Eda was reaching for. She looked up at him, then moved to the next one. Roul knew he would do her no favours by speaking up on her behalf.

The men paired off.

Usually, if there were odd numbers, Roul would join in, but Eda made three pairs. He was tempted to place her with Tollere, the weakest of the group, but the sooner she established her place in the hierarchy, the better it would be for everyone.

'Suttone, you'll pair with Tatum,' Roul said.

Blackmane looked over, then muttered. 'Perfect. Now we have to listen to her cry.'

'Watch yourself, Blackmane,' Roul said, 'or you'll be running laps also.'

He hoped they would quieten down once they saw what she could do. It was difficult for any man to comprehend that someone both petite and beautiful could also be lethal.

Yes, beautiful. Roul was not blind.

'Let's go,' he called.

Eda and Tatum moved closer to each other, watching the other with equal suspicion. Tatum was in his eighteenth year and took the title of cockiest recruit. He and Blackmane excelled at everything. Alveye and Hadewaye were improving, but they had to work hard at it. Tollere was decent with a bow, but that was about it. There was every chance he would not make it as a defender.

Eda tossed her sword into the air a few times, getting used to the weight of it.

'The idea is to poke me with the pointy end,' Tatum said, grinning at Eda.

Roul pressed his eyes shut, wishing the morning away

before it had barely begun. 'Less talking, more fighting. Once you've disarmed your partner, you bring your sword to me. The rest of you will run laps.'

'Oof,' Tatum said, circling Eda. 'You're going to be tired this afternoon.'

Eda rolled her eyes. 'Tired of your voice.'

'Promise me you won't cry. I never know what to do when women cry.'

'Are we fighting or courting?' Eda said, losing patience. 'You're holding weapons, yet I'm getting your life story.'

Tatum laughed at that. So did Hadewaye and Alveye.

'All right,' Tatum said, spinning his wooden sword, 'You want to fight? Then let's fight.'

Eda was determined not to be completely humiliated on her first day. Certainly not during the very first drill. Now that Roul had flexed a little muscle by making her run laps, she had her own point to make.

She waited for Tatum to strike first, wanting to see what his feet gave away in the process. This would help her for the rest of the fight. Once she understood his level of patience and self-control, then it was time to find out how strong he was.

Reasonably patient, it turned out. She noticed he held back on that first strike, suggesting that underneath all the bravado was a gentleman. When she blocked his strike with her shield, he nodded approvingly.

'Ah. The girl can keep hold of her weapon. Good.'

She let the comment blow past her.

The next time he struck her, it was hard. She had suspected that Harlan and Roul held back some when they were teaching her, but this confirmed it. She felt the force of the blow everywhere. It hummed through her bones all the way down to her toes. It was clear that if she wanted to win, she would need to be the one doing the hitting.

When he lunged for her again, she ducked, then shot up, moving to disarm him. But he was ready. His sword locked with hers.

'Someone's been teaching you defender tricks,' he said over the tops of their weapons. There was amusement in his eyes.

Eda shoved him back, but he came for her again. She spun, foot aimed at his leg in hope of knocking him off balance. But he stepped out of reach, and her foot sailed past him. It was his turn now. A foot slammed into her stomach before she had a chance to move out of its way. She doubled over, painfully winded. But she did not drop her weapon.

'Empty your stomach if you need to,' Tatum said, spinning his sword. 'I'll wait.'

She gasped for breath, eyes never leaving him. They were an even match so far as skill, but his heavy bones and muscular frame were undeniably an advantage.

'I'm good,' she managed to get out.

She was aware of Roul watching them. As much as he liked to play the tough, unfeeling commander, he would not enjoy seeing her hurt. She knew this because whenever he watched her spar with Harlan, he always averted his eyes when the sword connected with her.

It was around five minutes later when Eda realised the other pairs had already finished. They stood watching them, and she felt a small amount of pride at that. While she was by no means winning, she was upright and still holding her sword.

'You can choose to lay down your weapon at any time,' Roul called.

The words were for her, not Tatum.

'Did you hear our commander?' Eda panted. 'There's no shame in giving up.'

Tatum chuckled and wiped a hand down his sweaty face. He was tiring, but so was she.

While she was focused on that point, the recruit dropped, one foot hooking her ankle. Her feet went out from under her, and she landed on her back, winded once more. He came for her sword, but she rolled once and sprang back onto her feet, weapon pointed at Tatum as she coughed.

Hadewaye and Alveye cheered her.

'Almost had you,' Tatum said with a lopsided grin.

She coughed some more. 'Almost is not a win.' She ran at him, delivering a sequence of blows. He might have been strong, but he was not as fast as she was. If she could keep it up, he would make a mistake eventually.

Finally, her sword met his ribs. But just as hope took flight inside her, his shield crashed into her knee, sending pain shooting up her leg all the way to her hip. She bit her cheek to stop from crying out. The shield fell from her hand, but she still did not drop the sword.

'Stand down,' Roul called, walking over to them.

Tatum immediately stepped back from her.

'But I still have hold of my sword,' Eda coughed out, taking one step and almost falling in the process.

Roul's tall frame loomed over her. 'When I say stand down, you lower your weapon and step back from your opponent without question. Understand?'

She looked up at him. Seeing his dark expression, she nodded. 'Yes, Commander.'

His gaze fell to her knee. 'Do you need to go to the infirmary?'

'It's just a cramp,' she lied.

His eyes travelled back up to hers, and then he turned

away. 'Gather around. I have some tricks that might help you next time. Pay attention.'

Eda followed, trying to hide the slight limp as her leg throbbed. There was no way she would admit to being injured on her first day of training.

'That was impressive,' Hadewaye said, falling into step with her. 'No one normally lasts that long against him.'

She glanced sideways at the round-faced recruit. He was short and well built, with kind eyes. Younger than her judging by his distinct lack of facial hair. 'Thanks.'

They joined the others, watching the demonstration. Eda took mental notes for next time. She also took the opportunity to size up the other recruits. Alveye looked to be around the same age as Hadewaye, but a slimmer build. He had red hair and matching freckles that covered his face and hands. Tollere was the only one among them who really stood out as having come from a noble household. His speech was stiff, while the others had relaxed into a less formal way of communicating. He stood sniffing the whole time Roul was speaking, until Blackmane eventually shoved him to make him stop.

Blackmane.

There was no way Blackmane had come from the noble borough. It was evident in his speech, his stance, his alertness. The enormous chip on his shoulder. Eda did not know if he was in a bad mood that morning or if that was how he was normally. His black hair was swept to one side, falling over one eye. She was surprised Roul had not made him cut it. His jaw was sharp and his stare penetrating. He stood with his arms crossed over his chest, scowling. The scowl deepened when he spotted Eda staring at him.

She immediately looked away.

'We'll be heading to the butts for archery,' Roul was saying. 'Collect the weapons and take them to the armoury and get yourself a bow.'

Archery she could do. If he had told her to do a three-mile run, she would have probably cried—inwardly, of course.

Eda held back, wanting to walk behind everyone so they would not see her limp. But Roul also waited behind, eyes on her.

'Problem?' he asked.

'No, Commander.'

'Then catch up to the others.'

She began walking, concentrating so her steps were even. But they must have been too careful, because Roul called to her, 'You're injured.'

'I'm fine.'

He caught her arm, pulling her to a stop. 'Go to the port. Legs in the water for a half hour. If you can walk properly after that, you can come back. If not, go home. We don't train injured soldiers.'

She let out an exasperated breath. 'I just told you I'm fine.'

'We don't train liars either.'

She searched his eyes. 'If I leave, I look weak.'

'I don't care how you look. I care how you perform. Go.' He walked away before she had a chance to argue.

Eda watched his back for a moment, then, throwing her hands up, went to retrieve her cloak.

CHAPTER 7

*W*hen training finished for the day, the exhausted recruits announced they were going to the port borough for an ale. Roul decided to join them, because he wanted to check if Eda was still down at the water. She had not returned to training, which meant the so-called "cramp" in her leg had not subsided.

The port was quiet that afternoon. There were no supply ships moored to the dock, only a handful of fishermen dragging empty nets from the water. As the recruits filed into the tavern, Roul spotted Eda seated alone on the beach.

'I'll meet you inside,' he told the others before making his way over to her.

She sat with her legs stretched out and feet crossed at the ankles, staring out at the water. Her trousers were rolled up, ivory calves dusted with grainy sand. Her boots were next to her, woollen socks stuffed into them.

Dropping down onto the sand beside her, Roul drew up his knees and rested his arms upon them. He had a profile view of that pretty nose of hers. He really did not want to be around the first time it broke.

Whenever the pair sparred, he always took care not to hurt her. The recruits, on the other hand, would do whatever they needed to in order to advance. Roul had broken many noses in his time. One became immune to the pain of others after a while. Seeing Eda in pain was another matter. When that shield had crashed into her leg, he had felt it like it had collided with his own. It was the reason he had ended the fight—whether he cared to admit it or not.

She glanced in his direction, her eyebrows knitted together in annoyance. 'You and Harlan did me no favours by holding back when we sparred.'

'Did you honestly expect us to knock you unconscious to show you the way of things?' His gaze fell to her purple knee. 'I gather the cold water wasn't the miracle cure we had hoped.'

'It helped some.' She was silent for a long moment. 'Will I keep losing to them?'

'If you try to fight like them, you will. You need to fight smarter, because they're a lot stronger than you are.' He watched her face as she processed his words. 'You can always pull out, tell Queen Fayre you changed your mind.'

Her eyes closed. 'And then what? Marry the bootmaker and whittle the days away in his shop?'

He was torn on that. While he did not like the thought of her trapped in a life she did not want, he knew it would be a much safer existence. He also knew marriage would be the end of them spending time together. No sane husband would let his wife chase another man through the trees.

It was a difficult realisation to digest.

Eda was the only person within the walls who brought out his playful side. She was his escape from that harsh life. Her energy was contagious, addictive even. She made him forget the reason he boarded that boat and sailed to Chadora in the first place.

She made him *forget*.

'I'll take you home,' he said, rising and offering a hand. For once, she took it. He pulled her to her feet, keeping hold of her while she steadied herself. 'Your knee's swollen.'

She looked down at it. 'It barely hurts anymore.'

'Liar.'

Her gaze travelled up to meet his. 'Are the others at the tavern?'

'Yes.'

'Is that where you were going?'

He nodded. 'Roll your trousers down. We're not among the trees.'

He had seen her bare legs many times over the previous year. Sometimes they would swim in the creek, and she would strip down to her chemise without a second thought, as though he were a sibling immune to the sight of wet fabric clinging to her naked form. But his body did not react as a brother's would. There was a reason he waited in the water until she was dressed.

When Eda had finished fixing her trousers and putting her boots on, she straightened and asked, 'Can I come with you to the tavern?'

'It's not a place for ladies.'

She tilted her head. 'Do you see a lady before you?'

Fair point. 'Do you even drink ale?'

'Of course. It's my drink of choice.'

He exhaled, struggling to come up with a good reason to tell her no. 'Fine. One drink, and then I'm taking you home.'

Those pink lips stretched into a smile. 'One drink.'

~

Eda could barely stand the smell of ale, let alone the taste, but if that was what the recruits were drinking, then that was what she would drink also.

'There she is,' Tatum said when she slid onto the stool beside him. 'We were wondering where you disappeared to.'

She looked around the table at their curious faces awaiting her reply. 'I had to get some cold water on my knee.'

'Told you that you hurt her,' Hadewaye said to Tatum.

Tatum only shrugged. 'Never did get your sword though.'

'You would've had to pry it from my cold, dead hand,' she replied.

Alveye grinned into his cup. 'I don't care what Blackmane says. I like her.'

Eda looked over to where Roul and Blackmane were seated. The recruit had fled the table when she arrived. Roul had given her an apologetic smile before following him.

'Bit early for such a bold statement,' Tatum said, eyeing Eda over his drink. 'We haven't seen her shoot yet.'

Eda took a sip of her ale and fought to keep her face neutral as she swallowed the foul liquid. 'I can handle a bow.'

'Time will tell.'

She was worried her presence would upset the dynamic of the group, but they seemed relaxed enough. When she glanced in Roul's direction again, she found him looking at her. He winked before turning back to Blackmane. He had never learned to sign because there had not been a need. She had found her voice soon after they met. But they still found ways to communicate across a room.

'I heard the merchants have been catching mackerel off the dock,' Hadewaye was saying.

The conversation had moved on to fish.

'And garfish,' Eda said.

Everyone looked at her.

'I suppose you're an expert fisherman as well,' Tatum said, his blue eyes playful.

'I'm a merchant. You learn to fish or you starve.'

Alveye's freckled face creased in confusion. 'I thought you lived in the nobility borough with Commander Wright.'

'Now,' Tatum said. 'But only because her sister snagged herself a commander.'

Eda took a long drink.

Hadewaye watched her. 'What are you training with the likes of us for? Is the queen planning on sticking you on top of the wall?'

'I heard Queen Fayre is going to send her to Harlech Castle to seduce the prince and lure him home,' Tollere said.

Eda laughed. 'I'm the last woman they would send if that were the plan.' She glanced in Roul's direction, knowing he would have laughed at that comment too. The smile fell from her face when she found a woman standing behind him, arms wrapping Roul's neck and her mouth an inch from his ear. Lush honey hair fell over her face as she whispered something to him.

'Watch it,' Alveye said, reaching out and catching her hand. 'You're spilling liquid gold.'

Eda looked down at the pool of ale on the table in front of her, and her cheeks heated. 'Sorry.'

'Don't you go crying on us,' Tatum said with a hint of smile as he waved down one of the barmaids. 'We'll get it cleaned up.'

Someone arrived with a cloth. Eda held her drink off the table, eyes returning to Roul and the woman once more. Her chin now rested comfortably atop his head, her breasts brushing his back. She wore a simple yellow dress, belted in a way that showed off her round hips. While it was by no means news that Roul had been with women, seeing the evidence was oddly confronting. Eda felt sick suddenly and looked accusingly at the ale she was holding.

'Hopefully we shall get to use the lances tomorrow,' Tollere was saying.

She was thankful that conversation had continued without her.

'Because you need practise keeping hold of one?' Tatum said.

Hadewaye and Alveye laughed.

'You all right?' Hadewaye asked when he caught sight of Eda's unsmiling face. 'The ale's not the best.'

'The ale's fine,' she lied, forcing a smile. Then, clearing her throat, she asked as casually as she could manage, 'Who's that woman with Commander Thornton?'

Tatum looked in their direction. 'Ah. That's Hildred. Her father owns the tavern.'

She tried to remember if anyone had mentioned that name in front of her before but came up blank. She dared another glance and saw Roul was reaching back for Hildred now, holding on to her leg. It was such a familiar gesture. So intimate. She could not recall a time Roul had ever rested a hand on her in that way.

She caught that thought.

Of course he had not touched her in that way. They were friends, not lovers. A realisation hit her harder than any shield ever had. She was jealous. As illogical and childish as that was, she did not want him to put his hands on another woman's leg.

'Nice girl, and nice family,' Tatum was saying.

Eda swallowed. 'Is it serious between them?'

Alveye grinned. 'Well, she doesn't hold *us* that way

when we visit the tavern. I suppose that makes it serious enough.'

Roul chose that moment to look in her direction, and, as though reading her thoughts, his hand fell away from Hildred's leg.

She looked away, her heart pounding and stomach rolling. 'I should go.' She rose slowly, cautiously putting weight on her bad leg.

Alveye nodded towards her nearly full cup. 'You going to finish that?'

She slid the cup towards him. 'All yours.'

'Will you be there for all of training tomorrow?' Tatum asked with a smirk. 'Or just the first few minutes?'

Eda met his eyes as she stepped back from the table. 'All of it.'

'Are we supposed to stand up when she leaves?' Tollere asked. 'She is technically a lady.'

'She's wearing trousers,' Hadewaye replied.

Eda smiled. 'You're free to remain in your seats regardless of what I'm wearing.'

Tatum angled his head, looking her up and down. 'Having trouble picturing you in a dress, to be honest.'

Hadewaye shook his head.

'I'll see you tomorrow,' she said before fleeing for the door.

She was relieved when she stepped down onto the filthy street, the scent of salt and fish guts oddly comforting. A welcomed relief from the smell of sour ale that stickied the floors. She pressed her palms to her eyes, trying to remove the images of Roul and Hildred burned into her eyeballs. She had absolutely no right to feel jealous. He was her friend, nothing more. And she wanted him to be happy, to not be alone every night. She just did not want to bear witness to it.

She began walking, ignoring the pain in her knee.

'Eda!'

She stopped at the sound of her name from Roul's lips. She drew a breath, found a smile, and turned to face him.

'Where are you going?' he asked, jogging up to her. 'I told you I'd take you home.'

She looked past him instead of at him. 'You were busy. I didn't want to hassle you.'

'What are you talking about?' He began walking. 'We'll fetch a horse to save your knee.'

'There's really no need. It's feeling better with every passing minute.'

'If you rest it, it might actually hold you up tomorrow.' He glanced sideways at her. 'Or would you prefer to keep your pride intact instead?'

She watched her feet. 'We'll get a horse.'

He nodded.

They walked slowly to the royal gate, then made their way to the stables. Roul only asked the groom for one horse. She had ridden behind him more times than she could count, held on to him, but suddenly she caught herself needing some space.

He mounted, then reached for her.

She stepped back from his hand.

His eyebrows came together in confusion. 'What's the matter?'

She did not have an answer. At least, not one she was prepared to share. 'Nothing.' She stepped forwards and took his hand, and he hoisted her up behind him. He pushed the horse into a trot.

'Hold on,' he said over his shoulder.

She did. But not like Hildred had held on to him.

They headed for the gate, emerging into the merchant borough. When they were clear of the village, Roul pushed the horse into a canter. Eda was thankful for the fast pace because it meant they could not talk.

They were almost at Wright House when Roul finally slowed the horse to a walk. It was mid-afternoon, and the temperature was already dropping. Eda pulled her cloak tighter around her as they turned off the main road.

'I won't come in,' Roul said over his shoulder. 'I should get back.'

'Back to Hildred?' The question spilled out of her impulsive mouth, and she was so furious at her lack of control.

He turned in the saddle to look at her. 'Why would you ask that?'

She was conscious of how close his face was to hers as she grappled for a reply. 'Because I cut your meeting with her short.'

'My *meeting*?' Amusement filled his eyes before he faced forwards once more. 'Actually, I have to get back to the barracks.'

Whether that was true or not should not have mattered to her.

The moment Roul stopped the horse, Eda slid from its back, sucking in a breath when her feet hit the ground. She had forgotten about her knee.

Roul watched her from atop his horse. 'I would've helped you down, you know.'

'I don't need your help.' She sounded like a child. 'I'll see you in the morning.' She said all this without looking at him.

'Eda,' he called to her back.

She kept walking.

'Eda!'

She stopped, desperate not to turn, not to let him see the hurt and jealousy that would be so clear on her face. Why had she asked to go to the tavern? Everything had been fine until then. She turned, waiting.

He scrutinised her for the longest time. 'What's wrong with you?'

'Nothing's wrong with me.'

He continued to stare at her for what felt like an eternity. Then his gaze fell to her knee. 'If it's still sore tomorrow, don't come. I'll only send you home.'

'I can't not show up. Surely you of all people understand that.' If she expected any form of empathy, she did not get it.

He stared hard at her as he turned his horse. 'I mean it.'

She saluted in place of a reply, then headed for the house.

CHAPTER 8

*O*f course Eda showed up the following morning. What else had he expected? She also made a point of jogging from the gate to where the group was gathering, tugging up the belt of her brown trousers as she came to a stop in the middle of the training yard.

'Morning,' she chirped, stopping beside Hadewaye. She looked at Roul and nodded. 'Commander.'

At least she was in a good mood. She had barely been able to meet his eyes the day prior. There had been a brief moment where he had suspected her of being jealous, but then he reminded himself that this was Eda. If she was jealous, it was only because she did not like to come in second —ever. Everything was a competition with her.

'Today we're going over the wall,' Roul announced.

Tollere's mouth fell open. 'Already?'

Roul stared him down, then looked at Eda. 'If anyone here's not 100 percent up to it, then I suggest you tell me now. It's a challenging climb even at peak fitness. If you fall, there's every chance you'll die or never walk again.'

Nothing changed on Eda's face, stubborn woman that she was.

'How's the knee?' he asked when she did not speak up.

Eda lifted the leg and turned it in all directions. 'Good as new.' She always delivered her lies with confidence.

'All right,' Roul said, clapping his hands together. 'If everyone is up to it, then give me a sprint to the wall. Go.'

Eda took off before he had gotten the words out. The others pursued her, but they never caught up. She was first to reach the wall.

'What are you up to?' came Harlan's voice.

Roul turned to watch him approach. 'Just a casual trip down the cliff to keep the recruits on their toes.'

Harlan looked in their direction as he came to a stop beside Roul. 'If you're hoping she'll do something sensible, like pull out, prepare for disappointment. She was first to rise this morning and twice as determined as yesterday.'

'She tell you she hurt her knee? She was limping all over the place.'

'That wasn't the main topic at dinner, no.'

Roul narrowed his eyes. 'What does that mean?'

'We heard a lot about Hildred.'

So she *had* been angry about the barmaid. 'Really?'

'When Blake made a joke about her sounding like a jealous wife, she got up and left the table.'

She was likely angry at being excluded from that part of his life, but there was little to share from his perspective. He did not speak about Hildred to anyone. Their relationship, if you could call it that, was just a bit of mutual fun. Hildred was as busy as he was most of the time. Admittedly, Roul knew if he were to ask her to marry him, she would say yes in a heartbeat. But he had been honest from the beginning about his intentions without going into too much detail, and Hildred had assured him that she was content with their current arrangement.

The fact that Eda's mood was much improved meant

she had moved on from whatever she was feeling the day before.

'I better go catch up with them,' Roul said, exiting the conversation.

'She'll have no problem on the climb,' Harlan said. 'But just remember, if she drowns, the sisters will come for you.'

'Noted.' Drawing a deep breath, Roul jogged off to join the recruits by the wall.

When he came to a stop, he gestured to the defender above them, and a rope was thrown down. Walking to it, he turned to face the group. 'You'll climb up one at a time. Then you'll climb down the one on the other side. Black-mane, you'll go first.'

Blackmane took hold of the rope and began to climb.

'Tatum, you're next. Alveye, Hadewaye, Suttone, Tollere.'

The recruits appeared eager to get started, taking hold of the rope the second it was free. Eda flew up the thing like she had wings. Tollere was already sweating at the halfway mark.

When they were all standing safely atop the wall, Roul followed them up. Blackmane, Tatum, and Alveye had already climbed down and were waiting on the cliff's edge.

'You're really going to do this?' Roul asked Eda when she climbed up onto the embrasure.

She met his gaze as she took hold of the rope. 'These were *your* orders, Commander.' Then she disappeared.

A few minutes later, Roul stood with the group on the ledge, squinting against the damp wind. 'Test every foothold before you bear weight. If rock comes away, you warn those below you. This is important. And try not to panic. That's when mistakes happen. When you reach the bottom, wait. We'll swim to Flat Rock as a group.'

The men lowered themselves over the edge of the cliff

one at a time. When it was Eda's turn, she did not move. She was looking out at the rugged landscape. Her eyes were wide and filled with wonder. No fear to be seen. He had forgotten that her only perspective of outside the walls was Chadora's port.

Eda looked at him, and a wide smile spread across her face. 'Look how big the world is.'

Roul's mouth turned up involuntarily. He was constantly surprised by how much pleasure he got from watching her experience things. He looked around. The sea was vast and infinite from where they stood. These were the reminders she craved so much. These were the moments that would sustain her through a lifetime of walls and confinement.

When she moved to climb, he stepped in front of her. 'I'll go next. The two of you will follow me.'

Eda tilted her head, opened her mouth to say something, then closed it again.

Roul turned and carefully lowered himself over the edge.

Everything appeared to be going smoothly until Hadewaye reached the halfway point down the cliff face. His foot slipped, sending a spray of rock over Alveye and Tatum.

Swearing, Tatum caught a piece and threw it at the youngest recruit, hitting the back of his head. 'You're supposed to warn people below you, you arse!'

Hadewaye peered down at him. 'I was trying not to die!'

'Take a second,' Roul called. 'Then keep moving.'

'You're halfway,' Alveye said below him. 'The biggest risk of death is behind you.'

Hadewaye resumed climbing, muttering, 'But we still have to climb back up.'

Roul kept looking up to check on Eda, but there was no need. She climbed with confidence and grace. That was what came from spending most of one's life in trees. She was not afraid of heights. In fact, the only fear Roul had discovered in her so far was a fear of losing the people she loved.

It was a fear they shared.

Roul was nearing the halfway point when he heard Tollere yelp above him. He looked up as a large piece of rock came away from beneath the recruit's foot. 'Heads!' he shouted.

Eda pressed her cheek to the cliff face and held her breath.

The rock narrowly missed her, then passed a few inches from Roul's head. He was relieved when it bounced off course and away from those below him.

'Everyone all right?' Roul asked, looking up.

Eda nodded, not moving. Tollere was clinging to the rocks, hyperventilating. As tempting as it was to reprimand him, Roul knew he had to get him safely on the ground first.

'Eda, I want you to climb a few feet to the—' He did not get to finish his sentence, because the edge that Tollere's right foot was perched on crumbled beneath the weight of him. 'Heads!' Roul called again as rock and dust rained down on them.

Eda tucked her head beneath her arm as Tollere dangled above her, screaming.

'Tollere,' Roul said, his tone firm. 'I need you to calm down and find a foothold.'

The recruit's screams quietened to sharp, panicked breaths.

Eda spat dirt from her mouth and blinked. Then she pulled herself up the cliff face, reaching for his heel and guiding his toe to a foothold.

'You're all right,' she reassured him.

Roul's heart sped up. 'Eda, move aside—now.'

She did not have time. Tollere's foot slipped again, connecting with her face. Thankfully, she held tight. Roul began climbing up to them, but he was not fast enough. Tollere's hands slid from the rock, and he fell, crashing into Eda on his descent. But instead of falling with him, she caught the recruit by the arm. The weight jolted her. How she managed to stick to that rock, Roul had no idea. She winced with the effort.

Tollere dangled there for a moment while Roul scurried up at lightning speed. Roul grabbed hold of Tollere's ankle, taking as much of his weight as he could. He carefully guided Tollere's foot to the cliff, then did the same with the other one.

'Calm yourself before you kill us all,' Roul growled, moving up next to him.

Tollere took hold of the cliff and tried to slow his breathing. Only then did Eda let go of him. She rested her forehead on the icy rock, eyes closing as she collected herself.

No one spoke for a moment.

'All right,' Tollere said, taking control of his fear. He nodded, as though deciding on something. 'All right.' He was trembling all over as he started to climb again.

Roul looked up at Eda. 'What were you thinking? He's twice your weight.' His words came out harsher than he had intended.

She opened her eyes, chest still heaving. 'You said to take care of one another.'

He was not angry at her. It was fear working its way through his body—the fear of something happening to her. 'I need you to climb to the bottom before you tire. Can you do that?'

She nodded, licking blood from her lip. 'I can do that.'

He remained close as they slowly descended, directly beneath her and deliberately in her path so her feet were between his hands at all times. He wanted her within reach. Only when they neared the bottom did he increase the distance between them. He stepped down onto the slippery rock and moved aside for her, glaring in Tollere's direction. 'Just so we're clear, if by some miracle you make it back up that cliff face, you'll be running laps for the next five years.'

Tollere swallowed and looked at the ground. 'Yes, Commander.'

When Eda dropped down beside Roul, Alveye, Hadewaye, and Tatum applauded her. A smile played on Eda's lips as she held on to her hips and caught her breath.

'That was somewhat impressive,' Tatum said. 'I'll give you that.'

'I owe you,' Tollere said, his cheeks red.

Roul let them fuss. He might have even joined in the applause if he were not their commander. It had taken her one day to win over the group. One day. Everyone except for Blackmane, who was looking out at sea, ignoring what was taking place behind him.

'All right,' Roul said, quietening everyone down. 'I want this swim to be much less eventful than the climb down.' He ushered the group along the edge, where the water crashed against the rock and kicked into the air. 'Flat Rock is a half-mile swim. We stay together, and we look out for one another. If you can't swim, then now's the time to speak up.'

No one said anything.

Roul glanced at Eda, who was still peppered with debris. Her plait had come loose, and sections of hair blew in all directions. Her cheeks were red from the icy wind, her eyes two blinking emeralds against the sea spray. Swallowing, Roul turned his attention back to the men. 'All right. I suggest you strip down to the bare minimum. Suttone, you can go in as you are.'

'I hope you can swim as well as you can climb,' Tatum said as he unbelted his trousers.

She looked around the group now stripping to their braies. 'I can always call in my favour with Tollere if I start to struggle.'

'That would require Tollere to not drown,' Alveye replied.

Tollere shoved him as he was stepping out of his trousers, and he almost went into the water.

'You know, I think I'll remove my trousers too,' Eda said, reaching for her belt. 'I don't want heavy fabric slowing me down.'

Roul rubbed his forehead. 'As you wish.'

The others looked between themselves, then averted their eyes.

'Don't look so thoroughly uncomfortable,' Eda said. 'I'm keeping my shirt on.'

The men seemed to relax at hearing that.

'The water's dark, but look out for shadows,' Roul said. 'Shadows are likely rocks, and they'll slice you up good.' He blinked as a spray of water hit him. 'If a current wants to take you, don't fight it. You'll tire too quickly. Let it carry you for a bit—so long as it's not into a rock—then try again. Make sure you keep an eye on the person in front of you. Then no one will get left behind. I'll be at the back.'

'Then who's going to keep an eye on you?' Eda asked.

His eyes met hers. Of course she would ask that question. 'I don't need someone watching me. I just need you all not to drown. Can we all manage that?'

There was a collective murmur of 'Yes, Commander', and then Blackmane was first to dive in. The others followed, resurfacing with gasps and curse words describing the temperature of the water. Roul was last to dive in, popping up behind Eda.

'Let's go,' he called to Blackmane.

They all began to swim. Roul followed Eda so closely that her foot kept striking his chest as she kicked. She looked back at him.

'My toenails will shred you if you continue to swim that close.'

He did not slow. It was normal to feel protective of the most vulnerable member of the group. *Normal.* Except that she was not the most vulnerable member. Far from it. She had been a strong climber, despite her injury, and now she was proving to be an even stronger swimmer. So why did his pulse quicken every time her head disappeared under the water?

The half-mile swim was excruciating. Not only the physical demands of it but the mental. Roul was counting heads the whole time, the numbers going up and down with each rise and fall of the water. Blackmane and Tatum helped by pointing out any rocks they encountered. For all of Blackmane's faults, he always took care of his comrades.

The flat rock was within sight when Eda pulled up suddenly. Her back collided with Roul's chest.

'What's the matter?' he asked, looking around.

She turned in a circle, as though searching for something, her bare legs brushing his in the process. 'I saw something. A shadow.'

'A rock?'

'No, it moved.'

He caught her around her waist and swam forwards. 'We need to stay with the group.'

'There!' she said, pointing to a dorsal fin a few feet from them.

Tollere looked over his shoulder, and his eyes widened. 'Shark!' He began kicking out his feet.

Eda pulled a knife—from God only knew where—and readied herself for battle. 'Stay behind me.'

Stay *behind* her? Smiling, Roul took hold of her arm and said, 'It's a dolphin.'

Tollere stilled. 'It is? You sure?'

Roul took the knife from Eda's hand. 'Everyone relax. It's just a dolphin.'

'Everyone *is* relaxed,' Blackmane said, glaring in Tollere's direction.

Eda's exhale was so big, she disappeared under the surface of the water for a second. Roul tugged her back up by the waist.

'For future reference,' he said into her ear, 'if we do ever encounter a shark, I don't want you as my human shield.' He gave her a gentle shove to get her swimming.

'Do we just swim past them?' Hadewaye called as more dorsal fins popped up around him.

Roul's eyes creased at the corners. 'Yes. They're just curious. Keep going.'

They all moved forwards, continuing towards the rock. Every now and then, Eda would squeak and then laugh as dolphins dashed in all directions around them. Roul watched her, his smile hidden by the water. The mammals seemed to be drawn to her laughter. Not surprising. What mammal would not want to get closer to that sound?

The recruits dragged themselves from the water, collapsing onto the rock and catching their breath. Eda was also breathless but from play, from another experience lived.

It was with a heavy heart that Roul said, 'All right, Suttone. Time to get out.'

He watched as she hoisted herself up and out of the sea, trying not to look at her bare legs as they left the water. Only when she was safely on the rock did he follow her out.

CHAPTER 9

The next two weeks passed in a blur of fighting, weapons, horses, and exhaustion. Eda had thought herself prepared for the physical and mental demands, but Roul had a way of training them that always required slightly more than they could give. He pushed each recruit to their breaking point, and then he pushed a little further. Eda's mind and body took daily beatings, but she never complained. She never fell down. She never cried despite the ocean of tears that would build over the course of the day.

The others were expecting her to break. She saw it in their eyes whenever they paused to watch her, heard it in their voices when they made jokes.

Then one day the jokes stopped.

Her first battle won.

Eda showed up every morning, shivering in the eerie grey light as she waited for Roul to arrive with instructions. One day she would learn how to kill a man from thirty feet away with a lance while riding a horse at high speed, the next how to poison arrows. She learned to follow orders without thinking, to control fear, to control *others'* fear. She learned there were far worse outcomes than death in battle.

At the beginning of her third week, the warden came to watch the group train. The recruits were nervous—Eda could feel it. The longer the warden stood there watching them, the more mistakes they seemed to make.

'You have to work that clumsiness out of them,' she heard Shapur say to Roul. 'And send Tollere home. He doesn't have what it takes.'

Roul shifted his weight. 'He's a fine shooter, sir.'

'Shall we inform our enemy of that when they arrive with the wrong weapon?' Shapur replied, staring him down. 'I want him gone.'

Eda looked over to where Tollere was lying on the ground clutching his chin, blood seeping between his fingers. His parents would be humiliated by his dismissal, and he would carry their shame for the rest of his life no matter what came of him.

'Tollere,' Roul called. 'Collect your weapons and go clean yourself up. I'll come find you when we're done.'

Everyone stilled and lowered their weapons as Tollere rose to his feet and looked around.

'Just me, Commander?' he asked.

Roul nodded. 'Just you.'

Tollere picked up his sword and shield and walked off in the direction of the barracks, head hanging down to his chest.

'Did I tell the rest of you to stop?' Roul shouted. 'Tatum, you can join Blackmane and Hadewaye.'

Tatum nodded and walked over to them.

Needless to say, everyone else fought their best fight for the remainder of the time Shapur Wright stood there. That sparring session continued for another thirty minutes, each of them giving everything they had. It was the longest thirty minutes of Eda's life.

When the warden did finally leave the training yard, they all dropped their weapons and collapsed to the ground before Roul had even spoken the words 'Weapons down'. Tatum and Hadewaye lay on their backs, hands over their faces. Blackmane sat with his knees pulled up and forehead resting on one arm. Alveye emptied his stomach, and Eda tried very hard not to.

'I may never rise again,' Alveye said quietly, wiping his mouth with the back of his hand.

'Let's get you cooled down,' Roul said. 'On your feet.'

Eda pressed her eyes shut as the training yard spun around her, then prayed to any listening god that her legs would hold.

Get up.

'Let's go!' Roul shouted.

Blackmane was first up, but he immediately doubled over and threw up on the grass. Eda rose on shaky legs and looked around at the others. Hadewaye was on his hands and knees. She walked over to him and used what little strength she had left to pull him to his feet.

Roul gestured to the port gate. 'We'll finish with a swim.'

The group walked like newborn foals all the way down to the beach. As tempting as it was to fall down on the sand, Eda remained standing as she waited for instructions.

'To the end of the dock and back. Then you can return to the barracks,' Roul said, looking around at the group. 'Last one to step foot on the sand swims again. Off you go.'

This was what he did. They were all at their limit, and now he would push them past it. She told herself that a swim in the ocean would be refreshing. It would help with the muscle soreness they would all feel the next day.

Everyone began stripping. No one blinked when Eda did the same, because they no longer saw her as different.

Only Roul glanced in her direction, eyeing the colourful bruises that covered her calves. She saw him swallow.

They all waded into the water, and Eda went from boiling hot to shivering within seconds. When she was waist deep, she dove under and began swimming. She was second to reach the end of the dock behind Tatum, followed by Hadewaye, Alveye, then Blackmane. When she looked over her shoulder on the return swim, she saw Blackmane was fading fast, falling farther and farther behind. She should have kept her eyes forwards. Someone had to be last. Someone had to do the second swim—and it could not have happened to a nicer person.

With a resigned breath, Eda slowed. Hadewaye passed her. Then Alveye passed her. She was all but treading water as she neared the beach, willing Blackmane to hurry up. Their eyes met as he swam by, all pale-faced and barely able to lift his arms above his head. The men crawled up onto the beach, panting. Blackmane's dark eyes narrowed on Eda, his body trembling.

'You shouldn't have done that.' He sounded spent. 'I won't be returning the favour.'

Eda licked salt water from her lips and pushed off the sand to begin her second swim. 'Oh, I know.'

This time she moved at half the speed. By the time she was done, she could not even make it to the dry sand, instead lying like a beached whale with waves crashing over her legs. She could see by Roul's stance and rigid expression that he was angry, but not angry enough to leave her there.

He marched into the sea and pulled her to her feet. 'Enjoy your extra-long swim, soldier?' He hooked one of her arms around his neck and walked her to the pile of clothes sitting on the beach.

'Very refreshing.' The tops of her feet dragged along the sand like she was a rag doll.

'You couldn't just finish and get your arse out of the water, could you?'

It was a rhetorical question, so Eda did not bother responding.

Roul lowered her onto the sand, then sat next to her, removing his cloak and wrapping it around her. The warmth made Eda shudder.

'You're not doing Blackmane any favours long term,' he said. 'The resilience he builds during his training will see him through his entire career. Your interference only robs him of that.'

She closed her eyes and dropped her head to Roul's arm. 'Stop talking. Training's over. I don't have to listen to you anymore.'

He swore under his breath but wrapped an arm around her. 'You're infuriating.' He reached for her trousers, draping them over her legs since she did not have the energy to dress.

'And you're mean.'

He laughed at that. 'I should make you swim another lap.'

She tipped her face up to him, blinking. 'Then you'd be forced to save me.'

He stared back at her, knowing she was right. 'You weren't supposed to last this long.'

'I'm full of surprises.' She settled her head in the nook of his shoulder and stared out at the water. 'Tollere's gone, isn't he?'

'Yes.'

She exhaled. 'At least I wasn't the first to be sent home. That's something.'

'It's something.' He was silent a moment. 'You still have two more weeks to go. There's every chance you'll hate me by the end of it.'

'How do you know I don't hate you already?' She

looked up at him again so she could see his smile. And there it was.

'Fairly certain you hated me on your first day, but you came back for more.'

'You *wanted* me to hate you that first day. When it didn't happen at training, you resorted to trying to make me jealous at the tavern.'

His eyebrows came together. 'I did no such thing. If you were jealous, that's on you.'

They had never spoken about that day. Eda had pushed the memory, and all it conjured, from her mind in order to focus on her training. She did not have space for pointless feelings like jealousy—nor a justification for it. But since the topic had come up, there was a burning question on the tip of her tongue. 'Can I ask you something?'

He released a breath. 'I don't know why you say that when you always ask the question regardless of my reply.'

'Do you like her more than me?'

Roul shook his head. 'You'd think I would've grown accustomed to the things that come out of your mouth by now, but you still manage to surprise me. Why would you ask such a thing?'

'Because your taste in lovers is vastly different to your taste in friends. I suppose it threw me.'

He brushed a lock of dripping hair off her face. 'You're not so different.'

Eda's eyebrows rose. 'Is she good with weapons too?'

He bit back a smile. 'No, but she's smart and works hard like you.'

'She's also ridiculously beautiful.'

'So are you.'

She tilted her head. 'You think I'm beautiful? Or are you just saying that to hurry the conversation along?'

He sighed. 'I'm immune, not blind.'

She did not know how she felt about that response. She

77

wanted to know why he was immune, and at what point he became immune. And an even bigger part wanted to know if that immunity was for life. But she could not ask those things.

She looked out at the water, feeling far too comfortable tucked beneath his arm. 'Do you know I have a few bald patches on my scalp where weapons have caught my hair?'

He laughed at that, and the sound relaxed her.

'No, I didn't know that.'

'I don't know why that's funny to you.'

'It's the way you swing a conversation that's funny to me, not your baldness.'

She crinkled her nose. 'I'm not sure I could watch you suffer as I have suffered if our roles were reversed.'

'Because you're a better friend than me?'

'Because I'm a better person than you.'

She felt his body shake with silent laughter. Then his arm fell away, his warmth gone.

'That's why I'm a commander and you're swimming extra laps.' He snatched up her pants and held them in front of her face. 'Time to put some clothes on before this conversation gets any stranger.'

She took the trousers and began threading her legs through them. 'Then are you going to be all chivalric and offer to walk me home?'

He rose, brushing sand off his trousers. 'Probably.' He looked away as she slipped her tunic on. When she stood and tried to hand his cloak back to him, he shook his head. 'Keep it until we get yours. We don't want you turning into an ice block.'

Eda wrapped it around her. 'I'm going to succeed, you know. I'm going to complete the training, and Queen Fayre is going to send me to Harlech Castle.'

'That's one possibility.'

She searched his eyes for any clues as to his emotional

state, but he was an expert at masking his feelings—unless that feeling was anger. 'Will you worry about me when I'm gone?'

'Of course,' he said without hesitation.

'Will you miss me?' She was not sure exactly what she was fishing for. Perhaps she simply needed reassurance that she meant something to him after weeks of being pummelled at his request. Or maybe the conversation about Hildred had stirred some feelings she had tried very hard to bury.

His eyebrows came together. 'It'll certainly be boring with you gone.'

'That's not what I asked.'

He looked in the direction of the port. 'I suppose I will.'

Satisfied, she turned and began walking up the beach. He walked at her side.

'How long will you grieve if I die?' she asked.

Roul looked heavenward. 'Must we have this conversation?'

'How long?'

He threw his hands up. 'I don't know.'

'Months?'

He met her eyes. 'If I answer years, will this be over?'

'Years?' She studied him as she walked. 'That's a long time. Your feelings for me must be deeper than we both realised.'

'I'd trip you if I wasn't 100 percent sure you'd fall and not be able to get back up.'

Smiling, she looked ahead. 'That's just your future grief talking.'

He laughed quietly as they continued towards the port.

CHAPTER 10

*W*hen Eda asked Roul to stay for dinner, he should have said no. He had spent every day watching her obsessively on the training field for the past two weeks. It was too much. Every time a sword struck her, every time she fell from a horse, every time the air was knocked from her lungs, he felt it. Every blow, every knock, every gasp for air.

He was exhausted—and entirely responsible.

But if Queen Fayre's insane plan went ahead, Eda needed to be 100 percent ready for what lay before her. Going easy on her now might be a death sentence later.

If only he could care a little less. It would be so much easier then. Instead, his respect for her was growing, his feelings evolving and deepening. And he had rules about that. Friendship was perfectly acceptable. One could be friends with any number of people and go about living their lives. But when an attachment formed between two people, separating them became problematic—and separation was inevitable.

Five years.

He was in the latter half of his service now, a couple of

years from leaving Chadora and never returning. Eda still did not know, and he knew the news would crush her when she eventually found out. She would not want him to leave, and if he were being honest, the reality of leaving her behind was starting to eat away at him.

'I wish I could offer you some meat,' Candace said, taking a seat at the table. 'Unfortunately there was nothing at the market this morning, and Blake still refuses to slaughter the goats because they were a gift from Harlan.'

Blake rolled her eyes. 'Clove is a milking goat, Mother. You're not supposed to eat animals you get milk from.'

Candace laughed. 'And where is this mythical milk?'

'It will come.' Blake passed the plate of boiled eggs to Roul. 'We can't breed a dead goat.'

Harlan scooped Luella off the floor and kissed her face until she squealed, then placed her back on the ground with the duck. 'This family has a history of getting attached to its food.' He nodded at Garlic, who was now quacking at his feet for attention. 'Blake still hasn't eaten the first meal I gave her.'

Blake turned in her chair. 'Whose eggs do you think we're eating?'

'The chickens,' Candace replied dryly, picking up the plate of boiled carrots.

The smug expression fell from Blake's face, and Harlan smiled at his plate.

Roul noticed Eda staring longingly at the tray of roasted onions, then realised her arms were probably too tired to lift it. He picked it up and dropped a few onto her plate.

'What did you do to my sister today?' Blake asked Roul. 'She came home frozen to the bone, and then I had to fill the tub for her because she couldn't lift the pail—and it was empty at the time.'

'Sounds like he did his job,' Harlan said.

When Eda picked up her fork, the sleeve of her dress slid up. Candace sucked in a breath when she saw Eda's yellow-and-purple arm. She caught Eda by the elbow, dragging the sleeve higher to inspect the bruises.

'Oh my goodness,' Candace breathed.

Blake wiped her mouth with a napkin. 'That's nothing. You should see the rest of her.'

Eda glared at her sister. 'Stop. I'm always peppered with bruises—many of them from Harlan.'

'Harlan has never bruised you like that,' Blake replied. 'Your back looks as though someone took a hammer to it.'

Candace looked accusingly at Roul. 'Are you permitting grown men to use my youngest daughter as a pell, Commander?'

'Mother, please,' Eda said. 'I give as good as I get.'

Candace released her arm, tutting.

Roul found himself without an appetite suddenly, but he forced himself to eat the small amount of food on his plate.

'Eda's free to withdraw at any time,' Harlan pointed out. 'All she need do is speak up.'

'She's far too stubborn for that,' Blake said as she passed a boiled egg down to Luella. 'She'd sooner die of internal bleeding than admit she's not up to it.'

'I am up to it,' Eda snapped, looking to Roul for support. 'Tell them.'

Roul swallowed his last mouthful of food, then laid his knife and fork on his plate and rose from his chair. 'Thank you for dinner.' He looked at Candace. 'I apologise for rushing off, but I have to get back to the barracks.'

Candace looked up in surprise. 'But you barely ate a thing.'

'That was plenty, really.' He stepped back from the table before anyone could object and headed for the front door. He heard a chair scrape the floor behind him, and a moment later, Eda followed him out of the house. Outside, the light had faded, and everything was washed in grey light.

'Roul,' Eda called.

He continued to where his horse was tethered. 'Go back inside and eat. I'll see you in the morning.'

Naturally, she did not listen. 'I hope you're not doing something foolish like feeling guilty.' She followed him all the way to his horse. 'She's my mother. Worrying is what mothers do. Clearly I'm fine.'

He untied his horse. 'It's not always about you. I do have a life and problems outside of you, you know.' The second those words passed his lips, he closed his eyes. Now he was delivering blows during her recuperation time. He turned to face her, noting her slightly wounded expression. 'I'm sorry.'

She crossed her arms and shrugged. 'What for? It's true.'

While it was true, Eda remained one of the most important pieces of his life at that time. But he could never tell her that, because that would only deepen the attachment.

'Are you going to her?' Eda asked, her voice quiet suddenly.

He had done that. He had stolen her confidence with a few thoughtless words. 'Why do you ask such things?'

'I don't know.' She wet her lips and looked around. 'Perhaps I want you to choose time with me over time with her.'

He stared at her, his chest tight and palms heating. 'Eda. I've come here nearly every afternoon for the past year.'

'Then at night, you go to her.'

He gathered the reins and prepared to mount, knowing they were stepping into dangerous territory. 'I have to go.' She took hold of the horse's bridle, and he was forced to face her again. 'What now? What ridiculous question are you going to ask now? Do you want to know how long I'd grieve if Hildred died? Is that it? That way you can gauge where you're positioned in this competition you've created? Because heaven forbid you ever place second.'

If he did not hate himself enough before, he thoroughly hated himself now.

Eda let go of the bridle and stepped back from the horse, assessing him for a moment before turning away.

'Eda—'

'Leave.' She hurried for the door, shoulders rounded. 'I'll see you in the morning.'

Roul swore and raked a hand through his hair. He thought about going after her, then realised he could not say the things he wanted to anyway.

Mounting his horse, he galloped away from Wright House.

CHAPTER 11

*I*f Roul had a penny for every time Eda glared in his direction, he would have been the wealthiest defender in the borough. She had arrived that morning with a strange energy and hungry for a fight. There was sharpness to her manner, an edge to her tone whenever she spoke. The recruits noticed it too, looking between themselves every time she threw a spear or knocked someone else's knife from the pell with her own.

It was nearing noon, and Eda was showing no signs of slowing down.

'I want you on elbows and toes all the way to the wall,' Roul called to the group. 'Then run back to me. If I see a knee touch the ground, you'll start over.'

Eda was crawling off before the others had even made it to the ground. Roul watched her speed ahead, wondering how long it would take her to forgive him and what he would need to do to make that happen. He was so absorbed by the sight of her scurrying along the wet grass that he did not notice Queen Fayre and her guard approaching.

'Good morning, Commander,' the queen regent called to him.

He looked in her direction, then straightened. 'Your Majesty.'

Fayre came to a stop, eyes going to Eda, who was still well ahead of the others. 'How is our newest recruit doing?'

'She's doing well.' She was always going to do well.

They watched Eda touch the wall, spring to her feet, then run back in their direction.

'I have received reports that King Edward and his wife have left Harlech Castle for Windsor,' Fayre said without looking at him.

Roul crossed his arms. 'And Prince Becket?'

'He remains at Harlech Castle with the queen mother and Lord Roger Mortimer. For how long or what purpose, I do not know.' She paused. 'I fear we are running out of time.'

Roul knew what was coming next.

'Is she ready?'

And yet the question still hit him like ice to the face. 'She's only been training a few weeks.'

She turned her head to look at him. 'Yes, Commander. I can count the days. Is she *ready*?'

'Physically, absolutely. Mentally, it's too early to tell.'

'She can fight,' Fayre said, clasping her hands together. 'But can she follow orders under pressure?'

Eda came to a stop in front of them, breathless and sweating. 'Your Majesty.'

When she went to curtsy, Queen Fayre held up a hand. 'That is quite all right.'

'Did you come to see me in action?' There was childlike hope in Eda's voice.

Fayre nodded once. 'It seems you are keeping up with

the men.' Her eyes creased at the corners in place of a smile. 'How do *you* feel it is going?'

'I feel it's going great, but I suppose Commander Thornton's opinion is of more value to you.' She somehow managed yet another glare in his direction.

'I wonder if you might be up to a little test this afternoon to gauge your progress,' Fayre asked, chin lifting slightly.

Roul looked down at the ground. He had known she would be tested eventually but wanted longer to prepare her.

Eda's eyes were wide with excitement. 'Really? Of course. I can do whatever you need me to.'

'The point of the test is to find out if that is true,' Fayre replied.

The others had returned from the wall and were waiting for instructions.

'Three laps to cool down,' Roul told them. He looked to Eda. 'You too, Suttone.'

Another glare, another penny earned. She jogged off after the others.

Roul turned to face Queen Fayre and found her looking over at the tower.

'We have a merchant man in our custody at present who choked his own son to death,' she said, her expression thoughtful. 'He is due to be executed tomorrow.'

It took Roul a moment to catch up to her thinking. An uneasy feeling enveloped him. 'You want to use him for the test?'

Fayre's eyes met his. 'I shall have Commander Wright take care of everything. Say nothing to her beforehand.' She bowed her head before turning and leaving.

With his stomach in knots, Roul watched her walk away.

CHAPTER 12

'How much farther?' Eda asked as they headed to the centre of the forest in the merchant borough.

Roul glanced over his shoulder, his expression heavy. 'We're almost there.'

Eda felt hot and twitchy as she followed him through the trees. She was having trouble differentiating between excitement and fear. Roul had provided no details of the test so far, shutting down all her questions. 'Will Queen Fayre be there?'

He was choosing to simply ignore her now. While he claimed he was not permitted to discuss the test with her, she suspected it had more to do with her treatment of him that morning. She had not planned to arrive and melt him with her stares, but she was still getting over the hurt and embarrassment lingering from the night prior.

They walked for another thirty minutes before Eda spotted Harlan leaning against the trunk of a sequoia tree up ahead. She broke into a jog, eyes going to the collection of weapons at his feet.

'You're absolutely sure you want to do this?' Those

were the first words from Harlan's mouth as she came to a stop in front of him.

'While I'm not entirely sure what "this" is, I'm going to answer yes.'

Roul bent to pick up two daggers and began strapping them onto her body.

'You're going to track me to the village,' Harlan said, gesturing south.

Her eyebrows came together. 'All right. What are the weapons for? Am I to shoot you in the back?'

Roul slipped the quiver of arrows over Eda's head. 'You're going to encounter targets along the way. *That's* what the weapons are for.'

Digging into his pocket, Harlan pulled out a piece of red ribbon and showed it to her. 'Your targets are marked with one of these ribbons. If you miss any targets, that's a fail.'

She took the ribbon from him, kneading it between her fingers. 'Are these targets moving?'

Harlan met her eyes. 'That's a smart assumption.'

Roul took the ribbon from her hand and replaced it with a bow. 'As important as it is to hit the targets, it's equally as important not to shoot, stab, or kill anything that doesn't have a ribbon on it.'

She laughed despite nothing being funny. 'Kill?'

'You must think of the targets as your enemy,' Harlan said. 'There are defenders posted near each one, but you won't see them. If at any time you want out of the test, you must raise your weapon and shout "surrender". But don't leave it too late.'

Eda blinked. 'Who would I be surrendering to?'

'The experience,' Roul replied. 'And you wouldn't be the first. Remember that each test is uniquely designed for the individual, each with their unique limits. If you were Tollere, we'd be standing on the edge of a cliff right now.' He bent to pick up the sword, belting it around her waist.

'Is the blade sharp?' she asked.

Roul straightened. 'Yes. If you're not up to this, you need to speak up now. You're free to go home.'

She noted the subtle plea in his voice, but shook her head. 'I'll go home once I've passed the test.'

Harlan rubbed his forehead, then said, 'Listen for the horn. That's your cue. Track carefully, because if you miss a target along the way, that's a fail.'

She did not have to be told to track carefully. There was no way she was going to mess this up. 'I understand.'

'Good luck,' Harlan said before turning and jogging off.

Eda watched him disappear into the trees, feeling Roul's eyes on her. 'You don't think I can do it.'

A statement, not a question.

'I think you can. I just don't want you to.'

She looked at him, noting his sincerity.

Before she could reply, a horn sounded in the distance. It was time.

'Remember what Harlan said. If you need to surrender, you put your—'

'I know what to do.'

He nodded slowly. 'Then I'll see you at the other end.'

She reached back for an arrow, loaded her bow, then ran off in the direction Harlan had gone. When she glanced over her shoulder, Roul was no longer in sight. Drawing a deep breath, she focused on the task ahead of her.

Slowing, she followed the impressions on the ground left by Harlan's enormous boots. They led her to a fallen log, which he appeared to have climbed over. She did the same, then stopped. The earth was firmer that side of the tree, but even still, she would have expected to pick up his tracks. But the thick debris covering the ground lay undisturbed. She looked left, then right to where a few threads of broken cobweb blew gently in the breeze. Climbing back up onto the log, she walked carefully along it until she reached the base of the tree where moss-covered roots rose before her. The moss where she walked was shredded, which gave her hope. She looked around until she finally spotted Harlan's footprints.

'Found you,' she whispered.

From the moment she climbed down, she knew she was not alone. She was being watched, and that meant she was nearing her first target.

Lifting her bow, she moved between the trees like a cat, her feet soundless and ears straining. She heard a rustle in the trees overhead and looked up just as something fell from the branches. A plank of wood came swinging towards her, a single piece of red ribbon nailed to the centre. Eda released the arrow, striking the ribbon, then leaped out of its way. Loose hair lifted off her face as wood wooshed past her before disappearing into the trees.

Her heart raced, but in a good way. She was ready for whatever came next.

Reaching back for another arrow, she continued forwards. She had barely taken two steps when she felt something press against her ankle. Looking down, she saw it was a piece of string.

Oh no.

She leapt backwards at the same time a pell sprang up from the ground, a red ribbon flying. Through a flurry of soggy leaves and dirt, she shot it. Down it went, flattening against the ground where it had been hidden under debris. Eda reloaded her bow and swung it side to side as leaves floated down around her, settling on the ground once more. When nothing else popped up, she looked around for Harlan's footprints but did not find them.

Stepping over the string, she looked up and down and

side to side, searching for clues as to which way Harlan had gone. Her vision snagged on a tree trunk, a section of scuffed bark. She walked over and ran her fingers over it. Judging by the colour, the damage was recent. A smile flickered on her face when she looked down and saw prints in the earth that indicated Harlan had passed by at a run.

Eda followed them.

It was around five minutes later when she heard the croon of a seagull. The small hairs on the back of her neck stood up at the sound of a seabird in a forest where seabirds did not dare venture. Raising her bow to the sky, she watched the branches above, body still and bow string taut beneath her fingers. A herring gull took flight, a red ribbon dangling from one leg. She shot the bird from the sky, watching it tumble through the branches before landing with a soft thud nearby. Reloading her bow, she scanned the treetops, but no more birds took flight. She exhaled and lowered her weapon.

Eda went to collect the arrow from the dead bird, then took a moment to get her bearings. She was close to the village now. Harlan's footprints laid out a clear path for her to follow.

It all felt a bit easy suddenly.

Before she had even finished that thought, a low growl reached her, the sound carried on the westerly breeze. She swung around, lifting her bow, gaze darting from tree to tree. Nothing moved. For a moment she wondered if she had imagined it. But then she heard it again, closer this time. Her muscles grew tense. It sounded like a dog—and she despised dogs. Her only experience with them was being hunted by them. In the past, defenders would set them free in the borough to track down merchants coming in and out of the tunnels. Eda had watched many times from the safety of the treetops as they tackled and mauled men twice her size. She had sat frozen with her heart in her throat as the dogs turned in circles below her, her scent drifting down to them.

She was not in the treetops this time.

A whistle sounded, an instruction. *Find them,* she had always imagined the translation to be. *Hold them down with teeth and paws so we can hang them from the walls.*

Sweat beaded on Eda's brow as she waited, a slight tremble in her hands that she really needed to get under control. For a moment, all was silent. Then a dog leapt from the brush, its sleek black-and-brown coat blending with its surroundings. Enormous paws stretched in her direction, black eyes fixed on Eda. She took aim, ready to shoot, but then a cold realisation hit her.

There was no ribbon attached to the dog.

Roul's words sounded in her head. *'It's equally as important not to shoot, stab, or kill anything that doesn't have a ribbon on it.'*

What was she supposed to do? Stand there and wait to be mauled?

She turned and took off at a sprint, legs pumping as she listened for the dog behind her. Of course, it was faster than she was, and the gap between them started to close.

Through the trees ahead, she could see the village, but she would not make it. Turning, she swung her bow at the dog, and it was forced to pull up in order to avoid being hit. Back and forth she swung. The animal snapped and snarled each time the bow passed its face. Roul had never said she could not *hit* things without a ribbon, only that she could not shoot, stab, or kill them. But she reached for the dagger at her hip just in case. There was no point passing the test if she was going to die in the process.

She stared at the frothy-mouthed dog as she edged backwards in the direction of the village, wondering if she could make it all the way there in that manner. It would be a long, tiring walk, but a lot safer than trying to outrun an aggressive hound.

While she was focused on the dog, feathers burst into view, wings flapping in front of her face. The bird was either thrown into the mix to distract her or it had incredibly bad timing. She shoved it away with her free hand, trying to keep sight of the dog at the same time. The bird clucked, then squawked as it crash-landed on the ground a few feet from her. She dared a glance and saw it was a chicken. It continued to flap and carry on as it got to its feet. Eda prayed the dog would give chase, but it was too well trained.

Out of the corner of her eye, Eda saw a flash of red.

The bow in her hand all but came to a stop as her eyes narrowed on a red ribbon tied around the chicken's leg. And it was running for the trees.

'Oh, for the love of...'

Straightening her bow, Eda loaded it and shot the chicken just before it disappeared from sight. She was in no position to be chasing that thing through the forest.

The moment she moved the bow, the dog lunged at her, mouth open and lips curled up. Expecting it, Eda leapt sideways as she took the shot. The dog flew past her, pivoting as it landed, and came for her again. She swung the bow, this time knocking the animal sideways. It landed with a yelp and rose with a snarl. Reaching for another arrow, she loaded her weapon and pointed it at the dog. If she shot it, this would all be over. If she surrendered, this would all be over.

But she did neither of those things.

She dropped her aim and shot at the ground between the dog's front paws. A warning.

'If I find out your ribbon fell off, I'm going to be *very* angry.' Her voice shook.

The snarling stopped, but the dog continued to watch her.

Just when Eda thought she had taken control of the situation, she heard another growl—and it did not come from the dog standing before her. Slowly, she turned her head and looked over her shoulder as a second dog emerged from between two trees. It approached at an angle, eyes locked on hers. Eda's mouth was so dry she could barely swallow. She kept the bow between herself and the first dog as she slowly reached for a dagger. Not a red ribbon to be found anywhere.

It's a test, she reminded herself. Queen Fayre was expecting her to kill them. *Just breathe.*

If she planned to surrender, now was the time. The dogs would be recalled, and she would go home with everything except her ego intact.

The dogs edged closer. The second crouched, preparing to launch itself at her. Eda's breath sped up, and her mind raced. She lifted the knife, ready to throw it, still undecided how far she would let this situation play out.

As she was preparing herself to be mauled, a whistle reached them. The dogs stopped, ears pricked in the direction of the noise. A second whistle had them running off in search of their handler.

Eda half laughed and half cried as she sheathed her dagger. She turned in a circle, eyes on the surrounding trees as she drew greedy breaths. The dogs did not return. Leaning on her knees, she took a moment to collect herself.

She had to keep moving.

The village was so close. All she had to do was follow the trail still before her.

Loading her bow again, she took off at a jog. No planks fell from the sky. No birds took flight. Nothing chased her.

The village was right in front of her.

As she emerged from the forest onto the water-logged grass, she stopped. On the other side of the pasture stood Queen Fayre and Harlan. One look at their expressions confirmed her suspicion.

She was not done yet.

Eda looked around, bracing for a boar to charge at her or a vulture to swoop down. But nothing charged, and nothing swooped.

Her eyes returned to Queen Fayre when she waved a hand, not in greeting but a signal. Eda edged forwards, then stopped when two men emerged from between the shops behind the queen. One of the men was a defender, the other shackled. Blood roared in her ears as the defender pulled the prisoner to a stop and turned to unlock the cuffs. He shoved the man forwards, and he stepped out onto the same soggy grass Eda stood on.

That was when she noticed the red ribbon tied around the man's upper arm.

Her lungs stopped.

She looked to Harlan and discovered the same expression Roul had been wearing when she left him standing in the forest—sombre resignation.

The now free prisoner looked from Queen Fayre to Eda, eyes wide, then ran. He moved east, away from the defenders and the queen. Away from Eda. For a moment, she simply watched him. Watched him stumble, then recover. Watched his fear. And she was supposed to chase him. He *was* a target. She was supposed to shoot, stab, kill.

Move, she told herself.

She took a step in his direction, then another, then another, her hands finally thawing at her sides. She lifted her bow, took aim, knowing she would not miss at that distance. Blood roared in her ears as she watched him down her arrow. Instead of shooting him in the back, she dropped her aim and shot him in the foot. He tripped, roared, rolled. Then he got up and hopped away, dragging his foot behind him.

'Stop!' she shouted, running now. 'Just stop!'

But he had no reason to stop and every reason to continue.

When she was within range, she drew a dagger and threw it, striking his calf. He could not run with a knife in his leg. He fell to the ground, clutching above the wound.

'Don't kill me, please,' he begged as she approached. 'I have a family who needs me.'

Eda came to a stop four feet from him, eyes moving over the man's clothes. He was a merchant man. Now she understood what Roul had meant when he told her the test was unique to her. The queen wanted to know if she would kill one of her own if ordered to, without question, without hesitation. And she was hesitating.

She fought the urge to be sick.

'Please,' he said again, tears squeezing from his eyes as he trembled on the ground.

Eda stared at him as she reloaded her bow. 'Why did they choose you?'

'I don't know.' He shook his head, pleading.

'What did you do?'

'Nothing! I swear before Belenus.'

Eda pointed her weapon at the man, still not sure if she could actually let go of the string. Surely Queen Fayre would not pluck an innocent merchant for her to kill. And Harlan would not stand by while an innocent man was used as bait in one of her games.

'You're lying.' Her words lacked conviction. She studied the marks on his wrists left from the shackles. They were not fresh. He had been imprisoned for some time.

'They say I killed him,' he said, eyes as wide as plates. 'All lies. I killed no one.'

The string slackened beneath her fingers, and she stepped closer. 'Who did you not kill?'

Instead of replying, the man yanked the knife from his leg and lurched at her. An arrow struck his neck before he had a chance to use the weapon, sending him flying backwards.

It was not Eda's arrow but someone else's.

She flinched as his body hit the ground, and the bow slipped from her fingers. She watched it land, then looked over her shoulder, searching for the shooter.

Roul stood at the edge of the tree line, a second arrow pointed at the man as though expecting him to rise again. But the man was already dead.

It was over.

She had failed.

When she looked in Queen Fayre's direction, all she saw was the tail of her blue velvet cloak disappear between the shops.

CHAPTER 13

'*Y*ou are not ready,' Queen Fayre said as they walked down the main street of the village towards her waiting carriage.

'I *am* ready,' Eda replied, slightly breathless from running after her. A warning glance from the guard had her moving away. 'I missed nothing in that forest.'

The merchants had all moved to either side of the street, bowing before the queen.

Queen Fayre waved and nodded as she passed them. 'This is not about your skills but your ability to follow orders.'

Eda quickened her pace. 'When did I not follow orders?'

'Commander,' Fayre said to Harlan, who was walking on the other side of her. 'When a defender means to kill a target, do they shoot said target in the foot?'

Harlan glanced sideways at her. 'No.'

'Under what circumstances would one throw a knife at someone's leg?'

'When trying to prevent them from fleeing' was Harlan's very unhelpful reply.

'Not when trying to kill them?' Fayre was clearly wanting to nail in her point.

'I was aiming for the artery behind the knee,' Eda lied. 'It's a lethal injury.'

Fayre finally looked at her. 'Then you missed, because he was still very much alive when Commander Thornton stepped in.'

Eda looked over her shoulder to where Roul trailed behind, listening. 'Perhaps if someone had taken the time to explain to me that he was a murderer—'

Fayre stopped and turned to her. 'No one owes you an explanation. Therein lies the difference between a civilian and a soldier. When a defender is given an order, that defender will carry out that order without question. He does not play jury. I would have hoped that was clear at this point. I need to send someone I can trust to follow orders.'

Eda stood with her hands open and eyes pleading. 'You can trust me. Give me another chance. Let me finish the month. Then you can test me again.'

Fayre resumed walking. 'I am afraid we are out of time. Now, if you will excuse me, I have some business to tend to in the borough prior to departing. Good day, Eda.'

Not one to be dismissed, Eda continued to follow her. 'You can't send your army, so your point is redundant. And your advisors are all ancient, with little fighting experience. If you send them, they won't even survive the journey there.'

Fayre's eyes burned in her direction. 'Once again, you seem to be struggling with the basics. When a queen says, "Good day", the conversation is over.'

Eda stopped in the middle of the muddy street and watched her walk away. Her disappointment was suffocating her. Taking hold of the leather strap of the quiver she was still wearing, she tugged it over her head and threw it to the ground. It bounced across the street, arrows scattering in all directions. One of them hit the foot of a passer-by.

'Sorry,' she said, giving him an apologetic wave.

'You all right?' Roul asked behind her.

She rounded on him, anger bubbling inside her. 'How could you?' Closing the distance between them, she shoved him with both hands. 'This is all your fault.'

His feet barely moved. '*My* fault?'

'I had the situation under control. I was handling it.'

His face hardened. 'The target was about to stab you.'

'I would've stopped him.' Groaning, she marched off, too angry to even finish the conversation. She had been so close, and now it was over.

'Eda!'

She turned left into one of the dark alleyways that ran between the shopfronts, and he followed.

'Go away,' she shouted.

He caught her arm, turning her to him. 'I saved your goddamn life, and this is what I get in place of a thank you?'

She tried to pull her arm free, but he held tight. 'Your interference cost me this opportunity. Do you understand that?'

He brought his face close to hers. 'You don't get to put your failure on me.'

She pushed up on her toes, trying to match his height. 'Failure? How exactly did I fail? I did everything she wanted.'

'You hesitated.'

She punched the hand holding her, but still he did not let go. 'You know, it wouldn't hurt your kind to hesitate occasionally. Maybe there would be a few less deaths around this place if you bothered to stop and ask questions first.' She was hitting him where she knew it hurt. When he did not react the way she wanted, she shoved him again in frustration.

He backed her up against the wall of the shop, pinning her arms above her head and using his body to prevent her from kicking out. 'Careful. You're sounding a lot like a sore loser.'

She thrashed, trying to free herself.

'Calm down before you hurt yourself. You never win in a strength competition, remember?'

He was right, of course, but she still fought for a few more breaths before finally going still. 'How can I forget when you throw it in my face every five minutes?' Her head flopped back, resting on the wall. 'That's it for me. It's over. I don't have other opportunities. Now Uncle marries me off. Now I mean nothing in this world.'

He relaxed his grip slightly. 'What are you talking about? You speak as if marriage is the end of your life, a death sentence. All you need do is look to your sisters to see that isn't true.'

'Their situation is very different, and you know it. They're *loved*.' The fight drained from her. 'Men don't love women like me.'

'That's utter horseshit.'

She stared at him. 'You were there when Blake said at dinner a few months back that any man who shared my bed would have to sleep with one eye open and hide all the butter knives in the house.'

'Because she knows what you can do with a butter knife.'

'Then *you* said sane men know better than to court me.'

His eyes filled with remorse. 'Since when do you pay attention to anything I say? In truth, I don't know a man worthy of you.'

The tension in Eda's body dissipated but not the heat. She suddenly became aware of the intimate pose they found themselves in. A passer-by would assume them to be lovers, not quarrelling friends.

Roul should have let her go at that point. She was no longer a threat to him. He knew that. He should have stepped back. Instead, he remained where he was, his fingers curled around her wrists and body pressing against hers.

She should have pulled free, pushed him away, ducked beneath his arm out into the open space.

Yet neither of them moved.

Eda could feel his heart beating through his uniform. This was no longer a fight. Nor was it two friends making up. This was warmth and breath and a very distinct lack of words. She was waiting for something, bracing. She just was not sure exactly what that something was. But then his gaze fell to her lips, and she realised what it was. There was heat in his stare, heat and weight.

She swallowed. In case it was not clear enough that she wanted him to kiss her, she tilted her face up to him ever so slightly—an invitation. He leaned in, his breath on her skin. She waited, then waited some more.

But instead of kissing her, Roul released her wrists and stepped back.

'What was that?' Eda whispered.

He glanced in the direction of the street, visibly uncomfortable. 'It was just a fight. Now it's over.'

'I'm not talking about the fight. I'm talking about after the fight.'

He swallowed. 'I got carried away. Sorry.'

'Sorry?' She stepped up to him and took hold of his face. 'Didn't you feel that?'

He gently pulled her hands away. 'It's time to go.'

'Roul—'

'Must you push the boundaries with everything?' His

pleading eyes met hers. 'Even our friendship?' He gestured in the direction of the street. 'Let's go.'

She did not move. 'No. Not until you kiss me.'

He dragged a hand down his face.

'I may not have a lot of experience with these things,' she said, 'but I can recognise an almost kiss when I see one.'

'I'm not going to kiss you.'

'Because you don't want to?'

'Because I respect you too much to give in to my impulses.' He signalled for her to start walking. 'Now go.'

She crossed her arms. 'Does that mean you *don't* respect Hildred?'

'You're twisting my words.'

Still she did not move. '*Kiss me.*'

'That's not a good idea.'

'Why? It's just one kiss, not a commitment.'

He threw his hands up. 'What if it's good?'

'Then it's good.'

'No, then I'll want to do it again.'

She searched his eyes. 'Is that such a horrible thought?'

He linked his hands atop his head. 'I don't want to mislead you, and I don't want to ruin our friendship.'

'You're completely overthinking this. It's one moment. One experience I've not had before. Who better to give it to me than someone I trust, someone I care about, and who cares about me?' She took hold of the front of his uniform and backed up to the wall, brushing hair off her face in preparation.

'This is absurd,' he said.

'If I let this opportunity pass me by, my very first kiss will be with the bootmaker, clunky and awkward.'

He gestured between them. '*This* might be clunky and awkward.'

'And if it is, we'll laugh it off and never speak of it

again.' Her eyes moved between his, his face close to hers once more. 'Should I close my eyes?'

He laughed. 'Eda, your sisters are going to eat me alive.'

'I won't tell them. I won't tell anyone.'

He let out a shaky breath. He wanted to do this. She could feel it. He was just being chivalric, trying to protect her as he always did. But she did not need protecting from him.

Taking control of the situation, Eda tugged him closer until the palm of his hand landed on the wall beside her head. And there it was again, the heat, the draw.

Roul hooked a finger under her chin and tipped her face up. 'Promise me you won't hate me afterwards.'

'Not because of the kiss,' she whispered, her words coming out breathy.

He ran his thumb over her bottom lip as he studied her face. The heat inside her curled. Slowly, he lowered his mouth to hers, lips brushing lightly. Then he drew back slightly to see her reaction.

'More,' she breathed, knowing he was holding back.

Their mouths met again, and warmth spread through Eda this time, moving in all directions at once. Then she was reaching for him, her fingers brushing the short hairs on the back of his neck as she drew him closer. It felt better than she had imagined.

A warm hand landed on her waist, sliding to the middle of her back. Sensation travelled up and down her body. She deepened the kiss, not really knowing what she was doing yet more than willing to experiment.

Roul drew her closer until the warmth of his body met the warmth of hers. Her breath hitched this time, an involuntary response that made him break the kiss.

'Please tell me we're done,' he whispered.

The deep edge to his voice made the heat gather in her belly. It was the sound of Roul Thornton not in control.

She shook her head. 'No. No, we're not done.'

His mouth came down hard on hers this time, hungrier than before. His body was a delicious contrast to the icy stone at her back. His hand left the wall, feet edging closer to hers as fingers speared her hair. Her knees softened. Everything softened. She was certain she would be a pool of flesh on the ground by the time they were done.

Eda traced her fingers along his clean-shaven jaw, exploring the angles of his face. She wanted to taste those parts of him too. But when her mouth moved in that direction, his palm returned to the wall, and he drew back to look at her.

'We're done,' he said, stepping back and raking a hand through his hair. He took a moment to compose himself. He never looked away from her though. 'Tell me you don't hate me now.'

Hate him? She wanted to drag him to a darker part of the alleyway and demand he finish what he started. 'Of course not. Though I'm still angry that you shot my prisoner.'

He laughed at that, then backed away to the other side of the alleyway. He leaned against the wall, watching her from a safe distance. 'For what it's worth, you passed that test with flying colours right up until the end. You were honestly incredible.'

She played with the ends of her plait. 'Which test is that?'

Light danced in his eyes. 'Both.'

'What did I do wrong at the end of the second test?'

He drew a leg up, resting his foot on the wall. 'You went off course. That's very dangerous, especially for a new recruit.'

She could not stop her smile. They were all right. The kiss had not broken anything between them.

The light in his eyes faded, his expression turning serious. 'We can't do that again.'

The words stung a little. 'Because of Hildred?'

'Not because of Hildred.' His throat bobbed, and he opened his mouth to speak. But before he could say another word, a horn sounded in the distance.

They both straightened and looked south, to the sliver of wall visible at the end of the alleyway. Eda knew all the signals now.

'Intruders?' she asked.

Roul walked over to her. 'Go and tell the merchants to get off the street. They need to go inside and lock their doors.'

'Where are you going?'

'To the port. And no, you can't come.'

She tilted her head in a plea.

He pointed in the direction of the street. 'I'm not messing around here. Wait with Birtle at the shop. I'll come find you.' Then he was jogging away.

With a resigned sigh, Eda turned and ran towards the street.

CHAPTER 14

*R*oul drew his weapon as he neared the port gate. 'What's going on?' he called to a defender running past in the other direction.

'Sea warriors in the water.'

'Where's the warden?'

'Royal borough, readying an army.'

Roul continued towards the lowering portcullis. 'Are the taverns cleared out?'

The defender straightened when he saw Roul's gold cloak pin. 'Yes, Commander.'

'Good.' He knew Hildred had family in the merchant borough and would have gone straight there. 'No one's come ashore yet?'

'Not yet.'

Another horn sounded, prompting both men to look in the direction of the beach. It was abandoned, still, yet the signal told them the warriors were already ashore.

Another horn, the same warning again.

The men took cover, watching the sea through a gap in the latticed wood. Roul listened, but it was difficult to hear anything amid the noise inside the borough.

'Oh shit,' said the other defender, backing away from the wall.

Roul looked up at the same time a length of rope hit the ground beside him. He backed away, watching as more ropes were thrown down.

Not only were the sea warriors ashore, they were on the wall—preparing to descend.

'Shoot as many as you can,' Roul told the other defender as he took off at a run towards the turret, where the weapons were stored.

When he got there, he found Harlan handing out bows and quivers to both defenders and eager merchants.

'Where's Eda?' Harlan asked when he caught sight of Roul.

'I sent her to the shop.'

'Let's hope she stays there.' Harlan handed him some weapons, then slipped a quiver over his head before snatching up a bow. 'Ready?'

Roul already had his bow loaded and pointed at the wall. 'Ready.'

As if on cue, sea warriors descended the ropes like cockroaches, greeted by around fifty defenders and a hundred-plus armed merchant men. The two commanders strode parallel with the wall, shooting the warriors from the ropes before their feet touched the ground. They worked methodically alongside the other defenders, but more warriors spilled from the embrasures, and soon there were too many.

Roul was about to ask Harlan where the rest of their army was but then realised he already knew. If the sea warriors were on the wall, they could be anywhere. The harsh reality was that merchants were the last priority. Food was number one. Without it, the entire kingdom would perish.

Harlan cursed loudly when an axe flew past his head.

Soon it would be time to abandon their bows and draw their swords.

Roul looked behind him to the merchants. They would be no match for the warriors in hand-to-hand combat. 'Return to your families!'

'Where are the rest of the defenders?' one merchant shouted back.

'On their way,' Roul lied. 'Go. Quickly now.'

Thankfully, the merchants listened.

The first clash of weapons sounded farther along the line. Warriors surged forwards, shields raised and battle axes and swords ready. They descended on the defenders with a roar.

Roul drew his sword. The fighting had officially begun. He cut down anyone who came for him. There was nothing methodical about their approach now. They were outnumbered and had no choice but to take the fight moment by moment.

They were simply buying time.

'I thought Commander Thornton told you to wait here inside the shop,' Birtle said, following Eda to the door.

She looked back at the old man, who was rubbing his papery hands together. He was too old to fight warriors, and she could not bear to sit idle while the sound of fighting grew louder. She tapped her bow, the one she kept hidden under her old bed. 'I'm just going to climb up onto a rooftop and pluck off a few strays, make sure they don't make it all the way down to this end of the village.'

His watery eyes studied her. 'Your family will never forgive me if anything should happen to you on my watch.'

The fact that he felt she was under *his* protection in that moment made her heart swell. 'My family knows better than to blame others for my actions. I'll be back before you know it.'

She stepped through the door and tugged it shut before he could object, loading her bow as she looked both ways down the abandoned street. Satisfied it was safe, she stepped off the veranda and headed in the direction of the square.

When she neared the end of the street, she slipped between the shops and used the alleyways to get closer to the fighting. She froze when she caught sight of the sea warriors. There were hundreds of them. Hundreds of them *already inside the borough.*

Where were the rest of the defenders?

While she was watching, a group of warriors broke away from the fight and headed for the village. There was not one defender on the ground in the position to go after them—so Eda did. She climbed a wall into someone's courtyard, then crept to the edge of the shadows. She stilled when she caught sight of the queen's carriage parked outside of the goldsmith's shopfront. Queen Fayre had told Eda she had business to tend to in the borough. Those had been her final words before leaving her standing in the middle of the street. It was possible she had not gotten out in time.

The four warriors circled the carriage, peering inside it and saying things she could not hear. They reached inside and kneaded the expensive red curtains, then looked in the direction of the shop. They knew the carriage did not belong to anyone who lived inside this borough. Its elaborate details and lush trimmings screamed royalty.

There was every possibility that Queen Fayre was trapped inside the shop.

Raising her bow, Eda watched the men down her arrow, waiting to see what they would do. If she did decide to start shooting, she was going to have to be fast and efficient or they would be upon her in moments.

The string went taut beneath her fingers as two of the men headed for the veranda. But when they reached it, the door opened, and the queen's bodyguard stepped outside, sword in hand. The door locked behind him.

That confirmed it. Queen Fayre was inside the shop.

The moment the warriors made a move towards the bodyguard, Eda released the first arrow, hitting the warrior closest to the veranda through the chest. The others looked around, confused, then ran at the defender. But Eda's hands were faster than their feet. She shot two more before they reached the veranda, and the bodyguard took care of the fourth. As the defender pulled his sword from the warrior's stomach, he looked in Eda's direction. She was about to reveal herself when an arrow struck the bodyguard's neck. Eda flinched and watched as the sword slipped from his hand. It clanged against the hardwood. He reached for the arrow protruding from his neck, eyes as wide as plates. Eda knew there was no saving him.

She spotted them then, a fresh group of warriors striding in her direction. And more would follow. She needed to get the queen out of the shop. Blood roared in her ears as she ran to the back door, pounding her fist on it. 'Open up!'

She heard the latch, and then the goldsmith peered through a crack in the door.

'Queen Fayre's bodyguard is dead,' Eda said, voice low, 'and there are more warriors on the way. She needs to come with me now.'

The goldsmith looked her up and down, then pulled the door open, sheathing his sword. The queen stood behind him, looking less composed than usual.

'We need to move.' Eda reached inside and grabbed the

queen by the hand just as the front door of the shop banged open.

Fayre sucked in a breath as she was dragged outside. The goldsmith drew his sword and closed the door behind them. The women ran to the wall at the back of the courtyard. Eda leaned her bow against the fence and made a step with her hands. 'Over you go.'

Fayre hesitated.

'They'll kill you,' Eda said. 'Or worse. You know I'm right.'

Fayre closed her eyes, then lifted her gown before stepping into Eda's hands. Eda hoisted her up, guiding her carefully over the seven-foot wall, then climbed up after her. She dropped down beside the queen, looking around.

'If we alert the defenders, they will assist us,' Fayre said.

Eda shook her head. 'The few defenders inside the borough are completely overwhelmed, and we can't afford to draw attention to you. I'm going to get you to the royal borough.'

As they made their way towards the square, Eda saw the fighting had bled out into other parts of the borough, reaching almost to the square itself. They watched from the shadows. Eda thought about knocking on one of the doors and hiding the queen until it was all over, but if the warriors took control of the borough, they would drag Fayre out onto the street and do as they pleased with her. And there was no guarantee merchants would open their doors given all that was happening outside. The safest place for her was the royal borough. She would have all the protection she needed there.

'I want you to stay on my left,' Eda said, readying her bow. 'I'll match whatever pace you can manage. Just keep moving towards the gate no matter what.'

Fayre peeked around the corner, then looked in the direction of the portcullis, readying herself.

'What have we here?'

The women whipped their heads around at the sound of male voices behind them. Two warriors walked slowly towards them, eyes on Queen Fayre.

'Someone important judging by the looks of you,' said one.

Eda was not prepared to let the conversation play out. Raising her bow, she shot at the man who had spoken. He lifted his shield, smashing the arrow off course. Eda's hand slackened around the bow. She stood no chance against two men that size. Without taking her eyes off them, she whispered, 'Run.'

The women took off in the direction of the gate, Fayre raising the hem of her gown to stop from tripping. They were running, but it was too slow for Eda. Fayre still somehow managed to look every bit the queen with her jewelled fingers and expensive cloak sailing behind her. She was not built for running but rather for elegant entries and graceful transitions.

'Faster,' Eda instructed as they neared the portcullis. 'Open the gate! I have the queen!'

This drew the attention of nearby warriors. Soon they were being pursued from two directions. Reaching for an arrow, Eda loaded her bow and took aim at the largest man coming from the right. It hit, not killing him but bringing him to a halt. She did the same thing again, then again, until the only men chasing them were the two behind. When she reached back for another arrow, she found the quiver empty. Cursing, she threw the bow aside, relieved when the portcullis began to rise in front of them. Two defenders ran towards the queen.

'Keep going,' Eda said, falling back. She needed to buy the queen some time.

Fayre continued towards the defenders.

Eda drew her dagger and turned to face the men

behind her. They were forced to pull up in order to avoid her blade, though they did not avoid it for long. Ducking beneath one of the warrior's shields, she slashed his leg. The man cried out, and the other one came for her. She ducked beneath the swinging blade, then straightened, fighting back with her ridiculous knife until it eventually became lodged in his shield. The man snatched the shield out of reach before she had a chance to retrieve it.

'You made me bleed,' said the other warrior. 'Your turn.'

Eda had removed her belt in that time, and when he came for her, she flicked it so the buckle caught his face. The shield fell from his hand, and Eda caught it, using it to block the other warrior's sword. He shoved her backwards, and she hit the ground hard, sliding a few feet across the stone. She managed to keep hold of the shield, lifting it just in time. Frustrated, the warrior kicked it from her hand, sending it flying across the square.

She swung her belt at him, unable to get to her feet. She had put up a good fight. At least she would die in a manner she was proud of and be remembered. That was something.

Just as she was resigning herself to her fate, she heard the thud of arrows hitting flesh. Her attackers stilled, and Eda saw the arrows protruding from them. Chest and stomach. They each took a few unsteady steps backwards as they surveyed the damage.

Eda snuck a glance over her shoulder and saw Queen Fayre now tucked safely between two defenders beneath the portcullis, gesturing for her to come.

Scurrying to her feet, Eda sprinted for the gate.

CHAPTER 15

Finally, more defenders arrived, a hundred of them emerging through the royal borough gate and joining the fight. Their uniforms were still clean, their energy fresh. Roul's uniform was washed red, and his arms and legs shook with exhaustion. He snuck a glance at Harlan, whose face was blood-splattered and slick with sweat. He looked ready to fall down.

It all felt easier once the other defenders joined the fight. The warriors' attention was divided between the old fight and the new. Their distraction was welcomed, and the soldiers fought and killed until there was no one left to fight or kill.

When the last sea warrior finally collapsed to the ground, the defenders stood looking around at the mass grave, chests heaving and feet shuffling on the bloodied street. The air was metallic, as nauseating as the visual.

'The other boroughs?' Harlan asked a nearby defender. They knew nothing of what was happening elsewhere, and his first concern was Blake and Luella.

The defender wiped blood from his eye. 'Last I heard they were secure, Commander.'

Harlan exhaled. 'I want this borough checked. Every house, every nook. There may still be warriors inside.' He looked to Roul.

'Go,' Roul said. 'Make sure they're all right. I'll go to the shop and check on Eda.'

Harlan nodded. 'I'll be back as soon as I can.' Then he jogged off.

'Get the injured to the infirmary,' Roul instructed one of the defenders. He bent, wiping the blade of his sword on a warrior corpse before sheathing it. Then he made his way towards the shops, where merchants were slowly opening their shutters and doors, emerging cautiously to survey the damage. But every shop appeared to be intact.

The day had delivered surprise after surprise. He had woken prepared for another day of training and had instead watched Eda almost die at the hands of a criminal, then fought a battle no one had seen coming.

And then there was the kiss.

The kiss that had followed the almost kiss. The kiss she had insisted on and he had been terrified of. The kind of kiss that marked a person. He had known it would. He had been drawn to her long before that moment, long before she felt it. That was why he had said no. He knew tasting her would be another anchor to this place, another anchor to her. But she had pushed, and his objections had been pitiful.

He stopped when he spotted the queen's carriage parked outside one of the shops. The driver circled the horse, checking it for injury. Only then did it occur to Roul that Queen Fayre might never have made it out of the borough in time. He jogged over, slowing when he noticed the corpses trailing up to the door. 'Where's the queen?'

'At the castle—I hope. I was told to hide, so I hid.' The driver scrubbed a hand down his face. 'They killed the goldsmith, but his wife managed to hide in time. She says a woman came for the queen before they broke the door in.'

'A woman?'

The driver nodded. 'I'm heading to the castle now if you want me to take you.' His eyes moved over Roul's bloodied uniform. 'Or to the infirmary perhaps?'

Roul should have accepted the offer of a ride to the castle, but instead he turned away and broke into a run towards the Suttones' shop located at the other end of the village. When he arrived, he found the door locked. He pounded on it. 'Eda! Open up!'

There was an eternal wait as someone fumbled with the latch before finally tugging it open. Roul's stomach fell when he caught sight of Birtle's face. 'Where is she?'

The old man held on to the doorframe, his head dropping slightly on an exhale. 'She wanted to help. Said she would only shoot from a rooftop. Promised she would come back.'

Roul was already walking away. He stepped down onto the street, not bothering to check the rooftops, because he knew Eda was the woman who had come for the queen. She would have seen the carriage, and she would have done what Eda did. She *loved* to play the hero. And now he needed to find out if she had been successful.

He moved as fast as he could manage back through the village, across the square to the guard at the gate. 'Is Queen Fayre inside?'

The guard straightened. 'Yes, Commander. She's unharmed as far as I'm aware.'

'Was there a woman with her?'

The defender waved a stretcher through before replying. 'We held the gate for a woman at Her Majesty's request. I haven't seen her since, so she's likely still inside.'

Roul was hanging on his every word. 'What do you mean, you held the gate? Did they not arrive together?'

'The woman was caught up in the fighting.'

Roul's stomach dropped. 'Was she injured?'

'It was hard to tell in her state.' He waved through two more stretchers.

'What state is that?' But he already knew the answer.

The defender met his eyes once more. 'She was a bit of a mess. Not surprising given she was fighting armed warriors with nothing but her belt.'

Roul fought the urge to cover the man's mouth, to suffocate his words, to shout 'Why didn't you help her?' in his face. But the defender's job was to protect the gate. The gate and the queen, not the merchant woman in trousers whose name he did not know. 'She definitely made it inside?'

'Saw her run through with my own eyes, Commander.'

Roul nodded before stepping past him, walking beneath the archway.

The royal borough was buzzing with defenders. They rushed about carrying the injured and collecting weapons. Roul dodged men racing by and stepped around the stretchers laid out on the road. The infirmary was likely full.

'Do you need a physician, Commander?' a defender asked, falling into step with him.

Roul had not had time to evaluate his own injuries. The fact that he was upright and not leaving a trail of blood in his path was assessment enough. 'No, I'm fine.'

He watched the defender run off. Then his feet stopped when he caught sight of a woman walking between two rows of stretchers. It was Eda. All the tension his body had been holding seemed to melt away in a single glance. She moved slowly, taking in the face of every man. Her brow was pinched, one hand clutching her stomach. He could not tell if she felt sick or if she was holding her trousers up. A length of rope sat in place of a belt.

Relief hit Roul like a wagon, and he took a slow breath before calling to her. 'Eda!'

He saw the relief on her face, the sharp inhale of breath as she took off at a run in his direction. She had been looking for him among the injured. He swallowed, then braced as she flung herself at him. He caught her. Of course he caught her.

'You're in so much trouble, soldier,' he said.

She clung to him for a second, her feet a few inches off the gravel path. 'What took you so long?'

He reluctantly placed her on the ground before replying. 'I went to the shop looking for you, because that's where you were supposed to be, remember?'

She pressed her lips together, guilty as charged. 'Where's Harlan?'

'He went to the house.'

Her eyes closed with relief. 'The warriors never even made it off the walls in the other boroughs. The warden made sure of that. Of course, if he had known Queen Fayre was in the merchant borough, you would have gotten your reinforcements sooner.' A smile flickered. 'I witnessed some very strong words directed at a handful of defenders who failed to inform him.'

Roul should have been angry at her, but his relief seemed to extinguish every other emotion. He looked her over again. 'Are you hurt?'

'No.' She reached up and touched his torn sleeve. 'Are you?'

He shook his head, then looked around at the injured laid out on stretchers. 'I should get you home before your sisters come looking for you. Then I need to help here.' His eyes returned to her. 'Perhaps on the way you can tell me the story of how you came to lose your belt.'

Her nose crinkled as she crossed her arms over the rope holding up her pants. 'It's a very boring story.'

'I doubt that.' He swallowed. 'You're really all right?'

A nod. 'Are *we* all right?' She asked the question without looking at him.

He knew what she was asking. They had barely had a chance to process all the events *prior* to the battle. 'Of course we are,' he answered with confidence.

'Good.' She wet her parched lips. 'Good. Because I need you—alive, preferably. So if you could just not die moving forwards, that would be much appreciated.'

He searched her face, seeing how much this confession, this small glimpse of something she would consider weakness, pained her. He wanted to say he was not going anywhere, but that was not true. God, he wanted to say it though. 'Careful. You're sounding very human right now.'

'How dare you?' A ghost of a smile came and went on her face.

He looked at the ground between them. 'No one's managed to kill me yet.' It was the only reassurance he could offer her. Gesturing towards the stables, he said, 'Let's go.'

CHAPTER 16

*E*da watched Roul from the front step of Wright House until he was out of sight, feeling like the sun had just disappeared behind the clouds. They had shared a horse like usual, and she had held loosely to his tunic, her forehead occasionally tipping forwards to rest on his back.

'Don't you fall off,' Roul had said every time she rested against him.

But he would never let that happen. He would catch her before she hit the ground. The thought was as warm as his mouth had been on hers earlier that day. Now he was gone again, and her heart felt heavy at his absence. She did not know whether the intimate moment she forced upon him was to blame or if it was the time spent in the royal borough waiting to find out if he was alive.

As she turned to the door, it opened. Her mother stood there looking her up and down, then launched forwards, hugging her youngest daughter tightly. 'Thank goodness. Is Birtle all right?'

He's fine, Eda signed.

Candace held her at arm's length. 'You're speaking with your hands, which suggests otherwise.'

Had she? She cleared her throat. 'Sorry.'

Candace's eyes moved over her again. 'Whose blood is that?'

'Not mine.' She looked past her, then signed, *Where's Blake?*

Candace searched her eyes. 'Tell me what happened?'

The habit was harder to break with her family. She shrugged. 'I fought a little.'

Seeing she was going to get nothing more from her daughter, Candace exhaled and stepped aside. 'Blake is in the kitchen.'

Eda offered a reassuring smile as she stepped past. She found Blake and Luella standing at the bench with their backs to her. Blake looked over her shoulder at the approaching footsteps, then heavenward. 'Thank Belenus.'

Eda went to the other side of the bench, a hand pressed to her stomach.

Blake's eyebrows came together in concern as she held tightly to Luella. The tiny girl was attempting to beat eggs with a fork. The egg mixture was splashed from one end of the bench to the other. When Eda did not speak, Blake pried the fork from her daughter's hand and placed her down on the ground.

'All right,' she said, crossing her arms and looking at Eda. 'Out with it. What happened?'

So much. So much had happened. One topic in particular was burning on Eda's tongue, but she had promised Roul she would not tell her sisters.

Blake tilted her head. 'For goodness' sake. Out with it.'

I can't tell you.

Blake looked down at Eda's hands. 'The fact that you're signing suggests you really should.' She closed her eyes.

'Please don't tell me there's a body out front you need help burying.'

'No body.' Eda drew a breath. 'If I tell you, you must promise to never tell a soul.'

Blake looked past her to the back door. 'Before you go on—'

'I need to get this out.'

'Eda—'

'Roul and I kissed today. I mean, we *really* kissed. There was so much heat, I thought my skin was going to combust into flames at one point—'

A throat cleared behind her, and Eda whipped her head around. Harlan stood at the back door.

'That's what I was trying to tell you,' Blake said quietly.

Eda prayed the floor would open up and swallow her. 'Oh.'

Harlan stepped inside and walked over to Blake. 'I'm heading to the barracks. I'll be home as soon as I can.'

Blake pushed up on her toes and kissed him. 'Good luck.'

He kissed her again, then nodded a farewell at Eda before leaving.

Blake walked around the bench and took Eda's hand. The two women stared at the back door, not speaking for a long moment.

'Where's your belt?' Blake asked, breaking the silence.

'I used it as a whip when I lost my knife.'

Blake rubbed her forehead. 'Of course you did.'

'Harlan's not going to say anything to Roul, is he?'

Blake shrugged. 'He might.'

'He *might?*'

'He loves you like blood. He's going to watch out for you.' Blake ran her thumb over Eda's calloused palm. 'Lyndal and I wondered how long it was going to take the pair of you to fall in love. She said a year. I said two.'

Eda withdrew her hand. 'I confessed only to a kiss. I said nothing of love.' A lie. The words were a piece of armour.

Their mother rushed into the kitchen, a hand pressed to her chest. 'Queen Fayre's carriage just pulled up out front.' She looked between her daughters for an explanation.

Blake shrugged and looked to Eda, who raised her hands.

'I had no idea she was coming.'

Candace waved her out of the kitchen. 'Go and clean yourself up this instant.'

Eda rolled her eyes. 'She doesn't care what I look like, Mother—trust me.'

'Well, I care.' Candace pointed to the filthy rope holding up Eda's trousers. 'I care very much. Off you go. Quickly now.'

Blake followed Eda out of the kitchen and upstairs to the bedroom, throwing a washcloth at her as she filled a basin with clean water. Eda scrubbed her face, neck, and hands clean, then put on the undergarments and a dress Blake had gotten out for her.

'Much better,' Blake said. She combed out Eda's hair and twisted it into a bun at the nape of her neck.

They returned downstairs, and Candace informed Eda that Queen Fayre was waiting out front to speak with her.

'I invited her in. However, she insisted she was fine.'

Eda nodded and lifted her chin. 'Then I'll be back soon.'

Outside, the queen stood in front of her carriage looking up at Wright House. 'Such a big difference since the last time I laid eyes on it.'

Eda walked over to her and curtsied. 'Me or the house?'

Fayre ran her eyes over Eda. 'Both. It seems you really can play all the parts.' She nodded at the path. 'Shall we walk since the rain has stopped?'

Eda nodded and began strolling along the path that circled the house. The only sounds were their feet crunching on gravel and the bleating of distant goats.

'It is time for my son to come home,' the queen said after a long silence. 'Chadora is far too vulnerable without a king. News is spreading of our prosperity.'

"Prosperity" was a stretch, but the kingdom was certainly doing better than they had been under King Borin's rule.

Fayre lifted the skirts of her dress as they navigated a puddle of water. 'If I could only get an hour alone with my son, I could make him see sense. Belenus only knows what misinformation Queen Isabella is filling the prince's head with. There is a reason my letters are returned to me unopened.'

Eda said nothing, only listened.

'I always ask myself what is best for the Chadorian people at this point,' Fayre continued. 'It is a difficult thing to push aside one's pride in order to assess a situation in an honest manner.' She paused, looking to the trees at the edge of the lawn. 'I believe we shall soon fall under King Edward's rule if we do not act, and all our progress will be undone. England's food situation remains dire, which means the few food resources we have would be depleted in no time.' She glanced sideways at Eda. 'That is why Chadora must remain independent for now, until the world replenishes itself.'

Eda nodded. 'Can I ask you something?'

'Go ahead.'

'Why does the prince refuse your letters? Not returning to claim his crown is one thing, but his refusal to speak to you reeks of a falling-out.'

Fayre lifted her chin. 'It could be due to any number of my shortcomings as a mother, which is why I must approach him as a queen. First, we must free him from

England's clutches. Then I can mend what is broken between us. At present, he does not trust himself to lead—and he does not trust me to teach him.'

Eda stopped walking. 'You said *we*. Who is that exactly?'

Fayre turned to her, eyes gleaming. 'I am going to send you to Harlech Castle. I want you to bring my son home.'

Eda's hands went limp at her sides. It took her a moment to reply. 'You said I wasn't ready.'

'And then you proved me wrong. While it is important to follow orders, it is more important to be fearless and decisive in one's actions.'

Fayre resumed walking, and Eda followed her. They passed the stables and continued towards the front of the house.

'I shall have the warden put together a unit to escort you,' Fayre said when the carriage came into view. 'Tomorrow we shall spend the day preparing you, and then you will depart the following morning.'

Eda almost tripped over her own feet. 'You want me to leave in two days?'

'In truth, we barely have that to spare.'

And in truth, Eda would have left that very moment. All she needed was enough time to say goodbye to her family—and Roul.

Roul.

'Unless you have changed your mind,' Fayre asked when she did not immediately reply.

Eda looked at her. 'I'm as willing and ready as the day I broke into Eldon Castle to tell you I was willing and ready.'

They had done a full circle of the house now, and Queen Fayre stopped in front of her carriage. 'Come to me in the morning. We shall discuss everything then and have you fitted for some dresses.'

'I do actually own dresses.'

'Dresses fit for an English court?'

Eda swallowed. 'Not too many of those, no.'

Fayre pressed her lips together, holding back a smile. 'We may have made a soldier out of you, but we must make a lady out of you too.' She nodded once, a farewell.

Eda curtsied, lower this time to show just how much of a lady she could be. There was amusement in Fayre's eyes when she rose. The queen took the driver's hand and stepped up into the carriage, settling herself in the seat.

'No need to scale the wall,' Fayre said, eyes ahead. 'The gate will open for you this time.'

Eda watched the carriage pull away, then returned inside to face her family.

~

The infirmary was overflowing, so only those with life-threatening injuries made it inside. A tent was set up to house the rest of the injured defenders. The men sat on bloodied blankets, awaiting stitching and bandaging from exhausted physicians and healers doing rounds.

It was pitch black by the time Roul returned from the merchant borough, where he had assisted with the clean-up. His arms and legs ached, and his head pounded with fatigue as he made his way to the outdoor wash area. He stripped down, carefully cleaning the superficial cuts that peppered his body before scrubbing the rest of him clean. He had just finished dressing when Harlan appeared through the dark, leaning against the wall and crossing his arms.

Roul took in his body language. 'Everything all right?'

A small shrug from Harlan. 'You tell me.'

Roul turned to face him properly, brow pinched. 'Tell you what exactly?'

'How about what your intentions are with Eda?'

Roul's lips twitched. 'My *intentions*?'

'I heard about the kiss.'

Ah. So much for keeping it a secret. 'She told you about that?'

'I walked in when she was telling Blake.' Harlan's expression was serious. 'Does she know you're returning to Carno?'

'You told me not to tell anyone, remember?'

Harlan pushed off the wall. 'Well, I think it's time to share your plans with her before things get out of hand. Your family's waiting for you to return.'

Roul pinched the bridge of his nose. 'The kiss was... I tried to stop it.' That was absolutely sort of true.

'But the woman half your size forced herself upon you?'

Roul's hand fell away, but before he could reply, the warden appeared, looking between them as he came to a stop. The commanders straightened.

'I just came from Queen Fayre's quarters,' Shapur began. 'It seems the youngest Suttone sister will be going to Harlech Castle after all. I have been instructed to put together a unit.'

Roul glanced at Harlan, whose surprise matched his own. 'But she failed the test.'

'Then single-handedly saved the queen when every other defender in the borough failed to do so,' Shapur replied. 'She is capable, as you both know—and willing.'

Harlan exhaled. 'When?'

'We have two days.'

At first Roul thought he had misheard. 'Two days?'

Shapur nodded. 'I need five men.'

'Will five be enough?' Harlan asked.

'No,' Roul said immediately.

Shapur shot him a warning glance. 'Too large and they will attract unwanted attention.'

Five men was not enough. A hundred men was not enough.

'I'd like to volunteer to lead the unit, sir,' Roul said. 'I know the region and understand the risks better than anyone else inside these walls.'

The warden stared at him for what felt like a full minute before looking to Harlan. 'It is not the worst idea in the world.'

Harlan nodded in agreement. 'I think Eda will appreciate a familiar face, and Thornton will make sure *no one* lays a hand on her. Right, Commander Thornton?'

His meaning came through loud and clear. 'Of course.'

Harlan looked back at his father. 'We'll have a think about who else will make up the unit.'

Shapur nodded. 'Bring Eda to the castle in the morning. There will be a full briefing—and a dress fitting, apparently.'

'She's going to love that,' Harlan said.

'Make sure you are there for the briefing also,' Shapur said to Roul.

'Yes, sir.'

The warden strode off.

When he was gone, Roul linked his hands atop his head and turned in a circle. So many thoughts were crashing in at once. 'Five men? There are rebel groups the size of armies in Carmarthenshire.'

'Half our men are injured. We'll struggle to find an additional four defenders prepared to risk their necks for what they'll deem a suicide mission as it is.'

Roul stilled, his hands returning to his sides. 'What about four recruits?'

Harlan slowly nodded. 'A ready-made unit that Eda has already built trust with. Clever. Let's go see if they're willing.'

CHAPTER 17

When Eda arrived at the royal borough gate the next morning, she found Roul waiting for her on the other side. She watched his serious face through the latticed wood as the gate rose, sensing his mood before they had even exchanged a word. A lot had happened since their last meeting. She was going to Harlech Castle, and he was now responsible for getting her there. Admittedly, she had felt relieved when Harlan told her the news. It would all be so much more manageable with him at her side.

'I barely recognised you in a dress,' he said when she reached him.

'I barely recognise myself.'

He smiled at the ground as he fell into step with her.

'I'm sorry you got pulled into this,' she said.

'I didn't get pulled in. I volunteered.'

There was that light feeling in her chest again.

'It's what friends do,' he added.

The lightness dissipated at the pointed remark. 'Should we talk about yesterday?'

'Which part?'

She looked at him. 'The kiss, Roul. I'm talking about the kiss.'

He nodded. 'The one you went straight home and told Blake and Harlan all about?'

She winced. 'Sorry about that. To be fair, I only told Blake. Harlan chose that very inconvenient moment to enter the house. How bad was the lecture?'

'It wasn't bad. I like that he looks out for you.'

She regarded him, noting his heavy expression. 'But?' When he hesitated, she reached out and touched his arm. 'It's me. I'm listening.'

He moved closer until his cloak brushed hers. 'You know I don't speak much about myself.'

'Much? You share nothing about yourself whatsoever.'

He met her eyes. 'Well, there's a good reason for that. I've had to tread carefully since coming here. Everything that's been handed to me is fragile.' He paused. 'I need to know you'll not speak of this to anyone—despite your terrible track record with keeping secrets.'

Her feet slowed. 'You can trust me with this.'

He nodded. 'I didn't come to Chadora of my own accord. I came here because Queen Fayre sent me here. Our paths crossed at the Toryn border a few years back. I was in trouble. She spared my life in exchange for information.'

Eda's feet slowed. 'What information?'

'Army information, mostly.' Seeing her confusion, he added, 'She needed a trustworthy source inside an army with a growing reputation of brutality.'

'Chadora's army has always been loyal to its king. Any brutality that took place was ordered by *him*.' She stopped walking as a realisation hit her. 'She sent you here to spy on her husband.'

'Yes.'

She resumed walking, taking a moment to process this

new information. 'That woman has more resources at her disposal than she knows what to do with. Why send you?'

'I thought about that a lot. I think everyone she trusted was with her in Toryn.'

'So she sent you to be her eyes.' Eda watched her feet a moment. 'You said she spared your life.'

He stared ahead. 'When there's nothing left to steal in your own kingdom, you venture north to the next.'

'You got caught stealing?'

He nodded. 'She happened to be there, and she saw an opportunity.'

'You agreed to her terms in exchange for your life?'

He did not answer straight away. 'It wasn't really about me. I needed to stay alive in order to take care of my family. Queen Fayre promised to provide for them while I was gone, and so far she's kept her word.'

Eda watched him. 'So your family is in Carmarthenshire being provided for by Queen Fayre?'

'Yes.'

That led her to her next question. 'For how long? King Oswin is dead. How long are you expected to stay here?'

His eyes were heavy again. 'The minimum term of service is five years. I gave her five years.'

Eda stared back at him. 'Because you're a defender, and a defender must serve a minimum of five years.' Her hands had pins and needles. 'You arrived over three years ago.'

He struggled to hold her gaze. 'I have two years left. Then I'll return home to my family.'

Now she had all the pieces. 'You're leaving.' He did not reply, did not have to. 'Does Harlan know?'

Roul nodded. 'He was the only person I trusted inside these walls for the longest time. I hope you understand why I kept this from you. I can't afford to mess this up.'

Eda understood that better than anyone. She would do anything to protect her family.

She slowed as they neared the castle gate to give them more time. 'Tell me about your family.'

'I'm the eldest child and only son. I've two younger sisters, Lana and Odella. They're fourteen and fifteen.'

'Are both your parents alive?'

He nodded.

'What does your father do?'

'My father used to be a cartographer.'

She did not miss the flash of pain that crossed his face. 'Used to be?'

'After England cut Carmarthenshire loose, the work dried up. There was no way to earn money. My father eventually did what most people do in that place. He found other ways to survive.'

'He stole food?'

'Not well. He got caught. People in that kingdom make their own laws now. The farmer who caught him took two fingers from each hand. He knew exactly what he was doing.'

Eda pressed her eyes shut at the visual. 'I'm so sorry.'

Roul was watching his feet again. 'I think you know the rest of the story.'

They fell silent as they passed through the gate.

'I wish you had told me sooner, but I understand why you didn't,' she said once they were on the other side of the wall. 'I'll say nothing of this to anyone, I promise.'

He brushed a finger down his nose. 'I hope you understand why that kiss must remain between two friends. Even if I wanted to stay, I can't.'

She kept her expression as neutral as possible, because anything she felt, or he felt, was obsolete. Her feelings were not his fault, and the choices he had made were the same as she would have in his position.

'It was just a kiss.' The casualness in her voice surprised

even her. 'It didn't mean anything. I'm just glad it's out of the way.' The words soured on her tongue.

Roul nodded slowly, looking relieved—and something else.

'Let's focus on getting Prince Becket home,' she added. 'Shall we go and find out the details of this crazy plan?'

He watched her for a moment before replying. 'How would you like to go to the armoury afterwards and collect your new weapons?'

That made her smile. 'You always know how to cheer a lady up after a dress fitting.'

He laughed silently, and it eased some of the tension still hanging in the air between them. 'I've got your back, soldier. I hope you know that.'

A knot formed in Eda's stomach. 'Back at you, Commander.'

They climbed the castle steps in silence.

~

Eda left Eldon Castle with two swords, four daggers, a very fancy longbow, three gowns, a variety of pastes for her face and lashes, some new boots, an expensive chestnut gelding, some posh vocabulary, and a head filled with details of the royal family.

She was to play the role of Lady Hayley Peytone from Peytone House in Llanystumdwy, Prince Becket's English cousin who he had not seen since childhood.

'Next time we meet, I expect my son to be standing alongside you.' Those had been Queen Fayre's final words before dismissing her. They weighed more than her new weapons.

After the briefing, Eda went to the farming borough to say goodbye to Lyndal. The two women stood leaning against the back wall of the house, watching Astin put a new fence post in the distance.

'So you just stand here drooling over your husband all day?' Eda asked.

Lyndal pointed to her stomach. 'I work as hard as anyone around here when I'm not growing a human or at the almshouse. I'm still in charge of the pigs.'

Eda turned to her sister. 'You mean boars.'

Lyndal pinched her lightly, eyes remaining on her husband. 'He'll start getting all sweaty soon, and that shirt will cling to his muscled body.'

Eda screwed up her face. 'The man's practically blood. I can't have this conversation with you.'

Lyndal looked at her. 'Oh, I almost forgot. You only have eyes for *one* man now.'

Eda looked heavenward. 'I gather by that comment that you've spoken to Blake.'

'She came by this morning.'

Eda dropped her head into her hands. 'Can no one keep a secret in this family?'

Lyndal laughed. 'You tell one sister, you tell us both. You know that.' She waited for Eda to look at her. 'Is it serious?'

'Of course not,' Eda said immediately. 'It was just a moment of curiosity between friends. We've much more important things to focus on right now.'

Presley and Rose walked by on their way to join Astin. They waved at Eda as they passed. She waved back.

'Was it a good kiss though?' Lyndal asked once Presley and Rose were out of earshot.

Eda leaned her head against the wall. 'I thought my legs were going to give out.'

Lyndal's mouth lifted. 'Just a curious moment between friends, you say. It sounds like goodbye to the barmaid to me. And for the record, she has nothing on you.'

Eda met her eyes. 'What are you talking about? She's breathtaking.'

'*You* are breathtaking.' Lyndal took her hand. 'Inside and out.'

Eda looked down at her dress, the one she had spent two hours scrubbing grass stains from a week prior in order to avoid her mother's wrath. 'You're just saying that because you're my sister.'

'It also happens to be the truth. You're the best parts of every woman. Roul knows that. That's why he's been glued to your side for this past year.'

Eda blinked slowly. 'I should go. We're leaving at first light. I've much to do before then.'

Lyndal pulled Eda to her, holding tightly. 'You will come back in one piece, won't you?'

'That's the plan.' Her eyes closed. 'I'll miss you.'

'I'll miss you too. Make sure you bring us back a king so this separation is worthwhile.'

Eda stepped back and placed a hand on her sister's stomach. Bending, she whispered, 'Take care of your mother until I return.'

CHAPTER 18

*U*nsurprisingly, Eda did not sleep well that night. Her mind was busy and her body restless. When it was finally time to rise, she crept downstairs and stilled when she spotted her mother seated by the fireplace, sewing. She walked over to her, sinking down onto the floor and resting her chin on Candace's warm skirt. 'What are you doing up before me?'

Her mother gave her a triumphant smile. 'Finishing these.' Placing the needle between her lips, she held up a pair of trousers.

Frowning, Eda reached up and kneaded the expensive wool between her fingers. 'They're a bit small for Harlan, aren't they?'

'Yes.' Candace returned the needle to her sewing box and gestured for Eda to stand. Then, rising, she held them to Eda's waist. 'However, they are perfect for you.'

Eda looked up. 'You made these for me?'

'I could not very well let you leave here dressed in your brother's clothes. You are representing the family, after all.' She turned to the pile of neatly folded garments sitting beside her sewing box. 'Two shirts, two trousers, two tunics with flowers embroidered along the neckline—so Roul can tell you apart from the men.'

Eda's throat thickened as she ran a finger over the white flowers. 'They're perfect.' She threw her arms around her mother and whispered, 'Thank you.'

A hand landed softly on her back. 'You make sure you get back here safely and quickly, you hear me?'

Eda nodded. When she stepped back, she found Blake standing at the bottom of the stairs with Luella on her hip.

'We heard horses out front,' Blake said. 'Harlan's gone to saddle yours.'

Excitement and nerves churned in Eda's stomach as she flew up the stairs, kissing her sister's cheek as she passed. She had a quick wash, brushed her teeth, and braided her hair. Tugging off her nightdress, she put on her new clothes, the boots Queen Fayre had given her, strapped on as many weapons as she could comfortably wear, then swung her cloak around her. Everything else went into the canvas bag alongside the new dresses.

Eda walked over to the tall mirror that stood in the corner of the room, turning in a slow circle before it. The clothes fit perfectly. She had never felt more ready for anything in her life. She wondered if Queen Artemisia of Halicarnassus had felt this good before riding into battle. Snatching up her bag, she ran downstairs.

Out front, Candace and Blake stood to one side. Luella was seated on Eda's gelding, bouncing up and down in the saddle while Harlan kept a firm hold of her leg. Garlic sat on the rump of the horse, preening her feathers and looking far too comfortable.

Eda glanced past them to the six waiting horses, five carrying defenders and one loaded with supplies. One of the men dismounted and came forwards to take her bag. It took her a moment to realise who it was—Hadewaye.

'Morning,' he said, winking as he took her bag.

Her eyes returned to the other men, and she saw then that the group was made up of Roul, Alveye, Tatum, and Blackmane. 'You *all* drew the short straw?'

'Commander Thornton's idea,' Hadewaye said. 'We all agreed.'

'Everyone?'

Hadewaye knew she was asking about Blackmane. 'No one twisted his arm.'

Eda suspected he had agreed for the sake of his friends and the prince, not her.

She turned back to her horse as Harlan pulled Luella from the saddle. Her niece squealed in protest. Harlan held his squirming daughter in one hand and Garlic in the other.

'We'll see you soon,' he said.

Eda took her niece's hand and kissed it. She looked over at her mother and sister but did not go to them. She did not have another goodbye in her. They must have understood that, because they remained where they were and offered her a reassuring smile instead. Eda heard her mother sniff as she mounted.

'Looking sharp, Suttone,' Tatum said, riding up next to her.

She adjusted the bow on her back. 'Shut up.'

'It was a genuine compliment. We all know dressing isn't your strong suit.'

'And we all know archery isn't yours,' she replied. 'So I hope you brought your sword.'

Alveye and Hadewaye laughed.

Roul nudged his horse forwards. 'That's enough, you two. We haven't even left yet.' He nodded a farewell at Harlan.

'Bring them all home,' Harlan said in response.

'That's the plan.' Roul nudged his horse, and the defenders followed him.

Eda looked back at her family a final time and saw Blake's arm was around their mother. 'Please don't worry.'

'You just focus on what's ahead of you,' Harlan said. 'Make sure you listen to your commander at all times.' He clapped a hand on the gelding's rump, and it broke into a trot.

Eda watched her mother and sister over her shoulder until their faces blurred. Then Blake let go of Candace and signed, *Stand tall and strong, warrior.*

Eda blinked back tears as she faced forwards. Roul had slowed his horse and was waiting for her to catch up to the group. He said nothing as her horse fell into step with his.

An hour later, they reached the outer-wall. It all felt new to Eda, who rarely went to that part of the borough, because everything she needed and loved was in the opposite direction. The portcullis was heavily guarded, with defenders both on the ground and watching from the wall above. As they approached the gate, Roul looked at her.

'I need you to be the soldier we trained you to be on the other side of that wall. From this point, I'm no longer your friend, I'm your commander. That's the only way this works. That's how I keep everybody alive. Are we clear?'

She understood the pressure he felt to keep everyone safe. 'Yes, Commander.'

'You stay in my sight at all times. If anything happens to you, the entire mission is lost.'

'I know.'

A guard came forwards to speak with Roul. 'It's been very quiet these past few days. You should make it to the forest without incident.'

Tatum and Blackmane exchanged a look as the guard signalled to a defender atop the wall. A moment later, the portcullis began to rise.

Roul gestured to the group to proceed, and they walked their horses towards the rising portcullis, the noise cutting through the stillness of dawn. When it came to a stop, the only sound was the soft clap of hooves on the path.

Eda stared ahead at the heavy fog they were about to enter. She could not look away. Every muscle in her body tensed as they were swallowed up by the heavy mist. When the portcullis lowered behind them, Roul signalled for Tatum to watch east, Alveye west, and for Blackmane to fall back.

Mud sucked at the horses' hooves, causing them to trip on the changing terrain. Eda could see they were travelling on what was once a road but was now a jungle of ragwort and creeping thistle. She glanced over her shoulder at the wall, barely able to make out the defenders atop it.

'We'll be entering the forest in about five miles,' Roul said quietly beside her. 'We'll have more protection then.'

'I can't decide if the cloud cover is good or bad,' Eda replied.

Tatum glanced in her direction. 'It's both.'

A red kite passed overhead, its long wings flashing into view. Blackmane's horse sidestepped, and Alveye's emitted a low whinny.

'Easy,' Blackmane said.

The other horses seemed to feed off the nervous energy, their heads and tails lifting. Eda stroked the silky neck of her horse in an attempt to calm him.

The red kite appeared again, lower this time, swooping past Hadewaye. His horse stopped, front legs lifting off the ground. Blackmane reached for his bow, loaded it, and pointed it at the sky.

'He's probably hungry,' Alveye said. 'He's seeing if we have anything he might want.'

'Better put your hood up, Suttone,' Tatum said with a smirk. 'You'll be in trouble once he realises he can lift you.'

Eda glanced in his direction. 'And here I was thinking it

would fall to me to provide comedic relief.' Still, she tugged the hood of her cloak up.

It was another hour before the ground evened out and trees appeared on the horizon. There was no visible path into the forest, so Roul forged one. They moved in single file through the trees, Roul at the front and Eda behind him, then Tatum, Hadewaye, Alveye, and Blackmane at the back. He had finally relaxed enough to put his bow away. Nothing moved in the trees, the occasional call of a bird the only sign of life.

It was almost noon when they emerged on the other side of the forest. The cloud had finally lifted, so they could see what was ahead of them now: long grass and weeds all the way to the horizon. They had yet to encounter a person outside the walls they had built.

'We'll stop here for a bit,' Roul said, pulling his horse up and dismounting. 'Do your business, stretch your legs.'

The men dispersed to relieve themselves. Eda led her horse away from the group in search of privacy. She stopped when she stepped on something hard. When she looked down, she saw she was standing on a large bone. There was an identical one beside it. They led to more bones, and her heart sped up as she recognised a human skull with an arrow through it. She took a quick step back.

'That's what happens to people who are too proud to piss in front of an audience.'

Eda whipped her head around at the sound of Roul's voice.

'What did I tell you about leaving my sight?'

'Sorry.' She turned her horse, heading back in the direction she had come. 'I can hold it.'

Roul caught her arm when she stepped past him. 'We're not stopping again until we make camp.'

She looked down at the large hand holding her, the

memory of those fingers tangled in her hair still fresh in her mind. Roul let go.

'I'll watch your horse,' he said.

Eda shook her head and continued past him. 'I'm fine. Let's go.'

CHAPTER 19

*R*oul watched Eda squirm in the saddle for nearly four hours before he could not take it anymore. They were travelling through open land with nothing but animal carcasses for cover.

'Dismount, Suttone,' Roul said. 'The rest of you, eyes west.'

For once, Eda did not object. Swallowing her pride, she slipped from her horse and danced around while she unbelted her trousers. Only when she climbed back onto her horse did Roul look at her.

'Next time you go when the rest of the group goes.'

Her cheeks coloured. 'Yes, Commander.'

They reached the forest late in the afternoon. Roul was thankful for the cover of trees once more. It was better than spending the night out in the open, which would have left them vulnerable. He looked up at the long-reaching sequoia branches as they rode beneath them. It was not uncommon for rebels to drop from the trees, tackling riders to the ground and then riding off on their horses.

When they came across a stream, Roul veered his horse

left, heading alongside it until he found a clearing big enough for their tent.

'We'll set up camp here,' Roul said, pulling up his horse and looking over his shoulder at the others. 'If the rain gets heavy overnight, at least the tent won't flood.'

The light was beginning to fade as the group dismounted. They tethered their horses to nearby trees and took a moment to stretch. Eda stifled a yawn as she unbuckled her saddle and dragged it off her tired horse. It almost weighed as much as her. He had to stop himself from going to help her.

Hadewaye and Alveye erected the tent while Blackmane and Tatum went to see if they could scavenge anything to eat alongside their food rations. While Roul was lighting the fire, Eda fed and watered the horses, then went to the stream for a wash. She returned with a few large rocks, which she placed in the fire. They would help to keep the tent warm overnight.

Blackmane and Tatum returned with some lemon sorrel and aureate grubs. Tatum sank down beside Eda and opened his hand, revealing the grubs.

'I brought you dinner.'

Eda looked down at the squirming insects, then reached for one, tossing it into her mouth and chewing. 'Thanks.'

Alveye's eyes widened. 'I really didn't think you'd eat that.'

'How do you think I survived locked in the merchant borough with no food?'

Tatum looked impressed as he handed the grubs to the others.

'What was it like stuck in there for all that time?' Hadewaye asked.

Eda shrugged. 'You smelled the corpses from the nobility borough, did you not?'

Roul looked at the fire. He had arrived in Chadora prepared to play whatever role he needed to for the sake of his family, but he had not been prepared for the fallout of King Oswin's death. He had done what he could, collecting mussels for the children and tossing them through the port gate. But it had not been enough. He had not been acquainted with the Suttone family at that time, but he saw the impact their suffering had on Harlan.

Blackmane stared at Eda across the fire. 'You telling me your family survived on insects?'

'Insects and blind hope.' She picked up the lemon sorrel and dropped it into a small pan with some of the butter from their rations. The wilted leaves did not amount to much, but combined with some salted pork, they had a meal.

Roul noticed that Eda gave herself the smallest portion of everything. 'That's not enough for you,' he told her across the flames.

She shrugged. 'I'm half the size of the rest of you.'

He tore off a portion of his pork and held it out for her. 'Here.'

With a sigh, Eda took it and ate.

With their stomachs no longer growling, they settled into a comfortable silence, enjoying the warmth of the fire as the temperature continued to drop.

'Blackmane,' Hadewaye said. 'Why don't you tell us a Morrigan story?'

The defender's gaze slid to the youngest recruit. 'I'm not your fucking governess, and you're too old for bedtime stories.'

Tatum and Alveye stifled a laugh.

'I wouldn't have picked you for the storyteller of the group,' Eda said.

'His grandfather was Irish,' Tatum said. 'He knows every myth and folktale from that part of the world.'

Hadewaye nodded in agreement. 'The Morrigan was a goddess who could change form and influence wars.'

'Before he passed, my father told me the story of the battle between Tuatha Dé Danann and the Fomorions,' Eda said, looking back at Blackmane. 'Do you know it?'

Blackmane let out a resigned breath and sat up a little straighter. 'The Morrigan prophesied that the Tuatha Dé Danann would win the battle but that their victory would come at a terrible price. She foretold that she would slay the Fomorion king Indech and bring two handfuls of his blood and kidneys to the River Unshin.'

The group listened as Blackmane spoke of how the gods gathered for the Second Battle of Moytura. 'Lugh asked the Morrigan what she'd brought with her.'

'Pursuit, death, and subjugation,' Eda said quietly.

Blackmane nodded, then continued with details of the bloodbath that followed, how the Morrigan's grandfather Nuada was slain, and her husband, the Dagda, was mortally wounded. Finally, the Morrigan joined the fray, ending the battle with her prowess and a poem. 'The Fomorions fled from her and perished in the sea,' he finished.

The group sat contemplating the story in the dark, the only light that of the flames now. Eda was hugging her knees in an attempt to keep warm.

'All right. Story time is over,' Roul said. 'I'll take first watch. Blackmane, you'll take the second. Then Tatum, Alveye, Hadewaye, and Suttone.'

Eda sat a little straighter. 'Why am I last?'

Roul's eyebrows lifted slightly.

Realising her mistake, Eda shook her head. 'Never mind.'

'You can swap with me if it makes you feel like more of a man,' Tatum said. 'I'm happy to sleep for longer.'

'Suttone will follow orders,' Roul said, picking up his waterskin and the dirty pan. 'I'm going to the creek.'

Eda reached for her bow. 'I'll come with you. Someone has to watch your back in the dark while you're scrubbing dishes.'

Roul gave a small nod of approval.

The pair walked down to the water in silence. Roul crouched by the creek while Eda watched the trees around them. After rinsing the pan, he filled his waterskin, then gestured for hers. She passed it to him without taking her eyes off their surroundings.

'You could've stayed by the fire,' he said as he handed it back to her.

'But we promised to take care of each other, remember?'

He smiled at the water. 'I remember.' After having a wash, he rose and looked around. 'It's strange being this side of the wall again.'

She glanced at him. 'Just think, this time tomorrow you'll be reunited with your family.'

It was a surreal thought after so many years of separation. Roul had suggested the group spend their second night in Carno to Queen Fayre, and she had agreed. Of course she had. She owed him a visit with his family.

'I can't wait to see their faces when they see you,' Eda said, a smile on her lips.

He loved that she was excited on his behalf. He was more nervous than anything else, because every letter he had received from his family since his departure had spoken of the rise of crime and decay of their village. They had been forced to keep the aid they received a secret to avoid attracting attention. The only people who knew were friends also benefiting from the arrangement. His family were not the kind of people to live well while others suffered around them. They took what they needed in order to survive and discreetly distributed the rest. But it was nowhere near enough to sustain an entire village. Roul suspected his heart would be both full and broken in the same visit.

'Time for you to get some sleep,' he said, taking a step in the direction of the camp.

She began walking. 'I saw you put your things at the far end of the tent. Was that deliberate?'

The answer was yes. Lying beside her, not touching, would be a special kind of torture. 'I trust Hadewaye to keep his hands to himself.'

'But not you?'

He glanced at her. 'I'm not answering that.'

She shook her head. 'Well, I hope Hadewaye likes to snuggle, because it's very cold away from the fire.'

'There will be no judgement on my part if I find the pair of you spooning.' The sound of her laughter warmed him.

When they reached the tent, he turned to her. 'Thanks for having my back down there.'

'You don't have to thank me. I'll always have it.'

The sincerity in her eyes had him looking away. 'Goodnight, Suttone.'

'Goodnight, Commander.'

Roul was finishing his watch and was about to go wake Blackmane when he saw a shadow pass over the tent. He stepped back from the fire, a hand going to the hilt of his sword. If one of his unit had risen to relieve themselves, they would have surely said something to avoid a sword in the back.

He waited, watching and listening.

Then he felt it. The gentle weight of someone watching him.

His gaze snapped to the flap of the tent when it moved, eyes meeting Eda's. Whatever he had seen, whatever he was sensing, she had seen and felt it too. Now she was waiting for him to confirm it. He responded with the slightest nod. Then the flap moved again, and she was gone.

Roul stepped back from the fire and into the shadows, darkness falling like a cloak of safety over him. His ears strained to catch any thread of noise.

Snap.

A twig breaking underfoot made him look back at the tent. A dark figure appeared, casting a long shadow over the canvas. Roul lifted his sword, ready to throw it, but an arrow burst through the tent before he had a chance, striking the intruder through the chest. The defenders emerged then, weapons in hand. Eda had managed to rouse them with little fuss. She and Hadewaye watched the surrounding trees down their arrows while the others turned their swords in their hands.

They waited for the intruder to fall silent, to die. Then they waited for more of them to arrive.

An arrow sailed past Blackmane's face, and Eda returned fire, but she was shooting blind. Roul signalled for them to spread out, and the group dispersed, their footsteps careful and silent. He followed Eda because she was the job—and because he could not help it.

A man dropped from the trees, landing in front of Tatum amid a fluttering of leaves. The defender speared him with his sword before he had a chance to raise his weapon. Another figure appeared from the side, tackling Alveye from behind. Eda swung her bow in that direction and shot him through the ribcage.

Roul was almost to Eda when he felt the swoosh of a weapon pass by him. He spun around, lifting his sword just as the blade came back in the other direction. Rebels spilled from the shadows then, around thirty of them. An arrow pierced the neck of the man Roul was fighting, and he knew without looking back that Eda had fired it. He turned and ran for her, trying to reach her before their attackers did.

Out of the corner of his eye, he saw two men run at Tatum. Roul reached for his dagger and threw it, stopping one in his tracks. Tatum was ready for the other, disarming him in two strikes before cutting his throat. Eda pivoted on the spot, firing one arrow after another. Then a man twice her size stepped up behind her.

'Suttone, behind!' Roul shouted.

She turned, releasing an arrow into the man's face. Roul reached her then, kicking the man back and away from her.

'You all right?' he asked, panting and looking around.

She nodded, reloading her bow and turning at the sound of feet pounding the wet earth. Roul watched the trees on the other side of them, not taking any chances. He heard the arrow release behind him, heard it hit, heard the scream that tore from the rebel's throat. He turned at the sound, for it was not the scream of a man. There stood a boy, no older than ten, an arrow protruding from his neck. A sword slipped from his hand, and he toppled backwards. Eda clapped a hand over her mouth, frozen in place as she watched him writhe on the ground before falling still. With a sharp inhale, she ran towards the boy.

'Suttone,' Roul hissed.

When she did not stop, he followed her, watching as she dropped to her knees beside the boy and felt for a heartbeat. Roul did not need to check for a pulse to know he was dead. He took her by the arm, dragging her to her feet. 'Load that bow. This isn't over.'

Eda sank back down to the ground, the weapon slipping from her hand this time.

Roul looked to the trees, then back at her. 'I need you to pick up your weapon.'

She lifted her eyes to him, and even in the dark, he could tell the boy's death had broken something in her. Eda signed something he could not understand, her voice lost.

He bent to pick up her bow and placed it in her hands. 'Get on your feet. That's an order, soldier.'

Tatum appeared, announcing himself. 'The camp's secure, Commander.' He stopped when he caught sight of the corpse. 'Oh shit.'

Eda dropped the arrow she was trying to load and bent to pick it up with a shaky hand. As she straightened, a dagger flew past her head. She swung her bow in that direction, but Roul noticed the string was not as taut as it should have been. She was already hesitating. Tatum moved to the other side of her when a short man burst into view, his sword raised above his head. Still Eda did not fire the arrow.

'What are you waiting for, Suttone?' There was an edge in Tatum's voice. 'Another dagger?'

She let out a pained breath, hands trembling.

Roul stepped forwards and threw his sword, stopping the man a few feet from them. He watched the rebel fall to the ground before looking at Eda. She was still staring down her arrow, her breaths coming fast.

'Eda,' Roul said quietly, using her first name.

Slowly, she lowered her bow. 'I'm sorry.'

Then she fell to her knees.

CHAPTER 20

*T*here was no blood on her, yet Eda continued to scrub her hands in the freezing water. She was crouched in the stream in the grey light of predawn, her trousers removed. They sat atop her boots at the edge of the stream. The image of that dead boy's face was still sharp in her mind. Perhaps he had a mother waiting for him, a sister. How long until she found out? Would the grief steal away her words like it had Eda's?

Movement in her periphery made her turn her head, and there was Roul standing at the water's edge, watching her.

'Time to get out,' he said. 'The water's freezing.'

One minute, she signed, even though he could not understand her.

'You know I don't understand you when you sign.'

There was nothing she could do about that. The words would not come any other way.

She looked past him to where the tent was now packed up and the horses were being saddled. It was time to leave.

Releasing a heavy breath, Roul yanked off his boots and began rolling up his trousers.

What are you doing?

He trudged into the water.

I'm not dressed, she signed. *Go away.*

If he did not understand what she was signing, he likely knew what she was saying from expression alone, but he continued towards her anyway. He pulled her to her feet, eyebrows drawn together in an angry line.

'He was young,' he said. 'You feel bad. I get it. But we're in no position to take prisoners. If we had let him live, he would have returned home and told the rest of his group what happened. Then they would have come after us.' Eda went to sign something, but Roul took hold of her hands to still them. 'You have to speak. If you can't, then we may as well turn around and go home, and that boy's death will have been for nothing. We can't show up at Harlech Castle with you signing.'

She stared up at him, eyes burning. He was right.

'You *wanted* to play defender,' he continued. 'You chose this. Well, this is what we do. We kill people, and we go about our day, so don't act surprised.'

Eda pressed her eyes closed, then let her forehead drop to his chest. She could not bear the lecture, so she sought comfort instead, knowing he would not push her away.

Slowly, Roul released her hands and wrapped his arms around her. A second later, she felt his warm lips atop her head.

'Tell me you can still do this,' he whispered into her hair. 'Tell me you won't hesitate again. Because the next time you fail to release that arrow, it might cost you your life.'

She tipped her head back to look at him, then swallowed. 'I can do this.' If anyone could bring her words back, he could.

He searched her eyes, his face tense with concentration. 'Trust me to keep you safe. That means standing up when I tell you to stand up and picking up your weapon when I say so.' His hand moved to settle on her jaw. 'That's how I get you home to your family.'

His touch felt like it was burning a hole in her back. Maybe it was the proximity or the calloused hand cradling her face. Or maybe it was the words he had spoken. But the next thing she knew, she was pushing up on her toes to kiss him. He did not pull away. He remained still, lips soft against hers.

The kiss was different to the one in the alleyway. It was gentle, tender. Her mind went quiet. Her body melted against his. Then suddenly it was not, and Roul was lifting her out of the water, guiding her legs around him. She sucked in a breath at the sensation of cold leather on her bare thighs. His mouth travelled along her jaw to her neck, kissing softly, making her legs tighten around him. He stopped then, resting his forehead on her shoulder as he caught his breath.

'This is why I slept on the other side of the tent.' The words vibrated against her skin.

She held the back of his head, her eyes closed. 'I don't want you to sleep on the other side of the tent. I want to hold your hand in the dark.'

He lifted his head to look at her, his eyes a brilliant contrast of gold against the bleak light. 'You want to hold my hand?'

She shrugged. 'It's platonic, is it not?'

A throat clearing made them both look in the direction of their camp. Standing at the top of the rise was not one but all four defenders. Roul immediately lowered Eda back into the stream, and she tugged her shirt down as low as it would go.

'There's something you need to see, Commander,' Tatum said, trying very hard to hide his smile, while the others looked deliberately away.

Roul's eyes returned to Eda.

'Go,' she said. 'I'll be right behind you.'

Roul nodded, then exited the water. She watched him snatch up his boots and walk up the hill, and then she went to dress. She gave herself permission to put the events of the night aside and start the day afresh. There would be plenty of time to process her guilt once she was safely behind Chadora's walls. For now, she had a job to finish.

She went to join the rest of her unit, who were gathered together, looking at something. Her feet slowed when she saw what it was. In the middle of the group stood a donkey loaded mountain high with various supplies. How it was standing beneath the weight of its load she had no idea.

'Where did it come from?' she asked, stepping between Alveye and Hadewaye. The animal turned to her, and she extended a hand for it to sniff. With a bray, the donkey moved closer. She rubbed its face. 'Oh, you're just a big sweetheart.'

Roul inspected the items on its back, pulling an arrow from a quiver. He studied it a moment. 'This matches the arrows fired at us last night. I'd say the animal belonged to them.' He continued to ravage around for a minute. 'Nothing really of use except a few blankets.'

'Are we going to bring him with us?' Hadewaye asked.

'Absolutely not,' Roul replied. He unbuckled the girth and removed the load from the animal's back. Then he slipped the halter over its ears and gave it a gentle shove. 'Off you go.' When it did not move, he hissed and stomped his foot. Instead of running away, the donkey moved behind Eda, using her as a human shield.

Smiling, Eda turned to rub its long ears. 'What a smart'—she bent to check the gender—'boy you are.'

The donkey leaned in to her touch, thoroughly enjoying the attention.

'It's not going to leave if you keep petting it,' Blackmane said.

She ignored him. 'Don't worry, we'll take care of you.'

'No we won't,' Roul said. 'I've removed its load. Now it's time for it to leave.'

Eda met his eyes. 'It's a domesticated animal. He needs humans in order to survive.'

'Well, we don't need *him*, so say goodbye.' Roul waved his arms in another attempt to shoo it away.

Taking hold of the donkey's large head, Eda whispered, 'I'm sorry about him. He's actually very nice once you get to know him.'

Blackmane swore under his breath as he went to mount his horse. Tatum and Alveye followed him, laughing silently at the ground. Hadewaye was about to say something, but Roul held up a hand before he had a chance to speak.

'Not a word, or I'll leave you here with the donkey.'

Hadewaye gave Eda a sympathetic look before turning and going after the others.

Crinkling her nose, Eda said sweetly, 'Could we not bring him with us?'

'For what purpose?'

'As a spare pack horse.'

Roul stared hard at her. 'If we need to escape in a hurry, this thing will only slow us down. Now, go and get on your horse.'

Eda flattened her palm on the donkey's forelock with a sigh. 'I hope you find some humans worthy of you.'

'For the love of Belenus,' Blackmane called. 'Can we go now?'

Roul went to mount his horse, and Eda reluctantly followed him. She glanced a final time at the donkey before turning her gelding around. As she rode away, she heard braying behind her. It almost sounded like crying.

'Eyes forwards,' Roul said, riding alongside her.

She smiled at the sound of the donkey's short steps behind them.

'If you ignore it, it'll go away,' Roul said, eyes ahead.

Eda ignored the donkey the entire morning, even when they stopped to eat and water the horses. Then she ignored it for the entirety of the afternoon. Roul grew more and more frustrated throughout the course of the day. When they were a few miles from Carno, he pulled up his horse with an exasperated growl and turned in the saddle to glare at the animal. The donkey stopped also, watching Roul with a wary expression.

'We could slaughter it and have a proper meal,' Blackmane suggested.

Eda scowled in his direction before looking at Roul. 'Perhaps your family has use for him.'

Roul pinched the bridge of his nose. 'Perhaps.'

Relief filled Eda. 'We should give him a name.'

'We are absolutely not giving that thing a name,' Roul said, looking up.

'Basil.'

Hadewaye nodded appreciatively. 'That actually suits him.'

Roul kicked his horse into a trot. 'Hopefully someone steals him overnight.'

Smiling down at her saddle, Eda followed him.

CHAPTER 21

*T*he steeple of the church rose from a cluster of houses. It was the first thing Roul saw as they neared Carno. Only a handful of chimneys produced smoke. Many in the region had abandoned their dwellings long ago and headed north. He remembered seeing the paddocks dotted with livestock as a child. Now they were barren, muddy swamps.

'Keep to the left,' he said over his shoulder. 'The villagers cut sections of clay out of the roads. You can drown in the puddles here.' He eyed a murky pool of water as he passed by it.

'Maybe we'll get lucky and the donkey will fall in,' Tatum said.

Thankfully, Eda did not hear him.

Turning off the main road, they walked their horses along the muddy track that ran behind the houses. Roul sat straighter in the saddle when he finally laid eyes on the wattle and daub house he called home. It looked the same, except that the roof needed thatching, and it had a chicken pen attached to it. Two hens scratched around inside.

As they drew closer, he spotted his sisters out front

bent over a laundry tub. They straightened when they heard the horses approaching, calling to someone inside. They had gotten taller, their faces no longer pinched and gaunt. Queen Fayre had kept her promise.

His parents came out of the house, squinting in his direction. He knew the moment they recognised him, because his mother clapped a hand over her mouth, and his father's face contorted. His sisters broke into a run towards him. Roul dismounted, catching the youngest, Lana, as she flung herself at him. She was crying and laughing.

'Goodness,' he said, placing her down on the ground and holding her at arm's length to look at her properly. 'You're enormous now.'

She brushed tears off her cheeks. 'So are you. You're all… muscled.'

Odella pushed between them, wrapping her arms around him. He held her for a long moment.

'She's right,' she said when she stepped back. 'It's like hugging stone.'

'Do I get to greet my son now?' Wilona said behind them.

His sisters moved aside, and his beaming mother stepped forwards. She might have had a few more grey hairs and lines on her face, but she was still as beautiful as ever. She opened her arms to him, and Roul stepped into them.

'We've missed you,' she said into his ear.

Roul kissed her cheek before releasing her.

His father stood patiently awaiting his turn, eyes red and mouth turned up. His hair had begun to thin on top, but his face was round and healthy again.

'Look at you,' Clive said. 'What in God's name are they feeding you in that place?' He stepped up to hug his son, clapping him affectionately on the back.

Roul pressed his eyes closed.

'Goodness,' his mother said. 'You have a lady travelling with you.'

Roul looked back at his unit. They had all dismounted now and were watching the reunion from a distance.

'*Lady* is a bit of a stretch,' Eda said, walking over to them.

Roul stepped back from his father to do introductions. 'This is Eda Suttone.'

His mother's eyebrows rose. 'Oh. Is this the same Eda you mentioned in your letters?'

He could feel his men watching him. With a small nod, he continued with introductions and explained that they were on their way to Harlech Castle to retrieve Prince Becket. He did not tell them all the smaller details of the assignment, and they knew better than to probe when it came to royal business.

'You can stay in the Normans' house, right next door,' Lana suggested. 'It sits empty.'

Roul frowned. 'Where did they go?'

'They headed north about a year back.' Lana looked suitably heartbroken. 'We've not heard from them since.'

Wilona forced a smile. 'We tried to help, but with eight children...' She took a moment to compose herself. 'We keep the house tidy for them, in case they return one day.'

'It has two rooms,' Odella said, looking at Eda, 'so you won't have to share with the men.'

Eda smiled appreciatively. 'That's very thoughtful, but I'd honestly sleep anywhere right now. It's been a long day.'

Wilona brought a hand to her throat. 'What was I thinking? You must all be exhausted and frozen solid. Why don't you put your horses in the pigpen, then come inside for some soup? Perfect timing as the pot is full. The girls can go prepare the house for you.'

When his sisters went to leave, Roul said, 'Don't light

162

the hearth. Better not to draw attention to the fact that the house is occupied.'

'Why does your donkey not have a halter?' his father asked, peering around him.

Roul sighed. 'It's not our donkey. The animal followed us here.'

'His name is Basil,' Eda said. 'We thought you might have use for him.'

Clive laughed at the suggestion. 'We have enough trouble keeping chickens. Meat doesn't last long around these parts. An animal like that will make us a target.'

Roul's stomach twisted at the thought of thieves coming to his home when he was not here to protect his family. Queen Fayre could replace what was stolen, but she could not stop them from coming.

'They mean no harm,' his father said, reading his expression. 'If you give them what they want, they go on their way. I suggest you sell the donkey in Dolgellau when you pass through.'

Eda walked by with both their horses and the donkey.

'Let me do that,' Roul said, going after her. 'You go on inside.' Yes, he was breaking his own rules again. Perhaps the sight of her crouched in the stream trying to wash away her guilt was too fresh in his mind. He wanted her to rest.

'I can do it,' Eda said. 'You go spend time with your family.'

Wilona walked over and took Eda's arm, leading her towards the house. 'There will be plenty of time for that. Let's get you washed up and fed.'

'Don't worry, I'll help him,' Clive said, taking one of the horses. 'Many hands make light work. Finger count is irrelevant.' He chuckled at his own joke.

Eda looked back at Roul as she was led away. He winked, reassuring her, then headed for the pigpen.

Wilona ladled watery soup into bowls and handed them to Eda and the defenders. The men were seated at the table, playing dice. Eda was perched on a stool close to the hearth, savouring every hot mouthful as she edged closer to the flames.

'Any closer and your hair will catch alight,' Wilona said, pulling up another stool.

Eda swallowed another mouthful of soup. 'I didn't realise how cold I was until you sat me here.'

'You'll thaw out soon enough.' Wilona watched her eat for a moment. 'Tell me. How did you come to be stuck with this lot?'

'They needed a female who wouldn't die.' Eda placed the now empty bowl beside her and leaned on her knees.

'Roul mentioned in one of his letters that you were good with a bow.' She gestured to the weapon on the floor beside Eda. 'It appears you can handle a sword as well.'

Eda was curious as to what else Roul had said about her in those letters. 'I've been fortunate enough to have your son as a teacher. He's very good at what he does, and the men really respect him.'

'I've no doubt,' Wilona replied, pride in her voice. 'Does he seem happy there?' She waved a hand. 'It's so difficult to get a full picture of his life from his letters.'

Eda thought about what her own mother would want to hear under these circumstances. 'He's built a temporary life you would be proud of, but he misses his family.'

'It sounds as though he's built a temporary family too.' Her smile was sad. 'I'm glad for it. I would hate to think of him alone in that place.' She paused, watching Eda a moment. 'He mentions you so frequently that we've all been bracing for a letter declaring his love and announcing that he won't be returning to us after all.'

164

Eda leaned closer and said quietly, 'The others don't know of his plans to leave. He's been very careful with whom he tells. I only learned of the fact recently myself.'

Wilona searched her eyes. 'He clearly trusts you. My fears might prove true.'

'You don't need to worry about that,' Eda said, her throat closing. 'Commander Thornton is committed to returning to his family.'

Rising, Wilona walked over to the trunk by the wall and retrieved a piece of parchment, then returned to Eda. 'This is the last letter we received from him.' She opened it and held it out.

Eda took it and read the date at the top. It had been written three months earlier.

Wilona pointed to a section of the letter. 'As you can see, it's "Eda this" and "Eda that".'

Eda was so busy admiring the beautiful handwriting that she had not registered the words themselves. Sure enough, there were mentions of her peppered throughout. She read all the way to the signature at the bottom, resisting the urge to run a finger over it. The *R* in his name had a swirling tail that tapered off beneath the rest of the letters. It was obvious that he was the son of a cartographer. She handed it back to Wilona, who tucked it into her apron just as Roul entered the house.

He looked to where they were huddled in front of the hearth, eyes narrowing on Eda's guilty expression. 'Everything all right?'

She forced a smile. 'Your mother was just making sure my hair doesn't catch fire.'

Roul breathed out a laugh. 'You are rather close to the flames.' He sank down onto the trunk and leaned his head against the wall. 'Father insists he must watch the horses while we eat.'

Wilona rose and went to fetch him some soup. 'It's necessary, I'm afraid.'

As she was handing him the bowl, Roul's sisters walked in.

'The house is ready for you,' Lana said. Looking sympathetically at Eda, she added, 'Except there's no fire.'

'I'll be fine,' Eda assured her.

Wilona spoke up at that. 'I could set up a cot right there in front of the hearth.'

Roul shook his head. 'She must sleep where it's *safest*, and the safest place for her outside Chadora's walls is with me.' Seeing his mother's knowing expression, he added, 'Not me specifically, but with the unit.'

Wilona pressed her lips together to stop from smiling. 'I shall give you an extra blanket, dear.'

'Blackmane, you can take first watch,' Roul said, sitting atop the trunk to eat his soup. 'I'll take the second.'

Blackmane nodded, rose from the table, and stepped outside.

Taking advantage of his absence, Eda took his place at the table. 'Can you teach me how to play?' She wanted to give Roul time alone with his family.

'It's not a game for ladies,' Tatum said, throwing one of the dice at her.

She caught it and threw it back at him. 'Good thing there are no ladies at the table, then.'

'I'll teach you,' Alveye said.

Eda listened as he explained the rules, then joined in the game.

As she played, her gaze drifted in Roul's direction. His father had returned inside, and the family were gathered around the hearth, speaking in low voices. She loved how his sisters hung off Roul's every word as he told stories and answered their questions. They reciprocated with stories of their own.

Sometimes, Roul would glance at Eda and their eyes would meet. They could say so much with a single glance. Ask a question. Give an answer. Make a joke. Laugh at it.

Around an hour after the sun disappeared, everyone at the table began to yawn. The fatigue had caught up to them. Hadewaye was first to depart, thanking Roul's parents and bidding everyone goodnight. The others followed soon after, including Eda.

'Will someone wake me when it's my turn for watch?' Eda asked Roul as she prepared to leave.

'We'll be arriving at Harlech Castle tomorrow, so we need you nice and rested,' he replied. 'No one will be waking you tonight.'

Normally she would argue that she was capable of doing her part, but he was right. The others would not be going into the castle with her, so they could afford to be tired. Only Roul would join her. The logic behind that decision was that her presence needed to be as unthreatening as possible, and arriving with a small army might raise a flag or two.

'Thank you for the meal and opening your home to us,' Eda said to Wilona as she prepared to leave.

Roul's mother smiled. 'You are welcome here anytime.'

After spending time with his family, Roul went to relieve Blackmane. The defender bid him goodnight before heading off to get some sleep. Roul tugged the hood of his cloak up for warmth and stood beneath the small veranda of the house, just out of reach of the rain, watching the horses. They were huddled in the pig shelter, the donkey comfortably among them.

As he looked around, he felt homesick, which made no sense at all given he was finally home. The problem was it no longer felt like it, and the notion of returning to live there permanently sat like stone inside him. Of course, he would do it. He would not abandon those dependent on him.

Except that he would be abandoning Eda in the process.

'I want to hold your hand in the dark.'

He suspected she needed him as much as he needed her. She had kissed him like she needed him that morning. And despite knowing it was a bad idea, he had kissed her back. He would have given her anything in that moment, because the sight of her in a vulnerable state was both rare and heartbreaking.

A few hours into his watch, Roul's head began to drop with fatigue. He stepped out in the rain and walked to the house where they were staying. All was dark and still inside—and ice cold. He looked around at the sleeping bodies and, when he located Tatum, gave him a tap with his foot. The defender woke with a start, then reached for his boots.

Roul went to check on Eda in the next room. She was curled in a ball beneath a pile of blankets, shivering. He walked over to the bed his sisters had made for her, which was not much of a bed. There was nothing between the thin mattress and the icy floor. Her breaths came soft and even, indicating she was asleep.

He stood over her for the longest time, waiting for the shivering to stop. As he watched her, he imagined leaving her in a couple of years, imagined what that goodbye would sound like. What it would *feel* like. He knew they would probably never see each other again. Giving up his position was one thing, but walking away from her was something else entirely. She was the best part of his current life with her games and jokes and inappropriate conversations. She was spontaneous swims in the rain. She was racing through the trees and falling onto the grass. Her mind was free in a way his would never be.

How did one walk away from that?

Unable to watch her shiver any longer, Roul removed his cloak, boots, belt, and tunic and climbed in next to her. Instinctively, she moved closer until her legs met his beneath the blankets. Roul wrapped himself around her until every soft edge of her was moulded into the nooks of his body. After a few minutes, the shivering stopped, and a contented breath passed her lips.

Eyes sinking shut, Roul fell into a deep sleep beside her.

CHAPTER 22

$\mathcal{E}$da woke a little before dawn wrapped in warmth. She blinked her eyes open and looked down at the arm secured around her—Roul's arm. Her back was pressed to his chest, her head tucked beneath his chin. How was it possible to have such a contrast in size and yet fit so perfectly together? She did not want to move, because she did not want to wake him. If he woke, he would withdraw the arm, the warmth, the affection. It was inconvenient needing him for basic things like warmth. She was not supposed to need him for anything. She was not supposed to need anyone outside her family. But there she was, breathing Roul in like oxygen and setting herself up for heartbreak.

His palm lay open in front of her, tempting her. Carefully, she brought one arm from beneath the blanket and curled her hand into his. She just wanted to pretend for a moment that he belonged to her, that the arm around her was not that of a caring friend but a besotted lover.

She jumped when his hand enclosed hers suddenly.

Roul laughed quietly, his body vibrating against hers.

When she turned in his arms, she expected him to retreat, but his arm remained around her.

'What are you doing in my bed, Commander?'

'Running at around 50 percent of my usual body heat thanks to you.'

He was half asleep, his dark hair sticking up in all directions. She resisted the urge to run her fingers through it.

Neither of them spoke for a few minutes. They simply watched each other. Eda was aware of the change in her heart rate as she stared at him. All kinds of thoughts popped into her mind. At one point, she even pictured Roul and Hildred waking up together and wondered if they slept naked.

'What's going on in that head of yours?' Roul asked, reaching up to brush hair off her face.

'I'm just thinking about the day ahead,' she lied.

'Your performance of a lifetime?'

A nod.

'Are you nervous?'

She lifted one shoulder in a shrug. 'I'm nervous about the gown.'

The corners of his mouth lifted. 'You're nervous about putting on a dress?'

'Have you seen high fashion nowadays? It's very showy.'

He watched her for a moment. 'You're not allowed to be nervous with me at your side. That's the whole point of me.'

She wanted to reach up and touch his mouth, but she did not. 'I was also thinking about how inconveniently lovely your family is.'

'*Inconveniently* lovely?'

'Inconvenient in that your devotion to them is completely justified.'

He continued to stare down at her, his expression giving nothing away.

Wetting her lips, she said, 'Can I ask you something?'

He nodded.

'Did you ever think about bringing Hildred here?'

'For what purpose?'

'You know what purpose.'

He exhaled. 'Why would you ask me that?'

She bit her lip. 'You know why.'

He drew a breath. 'No. I've never thought about bringing Hildred here. It's not that kind of relationship.'

His answer made her feel guilty. It was unfair to expect him to return to Carno alone when she would likely marry in the time it took him to travel there. 'Did you ever think about bringing me here?' The question spilled out of her.

'I did bring you here.'

'You know what I mean.'

His eyebrows came together in a hard, disapproving line. 'What sort of man takes a woman he cares about from her loving family and brings her to a mostly abandoned village, where thieves come and go as they please and people live in a constant state of fear and starvation?'

He made some valid points. 'So you thought about it, then?'

'Eda.' He chuckled and shook his head. 'If I ever did, I quickly dismissed it.'

She stared straight ahead at his chest now. 'When we get back, I don't want you to visit Hildred anymore. Does that make me a horrible person?'

He shook his head. 'No. That doesn't make you a horrible person. It makes you human. And here I was believing you to be immortal.'

'Well, don't tell Blackmane. You know he views me as some sort of war god.'

Roul laughed quietly, then fell silent. 'Are you warm?'

'Yes.'

'Then I'm going to leave.'

Disappointment filled her. 'Why?'

'Because if I stay, I might kiss you again.'

'You've never kissed me. We've kissed twice, and both times were me. I'm the impulsive one. You have far too much self-control for such things.'

He looked down, studying her face. 'Then I'm going to leave in order to maintain my flawless record.' He swallowed, eyes moving over her face. 'I'll send one of the girls over and see you out front when you're ready.'

'Prepare yourself for visual splendour.'

He bit back a smile as he exited the bed. 'I'll do my best.'

She lay with her hand resting on the warm linen where he had been, watching him put on his boots, tunic, weapons, and finally his cloak. His eyes met hers a final time, and then he was gone.

Only when the linen went cold beneath her hand did she crawl out of her blanket cave. It was time to transform herself into a noblewoman.

Lana arrived shortly after Roul's departure with a basin of warm water, a handheld mirror, and a bowl of soup. 'Want me to stay and help you dress?'

Eda gave her an appreciative smile. 'I can manage, but thank you.'

'I'll leave you to it, then.'

Eda downed the soup in a few seconds, then had a wash. After laying everything out on the bed, she began the long process of dressing. Undergarments, breast band, chemise, stockings, then finally the very expensive, heavy gown. It was made from green silk, with lavish embroidery along the sleeves and neckline. Eda felt as though her breasts were pushed up to her chin, but upon inspecting herself in the mirror, she relaxed. While it was certainly more skin than she normally displayed, it was entirely appropriate for a noblewoman. Queen Fayre knew what she was doing. Not only was it flattering, but the colour matched her eyes, making them appear brighter than normal.

She spent the next half hour brushing knots from her hair, then braided it in the way Queen Fayre had shown her, half up and pinned in a loop at the back of her head. After applying some red paste to her lips, she picked up the grey cloak from the bed.

Done.

She was now Lady Hayley of Peytone House, cousin to Prince Becket. All she had to do now was convince everyone at Harlech Castle of it. If she could just get the prince alone in a room, she would tell him everything and persuade him to return to Chadora with them.

'No one laughs,' Eda warned as she exited the house and walked over to where the defenders stood with their horses.

And nobody did.

It was shock and confusion that registered on their faces. Not surprising given they had only ever seen her in trousers. They looked thoroughly uncomfortable.

Glancing at a gaping Hadewaye, Eda said, 'What? Say it.'

'You look like a lady,' Hadewaye said. 'But a proper one.'

'That's sort of the point' was Eda's reply.

Blackmane turned away, ignoring her completely.

Tatum crossed his arms, assessing her head to toe. 'Well, well, well. Who knew beneath all that sweat and grunt lay this feminine masterpiece?'

Eda stopped to greet Basil, rubbing his forelock. 'Glad you're getting all your jokes out of the way now.' She continued towards Alveye, who was holding her horse. He handed her the reins when she reached him.

'It's just going to take us a while to get used to it,' he said.

'I'd prefer you didn't get used to it,' Eda replied, preparing to mount. 'Because the second we leave Harlech Castle, I'll be changing.'

'Are you going to be able to ride in that thing?' Hadewaye called to her.

She rolled her eyes. 'I've worn dresses before.'

Alveye held the head of her horse. 'Do you need help getting up?'

She was about to tell him no, of course not, then realised the stiff, heavy fabric might prove to be problematic. There was no elegant way to mount a horse wearing such a dress. But before she had a chance to admit it aloud, hands landed on her waist, lifting her. She swung her leg over the saddle, eyes meeting Roul's as she adjusted her skirt atop the horse.

'Thank you.'

He nodded, gaze falling to the neckline of her dress. Her cloak had caught behind one shoulder on the way up. Swallowing, he said, 'You really look the part.'

She was surprised by the heat crawling over her skin. It was amazing what a simple drop of the gaze could do. It felt like a finger tracing her neckline. She reached up and fixed her cloak, prompting Roul to look away.

'We'll see you on the return journey,' Wilona called to Eda.

She looked over to where Roul's family were gathered. 'I'll take care of him.'

'You all take care of each other,' Clive said, wrapping an arm around his wife. 'We'll see you soon.'

When Roul went to say goodbye to his family, Blackmane rode off, apparently not one for farewells. Once Roul returned to his horse, Odella covered her face with her hands, unable to hold back her tears any longer. Eda felt sorry for them. They had only gotten a few precious hours

175

together, and for all they knew, it might be the last time they saw him.

Roul trotted after Blackmane without saying a word, and the others followed.

Only when they were outside the village did Roul address the group. 'It's a two-hour ride to Dolgellau.' He glanced at Basil, who was happily walking alongside Alveye's horse, unaware of his fate. 'We'll lose the donkey, then cross River Wnion via the bridge on the other side of the village.'

Everyone nodded, then returned to their thoughts for the next few hours. Every time Hadewaye began whistling a tune, Blackmane glared him into silence.

They reached Dolgellau mid-morning, and Eda was surprised by the absence of children. Normally they would be playing outside and on the road. Perhaps it was because the roads were nothing but slick mud and pooled water. She did spot a group of women on the side of the road, their faces drawn and pinched, but they fled upon seeing them. A few lone men walked by, their stares hard and their hands resting on their weapons. There were no dogs. No chickens. No babies crying in the run-down houses that lined the road. It all felt so sad.

Roul slowed his horse to ride alongside Eda. 'I think they're afraid of us.'

'You think?'

He glanced sideways at her. 'I hope you have at least one weapon hidden under that cloak.'

Eda nodded a greeting at a middle-aged man passing in the other direction. He did not reciprocate. 'I have four daggers, two in places that will be difficult to reach in a hurry.'

Roul suppressed a smile and looked forwards.

Soon they arrived in the centre of the village, where the

marketplace was supposed to be. They were met with bare tables and a handful of people wandering between them.

'Where is everyone?' Hadewaye asked.

Tatum looked around. 'Perhaps they came early.'

Stopping his horse and dismounting, Roul walked over to an older woman selling a single bolt of beige fabric. She rose as he neared, eyes moving over him with suspicion.

'Can I help you?'

'I have a donkey I'm looking to sell,' Roul answered. 'Do you know where I might find a buyer?'

Her eyes raked over him again before turning to the man at the next table. 'This lot are selling a donkey.'

That must have piqued the man's interest, because he stepped out from behind his table and walked over to them.

'Jankin's the name,' he said to Roul. 'Town's butcher.'

Confused, Eda looked to the table he had come from. A basket of onions sat on it. 'You're a butcher.'

'That's right.'

'But you don't have any meat.'

'Give me a moment, love,' Jankin replied. 'Things are looking up.' He limped over to inspect Basil. 'How much are you wanting?'

Eda opened her mouth to speak, but Blackmane cleared his throat. She glanced in his direction, noting the warning in his eyes.

'He's a working animal,' Roul said.

Jankin poked at Basil's rump. 'In case you've failed to notice, there's not much work around these parts right now. There *is* a famine though.' He turned to Roul. 'I'll give you two crowns.'

Roul looked to Eda, and her eyes pleaded with him. Jankin glanced between the two of them.

'Oh, I see,' he said with a chuckle. 'You want to sell him

as a *working* animal. Well, all right, then.' He pulled out his coin pouch and winked at Roul. 'Working animal it is.'

Eda rolled her eyes. 'We all know you'll slaughter the donkey before we even make it to the bridge.'

Jankin looked in her direction. 'Hope you lot didn't come all this way for the bridge.'

Roul narrowed his eyes. 'What does that mean?'

'The bridge was destroyed a few years back after some heavy rains,' Jankin said. 'Current tore it clean off. Just carried the whole thing away. There was talk of replacing it once everything settled down a bit, but the rain doesn't stop for long, does it?'

Roul and Tatum exchanged a look.

'How do boats get up and down the river if the current's that strong?' Eda asked.

The butcher practically laughed. 'Look around you, love. They don't. The few supplies we get come inland now —and that's not guaranteed.'

His words left them all speechless for a moment.

'So how do you cross the river, then?' Blackmane asked.

Jankin leaned his weight on his good leg and scratched his cheek. 'We don't. Safest not to cross at all. Even with horses as fine as those, the current is strong.'

'We need to get to Gwynedd,' Eda said. 'Where's our best chance of crossing on horseback?'

The butcher sucked his teeth, thinking a moment. 'You might see some improvement farther downstream as you get closer to the sea. Just be mindful that there are boulders as big as mountains hidden beneath the water's surface. And the banks are eroding, so you best take care exiting the water.' He held the two crowns out to Roul.

The commander drew a breath, then shook his head. 'I think we'll take the animal with us. I'm sorry to waste your time.'

Blackmane shook his head, and Hadewaye glanced at Eda, eyes smiling.

'Suit yourself,' Jankin said, waving them off. 'Might get the whole lot free if you drown.' He was smiling when he said it, broken teeth on display.

As they rode away, Eda trotted up beside Roul. 'Thank you.'

He shook his head, visibly annoyed. 'Don't thank me yet.'

CHAPTER 23

*I*t was not long before they heard the sound of running water, a sound that grew to a roar the closer they got. When the river finally came into view, they all shifted nervously in their saddles. The river was around one hundred and fifty yards wide and running at a speed that made it impossible to see what lay beneath the surface. The spray coming from it had the horses backing up.

Tatum emitted a long whistle. 'That onion butcher wasn't exaggerating, was he?'

'He said it would be better downstream,' Eda said.

Roul looked at her. '*Might*. He said it *might* be better.'

She shrugged. 'We try, or we turn around and go home.'

Everyone waited for Roul's response.

He swung his horse west. 'Fine. Let's see how it is farther down.'

'Not how I imagined dying,' Alveye whispered to Hadewaye.

Eda pressed her eyes closed and went to catch up to Roul.

The current did not change, but there were sections of

the river that were narrower than others. Every half mile, Roul would dismount to check the water level with a stick. The butcher had been right about the corroding banks. Twice Roul was forced to leap back as the ground he stood on was swept away.

'There must be another bridge somewhere,' Blackmane said when Roul returned to his horse for the fourth time. 'King Edward's clearly crossing somewhere.'

'He's likely going the long way around,' Roul replied. 'We could go searching for another bridge, but it'll potentially add days to our trip. And if we don't find one, the current will be twice as strong that close to the mountains.'

'Then we cross here,' Eda said, sounding braver than she felt.

'We could tie the horses together,' Alveye suggested. 'So we don't lose anyone.'

Blackmane shook his head. 'Then if one goes, we all drown.'

'What if one of us crosses with a length of rope,' Tatum said, 'and secures it to a tree on the other side? That way if we lose a horse, we'll still have its rider.'

'How much rope do we have?' Roul asked.

'Enough if we join it all together,' Alveye replied.

Eda held her breath as she waited for Roul to decide. He was hanging on to his horse's bridle, watching the water.

'All right,' he said. 'I'll take it across.'

'Shouldn't someone else take it in case it goes wrong?' Tatum asked.

Blackmane let out a heavy breath. 'I'll do it.'

Roul nodded his consent. 'Suttone, you'll cross with me. You have the smallest horse, which means you're at the highest risk of being swept away.'

Eda glanced at Basil. 'What about him?'

Roul walked over to the donkey and removed its halter. 'There's no way he'll make it across.' He gave her an apologetic look before returning to his own horse.

Now free, Basil walked over to stand with Eda, ears twitching back and forth.

'I suggest you stay away from the village,' she said quietly, 'unless you want to end up hanging from a hook.'

Everyone was busy removing boots and cloaks, packing them away in the vain hope of keeping them dry. Eda decided it was best to take off her dress. No one said anything as she stripped down to her chemise and packed the gown into her bag.

When everyone was ready, Alveye handed Blackmane one end of the rope and secured the other end to a nearby tree.

'We'll see you on the other side,' Tatum said as Blackmane nudged his horse towards the river.

Blackmane only nodded.

His mare needed a lot of encouragement, but the defender surprised Eda by being very patient with the animal, and eventually, they entered the water.

'Easy, girl,' Blackmane said as water rushed over the horse's legs and belly, causing her to panic. She lifted her head high as spray hit her face. Blackmane continued slowly forwards, the water rising to his thighs. They were halfway across when the river floor seemed to disappear from beneath his horse. The mare's head dropped beneath the water as they were swept downstream. Blackmane used the rope to slow their descent, enabling the mare to find her footing and get back on her feet. Steam now rose from her rump.

'We'll move the rope down when he exits,' Roul said. 'The depth seems to be more consistent in that part of the river.'

No one replied, because they were all watching Black-mane. There was a collective exhale when he finally reached the other side. It took him several tries to exit the water as the soft edges of the river crumbled underfoot, but eventually the mare scrambled up to safety.

Alveye untied the rope and moved it farther down-stream, and then Blackmane secured it to a tree on the other side.

'You sure about this?' Roul asked Eda.

She met his eyes. 'Can you imagine the look on Black-mane's face if I changed my mind?'

'He'd likely throw her in the river—assuming he made it back,' Tatum said behind them.

Roul glanced over his shoulder at the defender. 'Fair point. In that case, Suttone, you're up next. I'll follow.'

Eda looked back at Basil, who was a sensible distance from the water, watching them.

'Focus,' Roul said as he mounted his horse.

She turned to her own mount and gave him a soothing pat. 'We've got this.' Then she climbed up into the saddle, shivering from the cold and anticipation. She rode over to the rope and took hold of it, then clicked her tongue as she nudged her horse forwards. She thought she was ready, but when the cold water hit her bare feet, it felt like a thousand needles stabbing her at once. She shuddered, legs squeezing as the water climbed her calves. Her hand slid along the rope as her horse took panicked steps, suddenly in a rush to get to the other side.

'Slowly,' Roul said behind her.

Eda was trying—and failing.

She gripped the rope tighter when the gelding turned at an angle, losing the fight against the current. Next thing she knew, the horse was pulled out from beneath her, swept away, leaving Eda dangling from the rope with water pelting her. Roul was beside her a moment later, dragging her over the neck of his horse.

'Hold on,' he said. 'Don't you let go.'

It was not a matter of strength but getting her body to cooperate. She could not feel a thing below the waist. Every time Roul tried to lift her onto the saddle, the current pulled her down again. The horse began to turn sideways, as Eda's had done, but Roul managed to straighten it with his legs. It was too much weight for the animal. Eda knew it. Roul knew it.

She reached for the rope, but Roul immediately tried to pull her back.

'It's too much,' she told him.

Dismounting, he guided Eda to the saddle. Her legs would not cooperate, and she kept slipping off it. Finally, she got one leg over and looked to Roul. He gave her an encouraging nod.

'Go. I'll be right behind you.'

She gathered up the reins in one hand and took hold of the rope with the other, digging her heels into the horse's sides. She moved slowly, eyes darting between the riverbank and Roul, who was right up against the horse's rump. It was fine. He was fine. They were almost there.

No sooner had she had that thought than she heard Blackmane shout, 'Look out!'

She looked back just as an enormous branch went sailing into Roul. Somehow, he managed to keep hold of the rope, but his head was underwater. Eda reached for the branch, trying to pull it off him. To her horror, Roul's hand slipped from the rope.

'Roul!'

He popped up, gasping for air as he clung to the branch she was holding. Eda felt the horse lean as they were pulled by the weight. Then he disappeared beneath the water again. She needed to get him out. She tried to kick the horse forwards, to pull him to safety, but every time the horse took a step forwards, it was followed by a step back.

Blackmane was now knee deep in the water, holding the rope with one hand and reaching for the horse with the other.

'Go!' Eda screamed at the horse in frustration.

Roul surfaced with a gasp, and when their eyes met, a bad feeling filled her. She shook her head. *No.*

Then Roul let go of the branch.

She might have screamed if her lungs were not frozen. She watched in horror as he was dragged down into the water and carried away from her.

'Shit,' Blackmane said, grabbing hold of the bridle and tugging the horse forwards. Finally, her legs left the river, the excruciating pain reducing to a dull ache. Eda's gaze never shifted from the water though, searching for him.

The moment she was safely on land, Blackmane took off at a run downstream. Eda sat atop the horse, teeth chattering so hard she thought they might come loose in her mouth. When she was able, she slid from the saddle, her legs giving out beneath her. She used the stirrup to pull herself upright.

On the other side of the river, the other defenders were searching for Roul amid the rocks and white water. She desperately wanted to look for him but needed to wait for feeling to return to her legs. She leaned against the horse for what felt like half an hour but was probably only ten minutes, staring at the bend in the river, willing Roul to appear. She refused to cry, refused to show weakness after Roul had shown so much courage. He had let go so she could exit the water and be the soldier he had trained her to be.

She punched her thigh, relieved to feel pins and needles. It was better than numbness.

Just as she was taking her first few tentative steps, she

looked up and spotted two men rounding the bend on her side of the river. One of them was Blackmane, and the other was a living and breathing Roul. As if that sight alone was not magical enough, trailing behind him was her horse.

Eda bent and held on to her knees, eyes closing for a moment as relief gripped her. She straightened with the bravest face she could manage, taking slow steps towards him. He watched her the entire walk, right up until the moment he took hold of her face. His hands were ice.

'You hurt?' he asked.

She shook her head, but the strength of his grip prevented the action from being effective.

His fingers eased, but then his hands fell away. He turned to the men on the other side of the river, who were now walking back in the other direction. 'There's a sand-bank fifty yards downstream! Move the rope! Blackmane will show you where to cross!' He took Eda's hand and began walking. 'Come. We need to build a fire and get you warm.' When she did not move, he turned back to her. 'What's wrong?'

'Why did you let go of the branch?' Her voice was a croak.

He gave her a tired look. 'You know exactly why. And don't stand there and tell me I shouldn't have, because you would've done exactly the same thing in my situation.' When she *still* did not move, he added, 'Every swim out to Flat Rock has prepared me for that moment. I knew what I was doing.'

She blinked and swallowed. 'Well, don't ever do that again.' A shaky breath left her. 'You don't just let go like that—ever. We're supposed to take care of each other. You said you would be at my side. I'm not... I'm not going home without you.'

He searched her eyes, his expression softening. 'You

won't have to. I'm right here. I'll be at your side through all of it. All right?'

Her shoulders relaxed, and she was finally able to draw breath. 'We go home together.'

'We go home together.'

CHAPTER 24

*A*ll Roul could think about when he was underwater was Eda. Not only would she have to make it back to Chadora without him, but she would have to do it whilst grieving. She would insist on going to his home and telling his family in person, and then she would carry the weight of their grief also.

He had never been more grateful to hit a rock in his life. It had given him a moment to get his bearings, to surface. To *breathe*. From there, he had swum with all he had left to the river's edge, before being dragged from the water by Blackmane.

'Refreshing swim?' the defender had asked as he pulled him up onto the bank.

It had taken Roul a moment to speak. 'Is she all right?' Those were the first words from his mouth.

She had been blue-lipped and struggling to stand when he had finally laid eyes on her. He could see the relief on her face. He had let go of that branch without a second thought. Anything to ensure she got out safely.

Now she was seated in front of the fire with a blanket around her, rosy-cheeked with her hair out and falling down one shoulder. A contrast to when she had stepped out of the house that morning, but equally as beautiful. She did not need painted lips and expensive clothes to make him pause. Slightly dishevelled at all times was part of her charm.

Rain fell lightly, but they were protected by a canopy of trees. Every now and then the desperate bray of a donkey drew their gazes to the river. And each time, Eda pressed her eyes shut.

'Does everyone know what they're doing when we reach the castle?' Roul asked, trying to distract her.

Blackmane reached for his boots. 'We hide, and we wait.'

'Within hearing range in case something goes wrong,' Alveye said. 'You whistle, we come.'

Tatum's lips turned up. 'Like well-trained dogs. Ready to scale the walls at a moment's notice.'

'Hopefully it won't come to that,' Roul said. 'We should get moving while we still have plenty of light.'

She met his eyes. 'I'll dress.'

'I need you back as Lady Hayley in case we encounter anyone on the way.'

She nodded as she rose.

'If your gown's wet, blame Hadewaye,' Tatum said.

Hadewaye threw a stick at him. '*You* brought it across the river.'

'Because you were so afraid I thought you were going to piss yourself.'

Eda ruffled Hadewaye's hair as she passed him. 'Don't take the bait.'

The men put out the fire and readied the horses while Eda got dressed for the second time that day. She put on the gown, re-braided her hair, and painted her lips, but there was no hiding the fatigue brought about by the morning's events.

'Better?' she asked Roul, turning in a circle.

His eyes moved over her. 'Better. Try to keep your hands out of sight as much as possible. They'll be immediately suspicious of worked hands.' He helped her mount before climbing atop his own horse, then signalled to the men. 'Let's move out.'

It was close to four hours later when Harlech Castle finally appeared through the trees, perched atop a rocky crag at the edge of the sea. The group stopped to take in the sight. Its walls were as grey and bleak as the sky framing it.

'They say it's the smallest of the three castles in the region,' Hadewaye said, 'but it looks fairly big from here.'

'Not as heavily guarded as I was expecting,' Alveye said.

Blackmane glanced in his direction. 'That's because the king and queen aren't here.'

'But the king's mother is,' Tatum replied. 'You would think Queen Isabella has made enough enemies to justify the additional guards.'

Roul drew a breath. 'Doesn't matter, because we're walking straight through the main gate as welcomed guests.'

'Let's hope you leave in the same manner,' Tatum said. 'Our arrows can reach the wall from the edge of the moat if it all turns to shit.'

Roul looked to Eda. 'You ready for this?'

She was studying the castle, mind ticking. With a nod, she said, 'Let's go get us a future king.'

Roul looked around at his men. 'Stay safe until we return.' Then he followed her.

Access to the main entrance was via a bridge. The pair exchanged a glance when they reached it, knowing it was their last chance to turn around, then proceeded forwards. They walked their horses slowly along it, eyes sweeping the length of the curtain wall ahead of them.

'Do you think the guards have spotted us yet?' Eda said quietly.

Roul looked to the moat below. 'If they haven't, they're not doing their job properly.'

They fell silent then, eyes on the portcullis. Two guards stood on the other side of it, watching them approach. Each held a spear that could comfortably slip through the latticed wood, prompting Eda and Roul to stop their horses well back from the gate. The men looked Roul up and down before turning their attention to Eda.

'What's your business here?' asked the shorter of the men.

Eda flashed them a smile. 'I received word that my cousin, Prince Becket, is visiting. I wish to see him.'

The guard looked her over a second time. 'Name?'

'Lady Hayley Peytone.'

'Where have you travelled from?' asked the other man.

'Peytone House in Llanystumdwy,' Eda said without missing a beat.

The man nodded once, then turned and walked away. The other stood watching them, and Roul watched him right back while Eda tried not to look up at the wall walk above them.

Around twenty minutes later, Prince Becket strode into sight, looking much more of a man than the last time Roul had laid eyes on him. His hair was longer and features more defined. Gone were the round cheeks and disinterested stares. Now he wore the same stern expression his father always had.

Becket came to a stop in front of the gate, assessing them both.

'Good afternoon, Your Highness,' Eda said, speaking first. 'My goodness. I barely recognised you.'

The prince stared hard at her, as though trying to connect the woman before him with the eleven-year-old child he had once played with. 'Time has a habit of passing quickly.'

Roul forced his hands to relax.

'I do hope it is all right that I called upon you,' Eda said. 'I did not want to miss an opportunity to visit with my Chadorian family, for such opportunities are so infrequent nowadays.'

Roul was impressed. She had clearly been paying attention to the noblewomen in her life. She sounded just like her cousin, Lady Kendra.

There was an uncomfortable silence before Prince Becket finally said, 'I am always happy to see family. Please, come in.' He gestured to the guards. 'Open the gate.'

Eda had succeeded in the first part of the assignment.

Roul resisted the urge to look at her as the portcullis rose before them. When it came to a stop, they rode into the gatehouse. He saw there was a second portcullis at the other end. They passed by many arrow loops to get to it. Murder holes. When it did not go up, Roul's temperature rose and his hands twitched. Eda was completely vulnerable, and there was not a thing he could do about it without making a scene. His eyes kept going to the black holes in the walls on either side of them, expecting to glimpse an arrow tip, but nothing moved. Then the portcullis finally went up, and he could breathe again.

They emerged into the inner ward, where maids, servants, and other members of the household wandered about. There was a vegetable and herb garden, a chicken coop, and a small chapel. To the right of the chapel was a bakehouse.

Dismounting, Roul went to help Eda, feeling the prince's gaze on him the whole time. A groom appeared to tend their horses, and Eda tensed as they were led away.

'I heard you had a visitor' came a new male voice.

Roul turned to see a nobleman strolling towards

them. He looked to be in his forties, his hair neatly combed and reaching just below the ear. His beard was meticulously trimmed, and gold rings decorated both hands. A young boy followed at his heel, no older than twelve. The clothing he wore suggested he was a squire or servant.

Roul guessed who it was ahead of formal introductions.

'May I present my cousin, Lady Hayley,' the prince said, gesturing to Eda. 'This is Lord Roger Mortimer, 1st Earl of March.'

Eda lowered into a curtsy. 'A pleasure, my lord.' She gestured to Roul. 'And may I present Sir Bradley Hale. Sir Bradley is a close family friend who reluctantly agreed to escort me at my father's insistence.' She laughed lightly, releasing some of the tension she was holding.

Roul bowed his head. 'Your Highness. My lord.'

Roger scrutinised him for the longest time, then clicked his fingers at the boy behind him. 'You will need to surrender your weapon, Sir Bradley, at *my* insistence.'

The boy stepped forwards, hand extended to Roul. The commander reluctantly removed his sword and handed it over.

'What brings you to Harlech Castle, Lady Hayley?' Roger asked, gaze sweeping the length of her.

'I was quite desperate to visit with my cousin before he disappears again. He has proven to be quite the traveller.'

Roger smiled politely, but it did not quite reach his eyes. 'We hope to keep the prince as our guest for as long as possible. He makes for excellent company.' He fell silent a moment. 'How long has it been since you last saw your cousin?'

'Eight years,' Eda replied.

Prince Becket shifted his weight. 'Two, actually. You forget that I spent an evening at Peytone House when I travelled to Toryn after my father's death.'

Holy shit. There was a piece of information Queen Fayre had clearly missed.

The beat of silence that followed that statement rang out like a bell. The prince already knew Eda was not his cousin, but he had let her in anyway. Roul could not decide if that was a good or bad thing.

Eda recovered her smile. 'My goodness. You are quite right. The visit was so brief, and under such tragic circumstances, I barely registered it.'

Becket stared hard at her. 'It was a difficult time indeed.'

'Will you be staying the night at Harlech Castle?' Lord Roger asked Eda.

It was the second time Eda's response was delayed. 'I would hate to impose.'

'Stay,' Becket said, his expression giving nothing away. 'It will give us a chance to catch up on family news.'

Roul fought hard to keep still and quiet. He had to assume from that response that the prince was curious enough to hear her explanation for all this.

'I would like that very much,' Eda said, finding her smile once more.

Roger looked between them, then glanced behind him. 'In that case, I shall have the servants make up two rooms.'

'Thank you,' Roul said.

Eda curtsied. 'We appreciate you being so welcoming, my lord.'

The three of them watched Roger stride away, the boy scurrying after him. Then Prince Becket looked at Roul and said quietly, 'Uniform or not, I know a defender when I see one.'

Roul really wished he still had his sword.

'Listen—' Eda began.

'Perhaps we should speak in my private quarters,' Becket said, cutting her off. 'There are many keen ears within these walls, and they are always listening.' Without waiting for their response, he walked away, leaving the pair no choice but to follow.

They entered the castle, climbing steps to a corridor. They followed it all the way to a door at the far end. The man guarding it wore a defender uniform. He straightened when he caught sight of them.

'At ease, Woottone,' the prince said as they approached. Then he turned to Roul. 'You will wait out here.'

Roul went to object, but Eda shook her head. This was always the plan. *She* was the plan. He had no choice but to let her go in and do what she was sent to do.

'This is family time, Sir Bradley,' Prince Becket said, driving home his point, 'and you are in fine company out here.'

Roul's jaw tightened as the door closed in his face.

CHAPTER 25

*E*da followed Prince Becket into the room without hesitation. There was no cause for alarm. He was clearly willing to hear her out. That was why he told the guards to open the gate. He might have been driven by curiosity. Or perhaps he was lonely and missing home.

Hopefully the latter.

Eda came to a stop in the middle of the room and looked around. It contained a lounge, a wool rug, and a table and chairs. There was a small window up high for light and a door that probably opened to his bedchamber. The prince did not sit, nor did he offer her a seat. He simply turned, waiting for her to speak.

Eda cleared her throat. 'I suppose I owe you an explanation.'

'Let us make an agreement, shall we?'

Eda clasped her hands in front of her. 'I'm listening.'

'You shall speak the truth from this point. In return, I will hear you out before throwing you out.'

She appreciated his directness. 'That sounds fair.'

He crossed his arms, staring at her. 'Did my mother send you?'

'Yes.'

His face relaxed a little once he realised she was going to adhere to the verbal agreement. 'And what is your real name?'

'Eda Suttone.'

'No title?'

She shook her head. 'Merchant borough, born and raised.'

'And the man with you?'

'Commander Roul Thornton.'

He regarded her for the longest time. 'Why you two?'

'Commander Thornton was born in Carmarthenshire. He's familiar with the landscape and its people. He was a logical choice.'

Becket blinked. 'And you?'

'I offered. In fact, I insisted.'

He appeared immediately suspicious. 'And why would you do that?'

'Because we need you to return and take the crown. Your absence leaves us vulnerable. While things have greatly improved since Queen Fayre took control, she can't keep filling in for you forever.'

'Do not be so sure. There is nothing that woman cannot do. The lengths she will go to in order to get what she wants is evident in you being here.' He blinked slowly. 'Though I have no idea what she was thinking sending a merchant woman across Carmarthenshire with one defender for protection. You are quite lucky you made it here alive.'

'It wasn't luck, Your Highness, I assure you. Queen Fayre made sure I was up to the task before agreeing. I still have the bruises to prove it.'

With a resigned breath, he gestured for her to sit on the lounge, pulling up the chair for himself.

'There are more of us,' she said as she took a seat. 'Defenders waiting in the forest to escort you home.'

'I am quite capable of making my own way to Chadora if that is my desire.'

Eda leaned forwards, resting her elbows on her knees. 'Do you even realise who you're in bed with?'

'I beg your pardon?'

'I'm sure Lord Roger and Queen Isabella make for pleasant company, but they can't be trusted. And until King Edward is ready to step up and rule, he can't be trusted either.'

Becket stared back at her, emotionless. 'What exactly is your objective here? Was your plan really to show up and repeat the things my mother has already said numerous times in her endless flood of letters?'

'She speaks as queen regent and as your mother. I speak as a merchant who has suffered through your father and brother's mediocre attempts at ruling. I'm here asking you to come home and do a better job than they did.'

He blinked, taken aback.

'You asked for honesty. So here it is.'

He brought one foot up to rest on his knee. 'And what makes you think I can do a better job than them?'

'You've likely figured out by now that the tolerance for poor leadership is at an all-time low. You have no choice but to do better.'

He nodded slowly. 'Perhaps that is one of the reasons I am considering handing the reins to England.'

'If you do that, you'll jeopardise the little progress we've made.'

'My mother would be made regent. Everyone would be happy.'

Eda angled her head. 'I refuse to believe you're that naive.'

'Remember who you are speaking to.'

She drew a calming breath. 'How long do you think it'll be until the livestock disappears? What powers will your mother have as regent then?' She searched his eyes, desperate to see that he understood. 'A few years back, they tried to take everything from us. They would've happily let us starve.'

He was not looking at her anymore but at the ground between them. She wished she could crawl inside his mind and better understand his logic.

'They will likely take it from an inexperienced king anyway,' he said flatly.

'So you're just going to hand it to them instead? Save them the trouble?'

He lifted his gaze. 'Is war a better option?'

'It's certainly a faster death than starvation, but I don't expect you to understand that.'

His jaw tensed. 'I know nothing about fighting wars.'

'Your mother knows plenty. She'll help you every step of the way.' He all but flinched at her words, then averted his eyes. Eda sat back on the lounge as a realisation dawned on her. 'Something happened between you and your mother. This isn't so much about your ability to rule as it is your willingness to do it with *her*.'

Becket rose from his chair. 'I will not discuss my personal relationships with someone I have known five minutes—especially when that someone has already deceived me once in that short time.'

Eda stood also, undeterred. 'Your mother has her faults. Trust me, I know—'

'You know nothing.'

The venom in his voice took Eda by surprise.

Becket began pacing. 'If you truly knew her, you would not have risked your life to do her bidding.'

Eda observed him a moment. 'I won't stand here and

pretend to know what it's like to have her as a mother, but I can speak for her as a queen.'

'Oh yes. She is *spectacular* in that role.'

'Are you really going to let your feelings towards your mother keep you from your job?'

He stopped walking. 'You forget yourself.'

'Then I'm in fine company.'

'I could lock you up for speaking to me in such a manner.'

'Will that make what I said less true?'

They both fell silent, eyes remaining on the other.

'I was never supposed to rule,' Becket said, bringing calm back to the room.

'Well, too bad, because the crown has fallen to you.'

His face tightened. 'You are a merchant and therefore unable to comprehend the weight of such a responsibility.'

'You know, underestimating people like me seems to be a family trait, one that hasn't worked out well for royalty in the past.'

A scowl settled on Becket's face. 'Your sister is Lyndal Suttone, correct? She was betrothed to my brother.' He shook his head when she did not respond straight away. 'Another one of Mother's well-intentioned plans that led to him being beaten to death by his own people. And yes, I still know what goes on inside my kingdom in my absence.'

The fact that he referred to it as *his* kingdom gave her hope. 'Your brother wasn't fit to rule, and I think you knew that. It's why you left.'

'It is *not* why I left.' He leaned his weight on one foot. 'Though it was a nice perk.' He studied her a moment. 'How do you know I will do a better job than him?'

'Honestly, a seal could do a better job. I assure you, you'll be perfectly adequate.'

'You flatter me.' He turned in a circle, head shaking. 'I shall play along with this charade for the sake of peace.

Then in the morning, you will leave here. Our hosts will be none the wiser.'

Her stomach fell as hope abandoned her. 'And what am I to say to every merchant, farmer, and nobleman waiting for you?'

She saw it on his face then: the weight of these past few years, the exhaustion—and guilt. But before she could question him about it, there was a knock at the door.

Becket wet his lips and pressed his eyes closed. 'Enter.'

His guard stepped inside. 'Queen Isabella, Your Highness.'

The queen mother swanned in, eyes locking with Eda's.

Eda had only ever seen a picture of her depicted as a twelve-year-old bride. She had been thirteen when her mother told her the story of how Isabella came to be queen of England. She could barely comprehend leaving one's family, let alone moving to a new country and marrying a stranger.

The room felt smaller with her in it. Perhaps it was the dramatic flair of her sleeves taking up all that extra space, or the bold colour of her dress demanding their attention. Or maybe it was the headdress that added a foot to her height.

'Do forgive the interruption,' Isabella said. 'I heard your cousin was visiting and was quite impatient to meet her.'

Becket gestured to Eda. 'May I present Lady Hayley of Peytone House.'

Eda curtsied. 'Your Majesty.'

Isabella bowed her head, assessing her all the while. 'You must be quite exhausted after such a tedious journey.'

Eda smiled. 'Llanystumdwy is only a day's ride from here, and Sir Bradley kept me entertained. He is fine company when he is not ignoring me entirely.'

The queen mother's eyes creased at the corners. 'I

understand we have the pleasure of your company overnight.'

'Only if it is not too much trouble.'

Isabella looked to Becket. 'We want the prince to feel at home here, so we welcome his family with equal enthusiasm.'

Eda wondered if he saw through the act.

'The servants have made up your rooms. I shall escort you so that you might rest before dinner. I imagine you have had quite enough male company for one day.' She smiled at the prince as she turned and exited the room, clearly expecting Eda to follow her.

Eda looked at Becket. 'I suppose I shall see you at dinner, then.'

She could feel the tension coming from Roul as she stepped outside. His eyes moved over her vigorously, as though searching for stab wounds. She held his gaze until he relaxed a little, then hurried after the queen. Roul followed so closely, she half expected the toe of his boot to clip her heel.

'I have not visited Peytone House before,' the queen mother said, striking up a conversation. 'Is it along the coastline?'

'The manor is a little over half a mile from the water.' Eda was no fool. She had done her research thoroughly. 'And a few miles west of Castell Criccieth.'

Isabella nodded. 'I visited Castell Criccieth some time ago. Back when there used to be sheep grazing in the nearby paddocks.'

'We gave up trying to keep sheep on account of sea warriors. It is better not to tempt them to our shores.'

Isabella glanced sideways at her. 'And where is your brother residing these days?'

Brother? There had been no mention of a brother, only a younger sister. Eda felt her palms heat as the queen mother waited for a response. It felt like a test, so she decided to stand by what she knew. 'I am afraid you must be confused. I have no living brothers.'

'Forgive me,' Isabella replied. 'I must be confused.' She stopped out front of a door near the end of the corridor, turned, and gestured gracefully. 'I do hope you will be comfortable.' And to Roul, she said, 'Your bedchamber is right next door, Sir Bradley.'

Roul nodded. 'Thank you, Your Majesty.'

'Do you require a lady's maid for the evening?' Isabella asked Eda.

'I shall manage fine without one, but thank you.'

Isabella looked between them. 'Rest up, and I shall see you both later.'

Roul bowed, and Eda curtsied. Only once the queen mother had rounded the corner of the corridor did Roul follow Eda into the room. He searched every inch of the small bedchamber, including Eda's canvas bag that one of the servants had brought up. Satisfied, he turned his attention to her.

'All right. Tell me everything.'

She sat on the edge of the bed, repeating every detail of the earlier conversation that she could remember. Afterwards, they sat in silence, processing the information.

'Something happened between him and his mother,' Eda said, rubbing her forehead. 'Some betrayal he can't move past.'

Roul did not respond.

'I can see he cares,' she continued. 'There's a desire to do the right thing buried beneath misplaced pride.'

Roul looked to the door. 'We still have tonight to convince him that whatever it is, it can be fixed.'

'No pressure.' Eda looked around the bedchamber, suddenly aware of just how alone they were. It was improper for a lady of her standing to be alone with a knight in a bedchamber.

'I don't want to leave you alone, but I should probably go next door,' Roul said, clearly having the same thought. 'We wouldn't want to start a scandal at court.'

She really did not want him to go. She wanted to lie down on the bed with him and feel the weight of his arm on her again.

A knock at the door chased the thought away. Roul took a large step back when she called, 'Come in.'

A maid entered with a basin of water and a towel, glancing curiously at Roul before going to set it on the table.

'I'll come collect you before dinner,' Roul said, backing away to the door.

Eda swallowed and bowed her head. 'Thank you, Sir Bradley.'

*H*e was supposed to remain in his bedchamber, but every time footsteps sounded in the corridor, he found himself listening at the door to ensure they continued past Eda's room. Eventually, he gave up on the facade and waited out in the corridor instead.

A servant arrived an hour into his watch to tell them it was time to go down to dinner. Roul knocked on Eda's door, and when she opened it, he felt the same thickening in his throat he had felt that morning when she stepped out of the house. His gaze travelled from her painted lips to the low neckline of the new dress, then down the tightly fitted bodice.

'You look as beautiful as ever, Lady Hayley,' he said, aware the servant watching them.

Her expression softened at the compliment. If they had been safely at home inside Chadora's walls, she would have responded. But they were not free among the trees that day.

Turning, Roul offered Eda his arm. She straightened as she took it.

'Always the chivalric knight, Sir Bradley.'

Roul said nothing as they followed the servant.

When they arrived at the great hall, the first thing he noticed was that there were no other guests at dinner. The second was that Prince Becket was seated between Queen Isabella and Lord Roger like a guarded child. They were going to have to get creative if they wanted to get the prince alone.

The servant showed them to their seats. Eda was placed on the other side of Queen Isabella, Roul next to Lord Roger. Not only were they to be kept separate from the prince but also from each other.

The moment they took their seats, out came the food. Trays of eggs, poultry, and root vegetables. Despite the abundance of colourful options before him, Roul had no appetite. His eyes kept going to Eda, who was being kept busy by the queen mother. Roul had to settle for time with the prince with Roger as mediator. He noticed the prince did not shy away from tough topics.

'What is King Edward's plan with regards to the situation in Carmarthenshire?' Becket asked the lord upon finishing his meal.

Roger laid his knife and fork on his plate. 'He has the resources to go in. The desire to do so is another matter.'

Becket nodded slowly. 'Go in and do what exactly? Reform can be very complicated.'

'I would argue that the region is beyond reform' was Roger's reply. 'It would be more of a clean-up.'

He spoke as though it were a spilled drink instead of an entire kingdom of displaced and suffering people.

Roul could not help but ask, 'What would such a clean-up entail?'

'A healthy cull of rebel groups for one.'

Roul's eyes met the prince's, and he saw his own

thoughts mirrored back at him. 'Are there not women and children in these groups?'

Roger nodded. 'I am not suggesting genocide here. We would find a use for the women and children.'

Becket frowned. 'Would they not be uncooperative after seeing their husbands, fathers, and brothers slaughtered in front of them?'

'They would have no choice but to cooperate.'

Roul pushed his own plate away. 'Sounds like you mean to enslave them.'

The lord fixed his eyes on Roul. 'I imagine, Sir Bradley, that you will be the first person to take up arms given your encounters with such groups. They have ventured north recently, have they not?'

Roul stared back at him. 'Indeed they have.'

Queen Isabella placed her napkin on the table and announced, 'I thought Lady Hayley and I might visit the chapel.'

'Splendid idea,' Eda agreed, glancing at Roul.

There was no way Roul was going to let her leave this room without him. He rose from his chair. 'I shall escort you there.'

Roger eyed him. 'My. You are indeed committed to the family, Sir Bradley.'

'And I shall go for some air,' Prince Becket said, rising from his chair.

'Shall I accompany you, Your Highness?' Roger asked.

Becket gave him a polite smile. 'No need.' He bowed to Queen Isabella. 'Excuse me.' He left the room with Woottone at his heel.

Roger stood anyway. 'I think I shall get some air myself.'

Roul gave Eda a knowing look.

'It is important to give thanks to God for the things we have,' Queen Isabella said, standing. 'Such as new friends at court.'

Eda smiled as she got to her feet. 'Indeed.'

The air was cold outside, but the chapel was only a short distance away.

'You can wait out here, Sir Bradley,' Eda said in the doorway of the chapel. 'My prayers are for God's ears only.'

He reminded himself that Eda was quite safe inside a chapel. He nodded and watched her enter.

While he waited for her to return, he paced, looking up at the thick cloud above. He could smell the pending rain.

A murmur of voices made him still and listen. They were coming from the gap between the chapel and the bakehouse. Roul rounded the corner and came face to face with a glaring Woottone.

'Easy, defender,' Roul said. 'We're on the same side.'

Woottone's scowl deepened. 'The prince wishes to be alone.'

Roul looked past him to where the prince was leaning against the bakehouse wall in the shadows, Lord Roger nowhere in sight. He clapped Woottone on the shoulder as he stepped past him, feeling the heat of the guard's glower upon him.

Becket glanced in his direction. 'There is a reason I am hiding, Commander.'

Roul leaned casually on the wall opposite him. 'Sorry, but getting you alone seems to be an impossible feat.'

Becket rubbed his forehead. 'Is there something Ms Suttone forgot to say during her verbal attack earlier?'

'She can be a little direct.'

'I can see why my mother likes her. Two peas in a pod.' Becket regarded him a moment. 'Ms Suttone told me you are from Carmarthenshire. I did not know whether to believe her, but then I saw your face when Lord Roger mentioned "cleaning out" the kingdom and saw it was true.' He leaned his head back and was silent a moment.

'Tell me, how does a man from Carmarthenshire come to be a commander in Chadora's army?'

He was curious, which meant he was willing to listen. Roul took full advantage. 'I have your mother to thank for that.'

Becket shook his head. 'Of course you do.'

'We met in Toryn nearly four years ago. She saved my life, actually.'

The prince's hands fell away. 'This feels like a long story. You better tell me the quick version, because Lord Roger is currently walking laps of the castle searching for me.'

Roul smiled at the ground, then looked over at Woottone. 'Can you tell me if she leaves that chapel?'

Glaring, Woottone looked to Becket. The prince nodded. Only then did the bodyguard wander off to watch the door.

Once they were alone, Roul told his story—or rather the parts he could. When he was done, Becket stared at him for the longest time.

'So in your mind she is a hero,' he said after a long silence.

'I see her more as a contradiction. She can be one person's hero while being another's worse nightmare.'

Becket swallowed. 'You see it. A monster capable of good deeds.'

'I think that describes most people.'

The prince's eyes sank shut. 'I think you might be right.'

The response had Roul wondering if he knew more than he was supposed to. It would certainly explain the disdain. 'Tell me what she did.' His words were barely above a whisper.

Becket opened his eyes, and they were filled with pain. 'I cannot speak of it. I will not be responsible for her downfall.'

Roul's palms were sweating now. The prince knew things. That much was clear. Taking a huge risk, he said, 'There have been rumours.'

Becket stiffened. 'What rumours?'

'Rumours surrounding your father's death.'

And there it was. All the confirmation Roul needed in one averted glance. A few moments passed before Becket said, 'What if I told you they were not rumours?'

Roul took a moment to prepare himself for what was coming. 'Go on.'

Becket dropped his chin to his chest. After a long silence, he said, 'She orchestrated my father's death.'

Roul nodded slowly. He did not have it in him to act surprised. 'Have you confronted her?'

'No, because my brother needed her.' He swallowed. 'When he was alive.'

Roul stared at the ground between them, unsure what to say.

'And what did she do?' Becket continued. 'She sat back and watched him self-destruct.'

'She did not sit back. She fought hard on his behalf. His failure as a king, and his death, fall squarely upon him. I witnessed everything. Queen Fayre grieved the loss as any mother would.'

Becket shifted his feet. 'And now she expects me to step willingly into the role and spend the rest of my life looking over my shoulder.'

'You won't need to. She'll protect you.'

'Like she protected the rest of my family?'

The small amount of food Roul had eaten swirled in his stomach. 'Listen. Your father was headed down a dead-end path, and she was the only person brave enough to stop him. She didn't do it for power, or wealth, or any personal advantage but rather for the thousands of people suffering under his rule. Her actions are difficult to swallow, but they were well intentioned.'

Becket turned his pain-filled eyes away. 'It is impossible to trust her.'

It took Roul a moment to respond. 'Perhaps you can't trust her. I don't know. What I do know is she's held *your* kingdom together for the past two years. You owe it to everybody to at least have the conversation before you make a decision that affects so many lives.'

Woottone clicked his fingers to get their attention, then signalled that someone was coming. They were out of time.

'Leave with us in the morning,' Roul whispered. 'Tell them you want to escort your cousin home and have some time at Peytone House. Tell them whatever you want, just don't dismiss an entire kingdom of people in order to avoid a difficult conversation with your mother.'

Lord Roger stepped into sight, peering around Woottone. 'There you are, Your Highness. I was beginning to think you had retired early.'

Becket composed himself before walking over. 'What an excellent idea. I am rather tired.'

'But there is wine to finish.'

'I am afraid you will have to finish it without me.' Becket bowed his head. 'Goodnight, Lord Roger.' With that, he wandered away.

Woottone glanced once at Roul before following him.

Roul braced for questioning, but before Lord Roger had the chance, Eda and Queen Isabella exited the chapel. Roul felt himself relax.

'Where is Prince Becket?' Isabella asked as they walked over.

Roger appeared agitated. 'The prince has retired for the evening.'

Upon hearing that, Eda said, 'And I am afraid I must do

the same. It seems the day's riding has caught up with me.' She curtsied before the queen. 'Thank you for a pleasant evening and for being so welcoming.'

'Your company has been most refreshing.'

Roul offered Eda his arm. 'I will escort you to your room, then I shall retire also.' His eyes met Roger's a final time. 'My lord. Your Majesty.'

There was an exchange of courteous gestures, and then Roul led Eda away. He had never felt more uncomfortable turning his back on a man in his life, and he knew the feeling of distrust was mutual. The sooner they left Harlech Castle the better.

The smile fell from Eda's face the moment they were out of sight, but she kept hold of his arm. Neither of them spoke until they were safely inside Eda's bedchamber. The room was warm, and the embers from the fire provided soft light.

'What a fascinating woman,' Eda said as she removed her cloak. 'Clearly responsible for her husband's death, but to be honest, I'm surprised she held off as long as she did given some of the stories she shared.' She laid the cloak over the chair beneath the window and looked in his direction. 'I didn't get near the prince all night.'

The irony of what she had just said about Queen Isabella was not lost on Roul. 'I spoke to him, the prince. When you were in the chapel.'

Eda moved closer. 'And?'

'Well, funny you should bring up queens killing their husbands…'

She gave him a confused look.

He wished he could tell her everything, knew his soul would be lighter for it. But the secrets he kept protected those closest to him. 'He said Queen Fayre orchestrated his father's death. Apparently he has proof.'

Eda blinked. 'Oh.' Then she fell silent for a full minute.

'I suppose that makes sense. She's always been a better queen than wife. It explains the gaping rift between them.' She chewed her lip. 'Clearly she's unaware that he knows or she would never have sent us on this fool's mission.'

'It's not a fool's mission. He cares about the Chadorian people, and he made it very clear that he doesn't want to be responsible for his mother's downfall. The fact that he's still protective of her gives me hope of reconciliation.'

'If we can get them in the same room.' Eda thought a moment. 'We should go to his bedchamber and—'

'Or give him some time to think.'

'Then break down his door at first light and remind him that history is littered with stories of good queens killing bad kings.' She paused. 'From the loins of a legend, he came to sit upon the throne.'

Roul's lips twitched. 'I suggest you leave the door intact and think carefully about how you word your closing argument.'

'I still don't understand what he's even doing here. It's clear he's not a fan of Lord Roger based on the conversations I overheard at dinner.'

Roul shrugged. 'I suppose he's exploring every option available to him.'

Exhaling, Eda looked at him properly. A concerned expression settled on her face. 'Are you all right? You look a bit pale.'

It was the effort of keeping secrets from her. 'I think I'll remain outside your room tonight. Keep watch.'

'Surely you've watched me enough for one evening. I felt your eyes on me all through dinner.'

'I told you, I'm not taking chances.'

She sauntered closer. 'At first I thought you were concerned for my welfare, but now I'm beginning to suspect it was the dress.'

'Can't it be both?'

A smile spread across her face. 'You know, I've never really been one for fancy gowns, but I really like the way you look at me when I wear this one.'

Heat crawled up his neck.

'I was hoping there would be other guests present this evening,' she went on. 'An eligible lord to flirt with.'

'Why?'

'To see if you got jealous.'

He brushed a finger down his nose. 'You have a very twisted mind.'

'Would it have worked?'

'Yes,' he replied without hesitation. The thought alone made his blood heat.

She mulled his response over. 'I remember the first time I saw you at the tavern with Hildred. You reached back for her leg.' She scrunched up her nose. 'It felt a lot like being punched in the stomach. I think it was the familiarity of the gesture that got to me.'

The corners of his mouth lifted. 'You do understand that most of what comes from your mouth should never be said aloud?'

'Yes.'

'And my hands have been on your legs many times.'

She laughed. 'Grabbing hold of my ankles in order to trip me doesn't count.'

He searched her eyes. 'You never wanted me to touch you any other way until that day in the alleyway.'

Colour filled her cheeks. 'And ever since that day, I've imagined walking up behind you and leaning on your shoulders, like she did. I've wondered, many times, what she said in your ear that made you reach back for her.'

He crossed his arms. 'Really?'

'Whatever she said must've been highly amusing, because I saw your mouth lift slightly. Perhaps she told you a joke.'

He raised an eyebrow. 'You think she whispered a joke into my ear?'

'It's what I'd do.'

He tried not to laugh. 'But I've heard all your jokes, and they're not that amusing.'

She tilted her head. 'Have you heard the one about the sad defender who walks into the tavern holding a blunt weapon?'

'Go on.'

'The tavern maid turns to him and says, "Why the long mace?".'

The laughter escaped him. 'I was wrong. That would make me reach back for you.'

'It would?'

'Absolutely.'

Her eyes shone at him. 'Or perhaps I'd simply whisper, "Meet me in the alleyway".'

The smile fell from his face. 'That might also work.'

She walked around behind him, her movements slow. Out of the corner of his eye, he saw her rise up onto her toes. 'Commander,' she whispered.

He swallowed. 'Yes?'

'Did you know I like my wine the same way I like my castles?'

His breathing was shallow now. 'How's that?'

'Fortified.'

He grinned and reached back for her, taking her by the waist. She responded by wrapping her arms around his middle and pressing her cheek to his tunic. She had spoken of familiarity not realising she was the epitome of it.

'You reached for me,' she said quietly.

He nodded. 'The castle joke got me.'

When he turned, her arms fell to her sides, and she looked up at him expectantly. All that trust in her eyes. All that power she was handing him. The smart thing to do was leave before things got very out of hand, but his feet appeared to have grown roots, and now she was waiting for him to lead her through the next part. Always the eager student.

Naturally, Eda being Eda, she lost patience and made a move for him. He caught hold of her wrist. 'I'm worried you don't understand what you're initiating here, soldier.'

Her lips curved into a smile. 'Oh, Commander. I'm inexperienced, not naive.'

Letting go of her wrist, he trailed the tips of his fingers up her arm.

'I'm going to lock the door,' she said. 'Then you're going to teach me everything.'

'Everything?'

'*All* of it.'

The room felt stifling suddenly. 'That. *That* is what you whisper into my ear.'

Smiling, she went to lock the door, then returned. They stared into each other's eyes, not touching. He had no idea where to begin. The enormity of his feelings was impairing his ability to act.

Sensing his dilemma, Eda began unbuttoning her dress. He watched, hands clammy, as she removed every weapon and item of clothing until she was completely naked before him. Then she looked up at him. 'Your turn.'

He removed his own weapons, boots, and clothes. Her eyes travelled down, curiosity winning. If she was afraid, she did not let it show. He stepped closer, cradling her face in his hands as he dipped his head and kissed her slowly. Her breath hitched, and her hands landed on his chest. The naked warmth of her made every inch of him hard.

He continued to kiss her that way until he felt her nails dig into his skin. Pulling back slightly, he whispered into her open mouth, 'First I show you pleasure.'

She wound her arms around his neck and drew him

closer so every part of her was touching every part of him. His eyes sank shut, and he knew without a doubt that whatever happened next would change them both.

'You're sure?' he asked as he picked her up off the ground.

She wrapped her silky legs around him. 'When have I ever gotten cold feet?'

Carrying her to the bed, he laid her down on it and pressed a kiss to her neck. Then he brought his mouth to her ear and whispered, 'You're going to want to hold on to something.'

CHAPTER 27

*E*da woke to grey light, but she was not ready for morning. She kept her eyes firmly closed as she recalled every detail of her night with Roul. Every sensation. Smiling, she reached back for him, but he was not there. The smile fell from her face. She could not remember him leaving, though it was hardly surprising given how deeply she had slept afterwards. Roul had destroyed her, body and mind.

'He left an hour ago' came a voice that did not belong to Roul.

Eda sat up with a gasp, clutching the sheet to her naked body. It took her eyes a moment to adjust. She froze when she spotted Lord Roger sitting in the chair beneath the window.

'He must have heard us coming, because he stepped out into the corridor before I even had a chance to knock. It was all very civilised—at first.'

He was talking about Roul. Her Roul, who would never let a stranger into her bedchamber while she slept. She looked to the pile of clothes on the floor, where her weapons were buried.

'You know, this is an extraordinary number of knives for a lady of your standing to be carrying,' Roger said, drawing her attention back to him.

She saw then that he had them all laid out on his lap. He held one up, inspecting it closely. 'They are beautifully crafted.'

'Where is Sir Bradley?'

He lowered the weapon and angled his head. 'Perhaps you mean Commander Thornton?'

Her heart pounded in her chest. Something had gone very wrong while she slept.

'I had a few questions for him, so I took him to the prison tower,' he explained. 'It is the most suitable place for that sort of thing.'

Eda eyed the weapons on his lap. She could get to them if she needed to. But then what? Would she threaten him? *Kill* him? 'Does Prince Becket know you have imprisoned one of his guests?'

Roger stood, gaze dropping. She felt exposed despite the sheet covering her.

'I will be the one asking the questions this morning.' He gestured to the clothing on the floor. 'Get dressed. I shall be waiting for you in the corridor.'

He left without a fuss, the door clicking closed behind him.

Eda's mind raced as she looked from the dress on the floor to the window. She could climb up and squeeze through it if she needed to. But she did not even know where the prison tower was or how many guards stood between her and Roul. It was better to play the helpless woman for now.

Someone pounded on the door. 'Let's go!' There were guards waiting for her on the other side.

Eda slipped from the bed, but instead of picking up the dress from the floor, she pulled the far more conservative one from her bag. There was no chance she was doing this with her breasts on display. Dressing quickly, she shoved her feet into her boots, then searched her bag for a spare dagger. Nothing. It seemed someone else had already been through it. She pressed her palm to her forehead and took a moment to breathe. Then, straightening, she pushed her hair back from her face and tucked it behind her ears. There was no time to pin it.

She fetched her cloak, then pulled the door open. Two guards waited with Lord Roger. Never a good sign. Lifting her chin, she said, 'I won't answer any of your questions until I see Commander Thornton.'

Roger eyed her coolly. 'Whatever power you think you have right now, think again. You are in no position to be making demands.' He gestured with his head. 'Start walking.'

One of the guards took hold of her arm. She tried to pull free, but he held tight. She could have had him on the ground gasping for air with a few simple moves, but that would not help Roul. She needed to save the fight for a time when it was beneficial.

The party descended the stairs at the end of the corridor into the inner bailey. They were back indoors soon after, climbing up another set of stairs and emerging onto an open walkway. A bitter wind blew in off the sea. She blinked against it while mapping out her surroundings, committing every detail to memory. When they entered the turret at the end, it took her eyes a moment to adjust. Eda's pulse quickened as they descended another stairwell, passing a number of cells along the way. She searched for Roul in every shadow.

They were halfway to the bottom when the guard pulled her to a stop in front of a cell. It was so dark inside that it took Eda a moment to see the shackled man hanging from a chain. He was shirtless and blood-splattered. He lifted his head at the sound of keys rattling, and Eda sucked in a breath when she recognised Roul.

Blood covered one side of his face, and his eye was swollen. He tensed up upon seeing her, and the chains attached to his feet rattled.

'All right,' Lord Roger said, stepping inside. 'Now we will get some proper answers.'

Eda was led inside.

'Did they hurt you?' Those were the first words from Roul's mouth.

Eda went to reply, but nothing came out. *No, no, no. Not now.* She shook her head at him.

'First things first,' Lord Roger began, clapping his hands together and looking at Eda. 'What is your real name?'

Her mouth was so dry. She wet her lips and attempted to speak but failed yet again.

'There is no need to be nervous,' Roger said. 'We are all friends here.'

She signed a response because she did not know what else to do and feared they would hurt Roul further if they thought her defiant.

Roger emitted a confused laugh. 'What is all this?' He made a mockery of her signs and looked to the guard beside her, who was grinning.

Roul rattled the chain attached to his wrists to get his attention. 'I'll answer your questions.'

The lord glanced in his direction. 'We tried that earlier with little success. Look at the state of you. And all we got was your name. Now I am suddenly supposed to trust what you say?'

'She can't speak right now, so I'm all you've got.'

Lord Roger walked over to him, eyes remaining on Eda. 'Your *name.*'

Eda, she signed, knowing it was pointless.

Roger threw his elbow up, and it connected with Roul's

jaw. His head snapped back on impact, and a breath later, blood trickled from his mouth. Eda lurched at the lord, but the guard yanked her backwards.

'Name!' Roger shouted.

Eda's breathing was shallow. Her eyes met Roul's, filled with remorse. She was failing him. He would never fail her, but she was failing him now.

'I will start us off,' Roger said. 'I already know you are not the prince's cousin. I received confirmation from a close contact in Llanystumdwy early this morning.' He looked between them. 'I had no choice but to confine the prince to his quarters until I have a clear picture of what is going on here.'

'Prince Becket had no idea we were coming,' Roul said.

'And yet he knowingly let an impostor into the castle.' Roger pointed at Eda. 'This is your last chance. Then I shall have no choice but to start removing fingers.'

The chains went taut as Roul pulled against them. Eda might not have been able to speak in that moment, but she could certainly fight. Her eyes met Roul's. He must have known exactly what she was thinking, because he gave her the smallest nod.

That was the only communication she needed.

She kicked out, connecting with the guard's knee. His grip slackened just enough for her to pull free. She ducked, snatching his dagger from its sheath and slashing the back of his leg before rolling out of reach. She knew just where to cut. The other guard drew his sword. She threw the knife at him, striking his shoulder. She managed to catch the sword as it fell from his hand. Spinning around, she pointed it at Lord Roger. He stared at the tip, which sat a few inches from his face. The injured guard came for her, but Roul swung his body and knocked him into the wall.

A few tense seconds passed.

'You just made a big mistake,' Roger said. 'I will hang you both now.'

'Don't move from that spot,' Eda said as she backed up to the wall. She released the chain that was holding Roul up, then looked around for the keys to the shackles.

'Front pocket,' Roul said, gesturing to the man with a knife protruding from his shoulder.

Eda went to him.

'Do not let her touch those keys,' Roger hissed.

But she was not playing anymore. She cut the man's throat, then searched his pocket while he choked and writhed on the ground. The second her fingers closed around the keys, she threw them to Roul and returned to Lord Roger.

'You will never make it out of the castle,' he told her, growing more bitter with every passing second.

Eda heard the shackles hit the ground, and she could finally breathe again. 'I'm going to need your tunic.' She held out a hand.

With a shake of his head, Roger reached up and began unbuttoning the garment with sharp, angry movements. 'You are making this so much worse for yourself.'

Eda handed the tunic to Roul. He slipped it on without bothering with the buttons. Then, bending, he picked up the shackles and secured them around Roger's wrists. Eda ran to the wall and tugged on the chain until the lord's arms were stretched above his head, then secured it.

Not taking any risks, Roul finished off the remaining guard and retrieved all the weapons in the cell. Then he went and stood before Roger. 'I'm only letting you live because I don't want a war.' With that, he lifted the man's shirt and stuffed it into his mouth before turning to Eda. 'Time to go.'

Eda stared at the gagged lord. 'For the record, I think

Queen Isabella can do much, *much* better.' Then she followed Roul out of the cell.

Roul locked the door behind them, eyes meeting hers. 'You're really all right?'

'You're the one who's bleeding.' She hated seeing him in such a state.

He wiped at the blood on his face. 'I've received worse head wounds while training. Don't you worry about me.' He distributed the weapons evenly between them. 'I have a feeling Prince Becket is going to want to leave with us now.'

'But how will we get to him?'

'Using those sharp instincts of yours. You trained for this moment, remember?' He searched her eyes. 'Tell me you're ready.'

Was she?

He stepped up and pressed a kiss to her forehead, whispering, 'I'll be by your side the whole time, soldier, just like we agreed.'

She nodded. 'Then I'm ready.'

CHAPTER 28

*T*heir only option now was to escape, because no one was going to let them out after what they had done. Roul glanced sideways at Eda as they stepped out onto the open walkway. Her fingers were white around the hilt of her sword, and her eyes darted in all directions. She was ready to fight her way out, which was exactly what he needed from her.

'Straight ahead,' she whispered.

A guard came towards them. Even if by some miracle the man walked by, he was headed for the tower. They needed more time. The man's eyes moved over Roul as he drew closer, and his hand went to his weapon. Roul pounced before he had a chance to draw it, knocking him to the ground. Taking hold of the guard's head, he smashed it down onto the stone, and the man went limp beneath him.

Roul climbed off him and got to his feet, and the pair jogged off. Time was already running out.

They made it all the way to the prince's quarters without encountering anyone else but were met with two English guards parked at the door. The men drew their swords the moment they caught sight of them. Eda threw the dagger she was holding, striking the man closest to them in the throat. Roul ran at the other guard. After a short fight, the guard lay dead beside his comrade.

Eda went for the door and found it locked. Plucking the keys from the guard's belt, Roul tossed them to her. A minute later they were inside, face to face with an on-edge Woottone. Roul and Eda placed their weapons down and raised their hands to show they were no threat.

Prince Becket was standing in front of a dying fire, glaring at them. 'They think I liaised with you, deceived them.'

'We know,' Eda said. 'And because of that, we have to leave. All of us. You can't stay here. It's not safe.'

'It was perfectly safe until you arrived.' Becket linked his hands atop his head. 'They are not just going to let us leave.'

Roul gestured to Woottone to help him move the bodies.

'For the love of Belenus,' Becket said when the men dragged them into the room. 'They will hang you for that.'

'They'll more likely hang us for the things we did *before* that,' Eda replied. 'Which is why we really need to leave now.'

Becket took in Roul's bloodied and dishevelled state and narrowed his eyes. 'Is that Lord Roger's tunic?'

'We need to go,' Roul said quietly. 'We have a very small window of opportunity to get you home. If you would prefer to take your chances here, then speak up. We can't force you to come with us.'

Becket looked to Woottone for guidance.

'Never a good sign when they lock you in a room and confiscate your weapons,' the bodyguard said.

Becket exhaled a slow breath, then went to fetch his cloak. 'If I die here today, I am going to be very cross.'

Roul and Woottone took the scabbards from the dead guards while Eda distributed all the weapons among the living.

'What exactly is the plan?' the prince asked as they stepped out into the corridor.

Roul looked both ways before speaking. 'We have some men outside the castle who'll assist in whatever way they can.'

'Can they get us through the gatehouse?'

'We're not leaving via the gate,' Roul replied. 'We're going over the wall.'

The prince nearly tripped over his own feet. 'Please tell me you are joking.'

'There's a berm between the wall and the moat, and the moat's dry. We'll be fine.'

Becket glanced at Eda. 'You expect a woman to descend a wall?'

'I've been known to climb a wall or two in my time' was Eda's reply. 'I'll be just fine, Your Highness.'

They rounded the corner and descended the stairs, hit with the smell coming from the garderobe outflow.

'What if they shoot at us?' Becket asked.

Eda brought a finger to her lips and listened a moment. Footsteps approached. Roul gestured for everyone to keep moving, then pressed himself against the wall to wait. A guard appeared. Roul lurched out from the shadows, cutting the man's throat before he could utter a sound. He dragged the corpse beneath the stairs before running after the others.

'Are we good?' Woottone asked when Roul caught up to them.

Roul nodded.

The curtain wall now loomed before them, and they headed for the steps at its base. They flew up them. Two laundry maids in the courtyard paused their work to watch them.

'Halt!' A guard on the ground had spotted them. 'Stop right there.'

'That means go faster,' Roul called to Woottone, who was at the front of the group.

'I said halt!' the guard shouted below.

They had no bows and arrows, and even Eda could not throw a dagger accurately from that distance. Bringing two fingers to his mouth, Roul whistled as long and loud as he could, a signal to his men on the other side of the wall. Unfortunately, he got the attention of everyone *inside* the walls as well.

Footsteps sounded overhead, and the guard at the bottom was now on the steps behind them.

'Keep going,' Roul called as he dropped back to deal with the guard in pursuit. The man's sword was drawn, but he was no match for Roul. The commander disarmed him on his first strike, then kicked him backwards. He tumbled all the way to the bottom of the steps and did not get up again.

When Roul arrived on the wall walk, Eda was pulling her dagger from a guard's stomach while Woottone fought off another nearby.

'How do we get down without rope?' Becket asked, turning in a circle.

Roul stepped across the dead guard and peered over the embrasure. 'Everyone hand me your cloaks.'

'You must be joking,' Becket said.

Eda was already removing hers. Woottone had taken care of the other guard and was now doing the same. Cursing, Becket surrendered his cloak also. Roul tied expert knots in record time, testing their strength before throwing one end of the makeshift rope over the embrasure. It barely reached halfway down the wall, but he was confident they could drop from there without breaking any bones.

'Suttone, you're up,' Roul said, wrapping the fabric around his hand.

She shook her head. 'Woottone should go first so he can help the prince at the bottom.'

He should have known she would not go without him. 'Get your arse down that wall.'

'No.'

They did not have time to stand there arguing. 'Fine. Woottone, go.'

The defender leapt up onto the embrasure and began climbing down like he would have done during training a hundred times before. Roul placed one foot on the wall for balance. The moment the defender let go, Roul steadied himself and gestured to Becket. The prince appeared afraid.

Eda helped him up onto the embrasure. 'Try to keep your feet on the wall as you go down. Land with bent legs.'

Nodding, the prince lowered himself over the edge.

Voices coming from the turret made Eda and Roul look in that direction.

'Go,' Roul said, adjusting his grip. 'Now.'

Reluctantly, Eda tucked her weapons into her dress and climbed onto the embrasure. She looked back at him. 'Throw the cloaks the moment I let go.'

He nodded, gaze darting in the direction of the turret as the voices grew louder. 'Hurry.'

Eda descended quickly at first, then was held up by Becket, who was still making his way down. Roul gritted his teeth against the extra weight and leaned farther back. When Becket finally let go, he straightened a little and waited for Eda to follow.

The creak of a bow made him turn his head. He saw the arrow a split second before he felt it graze his arm. When

Eda let go of the rope, he immediately tossed the cloaks over the edge.

'You did not think this ridiculous plan would actually work, did you?' Lord Roger's voice carried along the wall walk. He was flanked by two men with loaded bows pointed at Roul.

The commander dashed for the embrasure. It was jump or die. So with blind faith, he leapt over it. He looked down as he fell, relieved to find one of the cloaks stretched out beneath him. The three of them repositioned themselves at the last moment so he landed in the middle of the cloak. He tumbled off it on impact, slamming shoulder first into the ground.

'You did not even check first,' Becket said, visibly shocked. 'What if we had still been navigating your impossible knots?'

Roul leapt to his feet and began ushering everyone towards the moat. '*Run*. Lord Roger's on the wall.'

An arrow struck the ground next to his foot.

Woottone moved behind the prince, and they were all running for their lives then.

'What's your plan for getting us up the other side of that moat?' Becket asked, between pants.

Roul brought his fingers to his mouth, whistling again. 'We're going to have help.'

Eda was struggling to run in the dress. Roul could see her frustration as she held it up.

'They're still shooting at us,' Becket said as an arrow flew past his head.

Eda glanced over her shoulder. 'Their accuracy will drop at around two hundred and fifty yards.'

'How far are we now?'

'Not two hundred and fifty yards.'

Roul slowed and moved behind her. 'I need you to go faster.'

'I know' was her reply.

An arrow tripped Woottone. 'Keep running,' he called to the prince as he fell. He was back on his feet a moment later.

The sound of a portcullis rising in the distance filled Roul with dread. But then four horses appeared on the other side of the moat, and Blackmane dismounted with a length of rope in hand.

'Please tell me those are your men,' Becket panted.

Roul nodded. 'That's them.'

When they reached the moat, they navigated the rocks all the way to the bottom. While it was technically a dry moat, the constant rain had turned the base of it into a bog. Still, they leapt into it without hesitating, sinking knee deep into the mud. Woottone took the prince's arm as they trudged through it. Roul resisted the urge to take Eda's.

Hiss, hiss.

Arrows flew past them, striking the cliff face they were about to climb up. Woottone ushered Becket to the rope, and the prince grabbed hold of it with both hands.

'Pull!' Roul shouted up at Blackmane.

Prince Becket was lifted out of the hungry mud as hooves pounded the bridge in the distance. Lord Roger's men were coming for them. Roul could hear his men returning fire above but knew they were severely outnumbered. All the while, archers continued to shoot arrows into the moat.

'Bow!' Eda called to the men above.

Hadewaye's head appeared, and he dropped a bow and quiver over the edge. Eda caught the bow, and Roul caught the quiver. He passed her a handful of arrows as she turned to face the wall. Loading the weapon, she took aim at the archers. She did not miss.

'I'll cover you,' she told Roul when the rope dropped for the third time.

Because she was safer in a ditch than atop the ledge, Roul went ahead of her.

Blackmane pulled him up, then took hold of Roul's arm to help him onto the ledge. He looked down at his bloodied hand when he let go. 'You injured, Commander?'

Roul glanced down at the wound. 'Just a graze.' He looked over to where the other three men were positioned in front of the horses, shooting at the riders on the bridge.

'Good to see you alive, Commander,' Hadewaye said.

'Alveye,' Roul called. 'Get the prince on a horse and get them to the river. We'll meet you there.'

Woottone had already mounted one of the geldings and was pulling the prince up behind him. Alveye leapt onto his mare, and a moment later, they were galloping towards the trees.

Blackmane was pulling Eda up now. She was almost to the top when an arrow struck the defender's shoulder. The rope slid from his hands. Roul dove onto the ground, catching hold of it. Blackmane lost his balance. Seeing he was about to go over the edge, Roul caught hold of the defender's cloak with his other hand, but the pin holding it together released, and Blackmane toppled forwards. Eda caught him by the trousers as he fell. The extra weight dragged Roul to the edge of the ledge, but he managed to anchor himself with his foot before going over.

His eyes met Eda's panic-filled ones.

'I can't hold him.' As she spoke the words, Blackmane slipped from her grasp and fell. His head clipped a rock on the way to the bottom.

Roul reached for Eda's hand and pulled her up. She caught hold of a rock near the top and met his eyes. 'I can get him,' she said. 'I'll tie the rope to him, and you can pull him up. I can do it.'

Blackmane's groans reached them from the bottom of the moat. He was still alive, and Roul knew they would not leave without him. While it almost killed him to do it, he let go of Eda's hand.

'We're running out of arrows here,' Tatum called over his shoulder.

Roul pressed his eyes shut. 'I need two minutes.' He got to his feet and watched as Eda scaled the rocks to the bottom. She trudged over to Blackmane, slipping and falling in the mud as she tried to tie the rope around him. The second it was secure, Roul began pulling him up.

Hiss.

Roul felt the fletching of an arrow brush his ear. 'I need some cover here.'

Tatum swung his bow and took aim at the wall, but arrows continued to fall from the sky.

'Grab hold of his foot!' Roul called to Eda. They did not have time for two separate trips. Eda reached for Blackmane's boot and climbed while holding on to the injured defender. Her feet slipped constantly as they tangled in her skirts.

Hiss, hiss.

Finally, Roul dragged Blackmane over the edge. He was conscious but disorientated, his hair slick with blood and mud. Roul reached for Eda, pulling her up.

'I'm out of arrows,' Tatum shouted.

Eda still had a bow and quiver looped over her head and shoulder. She reached back, then looked down at her hand. She only had five left.

Blackmane attempted to get to his feet. 'Give me a sword.'

He could not even stand, let alone fight.

'Hadewaye, I need you on a horse—now!' Roul shouted.

The defender gave his remaining arrows to Tatum, then ran to his horse. Somehow, they managed to get Blackmane up onto the mare behind him.

'Hold on to him,' Roul told Hadewaye as the horse took off.

More hooves sounded on the bridge. It was time for them to go.

'Take Eda,' Roul said, drawing his sword.

Tatum leapt onto the remaining horse and held out his hand to her, but Eda was looking only at Roul.

'Eda,' Roul warned.

'You can't outrun horses.'

He grabbed her by the arm and dragged her over to the horse.

'Roul, stop.' There was panic in her voice. 'Stop!'

'Take her,' Roul told Tatum, passing her to him.

The defender hauled her up behind him despite a small struggle.

'You can't fend off mounted soldiers with one sword while on foot,' she pleaded.

'You're right.' He gestured to the five arrows still in her hand. 'So you better make those count on your way out.'

With that, he slapped the rump of the horse to get it moving.

CHAPTER 29

$\mathcal{E}$da's insides screamed. She thought about sliding from the horse's rump and returning to Roul, fighting alongside him the way they had planned, the way he would if it were her back there. But then the horses charging towards him split into two groups, half of them continuing towards Roul and the other half coming after them.

'We have company,' she told Tatum as she retrieved her bow.

The defender glanced over his shoulder. 'Shit.'

Eda took aim at the rider closest to Roul. The angle of her body combined with the speed at which they were travelling made it difficult to keep her hand steady. Breathing out slowly, she released the first arrow. It struck the guard through the ribs. Wasting no time, she reloaded her bow and shot the next rider. Her aim dropped slightly upon release, but she still managed to hit his leg, which would make him easy prey for Roul.

One of the men pursuing them was getting closer, so Eda used the third arrow on him. Trees appeared around them, and a moment later, Roul was gone from sight. Panic rose in her. He would have to face the remaining riders alone.

She fired the final two arrows and missed completely as Tatum weaved left and right between the trunks. They emerged onto a leafy path. Eda could no longer see the guards, but she could hear the horses.

Eda hooked the bow over her head and pulled out the dagger she had tucked in her dress. She looked up at the low-hanging branches dashing overhead and had an idea. 'I'm going to need you to circle around and come back.'

He looked at her, confused. 'What?'

'Just come back for me.' Reaching up, she grabbed hold of the next branch and swung herself up onto it.

Tatum looked back, then, realising what she was doing, pulled hard on the right rein and disappeared into the trees.

A moment later, the guards rode into sight. She readied herself. When the first horse was a few strides away, she dropped from the branch, plunging her knife into the rider's neck as she landed. She shoved the injured man off the horse, then moved onto the saddle and gathered the reins as she turned to face the second rider.

She was feeling good about her plan until horses appeared through the trees on either side of her. A blade came at her. She leaned so drastically in order to avoid it that she fell off the horse. Her back hit the ground. Her bow snapped, and the dagger flew from her hand. She was gasping for air as she crawled towards the knife.

'On your feet, and hands where we can see them,' said one of the men in a tone that suggested he was out of patience.

She was outnumbered with only a dagger to fight with —and the dagger was not even in her hand.

As she rose, Tatum chose that moment to return. He charged in, sword swinging. Eda used the opportunity to swoop down and snatch up the knife, throwing it at a nearby guard. It stuck. She ran to catch the sword as it fell from his hand. The horse spooked, almost trampling her as it fled. She turned, ready to fight, and found Tatum disarmed and surrounded by English soldiers.

'Solid plan, by the way,' Tatum said drily.

She looked around, knowing one sword was not enough. It would not have been enough for Roul either. Still, she would not lie down and die yet.

'Tatum.' She tossed the sword to him because she could not watch him die without a weapon. He caught it and looked around.

A guard came for Eda—to kill or capture, she had no idea. She would fight with her bare hands if that was all she had.

But she did not need to.

An arrow pierced the neck of the approaching man. The horses stirred, and the soldiers looked to the trees surrounding them.

Hiss.

Another rider was knocked from his mount by an arrow. Tatum used the opportunity to attack, taking off the hand of a nearby guard. Eda ran forwards and snatched up a weapon, but by the time she raised it, all the English guards were dead or bleeding on the ground around them. A man gurgled and writhed nearby. Tatum drove his sword through the man's heart, and he fell still.

Another horse came through the trees, and the pair spun around, bracing for another fight. Eda's eyes locked with Roul's, and the sting of tears was instant.

He was alive.

Dismounting, he went to her, pulling her into his arms and holding so tightly she could barely draw breath. They were both covered in blood and sweat and mud, but it did not matter, because they were both alive.

'Thank you for not dying,' she said.

He smoothed down her filthy hair, then kissed it. 'Thank you for making it an easier fight.'

'I'm fine, by the way,' Tatum said.

They both looked at him.

'Perhaps next time we can discuss the plan before you swing off like a monkey.'

Roul frowned. 'Do I want to know?'

Eda shook her head.

Tatum went to gather the scattered horses.

'We need to get to the river,' Roul said, letting go of Eda. 'We'll bring all the horses with us. The last thing we want is them returning to the castle without riders.'

Tatum removed his cloak and tossed it at Eda without saying a word. She had not realised how cold it was.

'Thank you.'

The others stole cloaks from the dead.

'I'm not leaving you behind again,' she told Roul when he brought her a horse. 'So don't ask me to.'

He nodded and helped her up into the saddle.

The three of them made their way south, moving at a canter until the horses tired. They were looking over their shoulders the whole time, expecting Lord Roger's men to burst through the trees at any moment. At one point, Eda thought she could hear hooves behind her, only to realise it was her pounding heart.

They finally reached the river, then made their way west along it until they reached the sandbank Roul had discovered by accident the day prior. They checked the ground for hoof prints or any evidence of their men nearby but found nothing.

'Maybe they're lost,' Eda said.

The others looked doubtful. Roul brought his fingers to his mouth and whistled. A moment later, a loud bray sounded from across the river.

Surely not. Eda straightened in the saddle as she looked across the water. A smile split her face as Basil trotted out into the open, stopping a safe distance from the water's edge.

Tatum chuckled. 'I can't believe that thing waited for you.'

Roul shook his head in disbelief and drew a breath. 'Let's cross and wait on the other side.'

'And if they don't show up?' Tatum asked.

'They'll show up.' Roul sounded confident.

The horses sidestepped suddenly and looked to the trees. Eda slipped her bow over her head and reached back for an arrow. Roul and Tatum went for their swords. The three of them watched and waited. The string went taut beneath Eda's fingers when something moved in the distance, then slackened when Alveye rode out into the open. Woottone and Prince Becket followed, then Hadewaye and Blackmane.

They were all there, everyone accounted for—even if Blackmane was half dead and slumped against Hadewaye.

'That was absolutely the worst escape plan ever implemented throughout history,' Prince Becket said when they came to a stop. His gaze drifted across the river. 'Is that a donkey?'

Alveye grinned. 'Not just any donkey. That's Basil.'

Eda went over to check on Blackmane. The arrow was still lodged in his shoulder, and his eyes were closed. 'How's he doing?' she asked Hadewaye.

Blackmane opened his eyes. 'I'm fine.'

A smile flickered on her face. 'Good to see you're still alert.'

He wet his cracked, pale lips and stared at her. 'You should've left while you had time.'

'Why? Because that's what you would do?'

He swallowed with great effort. 'Thank you for climbing down.'

'Don't thank me yet. This might be a slow and painful death for you. And if it turns out I planned it that way, you'll look the fool on your deathbed.' She patted his leg, then grabbed Hadewaye's waterskin and headed down to the river to fetch him some water.

'So what is next in this terrible plan?' the prince asked as he walked over to claim one of the spare horses. 'Blackmane is going to need a physician.'

'We could find one in Dolgellau,' Eda suggested as she lifted the waterskin to Blackmane's mouth.

Roul shook his head. 'It's too risky. Soldiers will be swarming the village soon. Better to take him to Carno, to my family.'

Eda retrieved a blanket and wrapped it around Blackmane. 'Can you hold on for that long?'

'I told you I'm fine. Stop fussing.'

She rolled her eyes and returned to her horse.

'Where's the bridge?' Prince Becket asked, looking both ways.

Eda's eyes met Roul's as she mounted. 'Should you tell His Highness, or should I?'

'There's no bridge,' Roul said plainly, nudging his horse forwards. 'But this should seem easy after the morning we've had. Slow and steady along the sandbank.' He looked back at the group as he entered the water. 'Tatum, you're at the rear. Suttone, you'll cross with me. No one is drowning today. We don't have time. And no one talk to the donkey when we get to the other side. I don't want it following us.'

Eda felt the beginnings of a smile as she walked her horse into the river.

CHAPTER 30

*R*oul spotted his father exiting the chicken coop as they neared the house. Clive Thornton paused, looked in their direction, then called to his wife. The entire family came out of the house, smiles fading when they saw the state of the group.

Wilona took one look at Blackmane when they pulled up, then turned to Lana. 'Run and fetch Yetta.' She gestured towards the house. 'Bring him inside.'

Alveye and Tatum helped him from his horse and took him inside. Eda followed. Hadewaye, sweating and stiff from his efforts of keeping the injured defender upright for the journey, limped around tending the horses.

'I see you've still got the donkey with you,' Clive said. Then he looked from Woottone to Prince Becket. 'And a few extras.' He bowed. 'Welcome to our very, very humble home, Your Highness.'

'Thank you.'

Blushing, Odella lowered into a curtsy. 'Welcome to Carno, Your Highness.'

He nodded in response.

Roul looked nervously back at the road, and his father noticed.

'Trouble follow you?' Clive asked.

'We'll soon find out. Is there somewhere we can hide the horses?'

Clive thought a moment.

'We could shut them in one of the abandoned houses,' Odella suggested.

Woottone appeared to like that idea. 'Whatever gets them out of sight. I should get the prince indoors also before someone sees him.'

'Of course, of course,' Clive said, waving them towards the house. 'This way.'

Roul heard Hadewaye coughing, so he went to help him with the horses. 'You all right?'

Hadewaye wiped his brow with the back of his hand. 'Just a bit hot after all the excitement.' He coughed into his hand as he led two horses away.

Roul watched him a moment before gathering up the rest of the horses and following after him.

When he went inside, he found Blackmane laid out on a cot near the hearth. Yetta had already removed the arrow and was now stitching the wound. She nodded at Roul as he entered, face creasing.

'Look who became a man.'

Roul leaned on the doorframe. 'Good to see you, Yetta. I wish it were under better circumstances.'

Eda was carefully washing the wound on Blackmane's head, eyes blinking with exhaustion.

'Let me do that,' Wilona said, taking the cloth from her hand. 'You go have a wash. Odella will find you something to wear. You're just about the same size.'

Odella took her by the arm and guided her to the next room.

When Roul went to follow, his mother said, 'I think

your sister has things under control in there.' She gave him a knowing smile. 'Why don't the rest of you head next door and get cleaned up also, give Yetta some space?'

The men filed out of the house. Roul glanced a final time at the room where Eda was, then followed.

Once they were clean and dressed, Lana arrived with a pot of soup, bowls, and spoons. She informed them that Blackmane was stitched up and now resting.

'Thank you,' Roul said. He then sent Alveye to watch the road and Hadewaye to guard the horses. Tatum and Woottone remained with the prince, and Roul went in search of Eda. She exited the house just as he reached the door.

'Sorry,' she said. 'It took your poor sister forever to comb the mud from my hair.'

Eda's wet hair was braided, and she wore a simple long-sleeve beige dress that was belted around the waist.

'Better?' he asked.

She nodded and looked to the road. 'Do you want me to keep watch?'

'Alveye's keeping watch.'

She reached up to touch the split above his eye. 'You could ask Yetta to stitch it.'

'It's fine.' He took hold of her hand and brought it to his lips.

Eda looked behind her. 'What if your family walks out?'

'I don't care. I watched you nearly die at least five times today. I need you close.'

She leaned her head on his chest. 'Will Lord Roger send more men after us?'

'I don't know.'

They were silent a moment. Roul was playing with the end of her braid while watching the road.

'What happens now?' she asked, her voice barely above a whisper.

He rubbed his stubbly cheek on her hair. 'Now we go home.'

She looked up at him. 'And then?'

His eyes met hers. He knew what she was asking. Hooking a finger under her chin, he lifted her face. 'Then we make a plan.'

'You already have a plan.'

He brushed his thumb down her cheek. 'Eda,' he whispered. 'What did you say to me in the forest earlier today?'

Her eyebrows came together as she tried to recall.

'You said, "I'm not leaving you behind again, so don't ask me to", remember?'

She nodded. 'I remember.'

'We'll figure all this out.'

She bit her lip to stop from speaking.

'What?'

'How? How will we figure it out? My family is there. Your family is here.'

He dipped his head to kiss her, lips melting against hers. He could feel the steady beat of her heart against his ribs. 'We'll figure it out.' He spoke the words into her mouth. 'No soldier left behind.'

Her lips turned up.

A whistle cut through the air. A warning.

Roul ushered Eda into the house, then went to peer out of the small window. He ducked when two riders trotted by.

'English soldiers?' Clive asked.

Roul nodded. He looked over at Blackmane, whose eyes were now wide open. 'Can you ride?'

Blackmane sat up. 'Of course I can ride. No point waiting until the place is swarming with soldiers.'

'Us being here puts your family in danger,' Eda added quietly.

Clive waved the comment away. 'Don't you rush off on our account.'

Hadewaye appeared in the doorway, looking around for Roul. 'Orders, Commander?'

'Ready the horses. Tell the others we're leaving.'

His mother sprang into action. 'I'll pack you some food to take with you.'

'Please don't leave yourselves short,' Eda said. 'We still have some salted meat left.'

'Wish I could offer you fresh horses,' his father said.

Eda touched his arm as she passed by. 'Our horses have had a decent rest. We'll be fine.'

The horses were saddled and ready to leave twenty minutes later. It was time for Roul to say goodbye to his family.

'You take care of yourself,' Clive said, hugging him.

'I will.' He moved to his sisters, kissing their wet cheeks before turning to his mother. 'I'll be back.'

'Or not.' Wilona glanced at Eda. 'Your eyes never leave her.' She gave a resigned shrug. 'What more could a mother want for her only son? I love you no matter what. I hope you know that.'

Roul kissed her. 'I'm coming back.' Of course he had to come back. He could not just leave them to wither in this place while he built a life elsewhere. He would figure out a plan once he got everyone safely back to Chadora.

Eda stepped up to them. 'Thank you for everything.'

'We hope to see you again,' Wilona said.

'Likewise.'

Roul waited until Eda was on her horse before mounting. 'Blackmane, if you need to stop, you speak up. We don't want any torn stitches.' He looked at Prince Becket. 'Any questions?'

The prince shook his head.

'Stay alert.' He nodded a final farewell at his family, then rode away from them.

The group moved off the road as soon as they could, keeping to the trees until dark. Only then did they move out into the open. Then the trees disappeared altogether, and all they had was open plains.

They continued until their horses' legs trembled and Blackmane looked ready to fall from the saddle. Roul stopped, dismounted, and looked around. 'We can't sleep out here. We're too exposed.' He clapped a hand on the neck of his exhausted horse. 'We'll continue on foot until we find cover. Put Blackmane on Eda's horse. It's the least tired.'

Prince Becket looked to the back of the group. 'Actually, the donkey is the least tired. Those things can go for days.'

Blackmane slid from his horse. 'I'm not riding a fucking donkey.' Then, remembering who he was talking to, he added, 'Your Highness.' He cleared his throat. 'I'll be fine on foot like the rest of you.'

Three hours later, they reached forest, then continued for another half hour until they found a stream. The horses drank greedily, then began tearing leaves off nearby shrubbery.

'No fire,' Roul said. 'No tent. And leave the saddles on the horses. We need to be ready to leave in a hurry if the need arises.'

Alveye and Hadeweye tended the horses while Eda filled the waterskins. Roul passed around the blankets, and Tatum distributed the food. They wrapped themselves in the blankets and leaned their backs on the trees while they ate. Prince Becket did not complain as he shivered alongside the rest of them.

'I'll take first watch,' Tatum said.

Roul nodded, then opened his blanket to Eda as the rain started to fall. She settled next to him, blinking heavily. He tucked both blankets around her, and they sat watching the rain. When he saw her head drop, he guided it to his chest.

'Sleep,' he said.

She pressed her palm to his heart. 'I'm so cold.'

He drew her closer. 'I wish I could build you a fire.'

She was silent a while, then said, 'What if our lungs freeze while we sleep and we never wake up?'

'No one's lungs are freezing. Try to sleep.'

He thought she had finally drifted off, but then she whispered, 'Do you think if your heart stopped beating, mine would stop also?'

He covered her freezing hand with his equally cold one. 'No.' He spoke into her hair. 'I think yours would beat twice as hard to compensate.'

They were silent a moment.

'Roul.'

'Mm?'

'Will you be angry if Basil makes it all the way to Chadora?'

His lips twitched. 'Angry? No. Surprised? Absolutely. Now go to sleep, or I'll be forced to knock you out.'

Eventually, her body went heavy against him. Only then did he lean his head against the trunk and drift off to sleep.

CHAPTER 31

When Eda blinked her eyes open the next morning, she was relieved to find that the rain had slowed to a drizzle. She could tell Roul was asleep by his breathing.

Alveye was keeping watch. He nodded a greeting at her when he noticed she was awake, and she returned the gesture. The others were curled against trunks beneath the largest branches. Fat drops of water dripped on them from the leaves above. Eda was surprised to find Prince Becket awake and reading a letter, Wootone snoring beside him. She slipped out of Roul's arms, careful not to wake him, then went to check on Blackmane. He was breathing. She made her way over to the prince, sinking down beside him.

'We're stuck in the middle of nowhere,' she whispered. 'Who could possibly be delivering you letters?'

He gave her a weak smile. 'Wootone's snoring woke me. I thought I should prepare for the reunion with my mother.'

She leaned her head against the tree. 'I should probably mention that Commander Thornton told me why you're reluctant to return.'

'I figured he would given how *close* the two of you are.' He raised one eyebrow at her.

Her cheeks heated. 'I was sorry to hear of it but not overly surprised. It must've been a very difficult time when you found out.'

'That is putting it mildly. Every time I read this letter, I feel every emotion all over again.'

'Who's it from?' Then, remembering who she was talking to, she quickly added, 'Sorry. That's really none of my business.'

He surprised her by handing it to her. 'Read it. I do not mind.'

She ran her eyes over the elegant handwriting. It took her a moment to realise what it was. It was a letter to Queen Fayre agreeing to carry out her orders. A letter from King Oswin's killer.

'For a while I had this ridiculous notion that it had come from Lord Roger,' the prince said. 'The well-formed letters combined with the signature at the bottom. That is the main reason I accepted his invitation to Harlech Castle, to know once and for all. I managed to intercept a letter he had written, but the signatures did not match.'

Eda looked down at the signature he was referring to and stopped breathing. She had thought the handwriting familiar, and now she knew why. She ran her thumb over the swirling tail of a single *R*. It was identical to the one in the letter Roul's mother had shown her during their first visit.

'My mother might have coordinated my father's death,' Becket said, swallowing thickly. 'However, this person'—he tapped the letter, making her jump—'this man shot the arrow that ended his life. I want a name. My mother owes me that.'

Eda stared at the letter at the bottom of the page, trying to put the pieces together. Roul was no killer. He did not go around assassinating kings. He protected them. 'You're sure this is the person who killed him?' Her voice faltered.

Becket took the parchment from her, folded it, and tucked it away. 'It is all there in ink.'

Eda looked over at Roul and found him awake and watching her. His eyebrows came together when he saw her face. She looked away, heart racing. 'What will you do when you find this person?'

He met her gaze. 'I do not know.'

'Everything all right?'

Eda jumped at the sound of Roul's voice above her. She had not seen him get up or heard him walk over.

Woottone's snoring stopped and his eyes opened, taking in the scene before him.

'I'll ready the horses,' Eda said, getting to her feet.

Roul caught her arm as she stepped past him. 'You should eat something first.'

She pulled free, making Becket and Woottone look up. She tried to relax her face. 'I'll eat later.' Then she was walking away again.

It was no surprise that Roul came after her. 'Eda.'

She lengthened her stride, needing to gather her thoughts before facing him. 'I'm just going to relieve myself.'

He broke into a jog to catch up, spinning her around to face him. 'What's going on?'

They were a safe distance from the others now, but she was still not prepared to take the risk. 'I think we should talk about it when we get home.'

He dropped his head, looking her in the eyes. 'If you can't even look at me, then we're going to talk about it now.' He let go of her arm and waited. When she did not speak, he said, 'Eda, it's me.'

It took her a moment to work up the courage to say the

words aloud. 'Prince Becket showed me a letter.' Seeing his confusion, she added, 'A letter you wrote.'

He shook his head. 'What are you talking about? I've never written him a letter.'

'It was a letter you wrote to Queen Fayre.' The words rushed out of her.

His face fell, extinguishing any lingering doubt. 'I see.'

'It said that—'

'I know what it said.' His expression was unreadable. 'How did you know it was from me?'

She swallowed. 'Your mother, she... she showed me one of the letters you wrote her. I recognised the signature. How could you keep something like that from me?'

He rubbed his forehead. 'I couldn't tell you. I couldn't tell *anyone*. That was the agreement. She would've wiped her hands of my family. I kept silent for them.'

Eda felt an unexpected flicker of anger in the pit of her belly. '*Your* family?' She brought her face closer to his and lowered her voice. 'What about *my* family? My family who bore the brunt of your actions? We were locked in that borough and starved. Corpses were piled along every wall.'

Pain flashed in his eyes. 'Do you honestly think I haven't carried the weight of that every day since?'

'You sleep fairly soundly from what I've observed.'

'Because I know if I hadn't done it, then someone else would have. Queen Fayre wasn't just going to call the whole thing off because I told her no. Either way, the king was going to die. So I chose to keep my family protected.'

She took a step back from him and dropped her gaze. 'We can't do this now.' She shook her head, wishing she could shake the knowledge from it completely. 'We have to focus on getting the prince home.' Then, looking up, she said, 'Or perhaps you don't want him to make it back to Chadora.'

His eyes darkened. 'I'm going to pretend you didn't say that.'

She stared back at him, unflinching. 'You could've told *me*.'

'And put a target on your back?' He waved away the suggestion. 'I'm not going to apologise for keeping you out of it.'

They both looked away, taking a moment to calm themselves.

'Let's just get to Chadora,' he said, quieter now. 'Then I'll tell you whatever you want to know.'

She left without saying another word.

CHAPTER 32

Seeing all that betrayal and disappointment in Eda's eyes was a special kind of torture. She rode at the back of the group now, as far away from him as she could manage. She was barely visible through the heavy sheets of rain. Five hours they had been riding, and still not so much as a glance in his direction.

'The horses are going to need a rest soon,' Tatum said, riding up alongside him.

Roul looked over his shoulder to where Eda's horse was throwing its head up, its body angled against the rain. The donkey walked beside her, seemingly unaffected by the weather or the rocky terrain they were navigating. Black-mane's bandage would need changing soon. 'We'll stop when we find some shelter.'

They had exited the forest a few hours earlier, before the rain started again. Now they had no choice but to push through it. Roul prayed the weather would deter anyone in pursuit of them.

'How many miles are we from Chadora at your guess?' Prince Becket called behind him.

Roul was struggling with his sense of direction due to

the thunderous grey clouds blocking the sun. Plus land-marks were barely recognisable in rain that heavy. 'Maybe fifty miles?'

'That sounds like a question.'

'Call it a conservative guess,' Roul replied.

Becket adjusted his soggy cloak. 'So we will not make it before nightfall.'

'No.'

'Another glorious night beneath the stars,' Tatum said.

They reached a hill where a pool of water had formed at the base of the slope. Tatum walked his horse through it first to check its depth, then signalled for the others to follow. They climbed the hill as a group, horses grunting with the effort and their hooves slipping on the mud. Eda's horse appeared to be struggling the most. It was down on its back hocks and sliding. Hadewaye reached for her when the horse began to tilt, but he was too late. The animal landed on its side, Eda managing to free her legs from the stirrups and leap out of the way just in time. She watched helplessly as the horse slid to the bottom of the hill.

Roul dismounted and made his way over to her. 'You all right?'

She nodded, flicking mud off her hands. 'I'm fine.'

Her horse now stood in the middle of the pool at the base of the hill. Alveye went to fetch it.

'Did you hit your head?' Roul asked.

'I told you I'm fine.' She headed off down the slope.

'Let Alveye get your horse,' he called after her.

She turned back. 'Stop! I'm not an infant. Stop fussing.' The cloak of her hood had fallen back. Her hair clung to her face and neck. 'Your concern is too late.'

Alveye, who was now making his way up the hill with her horse, stopped. Everyone else turned to look at Eda, appearing confused.

'Suttone, you've been in a foul mood all morning,' Tatum said. 'What's going on?'

Alveye approached cautiously, handing her the reins of her horse.

'Let's just keep moving before we all drown on this hill,' she said, tugging her horse to get it walking.

Tatum raised a brow. 'What have we missed here?'

Roul closed his eyes. 'Let it go.'

'What did our fearless commander do that has you in such an uptight state?' Tatum pushed.

When Roul opened his eyes, he found Prince Becket staring at him, a stare so piercing it almost knocked him backwards. The prince dismounted on the hill, water gushing over his feet, and made his way towards the commander. Everyone stopped and looked back, wondering what on earth he was doing.

'Your Highness,' Woottone called.

The prince ignored his bodyguard, reaching inside his cloak and pulling out a soggy piece of parchment. He held it up in the air. 'The signature. The *R*. Is it you?' When Roul did not respond, he unfolded it, accidentally tearing it in the process, then shoved it in Roul's face. 'Did you write this?'

Blackmane shifted in the saddle. 'What the hell is going on?'

The prince was no fool. He had put the pieces together easily enough. But all Roul could think about was his family, his agreement with Queen Fayre. He turned his face up to the rain.

'It was,' the prince said, nodding slowly. 'It was you.'

'What's he talking about?' Tatum asked.

Eda's hands went over her face.

'Speak!' Becket shouted.

Roul linked his hands atop his head and looked at him, desperate to speak yet not permitted to confess.

'You traitor,' the prince hissed.

Roul had thought a lot about how this conversation might go. Though he never pictured having it on the side of a hill in the blinding rain while his men bore witness. 'I'm sorry.' An apology was not the same as a confession. Surely he could give the prince that.

Becket's face twisted. He threw the soggy letter at Roul —hard.

Tatum was off his horse then, falling down the hill towards them.

'Do they all know?' Becket asked, water spraying from his lips.

'Know what?' Alveye asked.

Roul shook his head. 'Only Eda. Because of the letter. I couldn't tell a soul without endangering my family.'

Becket ran at him. Roul could have stepped out of the way or drawn his weapon. He could have pled his case. Instead, he stood still. The prince slammed into him, knocking him backwards into the mud. They hit the ground in one unified thud, then began rolling.

'Murderer,' Becket shouted before they splashed into the icy pool at the base of the hill. Water roared in Roul's ears as he was completely submerged. Then he was yanked upright, and a fist collided with his face. Roul's blood sprayed the prince, mixing with the rain.

'You have the audacity to show up at Harlech Castle and pretend to care about my kingdom!'

Roul braced for another punch, but then Eda came between them.

'Stop,' she said, facing Becket. She sat fearlessly in front of his clenched fist. 'He was just a pawn.' She searched his eyes. 'You know what she's like. You know better than anyone.'

The prince did not back down. 'So I am supposed to

ignore the fact that he murdered my father in cold blood and treat him as a victim?'

'Holy shit,' Tatum said slowly.

Eda shook her head. 'No. You'll never forget.'

Becket staggered back, glaring at Roul. Muddy water ran off him as he turned away and exited the pool. Eda exhaled slowly, then followed him.

Roul looked up the hill at the others. Their expressions ranged from shock to utter confusion. No one moved. They were all looking at him, waiting for him to fix the situation.

He climbed out of the water to address the group.

'I'm still your commander. Still responsible for your safety—and the prince's. So whatever you're feeling right now, put it aside. Not forever. Just until we reach Chadora's walls. We still have a job to complete, and we can't do it divided.'

Eda turned away and began walking up the hill. Not only had he broken her trust but her heart. Her family had suffered enormously during the lockdown that resulted from King Oswin's death. But no one could have predicted the aftermath—not even Queen Fayre.

Roul trudged up the hill towards his waiting horse. He passed Alveye on the way. The defender looked down and stepped back.

Snatching up the reins of his horse, Roul climbed the hill.

CHAPTER 33

*I*t was her fault that Prince Becket found out. *Her* fault. He likely would have found out eventually when he confronted his mother, but she had exposed Roul at the worst possible time. They were in rebel territory being pursued by English soldiers, and her careless actions had created a divide so large they were all at risk of falling in.

Woottone was watching Roul like he expected him to come for the prince at any moment. Tatum was watching Woottone like he was expecting him to come at Roul. Blackmane was quieter than his usual level of quiet. Alveye and Hadewaye had detached themselves from the group entirely. They looked heartbroken and understandably torn. They were the *king's* defenders, after all—and Roul was their teacher.

It made for a long and painful afternoon of riding.

The group reached the last forest on their journey a little before sunset. Roul positioned himself at the front and said he wanted to get as much space between the English soldiers and them as possible. No one objected.

They had been riding in the dark for nearly two hours

when Eda got the distinct feeling that they were being watched. She looked over her shoulder at Basil, who was still trailing behind her, then to Tatum, who was at the rear. He gave her a questioning look.

'Something's wrong,' she said.

A creak in the trees above had her looking up. Hadewaye must have heard it also, because he looked up at the same time.

'Talk to me,' Roul said over his shoulder.

Eda searched the branches but could not see a thing. 'I thought I heard some—'

A figure fell from the trees before she could finish, knocking Woottone from his horse. Everyone drew their swords at the same time. Roul swung his horse around and went for Woottone's attacker, but the man rolled beneath the blade. Two more men dropped from the trees. Alveye and Hadewaye were upon them in an instant. Eda's horse reared when more men appeared on either side of them, coming at them with daggers and swords. Eda and Tatum took care of them before they even had a chance to use their weapons.

A few hectic minutes later, the rebels lay dead on the ground. Prince Becket crouched beside his wounded bodyguard. A large cut ran from his shoulder to the base of his neck.

'I need eyes on the trees,' Roul said as he pressed down on the wound to slow the bleeding. 'And medical supplies.'

The defenders dispersed, and Eda returned with what supplies they had.

'Everything's wet,' she said, handing Roul some bandages.

He looked around. 'Who's watching the rear?'

Alveye immediately moved to the back.

Roul selected the driest bandage and began wrapping Woottone's shoulder and neck. 'Anyone else injured?'

'No, Commander' came a chorus of voices.

Becket was staring wide-eyed down at Woottone. 'That is a lot of blood.'

Roul nodded. 'It is.' He looked to Tatum. 'Are we clear?'

'For now.'

'Tie Woottone's horse to mine,' Roul said. 'Get him in the saddle. We need to leave before anyone else arrives.'

Roul and Tatum lifted Woottone onto his horse, and then everyone mounted.

'Let's go!' Roul called.

Eda went to check on Blackmane, but he waved her away.

Roul was waiting next to her horse. She did not object when he insisted on riding at her side.

It was near midnight when they finally stopped. There was no stream to fill their waterskins, but there was shelter beneath the trees. Everyone changed from drenched clothes into damp clothes. No one asked about food because no one had an appetite. Eda replaced Blackmane's bandages, then went to check on Woottone. His dressings were completely soaked through. Eda shared a concerned look with Hadewaye as they packed the wound tightly with the remaining bandages.

'He's freezing,' Becket said, looking worried.

They were all freezing, but it was dangerous for Woottone in his fragile state.

Eda looked over at Basil, who was now lying down. 'Carry him to the donkey.'

'Why?' Roul asked.

'Because it's warm.'

They carried him to the snoozing animal, leaning the bodyguard on him and then covering him with two blankets.

'I'll stay with him,' Eda said. Since taking warmth from Roul was no longer an option, she curled up against Basil instead, tucking her legs against Woottone's as the temperature continued to plummet. He was already asleep, or unconscious. Hopefully asleep.

Basil turned his head to her. 'Thank you,' she whispered, rubbing his head.

The group was silent beneath the trees. The only sound was the horses eating the shrubbery. Eda stared through the dark at Roul. She could not make out his face, but she could feel his eyes on her.

'Eda,' he said.

She blinked. 'Yes?'

'I'll be pleased if the donkey makes it all the way to Chadora.'

Her eyes sank shut, and she drifted off to sleep.

Eda woke to coughing. Her eyelids were heavy as she peeled them open. The fog was so thick she could barely see the bodies huddled against the trunks around her. Another cough. She pushed herself up and looked around, every muscle aching. It was Hadewaye. She reached out to check if Woottone was breathing next to her. He was.

Rising, she made her way over to Hadewaye. Crouching next to him, she saw his face was flushed red and beaded with sweat. She pressed a hand to his forehead. He was burning up.

'What's wrong?' Alveye asked, sitting up.

'He has a fever.'

Hadewaye opened his eyes, which were bloodshot.

'You can't get sick now,' she said with a smile. 'We're nearly home.'

He swallowed, and it looked like it hurt. 'Water.' The word was a croak from his mouth.

Eda looked around for his waterskin. Luckily, he had

some left. She brought it to his mouth so he could drink, and then he closed his eyes again.

Everyone was slowly rousing now, looking worse for wear.

Roul wandered over. 'Was that Hadewaye I heard coughing?'

Eda nodded.

'Will he be able to ride?' Tatum asked.

'We'll tie him to the saddle if we have to,' Roul said. 'See if you can get some food into him.' Then he was off to check on Woottone.

Eda and Alveye gave Hadewaye some torn-up pieces of pork, but he had a lot of difficulty both chewing and swallowing. They tried to get him to his feet, but he could not remain standing without support. Somehow, they had to get him to Chadora.

'He can ride behind me,' Alveye said.

'I weigh the least,' Eda said. 'Put him behind me.'

When everyone was ready to leave, Eda looked back and saw Basil was still lying down. She clicked her tongue. 'Come on, boy. You can't stay here by yourself.'

The donkey got to his feet, extraordinarily vocal about the ordeal.

Blackmane emitted an annoyed growl. 'If the rebels didn't know where we are, they do now.'

'In a few hours we'll exit the forest,' Roul said, addressing the group. 'Then it's open plains all the way to Chadora. We should arrive around noon.' He looked around. 'If anyone needs to stop, speak up. Tatum, you'll ride at the front. Alveye, you'll be our eyes at the back. Since Woottone's injured, I'll ride with Prince Becket.'

'I think it would be more appropriate if someone else rode at my side,' Becket replied.

Roul met his gaze. 'Let's focus on keeping you alive and

worry about what is and isn't appropriate once you're safely inside the walls.'

Roul would do his job until the very end. If he was committed to something, he saw it through. King Oswin being a fine example of that. While the prince sat upon his horse wishing Roul dead, the commander was still prepared to protect him with his life.

Orders were orders.

Hadewaye's head bounced into Eda's back when they began moving. 'Lean against me,' she told him. 'It's better than falling off.'

Coughing ensued, and then his forehead dropped to her shoulder.

It was around an hour later when she felt his head slide. She reached back to catch him before he fell. Roul trotted up beside her, a length of rope in hand. He secured it around Hadewaye's chest, then handed the end to Eda.

'At least this way if he falls, he won't land on his head,' he said before returning to the prince's side.

When the group finally emerged onto the open plains that would lead them to Chadora's walls, they were met with a gap in the clouds and a sliver of blue sky. They all stopped their horses and looked up at it. As if on cue, the sun peeked through, bathing them in light. Eda lifted her face, the illusion of warmth making her smile.

'Can you feel it, Hadewaye?'

His reply came in the form of a cough that rattled his chest.

Eda glanced at Prince Becket. 'What do you think, Your Highness? Is Belenus celebrating the return of our new king?'

'A tad prematurely,' Becket said, walking his horse on.

Roul followed him.

Midway across the plains, they stopped to rest. Eda's

back was aching from holding Hadewaye up, but she did not complain.

The horses grazed while everyone stretched their legs and tended the sick and injured. Woottone had bled through his bandages again, but they were all out of supplies. Seeing the dilemma, Prince Becket began to undress.

'What are you doing?' Woottone asked.

'Literally giving you the shirt off my back,' Becket replied as he tugged it over his head. 'It's wet, but it's clean.' He handed it to Eda.

She gave him an appreciative smile as she took it. 'Kind of you.' She removed the soiled bandages and wrapped the wound with the shirt, tying it as best she could. When she was done, something nudged her elbow. She turned to see Basil standing there. 'Just a few more miles. Then you get to meet our goats.'

'Why do you assume you'll get to keep him?' Tatum asked.

'Where are you going to keep a donkey?'

'Fair point.' As Tatum was mounting, his horse collapsed beneath him. It lay panting on the ground, making no effort to get up. 'Something I said?'

Everyone stared down at the animal.

'Put Woottone, Blackmane, and Hadewaye on the spares,' Roul said, taking charge. 'The rest of us will continue on foot.'

'Nothing wrong with my legs,' Blackmane said, stubborn as always.

Hadewaye appeared to be getting worse by the minute and had to be tied to the saddle. He lay against the horse's neck, eyes closed.

Eda met Roul's eyes across the horse, and she wished with her whole heart that she had never seen that damn letter. But every time she tried to rationalise his actions, her sixteen-year-old self started to scream.

She went to remove the saddle from the horse on the ground, then took hold of the reins, pulling. The horse did not move. She bent to stroke the gelding's face. 'If Basil can do it, you can absolutely do it. No weight means no excuses.'

'Eda,' Roul said quietly. 'We have to go.'

Eda had no choice but to leave the horse behind.

She led Hadewaye and one of the spares towards home, with Basil walking alongside her.

It was over an hour later when Chadora's walls finally came into view, dominating the landscape in front of them. Eda felt both relief and dread. What would happen to Roul when they stepped through that gate? Would Queen Fayre protect him? Eda was not even sure if she could protect herself now that the secret was out.

'Home sweet home,' Becket said, his tone dry.

Apparently she was not the only one with mixed feelings.

The whinny of a distant horse made them all turn. The small hairs on the back of Eda's neck stood up as she watched the horizon for any movement. Perhaps the horse they had left behind had a change of heart.

'How far out do you think that was, Commander?' Alveye asked.

Roul squinted. 'Maybe a mile.'

Becket took a few nervous steps.

Tatum's eyes narrowed on something in the distance. 'Oh shit.'

Eda saw what he was referring to. *Less* than a mile out, a group of around twenty horses appeared, moving at a trot. A dog barked, making Eda flinch. Oh, how she hated to be hunted by dogs.

Roul sprang into action. 'Dump everything that isn't a

weapon. Bags, saddles, all of it. Then get on a horse. If that horse falls down, get on another one. If that one falls, get on someone else's.'

Everyone dashed from horse to horse, releasing girths and shoving saddles and bags to the ground, only leaving them on for Woottone and Hadewaye.

Roul hoisted the prince onto one of the mares, then went to help Blackmane. 'We're about two miles from the wall. Consider this our bolt to the finish line.' He circled back to make sure Eda was on a horse, then went to Hadewaye. 'I'm going to need you to sit up and hold on.'

Hadewaye did not respond, but when Roul sat him up, he stayed there.

'Tatum and Alveye to the back, and bows at the ready,' Roul said as he swung himself up onto one of the remaining horses. 'Suttone, your job is to get Prince Becket to that gate no matter what's happening behind you. And I swear to God, if you wait for that donkey, I'll shoot it myself. Understand?'

Eda retrieved her bow and nodded. 'I understand.'

The dog barked again, more urgent this time.

'That's our cue,' Roul shouted, heels digging into the sides of his mount.

As if sensing the danger, the horses came alive, lifting their heads and flattening their ears as they sped up.

Eda did as she was told, remaining close to Becket while keeping a hold of Hadewaye's horse. The youngest defender was bouncing so hard in the saddle she was sure the rope holding him would snap and he would fall. Woottone just held on to the saddle, trusting his horse would follow the others.

Eda told herself she was not going to look back, but she could not help it. The soldiers had spotted them and were in pursuit now. They knew once they reached the gate it was all over.

266

The distressed bray of a donkey falling behind had Eda facing forwards again.

There was nothing she could do.

The dog was whining excitedly now.

'They're still too far out to shoot,' Roul said. 'Save your arrows.'

Behind her, Alveye's horse tripped, nose diving into the ground. Roul reached for the defender as he went down, swinging him up behind him. Eda tried to block it all out.

Get the prince to the gate.

Do not stop.

No matter what.

But she could not ignore the yelping and the thunderous hooves closing in on them—and they were still a mile from the wall.

Hiss.

The English released their first arrow, but it fell short. Eda waited until they were within range, then turned to shoot. So long as she did not slow or stop, she was not technically disobeying orders.

When they were half a mile out, Blackmane brought his fingers to his mouth, emitting a long whistle to warn the defenders atop the wall of their approach.

An arrow passed between Eda and the prince. Then another. Woottone somehow managed to manoeuvre his horse behind Becket's, shielding him. Eda turned once more and took aim, trying hard to ignore the galloping donkey caught in the crossfire. She hit a soldier through the chest. He toppled backwards off his horse.

A horn sounded from the wall, making the soldiers lower their bows and look up. Ahead, Eda could hear the comforting sound of the portcullis being raised.

They were so close now.

Facing forwards, Eda pushed her horse faster. 'Ha!' Prince Becket's horse lengthened its stride. Another arrow flew past Eda, but she barely noticed it because she was focused only on the gate. Another hundred yards and they would be through it.

But then Hadewaye's horse slowed suddenly, the reins of his horse pulling from her hand. When she looked back, she found Hadewaye hanging from the side of the horse, his feet dragging along the ground. Blackmane veered closer, reaching for the defender with his good arm. But the rope holding Hadewaye snapped, and he tumbled beneath Blackmane's horse.

She was supposed to get the prince to the gate. That was her job. But she could not leave Hadewaye behind.

'Make sure he gets to the gate,' she shouted at Blackmane before swinging her horse around and returning to the motionless defender. Dismounting, she dragged Hadewaye's arm around her shoulders. There was no way she could get him onto the horse alone, so they would have to finish on foot.

'Slow down and shield Suttone!' Roul shouted when he caught sight of her ahead of them.

Eda looked to the gate, relieved when she saw Becket, Woottone, and Blackmane pass through it. 'I need your help,' she told Hadewaye. 'I need you to run.'

His movements were sloppy but helpful.

The English soldiers pulled their horses up just out of reach of the arrows pointed at them from atop the wall, which meant the fight remained between those on the ground. Eda and Hadewaye were twenty yards from the gate when he fell, causing them both to go down. She was straight back up on her feet, dragging him forwards. Blackmane appeared, taking his other arm and wincing as he lifted the defender off the ground. Then they were running for the gate, then through it. *Alive.* Alive with no arrows in their backs. Eda lowered Hadewaye to the ground and turned back to make sure the others were behind her.

They were not.

'Turn around now and we'll let you live,' Roul shouted, competing with the barking dog. 'You can return to Harlech Castle and tell Lord Roger the good news. Prince Becket is safely home. Or you shoot us, and a hundred defenders on fresh horses, with superior aim, will hunt you down.'

The soldiers lowered their bows and silenced the dog, defeated and exhausted from their efforts. The three defenders turned their horses and cantered for the gate. As soon as they rode beneath the archway, the portcullis began to lower.

'Wait!' Eda called up to the defenders above her. 'Hold the gate.'

The gate continued to lower.

Eda watched Basil trot towards her, braying. Roul caught Eda around the waist and dragged her back from the gate as she went to duck below it. 'Wait!' she pleaded.

The gate shuddered to a standstill, and Basil came to a stop a few yards away, ears flicking back and forth as he realised he had been shut out.

Roul let go of Eda.

She turned to him. '*Please.*'

Cursing loudly, Roul looked up and shouted, 'Let the animal through!'

The portcullis rose once more, and a moment later, an utterly exhausted and completely chuffed donkey walked through.

They had made it—everyone. Relief gripped her in dizzying waves, and she bent to hold her knees. But the relief was short-lived.

'I want Commander Thornton taken into custody,' Prince Becket said behind her.

Eda straightened and looked at him, nausea rolling through her. For a moment, no one moved. Not even the defender whom Becket had given the order to.

'I trust you will go without a scene?' the prince asked.

Roul nodded slowly. 'Yes.'

Tatum and Alveye stared at their feet. Blackmane turned away, kicking the ground.

'Your Highness—' Eda started, stepping forwards.

'Go home to your family,' Roul said, stopping her before she could say anything more. 'They're waiting for you.'

CHAPTER 34

*R*oul was placed in the tower while Prince Becket went to reunite with his mother. He had been in his cell around thirty minutes when he heard someone climbing the steps.

Harlan emerged, eyes landing on him. 'You killed the fucking king?'

That was one way to start the conversation.

He marched over to the cell door, eyes ablaze. 'Tell me I'm wrong.'

Roul pushed off the wall and walked closer. 'You're not wrong.'

Harlan punched the bars, then reached through them, grabbing him by the front of his tunic. 'Look me in the eyes and tell me you shot King Oswin, then stayed silent while Blake and her family were starving to death waiting for the killer to reveal themselves.'

Roul did not struggle. He looked Harlan directly in the eyes when he said, 'I killed the king. I remained silent.'

Harlan released him with a shove. 'Never in my life would I imagine a time that I would call you a coward, but that's what you are.' He began pacing, eyes trained on Roul. 'I can't even make sense of it.'

There was so much he did not know. 'Who told you?'

'Tatum. For some reason I can't fathom, he wants me to save your arse. I'm going to need you to start talking. Is this the reason you came to Chadora?'

Roul resigned himself to the fact that the secret was well and truly out. Enough people knew now that one more was not going to make a difference. 'Queen Fayre sent me.'

'Of course she did.' Harlan shook his head. 'She loves getting peasants with no options to do her dirty work. Go on.'

'She wanted information. In exchange for taking care of my family.'

Harlan stopped walking as the pieces came together. 'Well, that escalated.' He ran a hand down his face. 'Shit. It's really hard to hate you when she has your family hostage.'

Roul stared at the bars between them. 'It wasn't all threats, if I'm being honest.' He raised his eyes. 'She also had a plan to fix this place. I just needed to stay quiet long enough for her to get here.' Roul looked down at the piss-stained floor. 'King Oswin was a terrible, terrible king. Everyone was suffering under his rule. Every defender I knew resented what was being asked of them.' He closed his eyes. 'Perhaps there was a moment there that I thought my actions heroic. If I'd known what Borin would do…'

Harlan walked over to the wall opposite and leaned his back on it. 'Well, she did what she said she would, I'll give her that.'

'I wrote to her, during the lockdown. I told her it was dire here, that it was time to put an end to the insanity. I said I would confess and say nothing of her part.' Roul swallowed. 'She told me to sit tight, that my family was waiting for me to return, that she was coming, that my confession would jeopardise the king's trust in his army and further fragment the kingdom. So I waited.'

Harlan watched him a moment. 'You could've come to me.'

'I couldn't. You know I couldn't.'

Harlan exhaled and looked up at the roof. 'I can't believe Prince Becket didn't kill you on that journey home.'

'Me neither.'

'I suspect Eda and your men would've protected you if he'd tried. They're extremely loyal to you.'

'They're good people. They don't deserve to be in this position.'

Harlan watched him. 'Are you sorry you did it?'

The question Roul had wrestled with since it happened. 'Some days. Then there are other days...' He looked away. 'I think about now versus then. Now is better.'

Harlan nodded. 'Now *is* better.'

More footsteps on the stairwell made them both turn their heads. The warden appeared this time, the grimace on his face suggesting he had been brought up-to-date.

'Prince Becket and Queen Fayre want to speak with you.' He glanced at Harlan. 'You can escort him, but you stay out of it. Am I clear?'

Harlan nodded and went to fetch the keys. 'Yes, sir.'

Queen Fayre and Prince Becket stood side by side in the throne room. Roul might have thought they were presenting as a unified front if there had not been such a large gap between them.

'Good work, Commander Thornton,' Queen Fayre said. 'You did splendidly under very difficult conditions.' She glanced in the direction of Harlan and the other guards. 'Leave us, please.'

They did as commanded, and then it was just the three of them left in the room.

'It has come to my attention that certain revelations were made during this journey, stemming from a stolen letter,' Queen Fayre began, glancing at her son. 'Given the nature of these revelations, I am very impressed that you did not let these things impact your work.' She paused. 'The truth is, it might have solved some of your personal problems had my son not made it back at all.'

Becket stared hard at the ground in front of him.

'I can see why my son might think me a criminal without proper context,' she went on. 'However, I believe in time he will come to understand why I did it. It is not about a few individuals but the population as a whole.' She paused for effect. 'This is not an easy notion to digest, as you well know.'

The prince looked to the window. 'Perhaps you should get to the point, Mother.'

'What point is that?' Roul asked.

Becket's gaze snapped to him. 'The main point. That you are a traitor and a murderer. I intend to stay in Chadora. I will accept the crown. And while I am forced to tolerate my mother's presence at court, for the health of this kingdom, I will not tolerate yours. In fact, I will not tolerate it anywhere.'

Roul gave a small nod. 'I understand.'

'I hereby strip you of your title, your position, and banish you from Chadora.'

Queen Fayre looked heavenward. 'That is a rather dramatic way of saying that you shall be returning to your family in Carno earlier than planned.' She gave him a small smile. 'I think this arrangement will suit everybody.'

He was going home. It really was the best possible outcome. An early reunion with his family. It was more of a reward than anything. Queen Fayre had come through for him.

'And we shall continue to provide for you and your family for as long as you need it,' she added.

What more could he possibly ask for? To want Eda on top of that was just greedy. But he wanted her anyway.

'You know, a little appreciation for sparing your life would not be misplaced right now,' Becket said, glaring in Roul's direction.

Roul gave a small bow. 'Thank you, Your Highness. Your Majesty.'

'Commander Wright,' Queen Fayre called.

Harlan entered the room. 'Your Majesty?'

'Provide Thornton with a horse and adequate weapons for his journey, along with any other supplies he needs.'

Harlan's eyebrows rose. 'Where's he going?'

'To Carno,' Roul said, trying to keep the devastation out of his voice. 'I'm going home to my family.'

CHAPTER 35

'Lyndal had her baby the day you left,' Blake said.

'Oh.' It was wonderful news. *What did she have?*

Blake frowned. 'You're signing again.'

'Sorry.'

'A boy.'

Eda smiled. 'I can't wait to meet him.' She leaned on the stall door to watch Basil eat.

'Mother will be home before dinner.'

'Good.'

'And Luella's asleep.'

A nod. 'All right.'

Blake reached up and scratched at a piece of the wall. 'So are we going to talk about the fact that Roul is locked in the tower, or should I wait until Harlan gets home and ask him for the details?'

'I'm not sure I'm allowed to talk about it.'

Blake angled her head. 'Eda.'

She faced her sister. Then, drawing a breath, she told Blake the entire story, only leaving out the part where they had slept together at Harlech Castle. It was not relevant.

When she was finished, Blake stood in silence for a long time.

'I can't even imagine being in that position, knowing Queen Fayre could dispose of your entire family on a whim.'

Eda blinked. 'Did you hear the part where I said he *killed* King Oswin?'

Blake crossed her arms. 'How many times did we stand in that square wishing him dead? How many times did we feel sick to our stomach at the things the defenders did to us? The things they were ordered to do. Now you want to be angry at the one man who did something about it?'

The response was not what Eda had been expecting at all. Blake was supposed to join her in her heartbreak and outrage, not pity him. 'You don't even look surprised.'

'I'm not. He's not one to stand idle, as you well know.'

'But he'll happily stand silent. Have you forgotten the aftermath that followed? All he had to do was raise his hand, confess, and all the suffering would've come to an end.'

Blake's eyebrows came together. 'Is that what you believe? That if Roul had confessed, all the suffering would've ended?'

Eda did not reply.

'The merchants suffered under King Borin's rule long after the port gate was opened,' Blake said. 'Those deaths that occurred in the aftermath, when we were caged in like dogs, they do not fall on Roul's shoulders. Those fall squarely on King Borin.' There was a bitter edge to her tone when she said that last part. 'No one, *no one* could've imagined the drastic measures he would take.'

Eda reminded herself to breathe. 'So you think he did the right thing?'

'The right thing for whom? It's not as straightforward as you're making it sound. Have you forgotten what

277

happened with Lyndal? If there's one thing we all learned from that experience, it's that Queen Fayre is always in control. The only reason Lyndal escaped her clutches was because Borin died. She still has control of Roul's family.'

Eda thought back to all the horrible things she had said to him during that journey home. She had made him feel unlovable, his actions unforgivable.

'I love you,' Blake said, 'but you can be very black-and-white sometimes. We all wished King Oswin dead. We all thought his death would solve our problems. Many people stood by while we were locked in that borough. Harlan could've opened that gate. Or Astin. But then what? At least Roul acted with a plan.' She eyed her sister. 'And don't forget that he was the first defender to stand beside Harlan when Borin trapped us in the square like fish in a net and began shooting at us.'

Eda closed her eyes at the memory.

'Tell me one thing,' Blake said.

Eda waited.

'If you were in his position, if that was *us*, and you were the only person who could keep us alive and fed, where would you draw the line?'

There was no line. There was nothing she would not do for her family.

'How many people died at your hand on the other side of that wall?' Blake continued, cutting deeper still. 'How many fathers, brothers, and sons did you take from families?'

Eda held the stall door for balance as the face of the young boy she had killed flashed in her mind.

'I say this not to make you feel guilty but to point out that good people do questionable things all the time. We're all just doing the best we can with the hand we've been dealt.'

'Hello?' came Lyndal's familiar voice. 'Where is everyone?'

Blake pulled Eda into her arms. 'I'm proud of you, by the way, in case I forgot to say it earlier. You brought us a king.' She released her. 'Now go meet your nephew. Then we'll sit down and make a plan to get Roul out of that tower.'

Lyndal appeared in the doorway of the stables, eyes widening when she saw Eda standing there. 'You're home!'

Eda went to her sister, kissing her face twice before turning her attention to the sleeping bundle in her arms. She ran her hand over the light covering of blond hair. 'He's absolutely perfect.'

'Of course he's perfect. I birthed him.'

Eda ignored that comment. 'What did you name him?'

'Easton. After Astin's father.' Lyndal looked Eda up and down. 'Oh. Did you just arrive?'

'Do I look that bad?'

'You really do.'

A bray sounded from the other end of the stables. Both Lyndal and the baby jumped.

'Was that a donkey?' Lyndal asked, looking alarmed.

'A long story,' Blake said, wandering closer. 'Among *other* long stories.'

Lyndal's face fell. 'Did you get the prince? Wait. Did someone die?' She sucked in a breath. 'Did Thornton die?'

'We got the prince,' Eda said.

Blake clicked her tongue. 'And Thornton's locked in the tower.'

'The tower?' Lyndal let out a strained laugh. 'Whatever for?'

'The murder of King Oswin,' Blake and Eda replied at the same time.

The colour drained from Lyndal's face. '*What?*'

Blake ushered both sisters towards the house. 'We're

going to put Eda in the tub with some soap, and then I'll explain everything.'

~

'If it were up to me, you would have been drawn and quartered,' Shapur said before turning on his heel.

Those were the last words Roul heard from Shapur Wright's mouth as he stood in his soon-to-be former room in the barracks. He did not take it personally. The warden had been loyal to King Oswin to the end. Well, almost to the end.

Roul glanced at Harlan, who was waiting to escort him to the gate. 'I'm going to miss him.'

Harlan's lips twitched. 'That's just his odd way of dealing with emotional situations.'

'Yes, I'm sure that's it.'

Roul had washed and changed into civilian clothes, leaving his uniform items in a pile at the end of his bed. He picked up the bag he had packed and adjusted his sword.

'Ready?' Harlan asked.

He was as ready as he was going to get. Nodding, he exited the room.

They headed out into the drizzle, where Roul found Tatum and Alveye waiting for him. It was clear by their expressions that they had heard the news.

'It's true, then?' Alveye said. 'You're leaving?'

Roul nodded. 'It was always the plan. This is just a bit sooner than expected.'

Tatum ran a finger down his nose. 'Doesn't seem fair that she remains in that castle while you're banished to the wastelands.'

'Those wastelands are my home. My family's there. There are worse places they could send me.'

The group wandered to the infirmary so Roul could say

goodbye to Blackmane and Hadewaye. Blackmane was sitting up in bed, complaining that he did not need to be there, and Hadewaye was asleep. Roul let him rest.

'At least he let you keep your head,' Blackmane said, tired eyes on him.

A nod. 'There's that.' He squeezed the defender's good shoulder. 'You keep out of trouble.'

Blackmane nodded. 'You too.'

As they were leaving, Roul stopped by Woottone's bed. He was sitting up, eating, his wound stitched and properly bandaged. There was colour back in his face.

'You rest up,' Roul said. 'You've got a king to protect.'

Woottone's brow furrowed. 'For what it's worth, your departure is our loss.'

Roul gave him a faint smile before leaving the infirmary. 'I'd like to go by the port, if that's all right,' he said to Harlan once they were outside. 'After we collect our horses.'

Harlan did not ask why. 'All right.'

It was late afternoon, and the port was slow moving. There were no ships docked, only a handful of small boats and fisherman wandering about. Roul found Hildred leaning against a veranda post, getting some fresh air. The noise from inside spilled out through the open window behind her.

Her face lit up when she saw him, then faded when she saw his face. She hugged herself against the cold wind.

'You're back,' she said.

He stopped six feet away. 'Not staying, I'm afraid. I came to tell you that I'm heading over the wall for good this time. I'm going home.'

She did not seem too surprised. 'I don't suppose you're here to ask me to go with you?'

He looked down. 'That was never the plan.'

'I know.'

'I'm sorry.'

'I know.' She drew a long breath and looked over at the boats. 'You always said you would leave. I guess I was hoping you would change your mind.' She gave him a sad smile. 'You know, I saw you on the beach the day you brought the recruits down to swim. The others left, but you waited for her to finish.'

Her. She was talking about Eda. 'It's my responsibility to make sure everyone makes it safely out of the water.'

Hildred crinkled her nose. 'I saw the way you watched her, the way you talked. Everything made sense then.'

He did not deny any of it. 'Well, she's not coming with me either.'

'Bet you wish she was though.' Hildred pushed off the post she was leaning on. 'Safe travels, defender. Maybe I'll see you back in our port one day.' With that, she turned and went inside the tavern.

Roul returned to Harlan and the horses.

'Where to now?' Harlan asked as they climbed. 'Wright House?'

Roul looked out at the water, breathing deeply. It would be a long time before he saw the sea again. 'I don't think that's a good idea.'

'You're not going to say goodbye?'

'It won't end well.'

'Because Eda will scale the royal borough wall and demand an audience with our new king?'

'Or worse.' He nudged his horse forwards. 'She'll say she's coming with me—and she'll mean it.' He shook his head. 'Better that she's angry at me for leaving.'

Harlan nodded. 'Did something happen between the two of you over the wall?'

Something life-changing. He had fallen in love. Or perhaps the correct term was deeper in love, because he had loved her long before then.

'Yes, something happened.'

~

Eda rehearsed all the things she was going to say to Prince Becket while she dressed. If all went well, Roul would be out of the tower before dark. Roul was a good man, the best kind, and Prince Becket knew it. He was simply too blinded by his anger to see it.

She heard Luella stirring in the next room. Taking a final look in the mirror, she went next door to fetch her niece from her bed. A wide grin spread across the infant's face when Eda appeared above her.

'Yes, you remember me. Your favourite aunt.' She picked Luella up and placed her on her hip, then headed downstairs. 'Let's go find your mama.'

It was time to act. Eda would not stand idle while Roul was unjustly disciplined—especially when she was the reason the secret got leaked to begin with. She would go to the castle and plead Roul's case on his behalf.

As she reached the top of the stairs, she heard people speaking below. She recognised Astin's voice and froze midstep when she heard him say, 'Harlan's escorting him there now.'

Lyndal, Blake, and Astin gathered near the front door, talking quietly.

Lyndal bit her lip. 'I feel like we should tell her. She'll never forgive us if we wait.'

'Tell who what?' Eda asked.

They all turned in her direction, looking suitably guilty.

'Well, I guess that answers that question,' Astin muttered.

An uneasy feeling grew in Eda's belly as she looked between them. 'Are you talking about Roul? Did they release him?'

Blake walked over and took Luella from her, which only made Eda more nervous. 'Can someone please start talking?'

Luella started to cry, and Blake bounced her. 'He's going home.'

Eda thought she must have misheard due to the noise. 'What?'

'Thornton is going home, to Carno.'

There was sympathy in Blake's voice, which irritated Eda. 'What do you mean, he's going home? He can't. He's not allowed. The minimum length of serv—'

'Prince Becket banished him,' Astin said quietly.

Eda blinked. 'Who told you that?' The pity on his face was unbearable. '*Who?*'

'Our paths crossed on my way here.'

She was having trouble comprehending. That was what came of being sleep-deprived for days on end. 'He told you that?'

'Yes.'

Roul had told Astin he was going home. He had said those words. She laughed, despite nothing being funny. 'He's leaving now? He's going to travel at night?' When no one spoke, she said, 'He wouldn't just leave without telling me.' Because that would break her, shatter her heart into shards so small they would be carried away by the slightest breeze.

'He didn't want to upset you further or risk you doing something rash,' Lyndal said, not quite meeting her eyes.

Eda took an involuntary step back. 'He thought *not* coming was better?'

Her stomach twisted, and her heart...

She could not be walled inside this kingdom without him. That was not a life. That was a sentence. Who would she laugh with? Play with? It would be half a life. 'How long ago did you see them?'

'Eda,' Blake warned.

She did not wait for a response. It was too urgent. Astin's horse was still tethered out front, so she ran for the door.

'Eda, wait!' Lyndal called after her.

There was not a chance in hell Eda was going to wait even one moment. She was out the door and running for Astin's horse in the next breath. Untying the reins, she sprang up into the saddle and galloped away from the house.

She did not have a plan as such, only knew she had to reach him. Then they could make a plan together like he promised.

'We'll figure it out.'

That was what he said. All their secrets were out in the open now. There was no need for them to quarrel about anything ever again. At least nothing as big as assassinating a king.

She was almost at the north gate when her horse began to tire. She pushed the animal through it, knowing she was nearly there. Up ahead, she heard the sound of the gate closing. Not opening—*closing*. She pushed the horse faster still.

Finally, she spotted Harlan. He was facing the gate, the one Roul had just passed through. He looked in her direction, and she saw the same irritating pity that had been all over Astin's face.

'Open the gate!' she shouted. 'Open it!'

Harlan moved his horse into her path, forcing her to pull up. Undeterred, she leapt from the saddle and dashed past him, running towards the portcullis. She glimpsed Roul through it, about fifty yards away.

'Roul!'

He whipped his head around when he heard her, and his horse came to a stop. The defender at the gate caught her as she flew past him. Panic reared inside her, and she struggled violently. 'Open it! Open the gate!'

Harlan appeared, taking her from him. 'I've got her.'

Eda kicked him in the leg, then snatched his sword from its sheath with absolutely no idea what she planned to do with it next. But this was not Harlan's first dance. He had her face down in the mud and disarmed before she could utter a plea.

'You know how this goes,' he said. 'When you're calm, I'll release you.'

She continued to thrash beneath him, head turned towards the gate. *Come back. Please.*

Only when she heard Roul's horse coming at a canter did she still.

'You finished?' Harlan asked, easing the pressure of his knee off her back.

She nodded. 'Yes.'

Slowly, she got to her feet, arms raised to show she was in control of herself. 'Permission to approach the gate.' Her voice shook.

Harlan exhaled and nodded.

Eda rushed to the gate, where Roul had dismounted and was waiting for her. She slipped her hand through the latticed wood, reaching for him, but Roul had stopped just out of reach.

'Are you trying to get yourself locked up?' he said, glancing down at her muddied dress.

Realising he was not coming any closer, she withdrew her arm. 'Why would you leave without coming to me?'

'You know why.'

'Because of the things I said? I didn't mean them. I'm sorry. I understand why you did what you did. Forget about it—everything. Just come back inside.'

The pain in his eyes struck her chest like an arrow. 'Everything you said... You were right. You deserve better.'

She was gripping the gate with both hands. 'What are you talking about? I'm a complete mess. A delinquent—'

'I happen to like that about you.'

She pressed her forehead to the wood, feeling him slipping away. 'Don't go.'

'Prince Becket wants me gone.'

'I'll speak to him.'

He shook his head.

'He'll listen to me.'

He dropped his gaze.

'Then I'll come with you,' she said, almost brightly, like she was suggesting a picnic.

He took a step back from her words, from *her*. 'This is why I didn't come to the house. You can't come with me. Your family is here.'

'You're my family too.' Her eyes burned.

'You would never see them again. Never. Your niece, your new nephew. They would be forced to grow up without you.'

She slapped the gate. 'If you leave, *I'll* be forced to grow up without *you*.'

He gave her a sad smile. 'I can't take you from them, not like this. They would never forgive me—nor should they. And you'd grow to resent me.'

'It's my choice.' Her voice broke. 'If the alternative is a life without you, then this is better.' She turned to the defender on duty. 'Open the gate. I'm going with him.'

'Don't open the gate,' Roul said.

Her breaths were coming faster now. 'Please.'

'Please what?' He walked right up to the gate, and she met him there, reaching through the wood once more. This time he took hold of both her hands, squeezing tightly. 'Please *what*? Please ruin your life? Break the hearts of your family? Take you to a dangerous place so you can live out your days worse off?'

287

The burning gave way to tears. It was mortifying, but she could do nothing to stop them.

He brought his face close to hers. 'I love you,' he whispered. 'I mean, I *really* love you. It's the only reason I'm able to walk away, knowing it's what's best for *you*.'

Her eyes searched his. 'What if you're what's best for me?'

'You can't possibly believe that.' He let go of her hands and stepped back. 'I'm the reason you almost died locked in that borough, remember?'

She shook her head, eyes pleading and words not coming.

Then he did the unthinkable.

He turned away, returned to his horse, and left.

CHAPTER 36

*R*oul expected to die on the journey home. Not only because he was a sole traveller riding a piece of food but because his mind could barely form a coherent thought. He doubted his ability to pull off a clever escape if he were attacked. But somehow, either by God's grace or pure luck, he slipped by the rebels without incident and arrived in Carno still riding his horse.

Next thing he knew, he was standing out front of his family home, his sisters' arms wrapped around him and his mother crying nearby. His father's grin was as wide as a plate.

'We weren't sure we'd ever see you again,' Wilona said, brushing tears from her cheeks.

Roul wanted to match their joy and share in their relief, but he felt only hollow and misplaced.

'You must be exhausted after such a long journey—and so soon,' his mother said, interpreting his silence as fatigue. 'Let's get some food into you, then let you rest.'

He was exhausted. And he was hungry. He was also hoping to high hell that he had done the right thing in leaving Eda behind at that gate. She never cried, and the image of her tear-stained face had been his constant companion for the duration of the journey.

'*Please*,' she had begged. *Begged*.

Walking away was the hardest thing he had ever done in his life.

'Did the prince make it safely to Eldon Castle?' Lana asked as they gathered around the table.

'Yes. He'll take his place as king.'

Clive appeared pleased by that news. 'Good. He seems like he has a decent head on his shoulders.'

'What of Blackmane?' Odella asked, playing with the ends of her hair. 'Did he survive the journey?'

'He did. Woottone was injured and Hadewaye fell ill, but everyone made it.'

His mother reached across the table and took his hand. 'How long are you staying this time?'

The next words from his mouth should have been the easiest, most joyful ones to say to his family, yet they stuck in his throat. 'I'm back for good.'

Tears of joy ensued around the table. His father clapped him on the shoulder as if he had earned his freedom through sacrifice and hard work. In a way he had. His mother rose from her seat to hug him. One day, he would tell them everything, but for now he let them enjoy this moment. They deserved it.

'I'd hoped Eda might return with you,' Wilona said as she took her seat. 'You two seemed smitten. I'm not usually wrong about these things.'

He had not been ready to hear her name aloud, so it took him a moment to reply. 'Eda belongs with her family.'

His mother gave him a sympathetic, knowing smile.

'But you love her,' Lana said, eyes wide. 'I saw it. We all did. And she loves you back.'

The fatigue was really hitting him now. 'That's not a good enough reason to ruin her life.'

Odella scowled at him. 'Ruin her life? Are we so far below her standard of living?'

Wilona was on her feet again. 'I think that's enough questions for now. We must let your brother wash up before he falls asleep at the table.'

Roul hated himself for making his family feel less in any way. 'I'm sorry,' he said as he rose. 'That came out wrong.'

His mother waved the apology away. 'Your sisters know you're tired.'

The girls forced a smile before looking down at the table.

Eda. Her name sounded repeatedly in his mind as he was ushered through to the next room. *Eda, I'm so sorry.*

CHAPTER 37

'Rise and shine,' Blake said, flinging the curtains open.

Eda turned her face away from the light. 'Close them.'

'Not a chance.' Blake walked over and sat on the bed. 'It's been three days. Time to pull yourself together. Queen Fayre has requested an audience with you, and Uncle is chomping at the bit to take you to Eldon Castle so he can take full credit for all you've done.'

Eda groaned. 'Why would you wake me for such terrible reasons? I don't want to go to the castle. I've no interest in seeing Queen Fayre, and the last person I want to see is our uncle.'

Blake bit her lip. 'What if I told you he's downstairs waiting for you?'

'Then I'd ask you to kindly hold this pillow over my head until I suffocate.'

Blake tugged the pillow out from beneath her and threw it. When Eda still did not move, she brushed the hair back from her sister's face. 'You must get up and keep going. It's what we merchants do.'

Eda met her sister's eyes. 'Can't you just wake me when he returns?'

Blake did not have to ask who "he" was. Rising, she said, 'I'll pick out a dress for you.'

'I want to wear trousers,' Eda said, sounding like a five-year-old.

'I know you do.' Blake examined the dresses hanging in the wardrobe. 'But it's time to pack away your pants and put on your big girl dress.' She tugged a garment from a hanger. 'Up—now.'

It took twenty painful minutes for Blake to comb the knots from Eda's hair. Then she was stuffed into a dress and pushed down the stairs to where her uncle was pacing. Candace was standing by the fireplace, looking thoroughly uncomfortable in his presence.

'Is that what you are wearing?' Thomas asked when he spotted her. 'I specifically said something fit for the occasion.'

Candace gave Eda a reassuring smile. 'It is perfectly adequate.'

'She is representing the entire family,' Thomas went on. 'She should give thought to that each time she dresses.' He was at the door now, waving her through it.

'Good to see you too, Uncle,' Eda said as she walked by him.

He scowled in place of words.

'No need to be nervous,' Candace said, following them. 'I am sure Queen Fayre is simply keen to thank you for your part.'

Eda looked over her shoulder as she headed for the waiting carriage. 'I'm not nervous. I'll see you later.' She ignored the offer of the driver's hand and climbed in, sitting backwards because she knew her uncle always insisted on travelling forwards. Thomas climbed in after her, and then the carriage rolled away.

Her uncle spoke incessantly the entire journey, telling her to remember this, remember that. Do not say this, and most definitely do not say that. This is an opportunity to... something or other.

Eda stared out of the window and let the words blow past her. She had no interest in his agenda. He could say and ask for whatever he wanted.

Eda focused on the landmarks they passed, each one bringing up a memory of Roul. He was everywhere. In every form. Serious Roul. Silent and broody Roul. Disapproving Roul. Grinning Roul. That image hit the hardest. Oh, how she loved to make him smile.

'If you have any questions, ask them now,' Thomas asked as the carriage rolled to a stop out front of Eldon Castle.

She shook her head. 'No questions.'

A servant led them inside, along the familiar corridors Eda had grown to resent during the time she spent there. Unsurprisingly, Queen Fayre was on the terrace, her favourite place. It was still a beautiful space with its trellis walkways and arbours, neatly trimmed hedges and colourful plants. There was one difference though. The birds that had once hung in cages along the wall were now gone. Some merchants had claimed seeing colourful birds the size of eagles flying free in the sky. The thought warmed Eda.

Queen Fayre was playing chess with a lady companion. When they were announced, she dismissed her opponent.

'Your Majesty,' Thomas said, bowing. 'Thank you for the invitation.'

Eda curtsied. 'Your Majesty.'

'It was rather a long wait for you to get here,' Fayre said. 'However, Commander Wright tells me Ms Suttone has been recovering from the journey.' She focused on Eda.

'My son speaks very highly of you, of your bravery and level head.'

'That's the first time anyone has described me as having a level head. I must remember to thank him.'

Queen Fayre's eyes shone with amusement. 'So, young lady, you wanted to see what was on the other side of the wall. What did you discover?'

It was a good question. 'That there's suffering on both sides. There's no escaping this famine.'

Thomas's face fell slightly. 'What my niece means is—'

'I know what she means, Lord Thomas. I do not require a translator, thank you.' Her eyes returned to Eda. 'Well, I am pleased that everyone made it home safely.' She paused. 'You have likely heard that Commander Thornton has returned home to his family, a gesture of the prince's appreciation.'

So that was the narrative they were going with. 'I am aware of the fact, yes.'

Queen Fayre folded her hands in her lap. 'I would like to express my appreciation to you also. The mission was your idea, and you brought me my son. So how can I repay you?'

Thomas cleared his throat. 'If I may—'

'In a moment. The question is for your niece, who risked her life and fought bravely on your behalf.'

It was the first time Eda had come close to smiling since Roul's departure. This was the moment she was supposed to rattle off the list of requests her uncle had briefed her on during their journey. 'I would really like to see Commander Thornton again. Perhaps you could personally invite him back.'

Queen Fayre lifted her chin. 'I think Thornton will be keen to spend time with his family after being away from them for so long.'

Eda ignored the warning in her uncle's eyes. 'When he tires of them, then.'

Fayre looked down at her lap. 'I understand the two of you are friends. You must miss him.'

Eda swallowed. 'Very much.'

A knowing look came over the queen. 'Perhaps you are also in love with him.'

The way she said it made it sound so small and insignificant when in fact the love she felt for Roul paced inside her like a wild beast.

'A young girl's infatuation,' Thomas said.

Eda pressed her eyes shut.

'Whatever feelings my niece has for the commander must be put aside as we ready her for marriage,' Thomas continued.

Eda bit her tongue.

Fayre stifled a sigh. 'It sounds as though you have a request, Lord Thomas. Go on.'

He ran a hand down his tunic. 'I thought you might be able to assist in finding Eda a suitor. I understand you have connections in Toryn.'

Eda's gaze snapped to him. *Toryn? Perhaps I should have listened to him on the way to the castle.*

'A Toryn suitor?' Queen Fayre regarded him coolly. 'And what is it you hope to gain from such a match?'

'My niece has a very adventurous soul, as you well know. I think she would be happy there. Second to her happiness, connections outside Chadora's walls are useful for business.'

'Second to her happiness'? Just how big a fool did he take Queen Fayre for? Eda tried not to be sick. 'I don't want to go to Toryn.' She could not stand quiet while her uncle dispatched her to lands afar.

Thomas rocked on his feet and cleared his throat. 'Well,

you cannot remain a burden to your family forever. We all wish to see you settled.'

'And happy,' Fayre added, tilting her head.

He nodded. 'As I said before.'

Eda took a step towards the queen. 'Or perhaps you have need for me in your army. I've surely proven myself by now.'

'Be silent,' Thomas said.

The queen mother raised a hand, gesturing for calm.

Before anyone could utter another word, Prince Becket strode out onto the terrace. He looked from Eda to her uncle as he walked. 'Ms Suttone. Lord Thomas.'

'Your Highness.'

Becket went to stand beside his mother. 'What are we discussing?'

'A suitor for Ms Suttone,' Fayre said. 'Lord Thomas is keen to see her settled and happy.' Her eyes shone with mischief. 'He thinks a Toryn suitor might be the best option for her.'

Becket looked to Eda. 'Is that your wish, Ms Suttone? To settle down?'

He knew very well that it was not her wish. 'Actually, I was just telling Queen Fayre that I would prefer to be useful here in Chadora. Perhaps serve in your army.'

'Being a wife is useful,' Thomas said.

Becket nodded. 'That is true. Wives play an important role in any household.'

Eda's heart sank.

'But finding suitable men nowadays can be a tedious task,' Becket said, looking to his mother. 'Can it not?'

'Very tedious. Such arrangements can take months.'

Becket turned to Thomas. 'Perhaps we can find something useful for your niece to do while we wait.' His gaze met Eda's. 'I am sure Commander Wright would happily find a position for you atop the wall. Is that useful enough for you?'

He was gifting her time. 'Yes. Thank you, Your Highness.'

Thomas's jaw tightened. 'Will such a thing not work against her? No sane lord is going to take on an armed wife.'

'A lord?' Becket's eyebrows rose. 'You must *really* care about her happiness if you are aiming to make her a lady.'

Eda looked down so no one would see her lips twitch.

'You shall be paid the same wage as the other first-year defenders,' Becket went on. 'We would not wish you to be a financial burden on your family while we wait.' He winked at Eda, then turned his attention back to Thomas. 'I trust you will be attending my coronation next week, Lord Thomas.'

That seemed to cheer her uncle up. 'A true honour.'

'And you, Ms Suttone?'

She smiled. 'I wouldn't miss it for the world, Your Highness.'

CHAPTER 38

*W*ilona came to a stop a safe distance from her son. 'If you keep chopping wood at this rate, there will be no forest left.'

Roul rested his axe on the ground and wiped his brow. 'You'll thank me come winter.'

That made his mother laugh. 'Winter? What is winter nowadays when there's snow on the mountains all year round?' She studied him a moment. 'You've been home nearly a month. When are you going to slow down?'

'This is slowing down.'

Wilona exhaled. 'You're not a defender anymore. You don't have to get up before the sun and punish your body for hours on end before you take your first bite of food for the day. You're allowed to sit, rest, *sleep*.'

Sleep was a problem. He could only manage a few hours at a time. His dreams were vivid and violent. Suffocating. He woke drenched in sweat despite the cooler temperatures that far north. Eda often featured in his dreams, but she was different. If they were being chased, she was slow. If they were fighting, she never drew her sword in time. And if she needed saving, he was always too far away to help her. When a defender's mind was poisoned with violence and heartbreak, hard work was the only medicine. So he raised the axe and continued chopping.

'You could write to her, you know,' Wilona said, looking around.

'Who?'

'You know exactly who.'

The axe came down, and the wood fell to either side of the block. 'Why would I do that? She's suffered enough.'

His mother looked heavenward. 'Firstly, because she doesn't even know if you made it safely home. And secondly, it might help if you put your feelings down on parchment.'

'I don't need to put my feelings anywhere, but I do need to protect Eda. I know her. If I start sending letters, she'll get ideas. Next thing she'll be climbing walls and travelling through Carmarthenshire alone on foot.'

'So you'll just let her wonder if you're still alive?'

'She'd know if I died.'

'How?'

He did not have an answer for that. Not one he could share, anyway.

Do you think if your heart stopped beating, mine would stop also?

He leaned his forehead on the top of the axe, dizzy with the memory of her palm pressed to his heart.

'You miss her,' his mother said quietly.

Miss her? He was mourning her.

Straightening, Roul picked up another large log and balanced it on the block. 'Go inside. It's freezing out here.'

With a resigned nod, his mother returned indoors.

~

Eda always requested the north wall. It was probably a bad idea to torture herself that way, but she did it anyway. Sometimes she would lean on the embrasure and watch the fog below, imagining a single horse appearing through it.

Roul.

He would stop and look up, eyes narrowing on her. He would recognise her, even at that distance. She had conjured up all kinds of romantic reunions that she would not dare speak aloud. Her sisters would fall down with shock if they knew. They thought her incapable of romantic thoughts. They did not know the extent of her attachment because she had not shared any details with them. As far as they were aware, she fell in love with a man she could not have, and now she was moving on. She gave them no reason to think otherwise. It was pointless to mark herself a ruined woman and risk her uncle finding out. So she never mentioned him, and she made a point of not reacting when someone did.

'Is there no way he can write and let us know he's home safe?' Eda overheard Blake whispering to Lyndal in the kitchen one night. They thought she was upstairs.

'I know he's home safe,' Lyndal whispered back. 'He wrote to Queen Fayre just last week requesting straw to rethatch their roof.'

He was home and safe. And he was doing the jobs his father could not. Everything was just as he wanted it. Never mind the gaping hole in her chest. She would fill it with work and training.

Her first payday was a nice distraction. Six shillings. She held them in her hand, enjoying the weight of them.

'Coming to the tavern?' Hadewaye asked.

She shook her head. 'Not today.'

'What a soft cock you've become,' Tatum said as he

passed her. 'What else are you going to spend your money on?'

'Maybe she just doesn't want to waste her wages on drink like the rest of us,' Alveye said, tucking his coin pouch into his uniform.

Blackmane gave him a shove to get him walking, then nodded once at Eda before following the others.

Yes, their relationship had progressed to polite gestures now.

That night, Eda gave the coins to her mother. Candace turned them over in her hand for a moment before saying, 'How much longer are you going to keep doing this?'

'Mother,' Blake said, shaking her head. 'She's keeping Chadora safe. Can't you just thank her and let her be?'

Her sister was seated in the chair in front of the fire, Luella curled up in her lap and Garlic beside her. It was the same lap Eda had curled up in her whole life. She looked down at her niece's pouty face. No cuter replacements could be found.

'I'm going to check on Basil.'

Candace sighed and called to her back, 'You are not going to fall asleep out there, are you?'

Eda snatched a cloak from the hook by the back door and swung it around her as she headed outside. Basil must have heard her coming because the braying began before she had even reached the stables.

'Hello, you.' Eda slipped into the stall and checked his water. It was still half full, saving her a trip to the creek. She took the wool blanket off the divider and wrapped it around her before sliding to the ground. Basil lay down next to her like a loyal dog.

'Any progress with the goats today?'

Basil's ears flicked back and forth, listening.

'No?' She made a sad face. 'What about Harlan's horse? He picks on your ears, doesn't he?'

The donkey blinked at her.

'Never mind that elegant, perfectly proportioned bastard. We'll find you a friend.'

Eda curled against him, resting her head on his back and stroking his fluffy coat. She closed her eyes when she felt the sting of tears. 'I miss him.'

CHAPTER 39

$\mathcal{I}$t had taken a long time for the materials to arrive for the roof, but Queen Fayre had delivered as always. Now Roul was atop a ladder, thatching and already thinking ahead to other maintenance that needed doing. He was running out of jobs and wondered if he should do the neighbours' roof in case one day they decided to return.

Roul paused his work when he heard a horse approaching at a trot. It was Alfred, one of his father's friends from the next village. He stopped his horse at the front of the house, nodding a greeting at Roul as he dismounted. Clive wandered outside, and the two men walked over to the empty pigpen to exchange news.

It was close to half an hour later when Alfred called a farewell to Roul on the way back to his horse, a chicken tucked under his arm. Roul saluted, then continued combing out the last section of roof.

'He wasn't brave enough to go inside and try your latest batch of ale, then?' Roul said when his father was close enough to hear.

Clive looked up, inspecting Roul's work. 'I think he was worried the roof would collapse on him.'

Roul picked up one of the leftover hazel spars and threw it at his father. Clive got an arm up to block it in time.

'What news did he have?' Roul asked, continuing his work.

'His cousin's travelled up from the south with her young son.' He hesitated. 'She claims England's going to war.'

Roul stilled and looked at his father. 'Why would she claim such a thing?'

Clive crossed his arms. 'She said she saw English troops numbering in the thousands march right through their village.'

Roul climbed down and walked over to him. 'Marching in which direction?'

His father shifted his feet. 'West.'

West.

'There could be any number of reasons why the king's army is on the move,' Clive said, reading his face.

'But only one probable one. King Becket now sits upon the throne, and Chadora's thriving under his rule.'

'Which means King Edward missed his chance.'

Roul looked south. 'King Edward is irrelevant at this point. Queen Isabella and Lord Roger remain in control of England for now. And you better believe Roger Mortimer will take King Becket's success as his own personal failure.'

'Then all we can do is wait and see. We'll learn of England's intentions soon enough.'

Roul went to speak, then turned in a circle. 'King Becket may have no idea they're coming.'

'We don't even know if they're going to Chadora.'

'Of course they are. Where else would they be going?'

Clive pinched the bridge of his nose. 'It's all hearsay at this point.'

'You're right.'

He looked up. 'I am?'

'It's all hearsay. So I have to go and see with my own eyes what's going on.'

His father swore and took a step back. 'You'll be pushing your luck if you head off alone again.'

'I know.'

'And if the rumours are true, then what? You going to take on an entire army in the name of a king you no longer serve?'

That last part stung more than it should have. 'I've no intention of fighting anyone. But there are people behind those walls I care about. If war's coming, they deserve to know.'

A pained expression crossed his father's face. 'We just got you back. More importantly, we just got you smiling.' He rubbed his forehead. 'I can't go with you—'

'I'd never ask you to. And it's *your* smile this family needs, not mine.' He glanced over his shoulder at the house. 'I need to travel south and find out what's going on. Can you manage here without me for a few days?'

Clive sighed. 'We've managed for the past three years. What's a few more days?'

Roul took hold of his father's shoulder and squeezed.

'Then you'll come home?' Clive asked, searching his eyes.

'Then I'll come home.'

~

'The eldest son is to inherit everything,' Lord Thomas said, looking around the table to ensure everyone was listening. 'A well-respected family in Toryn by all accounts, with more land than they know what to do with.'

Thomas had joined them for dinner to share the news that Queen Fayre had found a suitor for Eda.

'I have no idea why it took so long,' Thomas added, 'but we are finally here.'

Eda knew exactly why it had taken so long. Queen Fayre had been buying her time to heal from her heartbreak, and Eda would be eternally grateful for those extra months. The only problem was her heart had not healed. She had to accept that it might never be the same again. But life continued regardless. Missing him did not mean she could never be happy, only that she had to learn to be happy while missing him.

Even as her uncle sat there spelling out the details of her future, Roul was noticeably missing from the conversation. She could not glance in his direction. He could not wink back at her. She wondered what he would think of her marrying a future lord. It was laughable.

'I have sent word confirming that we will put Eda on a ship as soon as possible. We shall have to find a lady companion to travel with her. It would not reflect well on our family if she were to arrive alone.'

Blake pushed her plate away, and Harlan's arm went around her.

'It all sounds so romantic,' Kendra said. 'Whisked off to a foreign land to marry a future lord.'

Eda blinked. 'Does it? Then perhaps you should go in my place since you're also unwed.'

'And Kendra will remain that way for as long as King Becket is in the same position,' Thomas said pointedly.

Eda mentally rolled her eyes.

Kendra gave her a sympathetic look. 'You will miss your family, of course. But with a husband that rich, you will be able to travel frequently.'

'Exactly,' Thomas said. 'You should all be thrilled by this outcome.'

Blake rose from her chair. 'Excuse me. I need to check on Luella.'

'Have you really not employed a governess yet?' Thomas called to her back.

Candace drew a breath. 'The girls never had a governess growing up.'

'And it shows,' Thomas said, levelling her with a look.

Harlan's chair scraped the floor, making everyone flinch. With his fists clenched at his sides, he said, 'Excuse me,' then followed his wife.

Lady Victoria cleared her throat. 'Whatever happened to Leigh Appleton? He was very kind. If Eda were to marry him, she could remain here in Chadora.'

Thomas's fork clanged against the plate. 'The man is a bootmaker. Queen Fayre has found us a future *lord*. Eda should be falling at my feet with gratitude.'

'I will not even see her get married,' Candace said, eyes welling with tears.

Victoria reached for her hand. Any words of comfort spoken aloud would only aggravate her husband further.

'We have worked tirelessly to secure this match,' Thomas said. 'Some appreciation in place of moping would go a long way.'

Blake and Harlan returned to the room with Luella. Harlan looked at Eda as he took his seat. 'If you have objections, now is the time to speak up.'

Thomas rose abruptly. 'How dare you interfere with family business.'

Harlan glared up at him. 'This is my family too. If she doesn't want to go, I won't make her.'

Eda placed her fork down on her plate, exhausted by the tension. 'It's fine. I'll go.' She could not very well complain about being stuck within the walls and then turn down her only opportunity to leave. 'I've always wanted to travel on a ship.' She wanted the conversation over. At least with a wealthy husband, she would have her own bedchamber and plenty of space.

'He is marrying you as a favour to Queen Fayre, knowing full well that you do not have a penny to your name,' Thomas said. 'You would all do well to remember that.'

Eda stared at her uncle. 'I'm not penniless. I earn a wage.'

'Money that would be better spent on real soldiers,' Thomas said, taking his seat once more.

She had taken every blow the man had dealt, remaining silent all evening. But something snapped in her mind when those words left his mouth. She looked down at the knife she was holding, then threw it at her uncle. It pierced the edge of his tunic, pinning his arm to the chair.

Lady Victoria screamed, and Luella began to cry. Everyone else sat frozen. Thomas looked down at the knife, colour draining from his face.

'Eda,' Harlan warned.

Thomas dragged his gaze up to hers. 'You wretched girl. You are lucky you missed.'

Eda snatched up her mother's knife and threw it, pinning his other arm to the chair. 'I never miss,' she said calmly. Then she rose slowly and walked over to him. She bent down so they were eye level. 'You're lucky I love my aunt and cousin more than I hate you.' She yanked the knives free. 'I might not be a *real* defender, but I *am* a soldier. Make no mistake about that.'

Slamming the knives down on the table, she left the room.

CHAPTER 40

*R*oul waited until it was dark before moving any closer to the camp. While he was dressed in civilian clothes and looked like any other peasant in these parts, he knew anyone found loitering nearby would be treated with suspicion.

He climbed the tallest tree he could find and settled himself in the branches up high. His eyes went to the wagons covered in canvas, no doubt concealing weapons, then to the meticulously spaced tents. Roul watched the men come and go, doing some basic calculations in the process. He estimated around three thousand soldiers.

Three *thousand*.

He had tracked them east for the past two days, and now he was absolutely sure they were headed to Chadora. They showed no interest in the towns and villages along the way. They were simply passing through. Now Roul had to beat them to Chadora. According to the map his father had given him, he was a two-day ride from the wall. Less if he made do with only a few hours' sleep.

So that was what he did. He travelled solo through the

open plains and forests of Carmarthenshire, avoiding people and ready for trouble.

Everything was going fine until day two, when a man attempted to rob him while he slept. Roul woke when his horse stirred, snatched up his sword, and killed the man without hesitation. It was not until he was on his feet staring down at the body that he realised it was an old man. No one else came from the trees. He was not part of a rebel group. He was just a loner trying to survive in the wastelands. Guilt hit Roul, but he pushed it away. It was kill or be killed.

Seeing it was almost dawn, he saddled his horse and took out the map. He was only a half day's ride from the wall now.

As he was returning the map to his bag, he heard a stick snap behind him. Perhaps he had been wrong and the man had not been alone after all.

Roul spun, drawing his weapon and squinting in the predawn light. He lowered the sword when he caught sight of a donkey.

'You must be fucking joking,' he muttered.

The animal walked over to the corpse, sniffed it, then blinked in Roul's direction. It wore a halter with a piece of rope attached to it and a girth around its middle with a bag balancing on either side. Roul walked over and searched the bags. Seeing there was nothing of use besides a small blunt knife that smelled of offal, he removed the load from the donkey's back, then snatched up the rope.

'All right. Same donkey rules as always. If you slow me down, I'll leave you behind.' He returned to his horse, mounted, and continued with the donkey trailing behind him.

It was around four hours later when the wall came into view. Aware he could not enter via the east wall, he veered northwest so he was approaching directly in front of the north gate. He stopped out of shooting range, knowing better than to venture any closer for now. Bringing his fingers to his mouth, he emitted a long, loud whistle. He was no longer a defender, but they were far less likely to shoot him if he spoke their language.

The wait felt eternal. It was close to ten minutes later when a reply finally came. A sequence, a test, one that if he got it wrong, he might as well turn around and go home. But he need not worry, because the language would remain with him for life.

A whistle came back telling him to proceed to the gate.

Looking back at the donkey, he said, 'I want you on your best behaviour.'

Eda stood frozen atop the wall, holding on to the embrasure, blinking repeatedly and telling herself the sight before her was not real. This time her fantasy had gone too far. This was not just a sole man on a horse appearing through the fog but a sole man with a donkey in tow. That was how she knew she had finally lost her mind.

There had been much discussion atop the wall when the signal had reached them.

'But no one left,' Harlan was saying to Hadewaye. 'Someone has to have left to be returning.'

Harlan decided to test this so-called defender before telling him to proceed. Then, satisfied, he went to meet him at the gate.

The closer the man got, the more her mind played tricks on her.

'Holy hell,' Hadewaye said. 'That who I think it is?'

She wanted to ask him who he thought it was, just to be sure, but the words would not come.

'It is,' Hadewaye said, a grin splitting his face. 'It's Thornton.'

Eda could barely breathe. Below her, the portcullis was going up. Below her, Roul was preparing to pass through it.

Drawing an urgent breath, she ran to the other side of the wall walk and peered over. She panicked when he did not appear straight away, worried that losing sight of him meant the illusion was over. But then he rode into sight, stopping to speak with Harlan and the guard at the gate. Her gaze went to the donkey, which was smaller than Basil. Its coat was browner and the ears shorter.

Roul lowered his hood, drawing her attention back to him. Even from that angle she could see he was different. His hair was longer, reaching all the way to his eyes. There was no need to clip it short anymore. It would be pure silk in her hands.

When they finished speaking, she panicked, thinking he might turn around and exit. But he did not leave. Harlan called to another defender on horseback, gave instructions she could not make out, and then Roul followed the man.

Why had he returned?

She watched him ride off through the nobility borough, drinking in the sight of his familiar frame and broad back. He was almost to the bend in the road when he slowed his horse suddenly. It was like he felt the weight of her stare, because he turned his head and looked up—straight at her.

Her lungs stopped, and the powdered remains of her heart stirred as though caught by a sudden gust of wind. He was unshaven and heavy-eyed and beautiful and visibly surprised at seeing her atop the wall.

The defenders said something to him, and he faced forwards again. A moment later they rounded the corner, and he was gone from sight.

~

Eda was on the wall. Eda was on the wall in *uniform*. What on earth was going on? He expected to find her married to the bootmaker, playing house in the merchant borough. He had tortured himself with that thought for months. But in true Eda style, she had gone rogue. Now he was moving in the opposite direction—away from her—and the pull to turn back was as strong as ever.

He had hoped those feelings might have eased after so long apart, but their edges were as sharp as ever. First he was going to warn King Becket. Then he was going to return to the wall and remove her before the English troops arrived.

Along the quiet roads of the nobility borough they went, then through the busy streets of the merchant borough all the way to the royal gate. Inside, Roul looked to the training yard, searching for familiar faces. None could be found. He passed the barracks, the stables, and a few minutes later, he was dismounting in front of Eldon Castle. The groom gave Roul a confused look when he handed over both the reins to his horse and the donkey.

Roul requested an audience with Queen Fayre, knowing King Becket would cast him out. But to his surprise, he was brought before the king. Not a happy king, mind you. Becket sat upon his throne glaring at Roul.

'You have a lot of nerve returning here,' he said, rising and stepping forwards. 'This feels a lot like a kind gesture thrown back in my face.'

Roul bowed. 'Your Majesty.'

'My men tell me you have important information. I pray for your sake they are right.'

At least he was prepared to listen. 'There are English troops on their way to Chadora. I tracked the army through Carmarthenshire. They're a few hours east of here. I estimate around three thousand soldiers.'

Roul could see the mental turmoil as the king weighed his words.

Becket turned to his guards. 'Find the warden, and send some scouts east to investigate.'

'By all means, send scouts,' Roul said, 'but don't wait for them to return before preparing your army. I can't speak of England's intentions, but an army that size suggests this isn't a friendly chat.'

Becket raised his chin. 'Why are you here? You just happened to be in the south and noticed an army coming our way?'

'I heard rumours of their movements and went to investigate. When I realised they were headed here, I came to warn you.'

'Why?'

'You know why. I care about these people and this kingdom very much.'

Queen Fayre swanned into the room at that moment, looking from Roul to her son. 'Surely you have figured out by now that Commander Thornton's loyalty lies not with one man but with the kingdom he swore an oath to protect.' She went to stand next to her son.

'He is not a commander, Mother, and I do not recall inviting you to this meeting.'

Fayre's eyebrows rose. 'I believe the commander asked to see me.'

Roul shifted his feet. 'I'm happy to see anyone who'll listen at this point.'

'Why?' Fayre asked, turning to him. 'What have I missed?'

A horn sounded in the distance. They all stilled to listen.

When it stopped, Fayre asked, 'What on earth is going on?'

'English troops are heading this way,' Roul said. 'Sounds like they're closer than I hoped.'

Shapur marched in, not waiting to be announced. 'Your Majesties.'

Becket clasped his hands behind his back. 'English troops will soon be arriving. I need you to prepare for a large-scale attack.' He looked to Roul. 'Is there any other information you can provide that might be useful?'

If the warden was surprised to see him, he hid it well.

'They have concealed wagons,' Roul said. 'I wasn't able to see what's in them, but if I had to guess, I would say weapons of some kind.'

'Get word out to all the boroughs so people have time to account for family members,' Fayre said.

Shapur bowed, then turned on his heel and left.

Roul cleared his throat and straightened. 'I'd like your permission to fight alongside your army, Your Majesty.'

Becket considered the request for a moment. 'Fine. Take what you need from the armoury.' When Roul turned to leave, he said, 'Thornton.'

Roul looked back at him, waiting.

'Try not to shoot me in the back while you are protecting my people.'

CHAPTER 41

'Oh shit,' Hadewaye said, eyes north. 'I see them now.'

Eda stepped up to the embrasure and watched as English soldiers appeared in neat lines below them. They stopped a sensible distance away, out of shooting range. Judging by their numbers, they meant to succeed this time.

A horn sounded again, and a stampede of feet echoed from the turrets at the end of the wall walk. Defenders emerged at a run, carrying weapons, supplies, and open flames. She was one of them now. She was expected to defend that wall with her life. But she had never fought without Roul.

The warden marched into sight, barking orders left and right. 'Hadewaye, go help distribute the remaining weapons. Move.'

The only person she trusted at her side through this fight had just been sent away.

'Get those arrows lit,' Shapur boomed. 'I do not know what is in those wagons, and I do not want to find out. I want them burned to the ground.'

The problem was the wagons were at least three hundred yards away.

'Move,' a defender hissed at her, shoving her back from the embrasure.

Eda righted herself, then set her jaw. 'The warden said two men to each embrasure.'

'And when another man arrives, I'll move aside.' He spoke without even looking at her, continuing to smear the tips of his arrows with mutton fat.

'Suttone' came a familiar voice.

She turned to see Blackmane setting up ten feet away. He moved over to make space for her.

'Thank you,' she said quietly, squeezing in beside him.

'Make sure that fat is on the arrows only,' Shapur shouted. 'I do not want sloppy shooting due to slippery hands.'

Eda looked out at their enemy and whispered to Blackmane, 'I can't shoot that far.'

He glanced behind him to ensure the warden was not within hearing range, then said, 'None of us can. Unless they roll those wagons closer, there's going to be a lot of wasted arrows.'

'Light those arrows!' Shapur's voice boomed along the wall walk.

The defenders held the tips of their arrows to the torches until they caught light.

'Nock!'

They loaded their bows.

'Draw!'

Eda took aim at the wagon directly in front of her, then, knowing she could not reach her target, lifted her bow.

'Loose!'

It was a beautiful sight, the sky exploding with orange

flames, but many of the arrows went out mid-air, and none made the distance.

Shapur watched them land forty to fifty yards short, and his mouth set in a firm line. He did not reprimand them because he knew he was asking the impossible.

As if their enemy had been waiting for that exact moment, they gathered around the wagons and untied the canvases covering them. It was time for the big reveal.

'Shit,' Blackmane said as the canvases were pulled back.

Eda looked from him to the enormous structures. While she might not have known exactly what they were, she knew fear was the correct response. 'What do they do?'

'They're catapults. They turn walls to rubble.'

Shapur rushed to the other side of the wall, shouting, 'Get some horses out there now! I want those things burning in the next few minutes.'

The gate cranked below them, and hooves pounded the muddy earth. Eda watched through the embrasure as teams of soldiers worked together to prepare the catapults, loading each with a rock the size of a small child.

A hand grabbed Eda's arm, spinning her. She came face to face with Shapur Wright.

'This is your one and only chance to get off this wall. I won't offer again.'

He was giving her an out. She could leave. The problem was Blackmane could not leave, or Hadewaye, or any of the other defenders standing atop the wall. 'I'll stay, sir.'

He nodded, then marched off without saying another word.

'You should've left,' Blackmane said when she returned to his side. 'Staying here to die isn't brave, it's stupid.'

She watched Chadorian horses gallop out into the open below, their riders armed with burning arrows. 'Would you have left?'

Blackmane stared ahead, not responding.

'That's what I thought.'

The defenders did manage to set two of the catapults alight before they were shot dead, but the flames were extinguished by ready soldiers. A moment later, the catapults sprang into action, hoisting boulders into the air.

'Take cover!'

That was the warden behind them, prompting every man atop the wall to drop down. Eda pressed her eyes shut and braced for impact. The first boulder hit farther along the wall, an explosion of rock and dust flying in all directions. Blackmane's arm went across her body, pinning her to the wall. The second hit nearby, the noise deafening and the dust choking them. Eda heard the next one, the whistle of rock cutting through air at high speed. She dropped her bow and covered her ears.

But she never saw it land.

~

Roul ran into Harlan at the nobility gate. He was on horseback headed in the same direction. He glanced down at the weapons Roul had collected from the armoury.

'Staying for the fun, I see.'

'You know how I love a fight where we're completely outnumbered.'

Harlan slowed his horse to a trot as they passed beneath the archway, then returned to a canter. 'I assume you're headed to the north wall, since that's where Eda is.'

'Do I want to know why she's standing atop the wall wearing a defender's uniform?'

'I think you can probably hazard a guess.' He glanced back at the donkey with a questioning look. 'And do I want to know why you've returned with yet another one of those things?'

'It's a long story.'

Harlan did not ask for the details. 'She's going to Toryn in a few weeks, you know.'

Roul did not have to ask who he was talking about. 'What for?'

'She's to marry into a wealthy family. One of her uncle's brilliant ideas.' Harlan's tone was dry.

The news landed like lead. One of the main reasons he had refused to take her to Carno was because he did not want her separated from her family. 'Did no one object?'

'Everyone did. Everyone except Eda.'

Roul tugged on the rope to hurry the donkey along. This was his fault. He had broken her. He had broken her, then abandoned her, and she had given up the fight. But he did not have the space in his head for that right now. First he needed to get her off that wall and somewhere safe. 'I need to drop this thing at Wright House on the way.'

Harlan shook his head. 'Absolutely not. I'm still stuck with the last donkey you returned with. Eda's lucky Luella's attached or I would've sold him long ago.'

The road was quiet because everyone had retreated to their houses upon hearing the horn, so Roul was surprised when they spotted a cart up ahead. A horse rode alongside it.

'Is that Fletcher?' Roul asked.

Harlan squinted. 'Yes.'

Astin turned when he heard their horses approaching. He was stern-faced and heavily armed.

'Where are you going?' Harlan called to him.

Presley was driving the cart, her sister tucked at her side. Lyndal was on the other side of her, clutching her new baby.

'Thornton?' Lyndal said, turning to look at him. 'What are you doing here?'

Another long story.

'We'll have to postpone pleasantries,' Astin said.

'There's rumours circulating through the farming borough that English troops have broken through the north wall.'

A cold sensation washed over Roul. 'Catapults. That's what was beneath the canvases.'

'I'm taking the girls to Wright House, and then I'm going to the wall.'

Harlan snatched the rope from Roul and tossed it to Presley. 'Can you take this thing with you?'

Presley tied the donkey to the back of the wagon.

'Eda was on the wall,' Roul said.

'The warden would've sent her away the moment he realised,' Lyndal said, sounding not at all confident. 'Wouldn't he?'

Astin turned to his sister. 'I need you to—'

'Go,' Presley and Lyndal said in unison.

'We'll go straight to Wright House,' Presley assured him.

The three men took off at a gallop towards the wall.

They were half a mile out when Roul tasted it. Dust. Dust in a kingdom that knew nothing of dust and everything of mud. The others must have noticed it too, because they picked up their pace.

They heard the war zone before they saw it. None of them were prepared for the sight. Ruins. Entire sections of the wall in ruins. That wall had protected them for well over a decade. It was supposed to be impenetrable. That was the word King Oswin had used to describe it when he was alive.

There were defenders everywhere, running back and forth, covered in a thick layer of grey dust. Some were sifting through the rubble, pulling bloody and dazed defenders out of piles of stones. There were two rows of defenders on the other side of the wall, a human barrier keeping their enemy at bay with arrows.

'Hold that line!' the warden shouted. Dust and blood

covered his face and neck, making him barely recognisable.

Harlan and Astin ran over to him while Roul searched for Eda amid the chaos. Where was she? She would not just leave when there were soldiers in need of help. So why could he not find her?

'Thornton.'

Roul turned to see Blackmane approaching. His eyes were bloodshot and his face cut to pieces. Roul's stomach knotted. 'Have you seen Eda?'

He blinked slowly. 'She was right next to me on the wall. And then she wasn't. I've been looking…'

All the air left Roul's lungs. He looked around. Some of the rubble was large enough to crush an entire crowd. If she was buried in there, she was dead.

The ground shook, and the air turned grey. Another piece of wall fell before their eyes.

'We're going to destroy the catapults,' Harlan said, appearing next to him on horseback. 'Find her.'

Roul coughed and nodded.

Astin rode up with a lit torch and a lot of sulphur. 'Let's go burn some shit.'

A boulder landed mere feet away, sending a spray of rocks over Roul and Blackmane. Roul would have run out and killed every English soldier with his bare hands had Eda not been buried somewhere in the mess before him.

'We were up there,' Blackmane said, pointing.

Roul ran forwards and began lifting rocks and throwing them behind him. 'Eda!'

Blackmane worked alongside him, matching his speed. It was just as well, because many of the pieces required two men to lift them.

'Fucking hell' came a voice.

Roul looked back to see Tatum and Alveye standing at the edge of the rubble.

323

'Are there men buried under that mess?' Alveye asked.

Eda. Eda was buried under that mess.

'Suttone,' Blackmane said. 'Start digging.'

The pair exchanged a concerned look, then climbed up to help.

For the next thirty minutes they searched, occasionally coming across a corpse or an injured defender. They carried the injured to a wagon parked nearby, but none of those people were Eda.

The more time that passed, the more frantic Roul's search became. He called for her, over and over, barely aware of the fight happening around him. At some point the rocks had stopped falling, bright flames in the distance confirmation that Harlan and Astin had been successful.

Blackmane held up a hand, and everyone stilled. 'You hear that?'

Roul listened. He heard nothing at first, then a cough. A single cough that filled him with hope.

'It came from over here,' Alveye said, climbing atop the rubble and moving to a large section of wall lying at an angle.

'Careful you don't move anything,' Roul called. As impatient as he was to get to her, he knew they had to move slowly and cautiously.

Alveye crouched and turned an ear to the ground, listening. Another cough, barely audible against the sounds of war but blissfully feminine.

She was alive.

'We can't move this,' Tatum said, crawling over the rubble to Alveye. 'If we do, the rubble underneath will collapse on top of her.'

Roul and Blackmane moved to the other side, inspecting the area.

'We create one tunnel,' Roul said, pointing to a spot. 'Nothing else moves.'

Then began the slow process of making a tunnel by removing one tiny piece of debris at a time. Except they did not have time. The fighting was happening less than fifty yards away, the English soldiers edging closer despite Chadora's strong defence. Arrows landed around them, disappearing into the very crevices they stood upon.

'Fall back!' the warden shouted at them.

'Suttone's down there,' Roul called back. 'We can get her out.'

The warden scraped his teeth over his lower lip and nodded. 'As you were.'

They worked quicker now, forced to catch rocks left and right. Then there were no more rocks, only a black hole barely big enough for a child to squeeze through—or one tiny soldier. Carefully, Roul lay flat and reached into the darkness, feeling for her with every sense available to him. His fingers brushed fabric, and he exhaled. He turned his head to the hole. 'Eda.'

A hand landed on his arm, and he took hold of it, gently dragging her to the small opening. His heart squeezed when two green eyes blinked up at him.

'Hold on.' His voice was strangled. 'I'm going to pull you out.'

She was only holding on with one hand, and he tried not to think about the reason why. He pulled her through the narrow hole. When her shoulders came through, he saw her left one sat at a strange angle. The others moved closer to help.

'I think it's dislocated,' he told them, 'so be careful.'

The walls of the tunnel crumbled as her hips came through, but it did not matter now because she was out. She was in his arms.

She was *alive*.

They all climbed down, and Roul carried her to the nearly full cart, which was preparing to leave. Alveye,

Blackmane, and Tatum drew their swords behind him. They were ready to join the fight. Roul knew he had to stay with them, because once the English crossed the rubble, it would be over.

Roul was surprised to find a dazed and bloodied Hadewaye in the wagon. 'You all right?'

The young defender looked up at him, nodded, then noticed Eda in his arms. 'Praise Belenus.' He shuffled over, making room for her.

Roul laid her on her good side and said to the driver, 'I need you to take her to Wright House.'

He nodded.

'I'll make sure she gets there,' Hadewaye said, coughing.

Roul looked down at Eda and brushed sticky hair back from her face. 'You're going to be just fine, soldier.'

She reached up for him just as the wagon pulled away. He watched it until it was out of sight, then turned to join the fight.

CHAPTER 42

'Bite down on this,' Candace said, placing a leather belt between Eda's teeth.

She was laid out on the table in the main room. It was a full house that day. Lord Thomas had relocated his family there also to increase the distance between them and the fight. He stood looking out of the window while his wife and daughter sat in the best chairs, staring wide-eyed at Eda. Lyndal and Presley were tending Hadewaye, and Rose was entertaining Luella upstairs while the baby napped.

'I can put it back in,' the physician said. 'However, it is difficult to establish the amount of damage to the surrounding muscle and ligaments. That part will be a waiting game.' He took hold of her arm. 'Everyone ready?'

Blake held her hand, squeezing tightly.

Kendra rose from her chair, a hand pressed to her chest. 'Excuse me.' Then she fled the room.

Lady Victoria went after her. Suffering was not a part of their world, or rather, they were shielded from it.

'This is what comes of women playing war,' Thomas

said, turning to watch. 'You are lucky the damage was not to your face or the wedding would be off.'

'On three,' the physician said.

Eda's eyes were locked with Blake's as he counted down. Her sister gave her a reassuring smile at two, but the worry never left her face. If one of them was hurting, they were all hurting.

'Three.'

Eda roared through the leather as the shoulder popped back into place. The physician patted Eda's arm. 'The worst is over. Let us take a look at the rest of you.' He lifted her shirt and felt along both sides of her ribcage. Eda winced when he reached her left side. 'I suspect you have a broken rib. There is little that can be done for that outside of rest.'

Candace looked at the ceiling, trying to hold back tears.

'How long will that take to heal?' Thomas said, moving closer. He was thinking only about the upcoming wedding.

The physician glanced in his direction. 'Around six weeks. She will need to exercise caution during that time. No household chores for a while.'

'Oh, she'll hate that,' Lyndal said from the other side of the room.

Blake smiled. 'Poor thing. But you heard the physician. No laundry or scrubbing floors for six whole weeks.'

Eda might have smiled back if she had not been in pain.

The physician checked her arms, legs, hips, then felt around her abdomen for any internal injuries. His eyebrows came together as he pressed down firmly on the area above her pelvis.

'What is it?' Candace asked.

The physician cleared his throat and turned to Lord Thomas. 'Perhaps we should talk outside—in private.'

'What? No,' Blake said immediately. 'If it's to do with

my sister's health, then you shall speak here in front of all of us.'

He hesitated. 'No one mentioned that the patient is with child.'

Silence.

Long, deafening silence.

And cold. Eda felt like she had been plunged into a tub filled with ice.

'Oh.' That was Lyndal. Always the first to regroup in stressful situations.

The physician looked around the room, then down at Eda's shocked face. 'I gather from everyone's reaction that no one was aware of the fact?'

Eda pushed herself up to a sitting position, wincing when pain shot through her chest and shoulder. She stared at the man as she replayed two words over and over in her mind.

With child.

'I'm not pregnant,' she said, looking from the physician to Lyndal to Blake to her very pale mother. 'I'm not.' He was likely mistaking some internal rupture for a foetus.

Thomas's face had turned an ugly shade of red. 'Are you certain?'

'I have been doing this a long time,' the physician replied. 'I estimate around three months.'

The certainty Eda had felt moments earlier dissolved. *Three months.* Three months ago, she had been at Harlech Castle with Roul. Had she bled since? She could barely remember. Her cycles had been a mess for years. That was what came of famine.

Thomas was striding towards her now, and Blake stood tall between him and the table.

'Not a step farther, Uncle.'

Thomas looked past her to Eda. 'You little harlot. After everything I have done, this is how you repay me?'

Repay him for what? The man had done her no favours. They were living in Wright House, not Cardelle Manor.

Eda went to speak, but no words came, only shallow breaths and tightness that made her ribs ache.

'Let us all take a deep, calming breath,' Lyndal said, making her way over. 'Mother, go sit down before you fall down.'

Presley walked over and guided her to a chair. Hadewaye was glaring at Lord Thomas. He looked ready to leap up and tackle the man to the ground.

'There are a few options here,' the physician said in a calm voice. 'I know a family outside the walls that would house the girl until the child is born. No one need know.'

Disgusted, Thomas returned to the window and began pacing. 'That will take months.'

The physician nodded. 'Six, to be exact.'

'What is the other alternative?' Thomas asked.

'There are herbs we can try if time is not something you have. However, there is no guarantee.'

'Give her the herbs,' Thomas said, marching back over. 'Give them to her right now.'

Candace closed her eyes and dropped her head.

'No one is forcing anything down my sister's throat,' Blake said.

Lyndal moved to her side. 'She can't be expected to make such an important decision on the spot.'

'It is not her decision!' Thomas shouted.

Everyone looked at Eda. What was she supposed to say? She was unwed, alone. No man would marry her now.

Roul might. He would do the honourable thing. Wed her and take her back to Carno to raise their child.

'Checkmate. You're stuck with me now,' she could say as his face fell at the news.

The thought made her sick. Or was that the baby?

'Give her the herbs,' Thomas said after a long silence. 'If it works, we might be able to salvage the situation.'

'The father's here in Chadora,' Lyndal said in a calm voice. 'Let us speak with him first. He's a good man.'

'I know all about this *good man*,' Thomas said. 'Roul Thornton. A nobody. A wasteland rebel who weaselled his way into our kingdom only to be cast from its walls. And yes, I know he was banished for Belenus only knows what.'

Eda might have gotten up and choked the man if she had two available hands.

'His opportunity to do the right thing was three months ago!' He was pacing again. 'What am I to say to the man waiting for you in Toryn? Do any of you ever think about anyone other than yourselves?'

'All right. That's enough,' Blake said. 'My sister needs to rest.'

Thomas pointed at Eda. 'You will do what is best for the family.'

A knock had him lowering his hand before he went to open the front door. A messenger stood on the other side. Thomas stepped out to speak with him.

The physician produced a small bottle of oil and set it on the table beside Eda. 'Pennyroyal. Start with half. If contractions do not begin within a few hours, give her the rest. If there are any complications during the process, you can send for me.' He closed his bag and looked around the room. 'I shall see myself out.'

When he was gone, Candace rose and took herself upstairs, closing the bedchamber door behind her.

'It'll be all right,' Lyndal said. 'These things happen all the time. We'll figure it out.'

Blake was staring hard at Eda. 'You should've told us.'

'I didn't know. I swear it before Belenus.'

Silence.

'He'll do the right thing,' Hadewaye said quietly.

Blake picked up the piece of fabric the physician had left, folding it into a sling for her sister. 'Especially once I'm through with him.'

Eda rolled her eyes. 'He only came to warn the king. I refuse to trap him into marrying me.'

'It's hardly a trap,' Lyndal said. 'He clearly loves you.'

'Which is why he doesn't want me living in the waste-lands,' Eda replied. 'Away from all of you.'

Blake fitted the sling. 'You do have to tell him. The child is his too. He deserves to know.'

He deserved so much more than that.

'Or I could marry you,' Hadewaye said from the other side of the room. 'It might feel a bit like marrying my sister at first, but I think we'd get along.'

Eda smiled at him. 'That's incredibly chivalric, but I can't drag you into this.'

The front door opened, and Thomas stepped inside, looking less agitated than earlier.

'Message from Commander Wright,' he said. 'The defenders held the wall. England has retreated.'

The whole room exhaled.

'Is Astin with him?' Lyndal asked.

'Yes. They are staying to help with repairs.'

Eda swung her legs over the side of the table. 'And Thornton?'

Thomas's gaze slid to her. 'I did not ask.' He looked in the direction of the kitchen and shouted, 'We are leaving.'

The expression on the women's faces when they entered made it clear that they had heard the news.

'Ladies,' Kendra said, not knowing where to look.

'Do not dilly-dally,' Thomas said, ushering them both towards the front door.

When they heard the carriage pull away, Blake placed a hand on Eda's leg. 'If something had happened to him,

Harlan wouldn't be staying behind to repair the wall. Roul will be with them.'

She knew Blake was right.

'Can you walk?' Lyndal asked. 'Because I have something to show you that might cheer you up.'

Eda's ribs ached and her shoulder throbbed, but she nodded anyway.

The three of them exited the back door, and Eda followed her sisters to the stables. 'I don't even think Basil can cheer me up right now.'

Lyndal looked over her shoulder with a mischievous smile. 'No, but Basil's new lady friend might.'

Eda peered into the stall and saw not one but *two* donkeys. It was the donkey Roul had brought with him, the one she had spied from atop the wall. A smile came and went on Eda's face. 'They make a very sweet couple.'

Lyndal nodded. 'They really do.'

Basil came over to Eda while his lady friend eyed her cautiously from the other end of the stall.

'I don't want to take the herbs,' Eda said, rubbing Basil's head.

Lyndal brought a hand to her chest. 'Thank goodness.'

A throat cleared, and they all turned to see Presley standing at the stable's entrance.

'I'm sorry to interrupt,' she said, looking uncomfortable.

Lyndal waved her inside. 'Not at all. Is Hadewaye all right?'

'He's fine.' Presley walked over to them, stopping a few feet away and hugging herself as she looked around the stables. 'I know this isn't technically any of my business, but there is another option.'

Eda turned to face her, waiting.

'You could stay here until the birth. No one would blink if a baby was born in this house. Everyone would assume the baby belonged to Blake and Harlan. Luella would have a sibling, and you wouldn't have to be separated from your child.'

A soft smile appeared on Lyndal's face. 'That's a very clever and helpful suggestion.'

Eda sat with the idea for a moment, then looked at Blake. 'Would Harlan go along with such a thing?'

'Of course he would,' her sister replied. 'He loves you like blood. He'd do anything to help and protect you.'

Lyndal nodded in agreement. 'We all would.'

Eda looked to Presley.

'I would take the secret to my grave,' Presley said with a reassuring smile.

There was a sadness behind that smile, one that made Eda wonder if the idea had come from experiences with these things. But she was not one to pry. 'Mother can't even look at me.'

Lyndal pressed her hand to Eda's stomach. 'When this baby is born, she'll not be able to look away, I promise you that. Give her time.'

'She's ashamed of me.'

'Never,' Blake said quickly. 'She's afraid for you. And don't worry about Uncle. He'll have no choice but to go along with it in order to preserve his reputation. Just make sure Harlan's around when you break the news to him.'

Eda placed a hand over Lyndal's and looked around at the three women. 'I think it's a good plan, and I think Roul will agree.'

Lyndal perked up at hearing that. 'So you'll tell him?'

'Yes.' Because she did not know how to lie to him, to deceive him—nor did she want to. She looked over at the new donkey. 'Are you sure she's for me?'

Lyndal laughed at the question. 'Well, it wasn't a gift for Harlan, that's for sure.'

'Who's going to be thrilled, by the way,' Blake said.

Presley bit back a smile. 'What are you going to name her?'

Eda tilted her head and thought a moment. 'Rosemary.'

They all stood watching the donkeys for a moment, and then Blake said, 'Welcome to Wright House, Rosemary. Displaced and in need of a good feed. You're going to fit right in.'

CHAPTER 43

*T*he English retreated. Chadora's walls had proven to be impenetrable—even with parts of them missing. At the end of the day, it was not a single wall that kept the kingdom safe but the army of defenders who guarded it. Their arrows did not miss, nor did their swords when the time came. There was a precision to their fight that meant no matter how many men the English sent forth, the result was always the same.

Loss.

King Becket lost men too, but on a much smaller scale. The injured were carried to safety, never left to be trampled. And Roul fought as hard as he would have while wearing a defender's uniform. He killed as he would have before—without guilt or hesitation. He fought to protect the people inside the walls, atop it, and the men fighting alongside him. He fought until he could barely keep hold of his shield, until blood blurred his vision. Until every man wearing a uniform was safe. He fought until there was no one left to fight. Then he stayed to assist the injured and retrieve the dead.

It was late afternoon when he sank to the ground

beside Blackmane. Tatum and Alveye were seated close by with their knees pulled up and foreheads resting on their arms. Harlan and Astin were supervising repairs. The merchants and farmers had come to lend a hand with the labour.

'You should get those cuts looked at,' Roul told Blackmane.

'Later.' Which meant he would do no such thing.

Roul allowed himself one minute of rest, then got to his feet and went back to work. Blackmane followed.

The pair were halfway through clearing a pile of rubble when someone called Roul's name. He turned, blowing dust from his nostrils as he looked around.

King Becket was on horseback, a guard flanking him. He dismounted and gestured to Roul. 'Walk with me.'

Roul exchanged a look with Blackmane before following the king. Falling into step with Becket, he said, 'Don't worry. I'm leaving.'

The prince did not appear to hear him. He was too busy surveying the damage. 'Their army had a proper go at it.'

Roul followed his gaze to a large hole in the wall. 'They did, but they didn't succeed.'

'The warden tells me you had a part in that.'

'A very small part.'

Becket was silent a moment. 'This is not your kingdom, yet you continue to fight as if it were.'

Roul gestured to the people behind him. 'It's *their* kingdom, their home. I fought for them.'

'What about me?' Becket asked. 'Did you fight for me also?'

Roul frowned. 'Yes, actually. Though I don't expect you to believe that.'

'And why would you fight for me?'

Roul considered his answer. 'Because I think you might

be the best king Chadora has ever had, and these people deserve a good king.'

Becket stopped walking and turned to him. 'I am inclined to think you mean that.' He studied Roul for a long moment. 'I initially thought you kept me alive in hope that I might change my opinion of you. I see now that I was wrong. You did it for them, knowing I would not forgive you.'

Roul wiped a dusty hand down his face. 'I don't need your forgiveness. I just need you to be the leader these people deserve.'

The king watched the work going on around them, not speaking for some time. 'I would like to invite you to stay.'

Roul crossed his arms and squinted. 'I don't understand. Stay where?'

'Here in Chadora.' Becket nodded thoughtfully. 'If a peasant can push his own needs and desires aside for the greater good, then certainly a king can. I trust you to take care of these men. And rightly or wrongly, I trust you will take care of me also, so long as I continue to be the leader they deserve.' He met Roul's eyes once more. 'And since I intend to be that man for the entirety of my reign, I cannot foresee any problems between us.'

Roul was genuinely speechless.

'Your debt with my mother is paid. So if she comes to you with instructions to kill me, I expect you to tell her *no*.' There was a hint of humour in his eyes.

Roul did not trust his comprehension in that moment. 'So I'm clear, you're inviting me to stay here in Chadora, and you're just going to ignore that flicker of anger that rises every time you lay eyes on me?'

The young king's face turned serious. 'It is possible that my anger might have been somewhat misdirected.'

Roul almost fell over at that admission. 'Misdirected

how? I shot the arrow that killed your father. That hasn't changed.'

'You did.' Pain flashed on Becket's face. 'And I did not stop you.'

Now Roul was completely confused.

'You know I found the letter you wrote to my mother agreeing to her plan,' Becket continued. 'What you do not know is *when* I found it.'

'And why does that matter?'

'It matters.' Becket adjusted the folds of his cloaks. 'It matters because I found the letter soon after it was delivered.'

Roul's lungs stilled. Surely he was not saying what Roul thought he was saying. He stared at the king, waiting for him to continue.

'I found it while my father was still alive.' His words were strained.

Blood pulsed in Roul's ears.

'So, as you can now see'—he met Roul's gaze with some difficulty—'we all played a role in his death. My weapon of choice was silence.'

Roul did not move, could not move. Becket had not warned his father. 'Why?' It was the only word he could get out.

'I do not fully understand the reason. I certainly *wanted* to tell him. But I think deep down I knew he was not up to the task.' He paused. 'Naturally, I despised myself afterwards—still do. As I despise you. And I do not foresee that changing.'

There were no words Roul could speak that were adequate, so he chose silence instead—as the prince had once done.

'So stay,' Becket said, regaining composure. 'Help with the clean-up if that is your wish. Then go to Carno, collect your family, and bring them to Chadora. I believe they will be safest here.' He linked his hands behind his back. 'Then I wish to see you back in uniform and training recruits to the same standards as those who brought me home. Those men—and that woman—are a credit to you.'

The man was handing Roul everything he could possibly want. 'Your Majesty, I—'

'Your actions today say it all, Commander Thornton. There is really no need for words.'

Roul nodded, took a step back, turned, then turned again. He opened his mouth to speak, then closed it. He tried to leave a second time, then said, 'I'll get back to work.'

'And I shall await news of your family's arrival.' He attempted a smile. 'I believe I owe them a dinner invitation.'

CHAPTER 44

*E*da gave up on sleep and wandered out to the stables wrapped in a blanket. She sat in the donkeys' stall, watching them doze in the dark. Basil seemed particularly content. He did not come to Eda for affection that night. His loneliness was cured—and she was so happy for him.

She must have fallen asleep, because when she opened her eyes, warm, bright light filtered through the wood.

Warm, bright light.

The sun had not only risen, but it had broken through the clouds.

Getting to her feet, and wincing the entire time, Eda opened the stall door so the donkeys could go out and graze. Then she did the same for Harlan's horse. She smiled as she stepped out into the golden light. It drenched her face. Steam escaped her mouth with each breath, a reminder that the air's temperature was no warmer.

But it *felt* warmer.

Basil's head bumped her, making her clutch her side and momentarily lose her breath. 'You can't do that for another six weeks,' she reprimanded him while rubbing his face, rewarding the demanding behaviour. 'Do you want to come to the creek?'

The donkey brayed as though answering her.

'Yes, Rosemary can come too.'

Eda made her way down to the creek, then strolled downstream until she reached her favourite spot, where light dappled the ground, turning to full sun closer to the water. Basil and Rosemary lowered their heads to graze. Eda scooped up some water and drank, then splashed a few handfuls over her face, enjoying the prickle of cold on her skin. Afterwards, she sat in the sunniest spot, watching light dance across the water, trying not to think about the life growing inside her.

It still did not feel real. She did not know if it was because she had not had any symptoms or if she had been too broken to notice them. There had been many mornings when she had skipped breakfast and put the loss of appetite down to grief, because every time she opened her eyes and remembered Roul was on the other side of the wall, the heaviness hit her all over again.

Roul.

Surely he would not leave without saying goodbye again, not after last time. He was probably still at the wall with the others, helping.

She sat a little straighter. If she took the horse and left now, she would be gone before her mother woke. She stood, too fast, then doubled over, clutching her side.

'How many ribs broken?' came Roul's voice.

Eda straightened at the sound, causing herself more pain. He was between the donkeys, reluctantly petting both. 'One, apparently. But it feels like seven.'

He suppressed a smile and was almost knocked sideways by Rosemary when he withdrew his hand.

'If you've come for your donkey, it might be a fight to the death. Basil's very attached.'

He raised his hands. 'Oh no. She's all yours.'

Roul was so beautiful drenched in sunlight, even while covered in blood and dust. It almost made Eda wish she were not standing before him wearing a nightdress, muddy boots, a horse blanket, and a sling.

'It's such a relief to see you up and about. And to hear your voice.' He swallowed. 'I was worried about the shoulder when I saw it.'

'The physician just popped it back in. I barely felt a thing,' she lied.

Roul's liquid eyes never left her.

'How's the wall?' Eda asked, struggling with what to say next.

'Still a way to go to completion, but everyone's pitching in.'

'Good.' She pulled the blanket tighter around her. 'I think it's amazing that you came to warn the king after the way he treated you.'

'Wasn't much of a warning in the end.'

'Still, I'm sure he appreciated having an extra soldier of your calibre on his side for the fight.'

A smile flickered on his face. 'You could say that.' His eyes swept the length of her, and his expression turned serious. 'I've always marvelled at your ability to look like a goddess in a moth-eaten blanket you stole from an animal.'

She reached up and poked a finger through one hole. 'I'm quite confident that you're alone in that thought.' She decided to be brave and close the distance between them. He smelled of a thousand wounds. 'Are you hurt? It's difficult to tell how much of that blood is yours.'

'Just a few cuts and bruises.'

She reached up and dragged the neck of his tunic down, revealing red-and-purple marks. She let go when she heard his breath change. 'You should wash in the creek. You'll feel like a new person.'

He glanced at the water. 'There are some things I need to tell you before I leave.'

Leave.

The word landed like a punch, knocking her off balance. He reached out to steady her.

'Are you all right?'

'Just a bit tired,' Eda said, giving her best impression of a reassuring smile. 'Go wash. I'm not going to run away.' To prove it, she went and sat at the creek's edge to wait. 'I've something to tell you also.'

Roul nodded, removed his boots and socks, then stripped down to his braies before wading into the water. Eda studied his back, evaluating every cut and bruise. The cuts would fade to tiny silver lines like all the others. She watched him disappear below the water's surface, then looked away when he emerged facing her. But not before noticing the way his muscled shoulders glistened in the sun.

He spent a few minutes washing himself. And she spent a few minutes practicing what she was going to say in her head.

I just want you to know I'm pregnant. Yes, it's yours. And this is the plan I made yesterday without you. How do you feel about leaving me and your child? How do you feel about breaking my heart a second time?

Then he was out of the water and coming towards her, and she was panicking. She opened the blanket to him, but he shook his head and sank down on the grass beside her, wet and clean. He drew his knees up, hands resting on them, and turned his face to the sun.

'You once told me you wanted to build a house on this very spot,' he said. 'Remember?'

'I remember.'

'It's a great spot.' He looked at his hands. 'Harlan told me you're to marry a young lord in Toryn.'

She looked out at the water. 'A *future* lord.'

'Oh, that's much less impressive.' One corner of his mouth lifted.

She cleared her throat. 'But there's a slight hiccup with the plan.' She could feel Roul's eyes on her.

'Oh?'

This was it. The moment she would tell him of her dilemma and her solution. She would demonstrate that she was more than capable of managing the situation in his absence. That was what he needed from her, after all.

'I'm pregnant,' she said.

Roul did not move, did not speak, only stared.

'I always thought it was something mothers told their daughters to keep them chaste. "It only takes one time." But it turns out there might be some truth behind that warning.' Her palms were sweating now, her entire body heating under the blanket. 'And I know this is the last thing you want to hear before you leave, but I didn't think it fair to hide it from you. I only found out yesterday when the physician was examining me.' She swallowed. 'I think the best part of the story is that Uncle Thomas was present for the entire thing.'

Roul was gripping one of his wrists so tightly his fingers had turned white. Since he was not speaking, she decided to continue.

'Naturally, he wants me to get rid of the problem and try to salvage the plan. *His* plan. But I don't want to do that. Despite our rather dire situation, I'm greedy for any part of you I can get.' She licked her lips, surprised when she tasted tears. She brushed them away before continuing. 'So, Harlan and Blake will say the baby is theirs. No one outside the family need know otherwise. I'll get to be a part of his or her life, a big part. The main part. And one day, when our baby's old enough to understand, I'll tell them all about their amazing father and the sacrifices you made.'

Eda dragged her gaze from the water to look at him. He was staring down at the blanket where her stomach was hidden.

'I know you're probably expecting me to beg you to marry me and take me with you,' she added. 'But I won't beg, because I already know your answer, and whether I like it or not, I understand your reasons. You want us somewhere safe.' She was desperate for him to speak now. 'Aren't you going to say anything?'

His eyes travelled up to meet hers. 'You're… pregnant?'

At least he had retained the main point of her long speech. 'Yes.'

'Show me,' he said, his voice choked.

She swallowed. 'There's not a lot to see yet.'

She opened the blanket and guided his hand to the beginnings of a bump. His whole body softened as his hand landed, his lungs expelling air. He tipped towards her until his lips pressed lightly on her shoulder. 'Our baby.'

The warmth of his hand through her nightdress combined with the enormity of this moment had her trembling. He was not angry or disappointed. He was not pacing and tearing his hair out, trying to figure out a better plan than the one she had made. He was calm and *happy*.

And now tears fell down her cheeks faster than she could brush them away.

It was the first time she had allowed herself to feel anything other than blind panic and guilt. The rest of the world could fade away for a minute while she sat with the tiny flutters that felt a lot like joy. For a brief moment, they were just a young couple in love expecting their first child. It did not matter that everyone else was stressed and devastated by the news.

When Roul finally raised his eyes, she saw they were shiny with tears.

'I've got news too.'

The flutters stopped, replaced with dread. 'If you tell me King Becket is beheading you in the square this afternoon, it's going to *really* ruin the moment.'

He reached up, running his thumb across her damp cheek. 'I'm leaving soon to return to Carno.'

She had known it was coming, but the pain in her chest worsened anyway.

'I'm going to pack up my family, and I'm going to bring them to Chadora.'

Her eyes moved between his as she tried to make sense of that information. 'To... hang alongside you? What are you saying?'

Laughter filled his eyes. *Laughter.* 'Not to hang. To live here within these walls.'

She licked her lips. 'Your family's going to live here?'

He nodded.

'Are... are *you* going to live here?'

'Yes.'

She did not react with happiness because she was too afraid she had misunderstood. 'Does King Becket know?'

He laughed. Roul washed in sunlight was one thing. Roul washed in sunlight while laughing was everything. 'Yes, he knows. It was his idea. He wants me to return and resume my duties in his army.'

'He wants you to come back?' Now the joy crept in, making her heart race and throat close. 'Because you fought for him?'

'Among other reasons.'

The reasons were not important at that moment. 'Are you sure you heard him correctly?'

'Quite sure.' He leaned in and kissed her tear-soaked cheek. 'Before I go, I'm going to call upon your uncle and tell him we're getting married. And when I return, we're going to have a wedding with both our families present.'

Eda covered her face with her hands.

Roul carefully placed his arm around her. 'And this baby will grow up with *two* parents.'

Her hands fell away. 'And two donkeys.'

He kissed her gently, then rested his forehead against hers. 'And two pain-in-the-arse donkeys.'

EPILOGUE

$\mathcal{R}$oul watched them from the trees behind the house. They were swimming in the river. Playing, shivering, laughing.

His wife.

His daughter.

They had called her Starla, because she most definitely belonged to the heavens. She was pure light, from her dimpled cheeks to her infectious laugh. And she was walking—far too soon. Still a month from her first birthday.

Eda lifted her from the water and placed her on her feet at the edge of the creek. Summer was coming to an end, and they had been treated to snatches of sunshine. The weather was changing—very slowly, but changing. And he thanked God for it each day, because he did not want his daughter to suffer as they had.

Moving quietly between the trees, he made his way to the other side of the house, the one they had built by the creek in Eda's favourite spot. In his hand was a wooden sword.

As though sensing him, Eda stilled and looked in his

direction. Her eyes swept over the trees, but she did not spot him.

'Starla,' she said, turning their dripping daughter around and pointing to the trees. 'I sense danger in the forest. I think Mama needs to get her sword.'

The tiny girl managed a smile despite the thumb jammed in her mouth. This was her favourite game.

Roul waited for Eda to retrieve her weapon before emerging from his hiding place. Starla jumped, then squealed, then began running in circles, cheeks bulging and laughter ringing in the air. Eda's playful eyes went to him, and then she attacked. They sparred for a few minutes, until Roul fell to the ground and surrendered. Starla came for him then, legs wobbling beneath her. She ran straight into his open arms. He lifted her high, anything to see those dimples again.

Eda disappeared into the house to fetch towels. Then the three of them sat in the fading sun eating the blackberries the girls had picked earlier.

Yes, there were berries that summer.

'How was your day?' Eda asked, pushing wet hair back from her face.

He loved her that way: wearing only a chemise that was see-through when wet, hair out and dripping, her skin cold and flushed.

What had she asked him?

She looked down at herself. 'Don't worry. I'm planning on dressing for dinner.'

'Maybe we could eat here tonight.'

A knowing smile spread across her face. 'Absolutely not. That would require me to cook.'

He chuckled lightly and turned to Starla, who was stuffing another berry into her mouth.

Blake appeared from around the side of the house, slightly out of breath. 'It's happening.'

Eda got to her feet. 'Now?'

'Now.' Blake dashed off again.

Eda ran into the house to dress while Roul found clothes for their daughter. A few minutes later, they were making their way through the trees and stepping out onto the green lawn of Wright House.

'I hope Astin's here,' Eda said, chewing her lip. 'She may need help.'

Roul rolled his eyes. 'She'll be fine. Stop fretting.'

Ignoring his reassurances, Eda ran ahead.

'Here we go,' he whispered to Starla as they entered the stable. Everyone was gathered around Rosemary's stall. The donkey was lying on the ground, labouring hard. They had put Basil in the stall at the other end. The pair were rarely apart, so he looked suitably lost.

A smile lit up Candace's face the moment she spotted Starla, but then it faded when she noticed her wet hair. 'Eda, did you take my granddaughter into the creek again?'

'Busy, Mother,' Eda called from inside the stall.

Candace tutted and walked over to take Starla from Roul. 'Let us go see what the other children are doing.' Then off they went inside.

While Candace had spent a majority of Eda's pregnancy pointing out that her latest grandchild was conceived out of wedlock, she had also held Eda's hand through the entire birth. And six months later, when Eda announced she wanted to resume training at the barracks a few hours a week, her mother had been the first to put her hand up to care for Starla.

No one asked Eda why she was returning to training. It was Eda. She needed to feel ready for whatever life threw at her next, and Roul needed her happy. If that meant letting Blackmane, Tatum, Alveye, and Hadewaye beat her up a few times a week, then so be it.

Astin arrived at the stables just in time, clapping Roul on

the back as he passed by, then making his way into the stall where Eda and Blake were now crouched down, making soothing noises in an attempt to keep Rosemary calm. The women stepped outside so Astin had room to work.

Roul wrapped an arm around Eda, pulling her to his chest and kissing the top of her head. 'She's doing great.'

Twenty minutes later, the foal was born, a spitting image of Basil but much cuter.

'I guess there's no question as to who the father is,' Blake said.

Eda slipped quietly back into the stall to meet the foal. 'It's a boy.'

'A colt,' Astin corrected. 'What horrendous name are we giving this one?'

'Pepper,' Blake and Eda said at the same time.

Astin and Roul exchanged a look but said nothing.

Lyndal appeared at the stable door, the duck at her feet. 'Roul, your family's here. How's she doing?'

'It's a boy.'

'A colt,' Astin called.

Lyndal clapped her hands together and wandered inside to see.

Roul tapped on the stall door to get Eda's attention. 'Congratulations, soldier.'

She beamed up at him. 'I'll be in soon.'

Eda nursed Starla upstairs where there were fewer distractions, then made her way down to dinner. Their family gatherings were so enormous nowadays that Harlan and Astin had built two trestle tables to accommodate everyone.

Roul's family lived in the Suttones' old house in the

merchant borough. Birtle's idea. He was getting too old to manage the shop solo and had reached a point where it was no longer practical for him to live alone there.

'Birtle can move to Wright House,' Harlan had said without hesitation. 'And the Thornton family have a ready-made business waiting for them.'

The women had all agreed to gift the business to Roul's family, who were starting from scratch. Roul had initially insisted on buying the business, paying it off in small increments, but then Harlan pointed out that it was a family business, and he was now family.

Eda paused on the stairs on her way down, looking out at the room below her. She normally despised social gatherings, but these were her people. Scarred and experienced in the art of suffering. Soldiers, like her.

A knock at the front door had Eda descending. 'I'll get it.'

It was her aunt and cousin. Her uncle had once again, much to everyone's relief, declined the invitation.

'Where's Edmund?' Eda asked Kendra as she kissed her cheek.

Lady Kendra had recently married a very rich lord in his forties who needed an heir for his estate. Once it became clear to Thomas that King Becket had no interest in marriage at present, and with Kendra 'now in the latter part of her prime'—her father's words—he had agreed to the match. Her cousin described the man as kind and wealthy, but focused more on the wealthy part when socialising in noble circles. The lord was always polite when the families crossed paths and never stopped Kendra from visiting Wright House, but he came from a long line of noble snobs. He too declined any invitations that came his way.

'He is *so* busy at present,' Kendra said, making unnecessary excuses for his absence. 'However, he sends his regards.'

Eda suppressed a smile. 'How nice.'

After dinner, Harlan built a fire outside. The children ran around with Garlic and the goats while the adults enjoyed their blackberry wine beneath a starry sky. Birtle brought his lute out and played softly amid the hum of conversation.

'Father said the removal of the wall would be a *complete* disaster,' Kendra was saying to Roul. 'Though he has been oddly silent on the subject since it came down. It seems the wave of crime he predicted did not come to fruition.'

When King Becket had announced he would be removing the wall that separated merchants and nobility, the entire kingdom had spoken of nothing else. Everyone prayed it would go well, and it had—mostly. There would always be a few who would take advantage of the situation, because there would always be desperate people. But according to King Becket, that was not a good enough reason to keep them separate.

'So long as the farming borough wall remains in place, all will be well,' Lady Victoria said.

Clive spoke up at that. 'The gate's permanently open now. People are free to move between the boroughs.'

'But they have the ability to close the area off, should the need arise,' Wilona said, smiling at Victoria.

They spoke like merchants now, like they belonged. It warmed Eda's heart to see how well the family had settled in. Odella was even courting a young farmer Lyndal had introduced her to.

'Now we just need to find Presley a husband,' Lyndal had said loudly when she had shared the news, ensuring her sister-in-law heard.

Presley insisted she had no interest in marrying, despite

reports of flirtatious behaviour with a certain butcher who regularly visited the farm.

'Ready?' Roul asked, stopping in front of Eda.

She passed their sleeping daughter up to him, then rose, bidding everyone goodnight before going to check on the new foal. Mother and baby were doing splendidly. Basil not so much.

'You'll survive a few days,' Eda reassured him before they left.

The three of them disappeared into the quiet of the trees. The area was so familiar to them now that they easily navigated their way home in the dark.

Once they had tucked Starla into bed, they grabbed some blankets and went to sit by the creek with their own private bottle of wine.

'Your family seem happy,' Eda said, resting her head on Roul's shoulder. 'In fact, everyone appeared in good spirits tonight.'

Roul did not reply straight away. 'I always feel a bit nervous when things are going too well. Is that strange?'

'Why do you think I resumed training? I'm not used to this pleasant, easy existence. I'm always bracing for the next traumatic event.'

He drew her closer. 'But you're happy?'

'So happy—and terrified of it all being taken away.'

He kissed the top of her head. 'I won't let anyone take it away.'

She leaned into his warmth. If he said no one was taking it away, then no one would.

'Do you realise it's been a year since Lord Roger Mortimer was hanged in London for assuming royal power?' Roul asked.

'A year already. Thank goodness King Edward regained control before his army returned to smash down any more walls.' She stared out at the black water. 'I still sometimes think about Queen Isabella. I'm glad she didn't suffer the same fate.'

'Many say she should have.'

'Well, they're wrong.'

He laughed into her hair and whispered, 'Do you want to go swimming?'

Her mouth stretched into a smile. 'Yes.'

Quietly, they took off their clothes and waded into the creek, sucking in a breath as they ventured deeper. Eda was first to dive under. Roul followed, grabbing her by the ankle and dragging her back. She wrapped her legs around him, staring into his eyes, slightly breathless from her feeble attempt at fighting him off.

He dipped his head to kiss her collarbone. 'I'll guard your happiness like I would a king.'

'King Becket or King Oswin?'

He laughed into her neck, his warm breath making bumps break out over her skin. 'I'd prefer to keep you guessing.'

Her arms tightened around him. 'I love you.'

He drew her closer, nose brushing hers. 'I'm going to let you enjoy your swim. Then I'm going to take you inside and spend the rest of the night getting you warm.'

She smiled. 'Throw in a quick sparring session and some early morning fishing, and then we have the perfect life.'

'You really don't slow down for long, do you?'

'Do you want me to slow down?' A smile played on her lips. 'Perhaps you want a wife who greets you with a ready meal each night instead of a wooden sword.'

He kissed her, harder this time. 'You know exactly what I want.'

'I do, but tell me again anyway.'

His mouth went to her neck, teeth scraping flesh. 'I want a soldier.'

ACKNOWLEDGMENTS

I would like to express my gratitude to the many people who contributed to this book. My biggest thanks goes to my readers. Without you guys, I wouldn't get to do what I love. Next, a huge thank you to my rock star husband who supports and encourages me even though my writing takes time away from him. I love you to bits. A big thank you to McKinley, Kristin and the team at Hot Tree Editing for polishing the manuscript into something beautiful. A shout out to my proofreader, Rebecca, for catching everything I missed. A round of applause for my cover designer, Domi (Inspired Cover Designs), for another gorgeous cover. And finally, a huge thank you to my Launch Team for your encouragement, honest reviews, and being the final set of eyes on my work. You guys are amazing.

ALSO BY TANYA BIRD

You can find a complete list of published works at
tanyabird.com/books